"Amazing," Becca whispered as the moon vanished from sight. "I really am thankful we're here."

"We are most grateful, too," said a gruff voice behind them.

The three women whirled around, but saw no one. Then Alizon's sharp eyes caught some movement near the edge of the stone circle, close to the ground. A hedgehog, she thought. Perhaps a badger. Then she realized she couldn't see the gnomes any longer. Something grunted at the base of their menhir.

Raquel directed her flashlight at the noise. Seven gnomes blinked at them. The one in the center, the gnome with the checkered breeches, bowed, his hand over his waist. His partner, the rotund fellow with the book, doffed his hat, and the girl gnome curtsied. The others pleasantly nodded.

"How much Calvados did you put in that coffee?" Becca asked in a tiny voice.

Raquel didn't answer, but swept the flashlight over to the empty clearing, then back at the small figures directly below them. They squinted. The blue-garbed gnome threw up his walking stick to ward off the beam and cowered. The other six were smiling, but he looked as blue as his buttoned jacket.

"Please do not shine that in our faces," said the spiffy gnome with the shovel. His French was flawless, but for a _____ _____ accent. "We see very well at night.

Baen Books by HARRY TURTLEDOVE

The Enchanter Completed

A
Tribute Anthology for
L. Sprague de Camp

Edited
by

Harry
Turtledove

THE ENCHANTER COMPLETED

A Baen Books Original

Baen Publishing Enterprises
P.O. Box 1403
Riverdale, NY 10471
www.baen.com

ISBN: 0-7434-9904-2

Cover art by Tom Kidd

First printing, May 2005

Distributed by Simon & Schuster
1230 Avenue of the Americas
New York, NY 10020

Production by Windhaven Press, Auburn, NH (www.windhaven.com)
Printed in the United States of America

Contents

Sprague: An Introduction

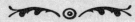

Harry Turtledove

L. SPRAGUE DE CAMP CHANGED my life.

About how many people can you say that? Not many, not if you're honest. A favorite teacher, perhaps, who pointed you in a direction you hadn't expected to go. That's what L. Sprague de Camp (Sprague, to his friends) did for me—and he did it more than twenty years before I ever met him, and, of course, altogether without knowing he'd done it or that I even existed. Writers, especially the good ones, can be dangerous people.

I was fifteen, I think, when I found a copy of *Lest Darkness Fall* in the secondhand bookstore I frequented in those days. For any who may not know it, it's one of the best *Connecticut Yankee in King Arthur's Court* stories ever written: right up there, in my admittedly biased opinion, with Twain's original. Before I read about Martin Padway's involuntary journey through time to the Italy of the sixth century A.D., I don't believe I'd ever heard of the Byzantine Empire. Because of Sprague, I got interested in it. If I hadn't happened across *Lest Darkness Fall*, I might well not have.

As things were, I got into Caltech, and flunked out at the end of my freshman year. When I got to UCLA, I'd left the sciences and become a history major—and ended up with a doctorate, Lord help me, in Byzantine history. I never would have done that had someone else picked up that book instead of me. I never would have written much of what I've written, a lot of which is either Byzantine-based or uses the historical and research skills I picked up acquiring my degree. I never would have met and married the lady who's now my wife, for we got to know each other when I was teaching at UCLA while the professor under whom I studied had a guest appointment at the University of Athens. I wouldn't have the three girls I have today.

Other than that, finding *Lest Darkness Fall* all those years ago didn't change my life at all.

De Camp had no small effect on the fields of science fiction and fantasy, either. Working alone and in collaboration with Fletcher Pratt, he helped expand the fields by using their techniques to examine not just the present and future but also the past, and by using modern viewpoint characters to get inside works of literature written from a very different perspective.

Along with *Lest Darkness Fall*, the Harold Shea stories collected in book form as *The Incomplete Enchanter*, *The Castle of Iron*, and *Wall of Serpents* have been in print almost continuously for the past sixty years.

Sprague's special virtues were logic, clarity, and a sympathetic understanding for the foibles of mankind. The heroes he created himself were always recognizably human and flawed, much more likely to try to work their way out of trouble with a quip and a smile than by smashing through whatever was in their way. (I am conscious of the irony of Sprague's having been a major factor in the rediscovery of Robert E. Howard's Conan, and in his often working in Howard's universe. Everyone's entitled to a little time off from what he usually does, and writers have to pay their bills no less than any other mortals—and I don't think anyone but Howard ever wrote Conan so well.) His own special science-fiction universe was that of the *Viagens Interplanetarias* ("Interplanetary Voyages" in Portuguese—Brazil is the leading country in this universe), which includes *Rogue Queen* (among other things, a splendid satire on Marxism), the stories collected in *The Continent Makers*, and many novels set on the low-tech world Krishna, which offers both science and swashbuckling a chance. Sprague did not believe faster-than-light travel was possible, and so did not include it in this universe; the Lorenz-Fitzgerald contractions play a role in more than one story.

This is typical. De Camp's worlds *always* feel real and thoroughly lived in. When he wrote of things, he knew whereof he spoke. He learned to fence and to ride a horse. He traveled widely all over the world, which helps make his series of historical novels set in classical Greek and Hellenistic times—*The Dragon of the Ishtar Gate, The Arrows of Hercules, An Elephant for Aristotle, The Bronze God of Rhodes,* and *The Golden Wind*—uniquely authoritative. Along with the novels of Mary Renault, de Camp's give the modern reader the best feel for what it was like to live in those times.

Trained as an engineer (unlike yours truly, he graduated from the California Institute of Technology), Sprague entered the job market during the Depression, when, essentially, there *was* no job market. The only time he worked in engineering was during World War II, as a naval officer stationed in Philadelphia, where he, Robert A. Heinlein, and Isaac Asimov fought the war with flashing slide rule, as he was fond of saying.

He used his technical training in his writing, though (to writers, nothing ever goes to waste), both in his fiction and in informative, lively nonfiction on subjects as diverse as engineering in the ancient world, Atlantis, the elephant, American inventions in the nineteenth and twentieth centuries, dinosaurs, and the Scopes monkey trial. He wrote an authoritative biography of H.P. Lovecraft, and another of Robert E. Howard.

I first made his acquaintance more than twenty years ago now, after I had a novelette in *Asimov's* and George Scithers, who was then editing the magazine, mentioned in the front material my debt to *Lest Darkness Fall.* Sprague sent George a postcard for forwarding to me, saying he'd liked the story and was pleased he'd had something to do with the shape of my career. I walked on air for days after that. When I published a translation of a Byzantine chronicle a year or so later, I sent him a copy, wondering if he might use incidents from it in fiction of his own (so far as I know, he never did).

We met in the flesh in Atlanta, at the 1986 World Science Fiction Convention. He was, as always, unfailingly kind to someone starting out. Later at that convention, we were on a panel together. He made a Byzantine allusion and then turned to me, asking if he'd got it right. He had, of course. That he made the gesture, though, speaks volumes about the sort of gentleman he was. After that, we'd see each other once or twice a year at conventions, and would write back and forth every couple of weeks or every month up till late 1999, not quite a year before he died. I'm not and never have been a whiskey drinker, but I'll always cherish the knocks of Johnnie Walker over ice I had in hotel rooms with him and Catherine.

Personally, he was tall, handsome, and elegant, and, till near the end, looked ten or fifteen years younger than he was. I was sad to watch him get slower and more frail as the years went by. The last convention where we met was in 1994 in Dallas, and he was not moving around well at all by then. (Even so, at dinner one evening there, he started talking in Swahili with another writer who'd recently been to Africa.) Later, he suffered a broken wrist, a broken hip, and perhaps a series of small strokes, and also had to endure his wife's sinking into Alzheimer's in the couple of years before she passed away.

Sprague and Catherine Crook de Camp were married for more than sixty years. It was, I think, the best marriage I ever saw. It made all the old cliches about finishing each other's sentences and putting up with each other's foibles look good. When he lost her the spring before he died, everyone knew he would join her again before long. And by what he, always a staunch rationalist, would undoubtedly have called pure coincidence, he died on her birthday, November 6, three weeks before his own ninety-third.

He won the Gandalf Grand Master Award from the World Science Fiction Convention, and was also named a Grand Master by the Science Fiction Writers of America. Even so, his works, these days, are less well remembered than they ought to be, not least because he was modest almost to a fault. When he appeared on one of the trading cards the 2000 Worldcon put out, his quote on the back read simply, "I've been lucky." Maybe he was, but he was also very, very good.

I count him as my spiritual father. When I told him that in a letter in 1998, he replied that I gave him too much credit and myself not enough—again, utterly in character. Back in the days when I was trying to get my feet wet as a writer, I would say to my friends, "I want to be L. Sprague de Camp when I grow up." That was more than half a lifetime ago; I realize now, as I didn't then, how foolish I was. There was, and could be, only one of Sprague. Even so, in another sense I wasn't so far wrong after all. I could have picked a great many worse models, and very few better ones. I miss him.

A Land of Romance

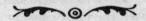

David Drake

THE MARKETING BULLPEN AT STRANGECO Head-quarters held seventy-five desks. Howard Jones was the only person in the huge room when the phone began ringing. He ignored the sound and went on with what he was doing.

It was a wrong number—it had to be. Nobody'd be calling seriously on a Sunday morning.

Dynamic 25-year-old executive . . . Howard sucked in his gut as he typed, not that there was much gut to worry about. *Ready to take on adventurous new challenges.* . . .

The phone continued to ring. It could be the

manager of one of the Middle Eastern outlets where they kept a Friday-Saturday weekend, with a problem that only a bold—a *swashbuckling*—marketing professional like Howard Jones could take on. Did Strangeco have a branch in the Casbah of Algiers?

The company slogan circled the ceiling in shimmering neon letters: IT'S NOT A SANDWICH—IT'S A STRANGEWICH! SLICES OF KANGAROO, CASSOWARY, AND ELK IN A SECRET DRESSING! STRANGEWICH—THE HEALTHY ALTERNATIVE!

The phone *still* rang. Howard's image staring from the resume on the screen had a stern look. Was he missing his big chance? The caller could be a headhunter who needed the hard-charging determination of a man willing to work all the hours on the clock.

Howard grabbed the phone and punched line one. "Strangeco Inc!" he said in what he hoped was a stalwart tone. "Howard Jones, Assistant Marketing Associate speaking. How may I help you?"

"Oh!" said the male voice on the other end of the line. "Oh, I'm very sorry, I didn't mean to disturb anybody important."

Sure, a wrong number. Well, Howard had known that there wouldn't really be a summons to a life of dizzying adventure when he—

"I'm at Mr. Strange's house," the voice continued, "and I was hoping somebody could come over to help me word an advertisement. I'm sorry to have—"

"Wait!" Howard said. He knew the call couldn't be what it sounded like, but it was sure the most interesting thing going this Sunday morning. It *sounded* like the most interesting thing of a lifetime for Howard Albing Jones.

"Ah, sir," he continued, hoping that the fellow wasn't offended that Howard had bellowed at him a moment ago. "You say you're calling from Mr. Strange's house. That would be, ah, which house?"

"Oh, dear, he probably does have a lot of them, doesn't he?" the voice said. "I mean the one right next door, though. Do you think that you could send somebody not too important over to help me, sir?"

Howard cleared his throat. "Well, as a matter of fact, I wouldn't mind visiting the Strange Mansion myself. But, ah, Strangeco staff isn't ordinarily allowed across the skyway, you know."

"Oh, that's all right," the voice said in obvious relief. "Mr. Strange said I could call on any of his people for whatever I wished. But I really don't like to disturb you, Mr. Jones."

"Quite all right, mister . . . ," Howard said. "Ah, I'm afraid I didn't catch your name?"

"Oh, I'm Wally Popple," the voice said. "Just come over whenever you're ready to, Mr. Jones. I'll tell the guards to send you down."

He hung up. Howard replaced his handset and stared at the resume photograph. That Howard Jones looked very professional in blue suit, blue shirt, and a tie with an insouciant slash of red. Whereas today—Sunday—Assistant Marketing Associate Jones wore jeans and a Fuqua School of Business sweatshirt.

Howard rose to his feet. Daring, swashbuckling Howard Jones was going to risk entering the Strange Mansion in casual clothes.

A transparent tube arched between the third floors of the Strange Mansion and Strangeco Headquarters to connect the two sprawling buildings. When Strange occasionally called an executive to the mansion, the rest of the staff lined the windows to watch the chosen person shuffle through open air in fear of what waited on the other side.

Shortly thereafter, sometimes only minutes later, the summoned parties returned. A few of them moved at once to larger offices; most began to clean out their desks.

Only executives were known to use the skyway, though rumor had it that sometimes Robert Strange himself crossed over at midnight to pace the halls of his headquarters silently as a bat. Now it was Howard Jones who looked out over cornfields and woodland in one direction and the vast staff parking lot in the other.

The skyway was hot and musty. That made sense when Howard thought about it: a clear plastic tube was going to heat up in the bright sun, and the arch meant the hottest air would hang in the middle like the bubble in a level. Howard had never before considered physics when he daydreamed of receiving Robert Strange's summons.

The wrought iron grill at the far end was delicate but still a real barrier, even without the two guards on the other side watching as Howard approached. They were alert, very big, and not in the least friendly.

Muscle-bound, Howard told himself. *I could slice them into lunchmeat with my rapier!*

He knew he was lying, and it didn't even make him feel better. Quite apart from big men *not* necessarily being slow, this pair held shotguns.

"Good morning!" Howard said, trying for "brightly"

and hitting "brittle" instead. "I have an urgent summons from Mr. Popple!"

Christ on a crutch! What if this was some kid's practical joke? *Let's see if we can scam some sucker into busting into the Strange Mansion! Maybe they'll shoot him right where we can watch!*

Howard glanced down, which probably wasn't the smartest thing to do now that he wasn't protected by the excitement of the thing. At least he didn't see kids with a cell phone and gleeful expressions peering up expectantly.

One of the guards said, "Who're you?" His tone would have been a little too grim for a judge passing a death sentence.

Howard's mind went blank. All he could think of was the accusing glare of his resume picture—but wait! Beside the picture was a name!

"Howard Albing Jones!" he said triumphantly.

"Nothing here about 'Albing,' " said the other guard.

The first guard shrugged. "Look, it's Sunday," he said to his partner. Fixing Howard with a glare that could've set rivets, he said, "We're letting you in, buddy. But as Howard Jones, that's all. That's how you sign the book."

"All right," said Howard. "I'm willing to be flexible."

One guard unlocked the grating; the other nodded Howard toward a folio bound in some unfamiliar form of leather, waiting open on a stand in the doorway. The last name above Howard's was that of a regional manager who'd been sobbing as he trudged into the parking lot for the last time.

The first guard pinned a blank metal badge on

Howard's sweatshirt, right in the center of Fuqua. "Keep it on," he said. "See the yellow strip?"

He gestured with his shotgun, then returned the muzzle to point just under where the badge rested.

An amber track lighted up in the center of the hallway beyond. The glow was so faint that it illuminated only itself. Focusing his eyes on it meant that Howard didn't have to stare at the shotgun.

"Right," he said. "Right!"

"You follow it," said the guard. "It'll take you where you're supposed to go. And you *don't* step off it, you understand?"

"Right," said Howard, afraid that he sounded brittle again. "I certainly don't want you gentlemen coming after me."

The other guard laughed. "Oh, we wouldn't do that," he said. "Pete and me watch—" he nodded to the bank of TV monitors, blanked during Howard's presence "—but we ain't cleared to go wandering around the mansion. Believe me, buddy, we're not ready to die."

Howard walked down the hall with a fixed smile until the amber strip led him around a corner. He risked a glance backwards then and saw that the light was fading behind him. He supposed it'd reappear when it was time for him to leave.

He supposed so.

Howard hadn't had any idea of what the inside of the Strange Mansion would be like. There were a thousand rumors about the Wizard of Fast Food but almost no facts. Howard himself had envisioned cathedral-vaulted ceilings and swaying chandeliers from which a bold man could swing one-handed while the blade of his rapier parried the thrusts of a score of minions.

There might be chandeliers, stone ledges, and high balconies on the other side of the blank gray walls but that no longer seemed likely. The corridor surfaces were extruded from some dense plastic, and the doors fitted like airlocks with no external latches.

The amber strip led through branching corridors, occasionally going downward by ramps. The building sighed and murmured like a sleeping beast.

Howard tried to imagine the Thief of Baghdad dancing away from foes in this featureless warren, but he quickly gave it up as a bad job. It was like trying to imagine King Kong on the set of *2001*.

The strip of light stopped at a closed door. Howard eyed the blank panel, then tried knocking. It was like rapping his knuckles on a bank vault, soundless and rather painful.

"Hello?" he said diffidently. "Hello!"

The corridor stretched to right and left, empty and silent. The amber glow had melted into the surrounding gray, leaving only a vague memory of itself. What would Robin Hood have done?

"*Hello!*" Howard shouted. "*Mister Popple!*"

"Hello," said the pleasant voice of the girl who'd come up behind him.

Howard executed a leap and pirouette that would have done Robin—or for that matter, a Bolshoi prima ballerina—proud. "Wha?" he said.

The girl was of middle height with short black hair and a perky expression that implied her pale skin was hereditary rather than a look. "I'm afraid Wally gets distracted," she said with a smile. "Come around through my rooms and I'll let you in from the side. The laboratory started out as a garage, you know."

"Ah, I was told not to leave . . . ," Howard said, tilting forward slightly without actually moving his feet from the point at which the guide strip had deposited him. After the guards' casual threats, he no longer believed that the worst thing that could happen to him in the Strange Mansion was that he'd lose his job.

"Oh, give me that," the girl said. She deftly unpinned the badge from Howard's sweatshirt and pressed her thumb in the middle of its blankness, then handed it back to him. "There, I've turned it off."

She walked toward the door she'd come out of, bringing Howard with her by her breezy nonchalance. He said, "Ah, you work here, miss?"

"Actually, the only people who work here are Wally and the cleaning crews," the girl said. "And my father, of course. I'm Genie Strange."

She led Howard into a room with low, Japanese-style furniture and translucent walls of pastel blue. It was like walking along the bottom of a shallow sea.

"Have you known Wally long?" Genie said, apparently unaware that she'd numbed Howard by telling him she was Robert Strange's daughter. "He's such a sweetheart, don't you think? Of course, I don't get to meet many people. Robert says that's for my safety, but . . . "

"I've enjoyed my contact with Mr. Popple so far," Howard said. He didn't see any reason to amplify the truthful comment. Well, the more or less truthful comment.

Genie opened another door at the end of the short hallway at the back of the suite. "Wally?" she called. "I brought your visitor."

The laboratory buzzed like a meadow full of bees.

The lighting was that of an ordinary office; Howard's eyes had adapted to the corridors' muted illumination, so he sneezed. If the room had been a garage, then it was intended for people who drove semis.

Black silk hangings concealed the walls. Though benches full of equipment filled much of the interior, the floor was incongruously covered in Turkish rugs—runners a meter wide and four meters long—except for a patch of bare concrete around a floor drain in an outside corner.

"Oh, my goodness, Mr. Jones!" said the wispy little man who'd been bent over a circuit board when they entered. He bustled toward them, raising his glasses to his forehead. "I'd meant to leave the door open but I forgot completely. Oh, Iphigenia, you must think I'm the greatest fool on Earth!"

"What I think is that you're the sweetest person I know, Wally," the girl said, patting his bald head. He blushed crimson. "But just a little absentminded, perhaps."

"Mr. Jones is going to help me advertise for a volunteer," Wally said to the girl. "I don't see how we can get anybody, and we really *must* have someone, you know."

"Pleased to meet you, Mr. Jones," Genie said, offering her hand with mock formality.

"Ah, Howard, please," Howard said. "Ah, I have a position with Strangeco. A very lowly one at present."

"That's what my father likes in employees," Genie said in a half-joking tone. "Lowliness. My step-father, I should say. Mother buried two husbands, but Robert buried her."

Howard shook her hand, aware that he was learning things about the Wizard of Fast Food that the
tabloids would pay good money for. Remembering
the uneasiness he'd felt while walking through the
mansion, he also realized that the money he'd get
for invading Strange's privacy couldn't possibly be
good enough.

An area twenty feet square in the center of the lab
was empty of equipment. Across it, beyond Wally as
Howard faced him, was what looked like an irregular,
razor-thin sheet of glass on which bright images flickered. If that was really the flat-plate computer display
it looked like, it was more advanced than anything
Howard had heard of on the market.

"Well, Mr. Popple . . . ," Howard said. If the conversation continued in the direction Genie was taking
it, Howard would learn things he didn't think he'd
be safe knowing. "If you could tell me just what you
need from me?"

"Oh, please call me Wally," the little man said,
taking Howard's hand and leading him toward the
thin display. "You see, this piece of mica is a, well,
a window you could call it."

Wally glanced over his shoulder, then averted his
eyes with another bright blush. As he'd obviously
hoped, Genie was following them.

"I noticed that shadows seemed to move in it," Wally
said, peering intently at what indeed was a piece of
mica rather than a high-tech construction. Hair-fine
wires from a buss at the back touched the sheet's
ragged circumference at perhaps a hundred places.
"That was six years ago. By modulating the current to
each sheet separately—it's not one crystal, you know,

it's a series of sheets like a stack of paper and there's a dielectric between each pair—I was able to sharpen the images to, well, what you see now."

Howard eyed the display. A group of brightly dressed people walked through a formal garden. The women wore dresses whose long trains were held by page boys, and the men were in tights and tunics with puffed sleeves. They carried swords as well, long-bladed rapiers with jeweled hilts.

"How do you generate the images, Wally?" Howard said. "This isn't fed from a broadcast signal, is it?"

"They aren't generated at all," Genie said. "They're real. Show Howard how you can move the point of view, Wally."

Obediently the little man stepped to the computer terminal on the bench beside the slab of mica. On the monitor was a graph with about thirty bars in each of two superimposed rows.

Wally touched keys, watching the mica. A bar shrank or increased at each stroke, and the picture shifted with the jerking clarity of a rotated kaleidoscope.

"Hey!" said Howard as what he thought was a lion turned and raised its feathered head. Its hooked beak opened and the long forked tongue vibrated in a cry which the mica didn't transmit. "That's a chimera!"

"I thought so at first," said Genie, "but they're supposed to be part goat too."

"I don't think it's anything that has a name in our world," Wally said, making further small adjustments. "Of course the people seem to be, well, normal."

"Not normal where I come from!" Howard said. Except maybe in his dreams. "And what do you mean about *our* world? Where's that?"

He pointed. The image tumbled into a scene of vividly-dressed gallants fencing while a semicircle of women and other men watched. The duellists were good, *damned* good, and they didn't have buttons on their swords.

"Robert thinks it's fairyland," Genie said. Her tone was neutral, but Howard heard emotion just beneath the surface of the words. "He thinks Wally's a wizard. Robert also thinks he's a wizard himself."

"Your father has been very generous in supporting my researches, Iphigenia," the little man said, glancing toward but not quite at Genie. "I wish I could convince him that these effects are ordinary science—"

He paused and added self-consciously, "Ordinary physics, at any rate. I'm afraid my researches have been too empirical to qualify as proper science. But the underlying laws are physical, not magic."

The mica showed the dim interior of a great hall, the sort of place that Howard had imagined the Strange Mansion might be. A troupe of acrobats capered on the rush-strewn flagstones, executing remarkable jumps while juggling lighted torches.

Splendid men and gorgeous women watched from tables around the margins of the hall, and over the balcony railings peered children and soberly-dressed servants. At the center of the high table was a grave, bearded man wearing a crown. He held a crystal staff in which violet sparks danced.

Beside the king, occasionally rubbing its scaly head on the back of his carved throne, was a dragon the size of a rhinoceros. It didn't look exactly unfriendly, but its eyes had the trick of constantly scanning in every direction.

"I . . . ," said Howard. "Wally, this is wonderful, just completely amazing, but I don't understand what you want me for. You've already succeeded!"

The image shifted again. Instead of answering, Wally gazed with rapt attention at the new scene. A spring shot from a wooded hillside to splash over rocks into a pool twenty feet below. Butterflies hovered in the flowery glade; in the surrounding forest were vine-woven bowers.

"Wally built the window on his own," Genie said in a low voice. "What Robert is interested in is opening a door into . . . that."

She nodded toward the mica. A couple, hand in hand, walked toward the pool. The man knelt, dipped a silver goblet into the limpid water, and offered it to the lovely woman at his side. She sipped, then returned the cup for him to drink in turn.

Wally shuddered as though he'd been dropped into the pool. He tapped his keyboard several times at random, blurring the image into a curtain of electronic snow.

He turned to Howard and said, speaking very quickly to focus his mind somewhere other than where it wanted to go, "Mr. Strange felt that if we could see the other place, we could enter it. A person could enter it. He's correct—I sent a rabbit through the portal last week—but I don't think anyone will be willing to go when they realize how dangerous it is. That's why I need you to help me write the advertisement for the volunteer, Mr. Jones."

This was going to work better if the little guy was relaxed . . . which probably wouldn't happen as long as Genie Strange was in the same room, *that* was obvious, but Howard at least had to try to calm him down.

"Howard, Wally," Howard said, patting Wally on the shoulder. "Please call me Howard. Now, what's dangerous about the trip? Do you wind up wearing a fly's head if things go wrong?"

"No, it wasn't that, Mister—ah, Howard," Wally said, pursing his lips. "The problem occurred later."

He adjusted the values on his display again, bringing the image of the royal entertainment back onto the mica. A young girl danced on the back of a horse which curvetted slowly, its hooves striking occasional sparks from the flagstones. It was pretty ordinary-looking except for the straight horn in the center of its forehead.

Seeing that Wally wasn't going to say more, Howard raised an eyebrow to Genie. She shrugged and said, "I didn't see it myself—Robert won't let me in here while the tests are going on. But all that really happened is that the rabbit hopped out, perfectly all right, and a lizard ate it. The same thing could have happened anywhere."

"The lizard stared at the poor rabbit and drew it straight into its jaws, step by step," Wally said without looking at the others. "It knew it was doomed but it went anyway. I've never in my life seen anything so horrible."

Then you don't watch the TV news a lot, Howard thought. Aloud he said, "It was a basilisk, you mean? Not just a lizard?"

"It was a lizard," Wally insisted stubbornly. "But it wasn't a lizard from, well, this world. It was horrible, and there are any number of other horrible things over there. It's really too dangerous to send somebody into that world, but that's the only way we can get . . . things."

"Well, an assault rifle ought to take care of any basilisks that come by," Howard said reasonably. "Or dragons either, which is more to the point. Basilisks aren't supposed to be big enough to eat people."

He sighed. "I hate to say this, Wally, but science always seems to win out over romance. I *really* hate to say it."

"But that's just what I mean, Howard," Wally said despairingly. "I had a leash on the bunny so I could pull it back, but it didn't pass through the portal. The leash was still lying on the floor when the bunny disappeared. The volunteer won't be able to take a gun or even clothes, and I really don't believe he'll be able to bring the scepter back for Mr. Strange."

"Robert thinks that purple scepter gives the fairy king his power," Genie said, her hands clasped behind her back as if to underscore the restraint in her voice. "Robert wants someone to go through Wally's portal and steal the scepter."

With absolutely no feeling she added, "Robert sacrificed a black hen the night Wally sent the rabbit through. He did it over the drain there—"

She nodded toward the bare concrete.

"—but you can still smell the blood caught in the pipe. Can't you?"

"Now, Iphigenia," Wally said, blushing again. "Your father has his ways, but he's been very generous with me."

Howard's nose wrinkled. He'd noticed a faint musty odor, but the room was so ripe with the smells of

electronics working—ozone, hot insulation, and flux—
that he hadn't given any thought to it. He still wasn't
sure that what he smelled was rotting blood rather
than mildew or wet wool, but now that Genie'd spoken he wouldn't be able to get the other notion out
of his mind.

"Wally, you're a genius!" the girl said so forcefully
as to sound hostile. "You could go anywhere and find
somebody to fund your work! I only wish you had."

Wally turned and looked her in the face for the first
time. "Thank you for saying that, Iphigenia," he said,
"but it isn't true. I went many places after I first saw
what the mica could do, and they all sent me away.
Your father thinks I'm a magician and he's wrong; but
he doesn't call me crazy or a charlatan."

A door—the door that the light had led Howard
to—opened. Robert Strange, identifiable from the
rare photos that appeared in news features but much
craggier and *harsher* in person, stepped through.
He wore a long-sleeved black robe embroidered
with symbols Howard didn't recognize, and through
the sash at his waist he'd thrust a curved dagger of
Arab style. Hilt and scabbard both were silver but
decorated with runes filled with black niello.

"Who are you?" Strange demanded, his eyes fixed on
Howard. His voice was like scales scraping on stone,
and his black pupils had a reptilian glitter.

The news photographs hadn't shown the long scar
down Strange's left cheekbone. There were many ways
he could've been cut, but only one reason Howard
could imagine that a man with Strange's money wouldn't
have had the scar removed by plastic surgery: pride.
It was a schlaeger scar, a vestige of the stylized duels

with heavy sabers that still went on secretly at the old German universities. The purpose of a schlaeger bout wasn't to defeat one's foe but rather to get the scar as proof of courage and disregard for the laws which banned the practice.

Mind you, Howard was pretty sure that Strange's opponent had left his share of blood on the hall's floor as well.

"He's a—" said Genie before either Howard or Wally could speak.

"Iphigenia, go to your quarters at once," Strange said in the same rustling tone as before. He didn't speak loudly, but his voice cut through the buzz of electronics as surely as a mower would the flowery meadow that Howard thought of when entering the room. "You disturb Master Popple. I've warned you about this."

"But there's nobody else to *talk* to!" Genie said. Though she complained, she walked quickly toward the door of her suite.

Strange returned his attention to Howard. "I said," he repeated, "who are you?"

"Mr. Strange, I asked M—that is, Howard to help me—" Wally said.

"I'm the volunteer you requested for your experiment, sir," Howard said without the least suggestion of a quaver in his voice. "Wally here—Mr. Popple—noted that the agent won't be able to carry a gun into the other realm, so my skill with a rapier is crucial."

"You know how to use a sword?" Strange snapped.

"Yes, sir," Howard said, standing very straight and keeping his eyes on the tycoon's, hoping that would

make him look open and honest. Even though Howard was telling the truth about the fencing, Strange's
whole tone and manner made it seem that everything
he was being told was a lie.

Besides considering that Strange might have him shot
as a spy, there was the possibility that the Wizard of
Fast Food would demand Howard duel him to prove
his skill. Beating Strange would be dangerous—rich
men were self-willed and explosive if they didn't get
what they wanted. Losing to Strange might be even
worse, especially since Howard didn't imagine he'd
have buttons on his swords any more than the folk
on the other side of the mica window did.

"Since I'm an employee of Strangeco," Howard
continued, visualizing the Thief of Baghdad dancing
over palace walls while monsters snarled beneath, "my
devotion to you is already assured."

"You work for me?" Strange said. Then, as if
he could remember each of the thirty thousand
Strangeco employees world-wide, he said, "What's
your name?"

The door swung *almost* shut behind Genie. "Howard
Albing Jones, sir," Howard said.

"Assistant Marketing Associate in the home office,"
Strange said. *My God, maybe he did know all thirty
thousand!* "Devoted, are you? Pull the other leg,
boy! But that doesn't matter if you've got the guts
for the job."

"Yes, sir, I do," Howard said. He cleared his throat
and went on, "I think I could honestly say I've been
training all my life for this opportunity."

"You practice the Art also, Jones?" Strange demanded,
the hectoring doubt back in his voice. "The Black Arts,

I mean. That's what they call it, the pigmies who adepts like me crush under our heels!"

"Ah, I can't claim to be an adept, sir," Howard said. He couldn't *honestly* claim to be anything but a guy who occasionally watched horror movies. As far as that went, he knew more about being a vampire than being a magician.

"No?" said Strange. "Well, I am, Jones. That's how I built Strangeco from a corner hot dog stand into what it is now. And by His Infernal Majesty! that's how I'll rule the world when I have the staff of power for myself. Nothing will stop me, Jones. Nothing!"

"Mr. Strange, I'm your man!" Howard said. He spoke enthusiastically despite his concern that Strange might reply something along the lines of, "Fine, I'll take your kidneys now to feed my pet ferrets."

"If you serve me well, you won't regret it," Strange said. Unspoken but much louder in Howard's mind was the corollary: *But if you fail, I won't leave enough of you to bury!*

"Master Popple, can you be ready to proceed in two hours?" Strange asked. When he talked to Wally, there was a respect in his tone that certainly hadn't been present when he spoke to Howard or Genie.

"Well, I suppose . . . ," Wally said. He frowned in concentration, then shrugged and said, "I don't see why not, if Howard is willing. I suppose we could start right now, Mr. Strange."

"It'll take me the two hours to make my own preparations," Strange said with a curt shake of his head. "I respect your art, Master Popple, but I won't depend on it alone."

As he strode toward the door, Strange added without

turning his head, "I'll have a black ewe sent over. And if that's not enough—we'll see!"

"Now hold your arms out from your shoulders, please, Howard," Wally said as he changed values on his display. Howard obeyed the way he would if a barber told him to tilt his head.

Waiting as the little man made adjustments gave Howard enough time to look over the room. Much of the racked equipment meant nothing to him, but his eyes kept coming back to a black cabinet that looked like a refrigerator-sized tube mating with a round sofa.

"Wally?" he said, his arms still out. "What's that in the northeast corner? Is it an air conditioner?"

"Oh, that's the computer that does the modulations," Wally said. "You can put your arms down now if you like. I used a Sun workstation to control the window, but the portal requires greatly more capacity. I'd thought we'd just couple a network of calculation servers to the workstation, but Mr. Strange provided a Cray instead to simplify the setup for the corrections."

"Oh," said Howard, wondering what a supercomputer cost. Pocket change to the Wizard of Fast Food, he supposed.

"Now if you'll turn counterclockwise, please . . . ," Wally said. "About fifteen degrees."

Howard wore a cotton caftan that came from Genie's suite. She'd brought it in when Howard protested at standing buck naked in the middle of the floor with security cameras watching. Howard was willing to accept that the clothes wouldn't go through the portal with him, but waiting while Pete and his partner chuckled about his masculine endowments was a different matter.

Not that there was anything wrong with his masculine endowments.

Genie didn't stay, but Howard knew she was keeping abreast of what went on through the part-open door. He wasn't sure whether he was glad of that or not.

The mica window looked onto the glade where Howard would enter the other world if everything went right. Occasionally a small animal appeared briefly—once Howard saw what looked very much like a pink bass swimming through the air—but Wally had chosen the site because it was isolated. There was only so much you could get from leaves quivering, even if they did seem to be solid gold.

The carpets, layered like roof shingles over the concrete, weren't the neutrally exotic designs you normally saw on Oriental rugs. Some of these had stylized camels and birds, sure; but one had tanks, jets, and bright explosions, while peacock-winged devils capered as they tortured people against the black background of the newer-looking rugs.

Around where Howard stood was a six-pointed star drawn in lime like the markings of a football field. Howard would've expected a pentacle, but he didn't doubt Strange knew what he was doing.

All Howard himself was sure of was that he was taking a chance at adventure when it appeared. If that was a bad idea, then he hoped he wouldn't have long to regret his decision.

It might be a very bad idea.

"There," said Wally. "There's nothing more I can

do until we actually begin building the charge. Then I may have to—"

Robert Strange entered through a pedestrian door set in one of the six vehicle doors along the outside wall. The black sheep he led looked puzzled, a feeling which Howard himself echoed.

"You're ready, Master Popple?" he asked.

"*Ey-eh-he-e*," said the sheep. Strange jerked the leash viciously. The cord looked like silver, but it was functional enough to choke the sheep to silence when Strange lifted his arm.

"Yes, Mr. Strange," Wally said. "I'm a little worried about Howard's mass, though. Eighty-seven kilos may be too much."

"Too much?" snapped Strange. "If you needed more transformers, you should have said so!"

"Too much for the fabric of the universe, Mr. Strange," said Wally, as mild as ever but completely undaunted at the anger of a man who scared the living crap out of Howard Jones. "I really don't want to go to more than thirty kilowatts."

Strange sniffed. "The subject's ready?" he said. "You, Jones; you're ready?"

"*Ey-eh-he?*" the sheep repeated, rolling its eyes. Her eyes, Howard assumed, since Strange said he was fetching a ewe. The tycoon's daggerhilt winked in the bright laboratory lighting.

"Yes, sir!" Howard said.

Strange grimaced, then bent and tied the leash around a ring set in the drain. He turned his head to Howard and said, "You know what you're going to do?"

"Sir, I'm going to enter the other land," Howard

said. "I'll take the scepter from the king of that land and return here to you with it."

As a statement of intent it was concise and accurate. As a plan of action it lacked detail, but there wasn't enough information on this side of the portal to form a real plan. Howard was uneasily aware that his foray, even if he wound up in a dragon's gullet, would provide information so that the next agent could do better.

"All right," Strange said. "Give me a moment and then proceed."

There were drapes bunched among the wall hangings. As Strange spoke, he drew them along a track in the ceiling to separate his corner of the room from Howard and Wally. The ewe bleated again.

"You may begin, Master Popple," Strange called, his voice muffled by the thick fabric. He broke into a musical chant. The sounds from his throat weren't words, or at least words in English.

"You're ready, Howard?" Wally said.

Howard nodded. His throat was dry and he didn't want to embarrass himself by having his voice crack in the middle of a simple word like, "Yes."

Wally rotated a switch, cutting the ceiling lights to red beads among the dimming ghosts of the fluorescent fixtures. The sheet of mica, bright with the daylight of another world, shone like a lantern beside the little man as he typed commands.

There was a reptilian viciousness to Strange's voice, and the sheep was managing to whimper like a frightened baby. The hair on Howard's arms and the back of his neck began to rise. For a moment he thought that was his reaction to the sounds coming from beyond the drapes, but as the fluorescents cooled to

absolute black Howard saw a faint violet aura clinging
to three racks of equipment.

Wally was generating very high frequency current
at a considerable voltage. Howard decided he didn't
want to think about *how* high the voltage was.

Wally muttered as he worked. Though Howard
could see his lips move, the words weren't audible
over the hum of five transformers along the outside
wall. The opening between Genie's door and the jamb
was faintly visible.

The air spluttered. Howard felt a directionless pull,
unpleasant without being really painful. Violet light
flickered through the mica, a momentary pulse from
the world across the barrier.

Strange shouted a final word. The sheep bleated on
a rising note ending in so awful a gurgle that Howard
pressed his hands to his ears before he remembered
that moving might affect Wally's calculations. The ewe's
hooves rattled on the concrete; the curtain billowed
as the animal thrashed.

Howard would've covered his ears even if he had
thought about Wally. The sound was *horrible*.

Wally typed, his eyes on the computer display. He'd
sucked his lower lip between his teeth to chew as he
concentrated. The transformers hummed louder but
didn't change tone.

Howard felt the indescribable pull again. In the
other world the violet haze formed again, this time
in the shape of a human being.

A blue flash and a *BANG!* like a cannon shot
engulfed the lab, stunning Howard into a wordless
shout. He clapped his hands, a reflex to prove that
he was still alive.

The air stank of burning tar. Dirty red flames licked from one of the transformers on the outside wall. Howard drew in a deep breath of relief. He immediately regretted it when acrid smoke brought on a fit of coughing.

Strange snatched open the curtains, his face a mask of cold fury. The ewe lay over the drain, her legs splayed like those of a squashed insect. Her eyes still had a puzzled look, but they were already beginning to glaze.

Wally changed values at his keyboard with a resigned expression. Howard looked for a fire extinguisher. He didn't see one, but he walked past Wally and turned the main lights back on. The transformer was smoldering itself out, though an occasional sizzle made Howard thankful that the floor was covered with non-conductive wool.

"What went wrong?" Strange said. "I know that the transformer failed; *why* did it fail?"

"The load was too great," Wally said simply. "We very nearly succeeded. If we replace the transformer—"

"We'll double the capacity," Strange said. "We'll make another attempt tonight, at midnight this time. I never thought you were careful enough with your timing, Master Popple."

"Sir, I don't think it would be safe to increase output beyond—" Wally said.

"We'll double it!" Strange said, his tone a rasp like steel grating on rib bones. "If we don't need the extra wattage, then we won't use it, but we'll use as much as it requires!"

He looked disgustedly at the dagger in his hand, then wiped the blade on the curtain and sheathed

the weapon. He strode past Howard and Wally to the
hall door; Howard watched him with a fixed smile,
uncomfortably aware that instinct tensed him to run
in case Strange leaped for his throat.

The Thief of Baghdad might've had a better idea.
On the other hand, Howard didn't remember the
Thief of Baghdad facing anything quite like Robert
Strange.

Strange thumped the hall door closed; it was too
heavy to bang. At the sound, Genie's door opened a
little wider and the slim girl returned. She grimaced
when she saw the ewe. It'd voided its bowels when it
died, so that odor mingled with the fresh blood and
burned insulation.

"Are you all right, Wally?" she asked. "And you,
Howard. I'm not used to there being anybody but
Wally here."

"I'm sorry you had to see that, Iphigenia," Wally
said with a perturbed glance toward the ewe. "You
really shouldn't have come in until the crew has
cleaned things up."

"Wally, I've lived with Robert for fifteen years,"
Genie said bluntly. "There've been worse things than
the occasional dead animal. I was worried about you
and Howard."

"It just tickled a little," Howard said. If he let
himself think about events in the right way, he was
pretty sure he could make the last ten minutes or
so sound more heroic than they'd seemed while they
were happening.

"There wasn't any risk, Iphigenia," Wally said. At
first he didn't look directly at her, but then he raised
his eyes with an effort of will. "Ah—I really appreciate

your concern, but right now I have something important to discuss with Mr.—with Howard, that is. Can you, I mean would you . . . ?"

"All right, Wally," the girl said, sounding puzzled and a little hurt. She nodded to Howard and walked to her room with swift, clean strides. This time the door shut firmly.

One of the vehicular doors in the outside wall started up with a rumble of heavy gears. A team of swarthy men, beardless but heavily mustached, stood beside a flatbed truck. They entered, paying no attention to Howard and Wally. One lifted the sheep over his shoulder and walked back to the truck with it; his three fellows started disconnecting the wrecked transformer. They talked among themselves in guttural singsongs.

"Will you come here please, Howard?" Wally said, showing no more interest in the workmen than they did in him. He adjusted the mica screen to show the spring again. "I, ah, have a favor to ask you."

A couple—not the same ones as before—sat on the pool's mossy coping, interlacing the fingers of one hand as they passed a cup back and forth with the other. Wally tightened the focus so that their mutually loving expressions were unmistakable.

"Yes, Wally?" Howard prodded.

"The water of this spring appears to have certain properties," Wally said. He looked fixedly at Howard to avoid watching the couple who'd begun to fondle one another. The statuesque blonde lay back on the sward and tugged her partner over her without bothering to walk to the privacy of the nearby bowers. "You'll have noticed that."

"I sure notice something," Howard said. He wasn't sure how he felt about the show: it was real people, not actors. Well, actors were real people too but they knew they were going to be watched.

The workmen hoisted the transformer by hand instead of bringing in a derrick for the job. It must weigh close to half a ton. They walked out and slid it onto the truck bed, forcing a squeal from the springs.

Wally grimaced and blurred the image to bright sparkles within the mica sheet. "If I succeed in opening the portal to the other world, Howard," he said, "you'll have a very difficult job to gain the king's scepter. I don't believe in magic, not here or there either one, but the animal guarding the king appears formidable."

"The dragon," Howard said. "Yeah, it does."

If Howard let himself consider the details of how he was going to get the scepter, it'd scare the spit out of him. By limiting his thoughts to vague swoops across the hall on a handy rope, followed by a mighty leap from a balcony-level window, he was managing to keep his aplomb.

"And of course we're not sure it'll be possible to bring inanimate objects through the portal in this direction, since we can't do it while going the other way," Wally continued with a solemn nod. He started to refocus on the spring, then snatched his hand back from the keyboard with a blush.

"I understand all the difficulties and dangers you'll face, Howard," Wally said. He stared in the direction of Genie's closed door; he looked as if he was about to cry. "Regardless, I'd like you to do me a favor if you can. I'd like you to bring me a phial of water from the spring we just looked at. I . . . I'd be very grateful."

You poor little guy! Howard thought. Aloud he said, "Ah, Wally? I'll do what I can—"

Which might not be a heck of a lot. *If* Howard arrived, he'd be bare-assed naked and in the middle of a bunch of guys with swords they knew how to use. Not to mention the occasional dragon.

"—but you know, it isn't that hard to, ah, meet girls." He paused to choose the next words carefully. "Lots of times just being around one for a while is enough to, you know, bring the two of you together. If you play your cards right."

The truck drove off with a snort of diesel exhaust as the garage door began to rumble down. The corpses of the sheep and transformer lay together in the bed of the vehicle.

"I've never played cards at all, Howard," the little man said with a sad smile. "I guess this is hard for a handsome young man like you to understand, but . . ."

He turned his head away and wiped his eyes fiercely.

"Hey, that's all right, Wally," Howard said, patting him on the back. "Sure, I'll take care of that if there's, you know, any way to do it. No problem."

Compared to the rest of the assignment, that was the gospel truth.

"Thank you, Howard," Wally said through a racking snuffle. "I'm, well, I'm lucky to have met a real hero like you in my time of need."

Only faintly audible through the heavy doors, another

big truck was pulling up outside. A relay clicked and the machinery began to rumble again.

"I feel sure we're going to succeed," Wally added. "If we have to double the field strength, well, that's just what we're going to do. No matter what!"

Wally sounded a lot more cheerful when he made that promise than Howard was to hear it.

With the six new transformers in place, the line almost filled the outside wall. On that side only the curtained-off corner—they were already drawn—didn't have machinery squatting on it. Howard could still smell burned insulation. He'd never thought he'd be thankful for a stink like that, but it covered other possible reminders of the afternoon's experiment.

Wally looked at Howard and tried to force a grin. His expression would've been more appropriate for somebody being raped by a Christmas tree.

"Hey, buck up, buddy," Howard said. "We're going to be fine!"

Funny, but telling the lie made Howard feel that the words might possibly be true. Logically he knew a lot better.

The door hidden behind the curtain opened. Howard heard a *clink* over the hum of machinery as something hard brushed against the raised lintel. He wondered what animal Strange was bringing in to sacrifice this time. Howard had expected a heifer or maybe an elephant, but Strange would've had to raise the vehicular door to bring in animals that big.

Strange stuck his head out between two curtain panels. "Are you ready to proceed, Master Popple?" he asked. He held the curtains together so that all

Howard could see was the throat of his garments. He seemed to be wearing the same silver-marked black satin as in the afternoon.

"I believe—" Wally said. He caught Howard's terse nod and continued, "Yes, we're ready, Mr. Strange. It'll take ninety seconds from whenever we start to build the field."

"Start now, then," Strange said curtly. He drew the curtains tight behind him and began to chant. His words had considerable musical power despite being complete gibberish. That was also true of opera, of course, so far as Howard was concerned.

Wally tried to smile again, then busied himself with his keyboard. The mica window looked onto the glade, empty save for trees and the flitting passage of a bird whose plumage was as purely blue as the summer sky. Howard watched the scientist, and he watched images on the mica; but more compelling than those, he listened through the curtains at his back to the sound of Robert Strange's voice chanting.

Howard felt the hairs lift from his body. Where those of his chest touched the loose caftan they tickled like the feeling at the back of a dry throat that you can't seem to swallow away. Violet haze blurred the air beyond the mica.

Genie Strange screamed.

Howard turned. The door to Genie's room was closed—closed and latched. The drapes around Strange and his activities bulged outward.

Genie hopped through and fell, dragging a section of the velvet down. The scarf used to gag her had slipped out of her mouth; it was the only garment she was wearing. Her wrists and ankles were tied together behind her back, but she'd managed to undo the cord that'd bound her to the drain.

Robert Strange, his face as hard and contorted as that of a marble demon, stepped out behind her. He grabbed a handful of Genie's black hair with his free hand.

"Hey!" Howard said. There was a bank of equipment between him and the Stranges. As gracefully as if he'd been practicing all his life, Howard took two running steps, planted his right palm on the rack, and leaped over with his legs swung off to his left side. Even the Thief of Baghdad would be impressed—

Until the caftan's billowing hem caught the chassis full of plug-in circuits on top of the rack. As Howard's legs straightened, the tightening cloth spilled him like a lassoed steer. Strange looked at him without expression.

Howard sprang up. The torn caftan, bunched now around his ankles, tripped him again.

Strange lifted Genie's head, avoiding her attempts to bite him. He poised the curved dagger in his right hand over her throat. Howard grabbed the sides of the rug on which he'd fallen and jerked with all his strength, snatching Strange's feet out from under him.

"You . . . !" shouted Strange as he toppled backward. Genie'd tossed her short hair free of his grip, but he didn't lose the dagger in his other hand. It was underneath when the Wizard of Fast Food hit the concrete.

The chassis that Howard'd dragged to the floor with him was popping and spluttering, but he wasn't prepared for the flash of violet light that filled the interior of the lab. It was so intense that Howard only vaguely noticed the accompanying thunderclap. He heard Wally cry out and turned.

Wally wasn't there. His clothing, from brown shoes to the pair of reading glasses he wore tilted up on his forehead, lay in the middle of the hexagram. The hundred and twenty-three pounds of Wally Popple had vanished.

Except for an image in the mica window.

Howard lifted Genie before he remembered that her stepfather and the dagger might be of more immediate concern. He looked back.

He'd been right the first time. Strange's face was turned toward Howard. He looked absolutely furious. He'd managed to thrash into a prone position while dying, but the silver hilt projecting from the middle of his back showed that dying was certainly what he'd done.

The transformer on the far left of the line shorted out. The one next to it went a heartbeat later, and when the third failed it showered the room with blobs of flaming tar. One of them slapped the mica window, and shattered it like a bomb.

"Can you please untie me, Howard?" asked the girl in his arms. "Though the way things are starting to happen in here, maybe that could wait till we're outside."

"Right!" said Howard. "Right!"

He paused to shrug off what was left of the caftan; it had started to burn as well. Somehow he couldn't get concerned about what the guards thought of him now.

Because he and Genie were going to be gone for at least three weeks and a fourth besides if the Chinese authorities agreed to open Tibet to Strangeco—which they would, Howard Jones wasn't called the Swashbuckler of Fast Food for nothing—Howard stopped by the mansion's former garage for a moment. He liked to, well, keep an eye on how things were going.

He'd had the big room cleaned and nearly emptied immediately after the wedding, but he still smelled the bitterness of burned insulation. He supposed it was mostly in his mind by now.

Genie'd wanted to tear the garage down completely since it held nothing but bad memories for her, but she'd agreed to let Howard keep the room so long as he'd had the door into her old suite welded shut. She wasn't the sort of girl to object to the whim of the man who'd saved her life; besides, she loved her husband.

Howard went to the skeletal apparatus on the one rack remaining in the room. Three hair-fine filaments were still attached to the top edge of a piece of mica no bigger than a quarter.

Howard bent to peer into it. If you looked carefully at the right times, you could see images in the mica.

The focus wandered. Howard hadn't tried to adjust the apparatus himself or let anybody else take a look at it. Mostly all there was to see was snow, but this time he was in luck.

The peephole looked out at the spring where couples used to cavort. Wally was there with his entourage, checking the generating turbine he'd built to power the first electric lights in his new home. If Howard understood the preparations he'd seen going on in the royal palace last week, telephones were about to follow.

When Wally turned with a satisfied expression, Howard waved. He knew the little fellow couldn't see him, but it made Howard feel he was sort of keeping in touch. Wally walked out of the image area surrounded by courtiers.

Howard checked his watch and sighed; he needed to get moving. He'd promised the company fencing team that he and Genie would at least drop in on their match with Princeton. After Howard instituted morning unity-building fencing exercises throughout Strangeco, a number of the employees had become fencing enthusiasts.

Howard took a last look at the pool in the other world. He'd never seen Wally take a sip of the water, and it didn't seem likely that he ever would.

After all, a powerful wizard like Master Popple had to beat off beautiful women with a stick.

The Ensorcelled ATM

~~~◉~~~

Michael F. Flynn

THE SALOON HAD BEEN DONE up remarkably well in its time, but its time was now demonstrably past. Years ago, when Gavagan bought the building, it had been even more run-down, drawing its clientele from the lowest strata of society, and was not at all the sort of place where a respectable man would take his thirst. Gavagan had renovated the place, having it in mind to cater to a more intellectual patronage. He did not quite achieve that lofty goal, but he at least lifted the saloon from its long decay.

Time, of course, had softened the renovations, and the odors of a great many beers had left their memory in the wood. The flooring was scuffed and planed from the passage of countless feet. Even the dark, rich surface of the bar had accumulated its share of nicks and scratches. A stuffed owl mounted on the back wall had a seedy appearance; and in the far corner near the ceiling could be seen the frayed straw of a nest, as if a bird had taken up residence.

The stranger at the far end of the bar, near the window, was a middle-aged man, though of uncertain years, for his gray hair seemed older than the rest of him. The three-piece suit marked him as a man of consequence, although the jacket had come off and the vest was unbuttoned. He'd had two cocktails already, but was not yet what you would call "under the weather." His face bore the soft look of far-off concentration.

The brass blonde, seated at the table with two gentlemen, tipped her head toward him and said, "Now there's a fellow with a few problems."

"We should all be so lucky, Mrs. Jonas," young Keating answered, "to have only a few of those."

Mr. Witherwax paid no attention to the interruption, for interruption it was. "All I said is that the neighborhood is changing. That's all I said." He was drinking boilermakers.

"Well, it's the sort of thing that always happens in a dynamic community," Keating said. "Times change."

Mr. Witherwax stuck his chin up. "Did I say they don't? I read in a book one time that . . ."

Mr. Gross, occupying a stool at the near end of the bar farther from the window, raised his glass to the bartender. "Mr. Cohan, another beer, if you please." Then, with a nod over his shoulder, "He's always reading *something* in a book."

The bartender smiled. "It's a fine thing in a man, to be after reading the books."

"Maybe so," Mr. Gross allowed, "but he doesn't have to go and recite them back to us, now does he? And while you're at it, see what that dapper gentleman down the other end is drinking, with my compliments."

"All I said is it's changing," Mr. Witherwax insisted. "I didn't say nothing about the immigrants."

"And a good thing, too," Mr. Cohan suggested as he busied himself with the bottles, "the half of them being Irish."

"Irish, sure," said Keating. "And Arab and Pakistani and . . ."

"Aren't Pakistanis Arabs?" said Mrs. Jonas.

"No, ma'am. No more than that Finns are French."

"That don't matter to me," insisted Mr. Witherwax. "All I said was it's not the same neighborhood it used to be."

"We don't get many of those Arabs in here," Mr. Cohan said. "But the Irish, now . . ."

"That's because their religion—Islam—doesn't let them drink alcohol." Keating worked at the library and in consequence had a great deal of miscellany in his head, perhaps as much as his companion, Mr. Witherwax, although, unlike the latter, he tended to keep it there and not let it go spilling about.

Mr. Cohan drew back in shock and turned to Gross. "Did you ever hear the like of it, Mr. Gross? I know there are those who cannot handle the creature, but a drink or two is a fine thing for a pleasant evening of talk." He turned to the stranger, wishing to include

him in the general conversation, for Gavagan had
always envisioned his establishment as much a salon
as a saloon. "Isn't that right?"

The stranger's eyes came into focus and he looked
around as if surprised to find himself present. "I'm
sorry . . . ?" he said.

Mr. Gross said helpfully, "We was talking about the
neighborhood and the Irish and—"

"Damn the Irish," the man said, draining his
glass.

A profound silence fell over the room. Witherwax
traded looks with his two companions. Gross studied
his beer. Mr. Cohan appeared to have something
lodged in his throat. After a moment's strangled
silence, that worthy said gently, "Gavagan does not
care for me to be chastising a patron. It's bad for
the trade. But I'll not be hearing such talk in this
establishment."

The stranger pushed his glass away and sighed. "I
shouldn't've had that second drink. I apologize . . . Mr.
Cohan, is it? I don't usually speak so intemperately, but
I have been having some troubles lately and the people
who have been giving them to me are Irish."

"There," said the brass blonde to her friends. "I
told you he had troubles."

"Troubles, is it?" Mr. Cohan said. "Well, the Irish
are good at giving those out, though we always seem
to have enough left over for ourselves. But it will do
you to know that we here at Gavagan's have heard
people's troubles before, but never once did they damn
anyone; not even that Italian joint around the corner,
which may even deserve the damning because they
pour short measure."

"Didn't that magician fellow damn someone one time?" said Witherwax.

"Theophrastus V. Abaris," said the bartender, drawing the syllables out. "I'd forgotten about him. Sure, he cursed poor Mr. Murdoch, when the young felly was after losing his dragon."

"What sort of troubles?" Mr. Gross asked the stranger.

"Do you remember Madame Lavoisin?" said Mrs. Jonas. "Now *she* was trouble."

Mr. Witherwax gestured toward the bar. "Does he look like a man who goes to a beauty parlor?"

"I asked . . . ," said Gross.

"These days they have unisex parlors," said Keating.

"And we'll have none of *that* talk in Gavagan's, either," said Mr. Cohan, who had only heard part of it. "'You need sex parlors.' What is the world coming to?"

"I asked . . . ," said Gross.

"No, no," said Keating. "I meant beauty parlors."

"Madame Lavoisin sometimes took in men . . . ," Mrs. Jonas said.

"Quiet!" cried Gross. Everyone turned to look at him.

"Now, there's no need to be shouting, Mr. Gross," said the bartender.

"I only wanted to know what sort of troubles our friend here has been having that he damns the Irish for them."

"I didn't mean it the way it sounded," the man said. "It was only my frustration talking. Look, I'll stand a round for the rest of you to make amends."

Mr. Cohan busied himself with the makings. Another boilermaker for Mr. Witherwax. A Presidente for both Keating and Mrs. Jonas. Gross, taking advantage of the offer, switched from beer to a whiskey sour with muddled fruit. The stranger asked for a club soda. "Two cocktails were one too many," he said.

"Now," said Mr. Cohan, having settled everyone with their libations, "perhaps you will tell us your story and let us be judging the fault of any Irish."

The man sat up straight on his stool and buttoned his vest. He looked about the room at five attentive pairs of eyes. "I don't know how you can help me, but . . ."

"My name is W. Wilson Newbury, and I am a banker by trade . . ."

"I knew it," Mr. Witherwax whispered to his companions. "Just look at his suit."

"Hush," said Mrs. Jonas. "Go on dear."

"You would think that my life would be all Kiwanis meetings and mortgages, and I'll be the first to admit that I've pretty much lived the standard, bourgeois life—married, two kids, both grown now, steady work and steady promotion—and I've never seen any reason to apologize for it. Even so, some strange things have happened to me . . ." Newbury sighed and shook his head. "It's not something I ask for, but sometimes it seems as if I'm a magnet of some sort."

"Say," said Gross to the bartender, "do you remember that young Van Nest fella, always had those critters following him? He was something of a magnet, too."

"Well," said Newbury, "my firm has been investing in out-of-state banks. You have to do that, to stay viable these days. A few months ago, the M & A people—that's Mergers and Acquisitions—tipped us to a good prospect in your city. A small immigrant bank on Maclean Avenue. Yes, Mr. Cohan, 'Irish Broadway.' We were interested because the Irish have a good history of bootstrapping. The Irish Emigrant Society, for example, during the nineteenth century, began as what we call today a 'microlender,' and grew to become Emigrant Bank. That was why we interested in this *Luchorpán Ltd*. It seemed poised for the same sort of growth."

"In my day," Witherwax said, "banks had real names. 'First National Bank.' 'Security Trust.' What do you see now? 'Rock Bank.' 'Fleet Bank.' Do they keep stones in their vaults? Do they loan only to sailors?"

"It's all marketing nowadays," said Mr. Gross.

Mrs. Jonas waved her hand in the air. "You're not letting Mr. Newbury talk."

The banker smiled his thanks at her. "Esau Drexel— that's my president—asked me to look into matters personally. Harrison Trust is an old-fashioned firm, and we believe in the personal touch. There is only so much you can learn from paperwork, regulatory filings, and web searches. He wanted me to form an impression of the people who ran this bank, to see if they were the sort we could work with.

"I'm used to these sudden trips out of town and Denise—my wife—has learned to live with them. I always keep a small carry-on suitcase packed and ready. The next morning, I took the early shuttle to LaGuardia, where the Luchorpán bank manager met me. Conn MacNai was a short fellow with flaming red hair—the sort of red you really only see in cartoon

Irish. I thought him rather young at first to be in such a position. His skin was very fine and there was not a trace of gray in his hair—not something I can say of myself any more, I'm afraid. Yet when I looked closer I received the impression that he was much older than he seemed. His eyes, I think. They had a cast to them that only age can give.

"Mr. MacNai had reserved a room for me at the Holiday Inn and he took me there first, so I could drop off my valise. He drove a compact car, an Escort I think, and it was no fun for me to fold myself into it. Fortunately, the bank was not too far from the hotel and the trip was a short one.

"When we pulled into the lot, I noticed several children clustered around the ATM, but when they saw us, they ran. I noticed some graffiti on the machine and asked MacNai if he ever had trouble with the local gangs, but he said no."

Mr. Cohan nodded. "I know the neighborhood."

"Well, MacNai showed me around the place. It was quite small and tidy, if you know what I mean. A teller line. One or two desks for loan officers. A room for confidential meetings. What surprised me was the vault for the safe deposit boxes, which was quite extensive—larger, I thought, than the size of the bank warranted. I said so to MacNai, but he told me that many of their depositors, being from the old country, like to keep their valuables in a secure place." Newbury lifted his club soda and sipped from it thoughtfully.

"There was one odd detail," he said when he set it down again. "The builder had managed some trick with the windows. They were leaded in some queer way and, though you wouldn't know it to look at them, they acted like prisms, so that the light inside the bank was split into colors as if by stained glass.

"While I was studying the windows trying to see how it was done—I used to work summers for a contractor when I was young—I saw a young boy walk up to the ATM, which was just outside and, when he tried his card and had apparently gotten nothing back, he spat on the cash slot."

"I've felt like doing that myself sometimes," Gross said.

"It's the human touch," Witherwax announced from the table. "That's what's missing in this day and age. When the machines misfunction, there's no one about to speak to."

"The young man," said Newbury, "turned as if he were going to stalk into the bank and make an issue of it, but he saw me looking and gave me such a glare of hatred and suspicion that it quite startled me and I took a step back. Because of that trick with the leaded glass, it seemed to me as if his eyes were as red as his hair.

"MacNai was standing there with me, explaining some arrangement with messenger tubes for drive-up banking, but when he saw what had happened, he took me by the elbow and led me away from the window. For the next minute or so, I kept craning my neck to see if the young hoodlum would come into the bank, for it seemed as if he had taken an instant dislike to me. But he never showed, so I thought I had been mistaken."

Witherwax shook his head. "What's the world coming to?" he asked. "These kids today, they don't show any respect. Mr. Co*han*, another boilermaker, if you please."

"It's not something you should normally worry about," the bartender assured the banker as he handled the bottles and jigger glass without looking. "Those punkas like to act tough, but it's mostly front. They won't *do* nothing to you when they think they'll be seen."

"At the time," Newbury said, "what bothered me was that the bank seemed awfully small for the assets they were claiming in their filings. So I asked to see their books. It wouldn't be unheard of for a small operation to pad their accounts so they'd be bought up at an inflated price. MacNai became very defensive, and that made me more suspicious. However, he must have wanted the capital we represented because he gave in eventually.

"He set me up in that private room and brought the books, which were old-fashioned bound ledgers, believe it or not. One of the reasons they were looking for capital was to modernize their systems. If he had just left me there with the books, I might only have given them a cursory look. The more detailed examination would come later—*if* I recommended we go ahead. But MacNai stood there beside me, fidgeting. Now, even the most honest man can grow nervous at such an examination—"

"It's all those laws," young Keating explained to his companions. "There are so many, you can't get through the day without stepping on one."

"—but I've learned to recognize when it goes beyond mere nervousness. MacNai was hiding something. So, I checked things a little more closely than I otherwise might have."

"And what was it you found?" Mr. Cohan asked. "For I take it you must have found something."

"There were an unusual number of small, unsecured loans, often to the same individuals. Now, that is just the sort of thing a microlender ought to be doing, except that these were consumer loans, pure and simple, not seed money for small businesses."

Mr. Cohan scratched his chin. "There ought to have been a shoe store or two in there."

Newbury waved a hand. "Oh, a few loans of that sort, but only a few. When I pointed out the excessive number of personal loans to MacNai, he hemmed and hawed and finally claimed that the loans were secured by jewels, coin, and other valuables those individuals had entrusted to the safe deposit boxes.

"'It's a new thing, we're after trying, Mr. Newbury,' he said to me. When I replied that microlending was hardly new, he said, 'It took a great deal of time and effort to convince my people to entrust their valuables to this institution. They are quite jealous and suspicious about their fortunes.'

"'Fortunes?' I asked, wondering if the safe deposit vault were as large as it was for some reason.

"MacNai seemed to flush ruddier than he was. 'Tis a manner of speaking in the old country.'

"I wasn't about to take MacNai's word for the contents of his vault. I know it was a matter for the auditors, but he had made me suspicious and I decided to press the issue. He had no legal obligation to show me their contents, but Harrison Trust was under no legal obligation to supply him with capital, either. Finally, he said he would consult with one or two of his depositors and see if he could get their permission to open their boxes for me.

"I had to leave it at that, as it was getting late. MacNai drove me back to the hotel and recommended a restaurant within walking distance—an Irish restaurant, of course. The food was quite good and a pint or two of stout ale added to this spare tire I've put around my waist. I was feeling pretty good when I made my way back to the hotel and had just about decided that there was nothing more to MacNai and his little bank than earnest amateurism and a rowdy neighborhood, but there in the lobby was that tough I had seen spitting at the ATM outside the bank.

"Seen up close, his eyes were gray, not red, and had that same indefinable look of age that MacNai had had. He might have been fifteen or he might have been fifty. I confess I took a step backward on seeing him, but he only smiled and offered me a drink from a flask he carried."

"You didn't drink from it, did you?" Mr. Cohan asked with sudden concern. "No, I can see that you did not, and a good thing, too."

"I should think so," said Newbury. "Who knew what germs it carried?"

"Go on," said Gross. "What did he say to you?"

"Well, despite the friendly gesture of the drink, he was quite rude. He accused me of trying to steal his money. 'I know why ye want to pry open those boxes. It's so ye can plunder what's in 'em.' His brogue was so thick I could scarcely understand him. I tried to assure him that I only wanted to verify the collateral on some loans, but he wouldn't have it. 'Ye're as bad as MacNai,' he said. 'He an' that machine o' his that won't give a bit o' coin when you ask it.'

" 'Is that why you spit at it?' I asked him, but he cried out and lifted his hand as if to strike me. I thought he *did* strike me, but all I felt was a brush of air."

"They don't have a bit of strength," Mr. Cohan said. "It's all in their wits."

"That was a bit too much. I'm a sedentary man, but I keep in shape and I won't shy away from a fight. I grabbed hold of him, but he was a nimble fellow and slipped my grasp. He ran out the door and I followed, but he was gone by the time I reached the parking lot. To make matters worse, the hotel manager lectured *me* about creating a scene in his lobby. I guess he felt he had to say something, and the other fellow had run off.

"I mentioned the incident to MacNai when he came to pick me up the next day. 'All this secrecy about the contents of the safe deposit boxes,' I warned him, 'could sound to some ears like illicit money laundering. And that could get the federal people interested in your operation.'

"That worried him and he brooded all during the drive. Just as we reached Luchorpán, he turned to me and said, 'Look here, Mr. Newbury, it's true that we've had problems with the ATM. It doesn't disburse the money, but it deducts from the depositors' accounts. We've been making those little loans to cover their losses until we figure out what the reason is. I know that's not proper, but we'll get things straight in a few weeks.'

"By that time, I had my doubts, but I decided to

say nothing and wrap up my visit as quickly as possible. I picked three safe deposit boxes at random and MacNai contacted the owners and asked them to come in. One of them refused and, rather than argue over it, I picked another box. While we waited, MacNai brought in some deli sandwiches—corned beef—but I had eaten a large breakfast and didn't touch them.

"The first owner was a little old woman named Maire ni Tuithe. MacNai carefully explained the reason for opening her box. She scowled and argued back and said her hoard—she actually used the word 'hoard'—was her own and no one else's. 'Now, Maire bawn,' said MacNai, 'remember what we all agreed. It does none of us any good to bury it in the ground. We need to make our money work for us. That means we must obey the banking laws, and this gentleman must confirm that the collateral exists. He's got you caught, fair and square, even if it is a rule that he's caught you by and not the scruff of your neck.'

"I can't say I cared much for the way MacNai explained things. He made it sound like I'd tackled the old lady and pinned her to the lobby floor. It seemed to work, though, for she became all sweetness and light after that. They went into the vault with their keys and emerged with a large metal box, which we took into the private room. Ni Tuithe actually locked the door and, after the box was opened, I could see why.

"I have never seen so much gold coin in my life. There were old double eagles and Krugerands and even, I swear, Spanish doubloons and Venetian ducats. That Maire bawn hadn't been kidding when she called it her 'hoard.' Melted down to ingots, the gold would have been worth a fortune; auctioned as coin to collectors, it was worth three fortunes. Museums would duel one another at twenty paces for some of the older pieces. My jaw must have dropped to the vicinity of my knees. 'How did you come by this?' I asked.

"''Tis me life savings,' the woman answered. 'All that stands between me an' a pauper's grave.' And I'll have to admit that her Social Security check would never come close to the income that brass deposit box would bring. I assured her that I had no intention of depriving her of her property, which actually seemed to shock her.

"Once she had gone, I questioned MacNai more closely on the security at the bank. It did not seem especially tight—if the rest of the boxes were as flush as the one I'd picked at random. 'We look out for our own,' MacNai said. 'First, no one would suspect such a trove in a small bank like this. Secondly, we have friends.'

"There was something in the way he said it that made my hairs curl. Then he muttered something about a black pig that I didn't catch. I began to reconsider my thoughts about the bank being a front for criminal elements.

"The other two box-holders came and it was just like the first. Brass containers full of golden coins—except the third, which had a significant amount of silver. That gentleman, O Beirne, was quite smug about it. 'You'll not find silver go like the morning's dew,' he said, much to MacNai's evident irritation. Neither of them made the sort of fuss about opening his box as did the Ni Tuithe woman earlier, but MacNai spoke with them quietly before introducing us, so I suppose he persuaded them the same way.

"In fact, I'm sure of it. For when I left the building I saw all three of them gathered in the parking lot listening to my friend of that morning. He was gesticulating wildly and I heard him say something like, 'not fairly caught,' when he caught sight of me and pointed. 'And there he is, making off with your treasures!'

"Now, they had all seen their safe deposit boxes locked safely back into the vault, so I don't know how they thought I'd be making off with anything, but they all turned to me and seemed almost to leap through the air. The woman, in particular, let out a horrific shriek that nearly froze the blood in my veins—and all this in broad daylight no more than a block from MacLean Avenue!

"I'm no coward, but I know when I'm outnumbered. Beside, Esau doesn't pay me to brawl in the Bronx. I sprinted up the block with them at my heels. It seemed to me as if they rode on the wind. Luck being with me, I found a cab at the corner. The cabbie was a Sikh. He saw my four pursuers and shook his head. 'What a terrible shame,' he said, 'what this neighborhood has come to. They are illegal aliens, you know. They come here and take jobs away from us Americans.'

"I hadn't had an experience like that since Decatur, Georgia. We drove for a while until I had regained a measure of calm. I saw your establishment, and told him to drop me here." Newbury spread his hands. "And now you know why I've had unkind thoughts about the Irish."

❀   ❀   ❀

"Well, as to that," said Mr. Cohan, "it wasn't rightly the Irish you had trouble with. *Luchorpán* was their old name in the Gaelic, but they've been called by other names. That sort has always meant trouble. They can be pleasant enough when they're rightly caught—and then it is all 'yes, sor' and 'no, sor' and 'as you please, sor'—but it doesn't do to turn your back for a moment. They are powerful jealous of their treasures, too. I hadn't heard that they was emigratin', but it doesn't surprise me, things being as they are in the old country."

"There is something I don't understand," Gross said. "I mean, I understand about the colors coming through the window—and it's not many men have the privilege of finding themselves at the rainbow's end—and about spitting at the ATM—"

"It's how you make sure the money doesn't disappear," Witherwax told him. "Didn't Councilman Maguire of the Fifth Ward have that very problem one time?"

Mr. Cohan nodded. "He did that. The poor felly, God rest him, was coming in here before every election to spit in the pot and get a little bit of the luck that was still in it."

"But that's not the part I don't understand," Gross insisted. "It's why the ATM wouldn't give out the money in the first place."

"Why, that sort of money," Mr. Cohan told him, "doesn't like the touch of cold iron—you'll recall that the lock boxes were brass—and I don't suppose paper money issued in place of it is any different. The money is only a symbol, after all."

"Oh, dear Lord," said young Keating. "We're in for a world of hurt."

Gross blinked and looked at the others. "Why's that?"

Newbury looked at Keating. Then he covered his face and groaned. "Money is fungible. Set them up, Mr. Cohan. We may as well spend it while we can."

Mr. Cohan set up another round, and while he did he whistled an old song:

"And did you meet Them riding down
A mile away from Galway town?"

Penthesilea

Judith Tarr

THE QUEEN OF THE AMAZONS came to the great
Alexander in the royal city of Zadrakarta, just after he
had become Great King of the Persians and Lord of
Asia. She rode into his hall with a company of bare-
breasted warriors, gleaming in bronze and gold, and
flung herself at his feet, and begged him to be the
father of her son. Alexander, men say, was flattered,
but he refused; and she went away unsatisfied, but
greatly in awe of the young conqueror.

So men say. Men tell tales to serve themselves.

Women, unless silenced, have better things to do with the life the Goddess has given them, than to boast and vaunt and tell lies round the fire at night. Women have a taste for the truth, even when that is too strange for men to endure.

The truth of the tale is altogether different, and altogether wonderful, though perhaps, to a man, it would be a horror past imagining.

The Queen of the Amazons had but one child, and that child was born without a soul. She lived, grew, thrived; she ate and slept and seemed to dream. But when the seers looked into her eyes, they saw only emptiness. Even in animals there is a soul, but in this strong young body there was none.

There was consternation among the priestesses and the council, and great outcry against the abomination. But the queen was unmoved. "The Goddess will mend what she has made," she said. "Be patient; protect her; wait and see."

They would not. She was a monstrous thing, they cried; a visitation of the Goddess' wrath upon the tribe.

At that the queen rose up, laid her hand upon the image of the Goddess that had dwelt in the tribe since the dawn time, and swore a great oath by heaven above and earth below, that this and no other would be Queen of the Amazons when she was dead.

She turned in ringing silence, lifted the child from the altar on which she had been laid, and strode away from the priestesses and the council and any word that might be spoken against her one and only and irrevocable heir.

❀   ❀   ❀

The queen's heir had no name, for a name requires a soul, and she had none. But with the turning of the years, she gained an epithet of sorts, a word that children used to signify a thing for which they knew no other name: *Etta*. She answered to it as well as she did to anything else, which was little if at all; for she never spoke, nor seemed to see or hear much that was of human making—except the arts of war. For those she had a gift that was pure instinct, and pure deadly skill.

In the twelfth year of Etta's life, the Great King of Persia fell at the hands of a traitor, and a vaunting boy from Macedon took the throne and the empire. Word came even to the far reaches of the steppe, to the tribes and villages where women ruled and men were permitted only on sufferance. It came swiftest of all to the queen where, led perhaps by prescience, she hunted in the hills not far from Zadrakarta.

She went down to the city between the mountains and the sea, to see for herself what new thing had come upon the world. She left her warriors behind, and her hunting companions, for she had no desire to make of it a state visit. Only Etta followed her, and I.

I was Etta's keeper then, her nursemaid as some were inclined to call me; I knew her ways, what she would eat, how she sustained life without wit or conscious will. She had an animal's instinct to protect herself, which made her a remarkably gifted warrior, and an equal instinct for her mother's presence. She was like a dog, trailing in the queen's shadow.

The queen had never made any effort to cast the child aside; no more did she do so now. As for me,

I was part of the child, as I had been since first I was given the keeping of her. The queen had not asked it lightly. I was and am rather more than a guard or a dry-nurse; my lineage is old and my rank not inconsiderable, and the Goddess called me to her priesthood before my breasts were budded. But I did not refuse the charge that was laid on me. I had no such clarity of vision as was granted to the queen my cousin; still I could sense a little of it, and be certain that this child must be protected.

We slipped away from the hunt in the quiet before dawn, covering our trail for some distance away from the camp. It was not that we mistrusted the queen's own warband and oath-sisters, but she was minded to see this Alexander for herself, outside the bonds of royal protocol. Therefore we rode as hunters from the plains, with no splendor of dress or ornament. Our clothes were good and our weapons well made, but it needed a keen eye to see their quality beneath the stains of travel.

Zadrakarta was full of Macedonians: big, rough-spoken men who filled the taverns and roistered in the streets. I had heard that this Alexander kept decent discipline in war, but in the flush of victory it seemed that the army could do as it pleased. There were games, to which women were not admitted, and which the townsfolk found frankly embarrassing: all the men in them were naked.

We were not women of town or army, nor would we bow to any man's will. In Persian dress, with scarves over our faces, we tarried for a day at the games. They were not unlike the games of spring and autumn among the tribes, when the young warriors tested their prowess, and men came to be judged for their fitness to be the fathers of our daughters. We saw a few here whom we might have been glad to take to our beds, but that was not our purpose in this place. We looked for the one who ruled them, the king who was still, by all accounts, little more than a boy.

He was not sitting in the high seat above the field, though that was surrounded by men of rank adorned with gold enough to ransom half of Persia. I had heard what people said; I looked for a sturdy man, not tall, with hair the color of new gold. Soon enough I found him, down on the field, running races with men who as often as not were bigger than he.

He did not always or even often win. The victors were not afraid of his rank and power, either, nor did they yield the prizes to him. The one who tried had to see it given to the man who had come in last, with a warning not to do such a thing again. Alexander, it seemed, wanted his victories whole, well and honestly won.

That was strikingly unusual in a man, and unheard of in a king. But this was not the usual run of either men or kings. Past that first, unknowing glance, when I saw him as those not touched by the Goddess could see, I was blinded, dazzled, confounded. He was like a rioting fire, like a blaze of the sun. Such a soul came direct from the spheres of heaven. It was too strong for living flesh to bear.

This one would never live to grow old. The fire of the spirit would burn his body to ash long before grey age took him. But oh, Goddess, what a light he would shed before he consumed himself!

I came back reluctantly to the duller world, and to my duty. My queen was watching Alexander, but not as one who is rapt in awe. She was studying him, narrow-eyed, judging as a queen must judge.

Her child between us, blank and soulless Etta, startled me by leaning forward over the tier of benches. I gripped her tightly before she tumbled down. She took no more notice of me than she ever did. Her eyes, for the first time that I could remember, had something like an expression. They were fixed on Alexander. They were full of his fire.

She who saw nothing human or animal, only weapons aimed at her, saw this child of light. She tugged at my hand, struggling to break free. I set my teeth and held on tighter. She began to fight in earnest.

Just before she escaped, I realized that her mother was no longer beside me. My queen had risen and begun a leaping descent through the tiers. On the field below, the races had ended. Men were challenging one another, offering tests of combat.

No one challenged Alexander—until a clear voice that I knew all too well rang out over the clamor of the crowd. "Alexander! Alexander of Macedon!"

He whipped about. He was fast, and light on his feet, even after a long day of games and, I did not doubt, an even longer night of wine and roistering. He looked up to where my queen was standing in her Persian guise. His eyes were grey—I could see them clearly, for I had come down beside the queen. Her daughter was crouched at her feet, clear blue eyes still fixed on Alexander.

"Alexander," said the queen, "I wager that you cannot best me in combat."

"Indeed?" Alexander said. His head tilted. "What will you wager?"

"This," she said, laying her hand on her daughter's head.

My breath caught. Alexander's brows were up. "A boy? He's pretty; I've seldom seen a prettier. But I'm no Persian king. I've no need of boys to ornament my palace."

"This is my own child," the queen said, "my blood and bone. What will you wager, king of Macedon? What will I take with me when I win?"

Alexander grinned at her. "You have gall, I grant you that. I'll give you . . ." He paused. His brows knit. Suddenly he laughed, light and free, as one who wagers everything on certain victory. "I'll give you whatever you ask, that is in my power to give. Only ask it, and it is yours."

She bowed to him. I could not see her expression beneath the scarf, but her eyes were full of mockery. "That is a good wager," she said. "Shall we fight?"

They fought with swords, sharp blades unblunted. Alexander's guards and servants were appalled. His men cheered him on. They loved his crazy courage, to fight naked against an unknown, shrouded and no doubt armored enemy. They would never know what Goddess was in him, driving him, giving him strength—but never as much as She gave her daughter, her beloved, my queen.

He was lethally fast and brilliant in battle, but my queen was the Penthesilea, the daughter of war, and her sword had been forged in the morning of the world. She danced a sword-dance about the heavier, slower, more quickly tiring man, with grace that caught at my throat.

In the midst of the dance, as he rallied and pressed hard against her, the bindings of her headdress parted, then fell away. Her hair, bright gold, made the watchers gasp. But Alexander, who could see her face, checked for the space of a breath, astonished: for like all Greeks and their kin, he never thought to see a woman in the field of battle.

She had been winning before then, in my estimation, but once he saw her face, there was no battle left. She beat him back with ringing blows, forcing him to defend himself, but he was crippled, defeated; he could not strike, only parry. She drove him to his knees, and thrust her sword in the sand between them, and said coolly, "I had thought better of you."

He was a high-colored man, ruddy even at rest, but as he knelt at her feet, he went crimson. He surged up in pure blind rage.

Her arm caught him and thrust him down again. But he was beyond reason. The third time he fell, her blade came softly to rest across his throat.

His eyes cleared. As suddenly as it had risen, his fury died.

She lowered her sword. He stood slowly, stiffly, bleeding from a score of small wounds. He was exactly as tall as she. "If I needed a child," she said, "I would ask you to give me one."

"If you asked," he said as civilly as a man could who had just been soundly and publicly defeated in battle by a woman, "I would respectfully decline to do the honors."

"Would you?"

"Some things cannot be forced."

"Yes," said the queen.

He looked hard at her, as if seeing her for the first time. I thought he might say something for all to hear, but when he spoke, it was only to say, "Come to dinner with me."

That was a royal command, but the queen of my people chose to suffer it. She followed Alexander out of the crowds and the sun, past men who stared and murmured, in a flurry of rumor and speculation. It had not been clear to any but Alexander, what had come forth to fight him; they still were thinking that my queen was a Persian, a fighting eunuch perhaps, intent on avenging the death of his king.

He fed us royally, but not in the crowds and confusion of a royal feast. There were a few friends and companions, somewhat wide-eyed when they saw us bathed and unveiled. Alexander with the courtesy for which he was famous had offered us a selection of garments, both women's dress and men's. We chose coats and Persian trousers, for comfort and because they were close enough to our own fashion.

We ate in a smaller dining hall of the palace, within sound and scent of the sea. I do not recall now what I ate; but I remember vividly the faces of these lords and generals, warriors all, as they understood at last what we were. Alexander laughed like a boy. "Legends! Old tales walking out of the plains. You are—you really are—Penthesilea?"

"I am the Penthesilea," my queen said. "My line has borne that title for years out of count."

"And you came to see me." He tilted his head in the way he had. "To teach me a lesson?"

"To see what you were." She smiled at him. "And to teach you a lesson."

"Did I learn it? Or am I still being taught?"

"That will be clear in time," she said.

"So," said Alexander. "You won a gift from me. What is your desire?"

"It is not yet yours to give," she said. "But when it is, I shall ask for it."

"What, the other half of Persia?" That was one of his generals, a big man, black-bearded, with an air about him of one who needed a good thrashing with the flat of a blade.

I would have been happy to oblige, but this was not our country. I could only watch him along with the rest, and tend Etta, who would not eat for her unceasing fascination with Alexander. I persuaded her at length to take a bit of bread sopped in honey, which she ate neatly as she always did; she was a clean creature, whatever she lacked in wits or will.

The black-bearded man was watching us. Looking for weaknesses, I thought, and greatly pleased to find one. "Well, Alexander," he said, "whatever you have to pay for losing the fight, at least you won't be nursemaid to an idiot."

I tensed to rise, to teach him the lesson he so badly needed, but my queen caught my hand. "Selene," she said: only my name, but it bound me. She regarded the Macedonian with the hint of a smile. "One may be forgiven a lack of understanding," she said. "This is my daughter, my heir. She is blessed of the Goddess.

If your king had won her, he would have won a queen of the Amazons."

The Macedonian's lip curled, but Alexander spoke before he could insult us further. "A great prize," he said, "and a great gift." He looked into Etta's face, and smiled. And she, who had never shown human expression, mirrored that smile exactly.

"She's very beautiful," he said. He did not add, even with his eyes, that it was a pity she had no heart or spirit to give that beauty substance. He reached out his hand. She reached in turn, to clasp it. "Good day to you," he said with courtesy that cannot be learned; it is born in a rare few, vanishingly few of whom are kings.

Of course she did not answer, but her eyes never left his face. She was basking in the light of him, as if he had been the sun.

He bade a servant bring a chair to set beside his own, and drew her to it. All the rest of that dinner, he ate with one hand, for she would not let go the other. He heard such tales of our people as my queen and even I, reluctantly, would tell; he was insatiably curious, eager to learn all that he could, and of us he had heard every myth and legend from the most preposterous to the merely foolish.

We sat there well past sunset, but although there was wine enough, it was well watered; we did not suffer the infamous excesses of a Macedonian banquet. Some of his companions, the black-bearded man among them, excused themselves—to escape, I supposed, to a more comfortably male gathering. The rest lingered with us. They had some share of Alexander's thirst for knowledge, and some of his quick intelligence. I caught myself warming to them, helped perhaps by the wine, though I drank little enough of that.

When it was time to go, we met a difficulty. Etta would not leave the king. I had anticipated that; I was ready for the silent battle. But Alexander said, "Beautiful one, you should sleep. In the morning you may come to me; we'll visit the horses together."

She could not have understood him; words to her held less meaning than the cries of birds. Yet she let go his hand. She took her eyes from him at last, bent them down, and permitted me to lead her away.

As long as Alexander was in Zadrakarta, we stayed as his guests, housed in the palace and given a servant, and a groom for our horses. Etta had abandoned her mother; as much as she could, she attached herself to Alexander, following him like a dog, crouching at his feet when he sat to eat or hold audience. He was remarkably gentle with her, and strikingly tolerant; he was fierce in protecting her against both mockery and disapproval. Soon enough, his people learned to take no notice of the odd blank-faced child in the king's shadow.

I was the shadow's shadow. Because I was possessed of both soul and wit, I could undertake to be inconspicuous. I cared for my charge as I could, as little as there was to do here, with servants to tend her and a king to guard her.

Duty tore at me. My queen came and went as she pleased, by Alexander's order; any who accused her of spying was swiftly silenced. I, seeing the queen's heir so manifestly safe, was sorely tempted to abandon the charge and follow where my heart truly was, with the queen. But I had given my word. I would serve the heir until the queen, or the queen's heir herself, set me free.

She came to me one evening as the year drew on toward winter. Alexander was out fighting; there was a great deal of Persia still to subdue, and he was much preoccupied with it. To my amazement, Etta had not tried to follow him to his war. As if some communication had passed between them, a promise that he would return, she settled into her old, blank calm.

She was sitting by the fire in the room that Alexander had given her, staring blindly at the flames, when her mother passed the door-guard. The queen was windblown and damp and spattered with mud, for it had been raining that day, a cold raw rain. She came in shivering. The servant, unprompted, ran to fetch dry clothes for her; I warmed her hands in mine, and led her to the fire, sitting her down beside her daughter. Etta was rapt in contemplation of the flames; she was oblivious to us both.

The queen ran a hand lightly over the bright gold curls. "It's time," she said. "Winter comes; the people need us. It's time to go home."

My heart leaped at the prospect, but I said, "This one may beg to differ."

"She may," said the queen. She was warming slowly; the chattering of her teeth had eased. She took the cup that the servant brought, and sipped wine heated with spices. Between sips she said, "If she wishes to stay, and if the king will agree to it, she may."

I was silent. I tried to be expressionless, but I was no Etta. My eyes, I have been told, never fail to give me away.

"I release you from your charge," she said. "You've kept it admirably, for years longer than you must ever have expected. Now you may lay it down. She herself has chosen her keeper. You are free."

"No," I said. I startled myself. "I can't be free. Not while her soul is bound apart from her body."

"Not even to go back to the people? Not even to be what you were born to be, priestess and warrior, protector of the tribe?"

"I protect my queen's heir," I said.

She might have said more, but she chose to say nothing. She bent her head. "As you will," she said.

My queen went back to her people, as duty bade her. I stayed where my duty bound me. My heart was dark and still; my prescience had fled. I only knew that where the soulless one went, there must I go.

It was a long journey, a tale of years. We saw the road through Asia, and the land of India, but never the stream of Ocean; Alexander's army refused to go so far. He, forever their lover, gave way. They say he wept that he had no more worlds to conquer. I know that he wept because his people would not follow him where he yearned to go.

Word came from my people through long chains of messengers, until it was stretched and distorted into little more than rumor. There was a war or two, a famine, a fire on the plain; but there were joys, too: rich hunting, strong victory, the birth of a white filly-foal among the horses. I was near to forgetting what I had been; my thoughts most often were in Greek, though my dress remained Persian, for modesty and for convenience.

The histories tell nothing of us. My doing: I could protect my charge from notoriety, and guard her against false rumor. There were so many followers about Alexander, after all, and more, the farther he traveled. We were too familiar to remark on, and too dull, in the end, to notice. What were we, after all, but a woman of a certain age, and a speechless idiot?

Etta grew from beautiful and empty child into even more beautiful and just as empty woman. She needed strong protection then against men who saw the shapely body and the vacant eyes, and thought to take what they pleased. I killed one or two, and maimed half a dozen more. After that they were wary, walking well shy of me and offering at least token respect to my charge.

My queen died while we followed Alexander home from India. We were in the Gedrosian desert then, in that horror of heat and sun and thirst, when even the strong shriveled and died. I endured because I must; I tended Etta, I saw to it that she had what water there was, and I kept her on her feet when she would have lain down on the march.

It was a long while since I had been scrupulous in keeping the rites of the Goddess. I worshipped her still, but in these foreign lands, in this foreign army, with no one of my own kind but a soulless child, I had let slip the observances one by one, until I could barely remember even the great ceremonies.

Yet in one thing I remained as I was. I still dreamed. The dreams came when they would, which was often enough; they were sometimes foreseeings, sometimes memories, and sometimes visions of the world as it was in that hour. I learned more of my people then than from any message or rumor; for a little while I was among them again, living the life to which I was born, and my heart eased immeasurably—until I woke and found myself again among strangers.

In Gedrosia we traveled by night in what cool there was, and slept through the burning heat of the day. That day I had found a sheltered hollow in the sand, and made a burrow for us both. There was water, rather brackish but not too scarce, and bread to wash down with it. I felt almost luxurious, and almost at ease, as I dozed beside Etta.

She was not as drawn with suffering as most of us. She was thin, certainly, and her cream-pale skin had burned dark gold, and her hair bleached from gold to almost white. Yet she showed no sign of weakness. She slept as a healthy young thing could, even in a pit of Tartarus.

As I slid in and out of sleep, I seemed to pass from this world of fire into a world of blessed water. Rain fell in torrents, running in rivers over the plain. I saw my queen, caught in the midst of the hunt, gathered in a circle with her companions. They all sheltered under cloaks, but she stood bareheaded in the storm.

She was older; we all were. But she was still strong, still beautiful. She laughed as the rain sheeted over her, flattening her hair to her skull and her garments to her body. She spread her arms and danced with the joy of life and living.

The Goddess took her just then, in supernal mercy, with great blessing. I saw the fire come down, the bolt from heaven. It pierced through her from crown to sole. It seared her body to ash; her soul spun free, brighter than the lightning, startled, singing like a lark as it soared up to heaven.

The body that I had believed must be waiting for it was still asleep beside me in the horror of Gedrosia. No soul came to fill it; no living spirit to fill her emptiness with splendor.

I had no tears, but still I wept. My queen was dead, gone, lost forever. I sprang up, staggering with the effort. But where would I go, what path would I take, that I had not set foot upon already? My horse was dead; my body clung to life by sheer will. I could go no faster, nor drive myself harder.

There was nothing I could do but sink down in my burrow of sand, and give myself up to mourning for my kinswoman, my beloved, my queen.

We survived Gedrosia, Etta and I, and Alexander whose spirit was unconquerable. Every step of that journey after my dream had come and gone, I yearned for my people and my country, my tribe without a queen. But when we had come to the end, to water and blessed green and relief, at last, from thirst and hunger and furnace heat, I dreamed again.

She came to me, my queen, as I had seen her in life, with her bow in her hand and her sword at her side. She smiled at me as she had so often before, that smile I would have followed to the ends of the earth—and for which I had let her leave me, and bound myself to follow a man, a mere king. "Selene," she said in an accent I had half forgotten, the accent of our people. "Dear cousin. Are you happy?"

Strange question for the dead to ask. I answered

honestly. "How can I be happy? I live in exile. And you, my queen, are dead."

She laughed as if my grief were a splendid jest. "Oh, yes!" she said. "I am dead. Is that why you creep about in such gloom? That's foolish. I'm with the Goddess now, in the land of everlasting."

"You should be here," I said in unslaked bitterness, "in this body that waits for you."

She frowned slightly, though her lips still smiled. "Body? Waiting? It's not my time to be reborn."

That startled me; it left me in confusion. "And yet—you said—your oath—"

"I swore that she would be queen after me," she said. "And so she will. That is as true a vision as it ever was."

"How can she be queen? The Goddess made her, but never finished her. She was never given a soul."

"One waits," said the queen. "Wait, and see. It's not long now. The time is coming."

"I am coming," I said, "to the plains where I was born."

"Wait," said the queen. "Be patient. Protect my heir. She is safer by far here than she ever would have been among the tribe. They go to war, cousin; my loyal friends, my warriors, my priestesses, fight against those who would proclaim a queen. If you bring her there, as she is now, she will die—and you with her. And she will never be reborn, for only souls may take flesh again, and she, as yet, has none."

I heard her in a kind of despair. The urgency in me to be gone, to go home, flared into ash.

She laid her hand on my head, both blessing and comfort. "Soon," she said. "The time will come; you will know. Wait, and see."

I waited. I guarded my charge, who was now, little though she was fit for it, my queen. I watched Alexander in the dregs of his great war of conquest. The fire in him was overwhelming the flesh at last. He was still young; he was barely come to his prime. Yet he had begun to fade.

Etta still followed him with unswerving devotion. The more he faded, the more devoted she seemed to be. When his dearest friend died, the lover who had been with him from his childhood, he would suffer no one else to see his grief. But she, his silent shadow, and I who was hers—we saw. She could offer no comfort but her presence. I had none that he would accept. I knew the pain that was in him, the anguish of loss; for I too had lost one whom I loved. Time had barely blunted the blow.

He never recovered, no more than I; but he learned to endure. The heart was not quite gone out of him. He was still Alexander; he still ruled the world. That gave him a little joy, even yet. In time, everyone murmured, he would remember his old bright self; he would be strong again, and lighthearted again, as he had been before.

They had no prescience. If he had reached the stream of Ocean, perhaps that would have cooled the fire of him. But his army had refused to go so far. The fire of his spirit had shrunk to an ember, and that was growing cold.

Alexander was dying. He lay in his golden bed in the palace of Babylon, in the hot and steaming summer of that country, and burned with fever. The ember, I thought, had flared. When the flame was gone, only ash would remain.

Etta would not leave him. She crouched at the foot of the bed, as motionless as one of the carved lions that upheld it, and her eyes, clear and empty blue, fixed on his face. The servants had long since grown accustomed to her. The great ones who came and went, some weeping, others narrow-eyed as they weighed their chances once the king was dead, eyed her askance but did not move to dislodge her. Even the most arrogant of them had learned long since to let her be.

I stood in shadow, silent and forgotten. As the long hours of the king's sickness stretched into days, I remembered my training long ago, fasting and cleansing the flesh so that the spirit could see more clearly. The heaviness of earth dropped away. Through the shadows of it, I saw the dim candles of men's souls, and the blazing fire that was Alexander. Etta I could not see. She had no substance here.

Alexander burned without measure or restraint. His consciousness hovered on the edge of dissolution.

He was nearly free of the flesh. It crumbled about his spirit, swollen with fever, racked with wounds, full of old pain.

The physicians gave up hope long after I knew that this fever would not pass. It was fear for their lives, I suppose, and a degree of wishful thinking. Many of them did love him; they wept as they tended him.

❀   ❀   ❀

My queen came to me in the night, after I had stopped reckoning time and merely lived from day into darkness. I had fed Etta when servants brought bread and possets which the king was too far gone to eat. I was empty even of hunger. When she came, I was waiting for her, standing guard over the gates of the dark.

She was not as pale as I was then, nor as far removed from living will as Alexander. She looked, indeed, as she had in the prime of her life: young, strong, beautiful. She stood over Alexander, looking down at the wreck of him. Her face had the remoteness of a cloud, or of a god.

I did not move or speak, but she turned to me. Through her I could see Etta sitting where she had been since he was laid in this bed, insubstantial as an image in water.

My queen held out her hands to me. I knew better than to touch the dead, but I met her eyes. They were dark and endlessly deep. "Help me," she said.

Old vows, old dreams bound me. I had sworn oaths to this shade of a queen, on behalf of her shadow of a daughter. Now they all came down upon me. I must see this thing done; must bear witness to it when the time came, before the council and the warriors of the tribe.

My queen laid her insubstantial hand on the husk that now barely housed the spirit of Alexander. It was more than human, more than mortal. What god had chosen to inhabit this flesh, I did not know, nor did it matter.

I took Etta's limp cool hand in mine. My free hand reached across the burning body of the king.

Never touch the dead. My old teachers' voices echoed in my skull, throbbing with urgency. They rose to a roar as my fingers closed about my lady's.

Her hand was cold. It had substance, which I had not expected. Chill wind gusted through me; I caught the scent of graves, and glimpsed, for an instant, a light so bright it came near to blinding me.

She tightened her grip until I gasped. The pain brought me back to this place and this time, precisely balanced between the living and the dead. Warmth in my right hand, living but soulless; cold in my left, dead to earth yet living in a realm which I could barely comprehend.

I was the link and the joining. I was the bridge. My queen opened the gate.

He stepped out of his dying body as from an out-worn garment. I saw once more the young king of Zadrakarta, naked without shame, light on his feet, with those remarkable eyes, and that tilt of the head as he looked all about him. He was ever quick of wit; his lips tightened as he looked down at the thing he had left, but I saw the understanding in him, and the refusal either to rage or to be afraid.

He did not understand all that he thought he did. He took us in, triune face of the Goddess if he had known it: maiden, mother, crone. His eyes widened slightly. "What, no winged Hermes?"

"He comes for your people's dead," said the queen.

"Indeed," said Alexander. "And what am I?"

"Dying," she said. "But with a choice. I bring it from my Goddess, king of men. Would you live? Would you look on the sun again?"

I saw the yearning in him, the longing that twisted his phantom heart with pain. Yet he said, "These things always have a price. What will I pay to be alive again?"

"Remarkably little," said the queen, "all things considered."

"What, my wealth? My titles? Half my empire? All of it?"

"Everything," she said. "Even your name."

He lifted his chin. I had seen that look in battle. He was smiling, but his eye had a gleam of steel. "Then what will I be?"

My queen swept her glance across me to the living shadow beyond. Etta had fixed her stare on Alexander. Even as bodiless spirit, he fascinated her.

I had understood some time since. It had a certain inevitability, and a certain monstrous tidiness, like one of the Greek plays Alexander was so fond of.

He laughed. If I could have killed him for it, I would have; but he was beyond any mortal harm. But he was not mocking any of us. He was laughing in incredulity. "*What* are you asking me to be?"

"Penthesilea," she said. It had been her name and title. No one now held it, though I had no doubt that some had tried to take it. The one they were all bound to accept as queen, by her own great oath, strained past me, stretching toward the shade that was Alexander.

As unwise as it might prove to be, I let her go. He recoiled, but she was both swift and strong. He was but a shade; his body was sinking from the heat of fever into the cold of death. She was alive, if only as a flower is, mindless and soulless but fixed on the sun.

"When she was born," my queen's voice said, sounding somewhat faint, as if it came from a little distance, "the Goddess gave her no soul. One was in the world for her, that was made clear to me, but it would not come until it had done its duty elsewhere."

"Impossible," said Alexander.

"For the Goddess, all things are possible." My queen was fading; my hand could not hold her, however tightly it clutched. "When first we met, we made a wager. I never asked for payment. I ask it now. Will you take this gift that the Goddess has given you?"

He stiffened, then eased with an effort that I could see. "And if I refuse? If I call the wager void, because you died before it could be paid?"

"You die," she said.

He looked down at himself, then up at Etta, as if she had not been as familiar as one of his dogs. But then, I thought, he had never imagined that this might be the flesh he wore when his own body had burned to ash.

He was a man like no other, but he was Greek enough to find women both alien and a little repellent. And of course there was his mother, who should have been one of us; she was never made for a life of meek submission. She had taught him both to love and loathe her sex.

I knew that he would refuse. He was Alexander; he was as near a god as living man could be. But he could not take this gift, which he would see as a bitter sacrifice.

"I . . . would rule?" he asked after a stretching pause.

"You would rule," my queen said. She was far away now, and faint.

"I would not be challenged?"

"You would be challenged," she said. "I am too long dead to protect you."

"Have you allies?"

"Selene knows," she said, now so distant that I could barely hear her. "Trust Selene. Listen to her. Take her counsel."

"But I haven't—"

She was gone. He looked from Etta to me, and back again. He looked long at the inert thing that had housed his spirit for nigh on three and thirty years.

I said nothing. He spun back to me. "Tell me there's another choice. I'm not dead. I won't be dead. There's too much to do."

"There is always too much to do," I said. "Your life is ended, king of Macedon. The dogs have already begun to squabble over your bones. This—who knows? You could be immortal."

"I could come back," he said as if it had just dawned on him. "I could take—I could be—"

I waited for him to come to his senses. It did not take long. He knew better than I, what the men of this world would say to such a thing. They would laugh. Then they would rise up in all their numbers, march against our people and destroy them.

He fell silent. Then: "Will I remember? Once I wake up—will I still be myself? Or will it be like being born again?"

I spread my hands. "I don't know," I said. "It has never been done before. The Goddess has never set a body in the world while its soul still inhabits another. Why She did it—who knows why the gods do anything?"

"Maybe She was curious," he said. "Or maybe She needed two of me, and Macedon needed me first."

He had a fine sense of his own worth. But it was very likely true, what he said; I could hardly contest it. When I spoke, it was to say, "You must choose soon—before the fire goes out in the body. Or you will die, and there will be no returning."

I had roused in him no fear, not of death. But of leaving this life—after all the grief and all the loss and all the pain of his wounds of both body and spirit, still he yearned to live.

"Better the lowest peasant in a living field," he said at last, "than king among the dead." He sighed, though he had neither breath nor lungs for it. Without pause, without further word, he strode toward Etta.

With her mother's departure she had faded again, nearly to vanishing. I could barely see her, but it seemed that his eyes were as clear as mine were clouded. As he drew nearer, she became more distinct. She was reflecting the light of him, the moon to his sun.

They stood face to face. I could have sworn that he was the living man and she the formless dead.

She raised her hand. He raised his to match her. They touched.

On the golden bed, the body gasped and convulsed. In the world between the living and the dead, Alexander blazed up like a beacon in the dark. As suddenly as he had caught fire, he winked out.

I fell headlong from world into world. The tiles of the floor were hard; they bruised my knees, and my hands flung out to break my fall. I smelled the reek of sickness, and beneath it, subtly, the sweet stench of death.

There was someone in the room, some strong presence. The skin prickled between my shoulderblades. I turned slowly.

It was only Etta. She had fallen from the bed and caught herself against one of its carved lions. She was breathing hard, as if she had been running. Her body trembled.

She lifted her head. My breath caught. I had expected it, prayed for it, and yet to see it . . . it was astonishing. Terrifying. Splendid.

There was life in those eyes, expression in that face. Memory—it was there; all of it, as she turned to look on what she had left behind. I wondered if it was a blessing, that she should remember; whether it would have been more merciful to veil her with forgetfulness, and let her be born all new.

It was not my place to judge the Goddess. She had done a great thing, as was well within Her power; a fearful thing, it might be, but as I met those clear blue eyes, I knew that I could serve this one whom She had made.

My young queen smiled at me, with a twist of wryness in it that I knew all too well, and a tilt of the head as she considered what I was now, and what she had chosen for herself. I looked for regret. I found none.

It had been so in all his battles, when Alexander was alive. Once he had set his armies in motion, he never looked back. He fought the battle to its conclusion.

People were coming. The physicians had fled; the servants were gone. These could only be the wolves and jackals, come to gnaw the bones of his empire.

Etta—no, I should not call her that; she was queen now by right of blood and spirit, Penthesilea of the Amazons. Penthesilea hesitated for a stretching moment. Old habits die hard, and she had never been a fool. She knew what must happen now: the wars of succession; the battles over the heirs; the struggle for rule of the empire.

She had died to all that, and risen again to a new realm, a new throne. There would be battle for that, too, after so many years; wars enough to keep even the great Alexander occupied.

"And maybe," she said to herself, "maybe even the stream of Ocean."

"Maybe," I said.

A thunderous crash brought us both about. Whoever was outside had found the door barred, and set about breaking it down.

My young queen caught my hand. I was running, borne along behind her, fleeing as any sensible servant would do, now that the lions were fighting over the spoils. No one tried to stop us. We were only women. Later they might be inclined toward rape, but for the moment they were intent on pillage. In my heart I thanked the Goddess for the frailty of men, and their feeble wits which could not fix on two thoughts at once.

I had prepared for flight, once Alexander was dead: there were horses, weapons, provisions waiting, well hidden outside the walls of the city. My young queen did not shame me with effusion, but her glance was approving. Already she was settled in this body; she mounted and rode as easily as she had in that other life.

She never looked back. I could not be certain what was in her heart; I could only see her face, which was eager, intent, and her eyes, which were full of living fire.

We were long gone when the war began in earnest. She had not forgotten who she had been, nor ever would, but her choice was made, and her wager paid. We rode north and east, away from the lands of men and the empires of Alexander, out upon the sea of grass, the plains of my people. What we did there, what battles we fought, what sufferings we endured in the winning back of my dead queen's title and her power, and how in the end there was once more a Penthesilea over the tribe of the Amazons, is a tale of its own, and has nothing to do with the legends of Alexander. Alexander, as the world knew, was dead. His like would never walk among men again.

But among women, and Amazons in particular . . .

"Well," she said to me one long warm evening, as she suckled her lively and strong-spirited daughter and watched the dances of the young warriors about the midsummer fires, "you still must admit, old friend, that even here, I'm hardly the common run of women."

We were speaking Greek. She still had a Macedonian accent; that had passed from life into life. I smiled at it, because it brought back memories that only we could share. "No, my queen," I said in that same language. "Even here, you are anything but ordinary."

Ripples

Richard Foss

THERE IS SOMETHING TO BE said for throwing
stones in the water and watching the ripples spread
outward. When compared to most of the diversions of
a ruler of men, it is the most innocent of pastimes.
I may toss them in one by one for an hour or more
and cause no harm to anyone save the man who
cleans the fountain of stones. Even to him I render
a service, for if I did not toss stones, the pond in
my palace would never need cleaning, and he would
have no job.

My life allows few such moments of peace and
contemplation, which is the curse of my profession. It

is an irony as well, for I once had much peace, was monumentally unimportant, and nobody cared what I thought about anything. Had I not had the time to formulate my philosophy, I should have been forgotten to the world, rather than ruler of the nation that is called the beacon of civilization wherever men know the meaning of the word.

It is a grand and glorious thing, when I think about it. I used to think about it more, but I haven't the time these days. Those who command men find that they are called upon to command often. Simpler and simpler questions are asked, either because worshipful subordinates think I shall know better on every question than they, or because they fear the consequences if they decide differently than I would have, and so ask of me and are safe. In vain do I question my officers of the ethics of actions, try to show them how to make up their own minds. This was not what I planned when I proposed an ideal system of government. Indeed, I scarcely thought such a system would ever come into being on this Earth, much less that I should live to see it, and not at all that I should be placed in charge of that which I proposed half in jest.

My tossing of stones in my courtyard was interrupted by the clash of heels on marble floors, the unmistakable sound of a struggling man being dragged forward by armed men. I tossed a pebble with greater violence than before, watching the ripples spread faster and wider, the drops of water hurled up on the marble paving. I resolved not to look, to try to hold on to the peace I had felt for a few moments longer.

It was not possible. I knew that the men-at-arms

were there, patiently waiting for me to notice them, and I knew from the small sounds that whoever they were holding on his knees was making occasional attempts to rise to his feet. In such circumstances it is not possible to hold on to the beauty of a ripple spreading across a pond, rebounding from the sides and clashing with the multiple reflections of itself. I turned from the pond to see who was there.

The captives are always more interesting than the captors. Captors look the same, the clothing and weaponry the same except for the insignia of rank, the hair neatly trimmed, the grim faces identical. Captives come in many flavors, from the iron-backed ones who want to usurp me to the wild-eyed ones who wish to abolish my very position and usher in anarchy. I find the latter more interesting for obvious reasons—I was one of them once, and the difference between them and me is merely that I succeeded.

This one was more interesting than usual. The face alone was diverting—he was balding even though still fairly young, with a broad forehead and dark, intense eyes. His clothing and bearing marked him as someone who had never worked for a living, and he reminded me of the professional students I had known when I was younger, the type who are always attending classes and never doing anything with the knowledge gained. Oh, that was unfair. Perhaps they used quotes from my lectures to argue fashionable politics with others of their own class, which is something, but not something useful.

He knelt uncomfortably, held there by the soldiers, while I studied him. The more I looked at him the more I was sure that I had seen him before.

Subtract years from the face, add a bit of hair to the head, though not very much, and he was someone I had known. Indeed, I suddenly knew who—from my own days when I argued perfect government to anyone who would listen, to an audience of aristocrats who prided themselves on how different they were from their parents, and then turned into them as soon as it was time to make a living. He had been my best student once, the one who promised to record my teachings so they would live forever, and stomped off angrily when I proved capable of doing so for myself.

He was watching me, saw the moment I knew who he was. "The student returns to learn at the feet of the teacher," he sneered.

I could not resist asking the question. "Then what have you learned?"

"That no matter what a man says, he will do something different when he achieves power."

"And have I?" I asked mildly. "I have endowed the schools, reformed the courts, and brought order into men's affairs."

"Schools teaching your doctrines, courts enforcing your will, order as you conceive order!" He spat on the tiles beside my pool, beside my pile of stones to throw into the fountain.

"Have I ever said I would do otherwise?" I asked. "What teacher would teach contrary to what he believed?"

He was silent for a moment, and I had to give him credit for thinking. Men rarely think in my presence, preferring to wait until an order is given and obey it. I resolved to find a way to spare his life if I could.

"A teacher who remembered that his own method was to question authority!" he finally replied. "A teacher who realized that he has killed the intellectual life he sought to nourish. Have you walked the streets, listened in the tavernas? Nobody argues politics, or questions their teachers, or speaks of anything important at all, because they are afraid of your spies, your minions. The city is full of people, but empty of opinions, and you are to blame!"

The guards looked shocked and shook their captive roughly. I addressed the senior of the two. "What is the crime?" I asked.

"Sire, inciting a riot, proclaiming that your kingdom should be abolished and resisting arrest," he answered crisply.

I looked at the captive again, at the sweat beading on his wide forehead. "Dear me, what should I do with you?" I asked him.

He looked back at me steadily as he replied. "Always more questions than answers, and always leading questions, questions that can only be answered the way you want them answered, until a man hangs himself with his words." He looked sad for a moment. "I believed in you once," he said softly. "I never thought it could come true, or that it could be so horrible when it did."

His leap toward me was completely unexpected, and I would have never thought that he had so much strength in him. His captors sprawled aside, and his hands were at my throat in a moment. I am not so feeble as I look, and I held him off long enough that my guards could recover themselves and club him into submission.

"Over the cliff with him, and onto the rocks," I croaked when at last I could speak.

"The philosopher-king's word is law," answered the senior of the soldiers. "Hail Socrates." He hesitated for a moment. "Sire, we shall need to know his name for the records."

"I have never known it myself," I answered. "Just his nickname. He was called 'Wide One' for his forehead—that is to say, Plato. It will do for the records."

They left and I drank some watered wine, rubbing my throat. It took a long time after that before I could find peace in my pastime of tossing stones. The actions of men are like stones that create ripples, and even someone so unimportant as that pampered aristocrat could interrupt the stillness of the great lake of my thought. I wish it were not so.

Gun, Not for Dinosaur

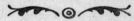

Chris Bunch

NOW, PAUL, YOU KNOW I can't talk about that, even if you keep pouring til I'm wooden-legged.

Oh.

And what's this you're taking from under the bar, with that little smile?

M'god. I didn't know there was a bottle of Old Rare Jack Dann east of Sydney.

You're trying to bribe me.

And I know what you want me to do my tra-las about. That damned safari the hacks are calling the Mystery Death of Sir Peter Kilbrew, or Murder in the Pleistocene or Strange Time Hunter Killing or . . . or whatever other cockup labels they can come up with.

Sir Peter my arse. Born and bred a Texan, which is hardly one of my favorite sports, and getting that courtesy knighthood from King Willie just because he got the Royal Army's computer system to quit having the technicolor spits.

Damned glad you Americans beat hell out of the Brits back when, so when I'm here I don't have to worry about damned titles, theirs or mine.

I need another drink.

'Tis misfortune that I'm feeling bribable right now about Sir Peter, for the truth. Most likely it was that damned taxman, who wanted to look at all the records, and wouldn't let me get any real work done today.

I'm just a bit red-arsed about the bloody government, to tell the truth.

For it's not only their wandering about with their thumb up that kept proper sanctions from being put in place, which brought the whole bloody disaster to term, but now they're going to pass laws and regulations and call in air strikes for anyone who's not a proper civilized nation who even thinks about setting up a time machine.

You'd think it was the old days, when everybody who had a nuclear bomb was piss-scared somebody else, generally somebody of a darker complexion, might get one too.

But keep me off politics. I get into raving, and then my wife has got to take hell's own forever to calm me down.

But pour me about six fingers of that Jack Dann, and I'll tell you most, maybe even all, the truth.

I'll even start at the top, with the questions all of these hacks are running about, trying to find the answer to:

Why was Peter Kilgrew killed?

That one's very simple. The stupid git was trying to wipe out all of humanity, though he was too stupid to realize it.

And who killed him?

Everyone is saying I did it, and I'm content to live with whatever blame that brings.

But it's not the truth, and there's the story.

The disaster wasn't the first meeting, or contract, I'd had with Peter Kilgrew.

He'd come to me, about a year before, wanting to shoot an allosaur.

I knew who he was, of course. The third or fourth richest man in the world, depending on whether you included the current president of China.

I don't know if you remember all the press about him—only comparable to the late Bill Gates, the pirate who formed a computer company named Microsoft and then destroyed it. Except that Kilgrew had inherited most of his wealth, determined to build it early on, and in the process became one of the most publicized computer wonks in the world, building not only that stock monitor you've got over there to super-speed series blaggards, plus their software.

Kilgrew was slender, slight, balding, and would pass for any other computer wimbler if you didn't note the hard look of determination in his eye.

Maybe determination isn't the right word, since I've seen the same expression in paintings of Napoleon, and films of Hitler, Stalin, Cho Ke. More a look of power, power that should righteously be given to the eyes' owner.

If you look into the eyes of madmen, you'll see the same thing.

I had seen that look, over the years, but was too thick to take note of it in Kilgrew.

Possibly because I was getting ready to go into the standard speech—no, I won't take you back into the Jurassic to pot a big lizard, for you're too light in the bum, as the late Mister Holzinger proved rather thoroughly, almost getting me dead in the process.

He let me get about two polite sentences into my spiel, when he started shaking his head. I shut up, looked inquiring.

"I don't think that applies to me," he said.

I looked at him pointedly. He grinned, as if a synapse had closed in his brain, telling him what facial expression he should put on. It vanished in a second.

"I assume you have a range about?"

I told him of course, down in the basement.

"Then let me show you something."

He went out to his Bentley hovership, came back in with an aluminum guncase, and followed me down-cellar.

In the case was an almost impossibly ugly bolt action rifle. Most of the ugliness came from the bulky receiver group that looked as if it should have belonged to a military semiautomatic.

It didn't help that the stock was black synthetic, rather than the usual highly-polished Circassian walnut most people who can afford a custom gun, which this clearly was, prefer.

It also had an amazingly large bore.

".500 A-Square," I guessed.

He shook his head. ".577 Tyrannosaur. I figured if I was going to mess about with guns, there was little point in going for anything except the heaviest."

Which was true. The Tyrannosaur is an obsolete shoulder cannon, obsolete mainly because it will kick you swilly and also, until the time machine came around, because it was utterly impractical after the near demise of contemporary big game hunting.

Amused at the name, I fired two rounds from one once, that belonged to a friend who was both an antiquarian and, I think, a masochist, and I had no desire at all to fire a third time.

The bullet was huge—over half an inch in diameter, using the archaic system it was invented under. The bullet weighed 750 grains, and was punted out with 170 or so grains of powder, which gave it a muzzle velocity of 755 meters per second, and an incredible muzzle energy of 10,240-foot pounds, although ME is a rather precarious measurement to base real-world impact on.

It would, in the vernacular, knock anything on its ass. On either end of the barrel.

"Take a look at it," Kilgrew invited. "There's only one like it in the world."

The rifle was heavy, probably touching seven kilograms empty, which was good. A heavy rifle may be a bitch to haul through the brush, but it'll soak up recoil far better than a light spitkit.

It was fitted with a wide aperture scope, no more than a 3x magnification, ideal for use in brush or jungle.

"I'd read about your exploits," Kilgrew went on,

"and knew of your problem with clients who aren't that heavy in the avoirdupois, and started researching.

"Actually, I had some of my staff do the work. One of them came up with a couple of interesting rifles from last century. One was the AR15, which was made in various permutations by America, the other was the FN, originally made by Fabrique National, in Belgium, licensed on out to other companies.

"Both were service rifles, both semiautomatic and fully automatic, and both had a singular device. In the plastic stocks were springs, so that when the weapon was fired, the bolt recoiled against this spring, called a buffer group, into the stock.

"I found old examples, fired them, and they had no recoil. I mean, none. You could shoot them against your nose . . . or your balls . . . without the slightest problem."

Now that big, bulky receiver made sense. It sat in a subreceiver, and there was about three centimeters the upper receiver, bolt and barrel could slide back into.

"That's not much room to move," I ventured.

"It's enough," Kilbrew said. "I've got an eight-hundred-pound spring in the stock for the buffer group. Plus magnaporting up front, and a good hold.

"Do you want a demonstration?"

I nodded, and he took three enormous rounds from the case, shoved them down into the magazine, snicked the bolt closed.

We put on earmuffs, and I touched the button that brought a target, a conventional bulls-eye, up at fifty meters, the best my range could offer.

He braced, and squeezed, not jerked, the trigger.

Even through the protective earmuffs, the slam was shocking. Kilbrew's hair stood up at the blast, and he rocked back.

But he didn't lose his footing, and ejected the case, chambered a new round, and fired again.

I noticed that he showed no sign of flinching and the two holes in the target were touching.

"Here," he said, holding the rifle out to me, with a grin. "At fifty dollars a shot, have one on me."

I aimed, put pressure on the trigger. At about two kilos, the rifle crashed back into my shoulder. I let the muzzle climb a bit instead of fighting it.

I set the rifle back down.

"Well?"

"Whew," was the best I could manage, rubbing my shoulder.

"Not as bad," I grudged, "as a .510 Welles. But still not much fun."

"I've done some hunting up in Alaska, helping the wardens on the Kodiak game preserve, culling brown bear," Kilbrew said. "Not with the Monster, though. Mostly .375s and such. And once I had something in my sights, I never noticed the recoil."

True enough, I admitted to myself.

"What about accuracy?" I asked. "There's got to be some receiver wiggle."

"Probably," Kilbrew said. "But not enough to throw the bullet strike off at the range I plan on shooting at. Fifty, maybe seventy meters at the most. This isn't a long-distance gun, after all."

I nodded agreement. One problem many shooters have when they graduate to a monster caliber is forgetting that, with an incredibly heavy bullet, the point of aim is going to change radically over, say, 300 meters, unlike their favorite ultrasonic wildcat round, which is why the classic elephant rifles were intended for use close in.

But I was still skeptical about Kilbrew's invention. A physicist once told me there's no such thing as a free lunch, and I believe it.

It's a pity . . . for Kilbrew that he didn't, and a blessing that I did.

"I'll ask 'well?' again," Kilbrew said. "This time about whether you'll take me out for an allosaur."

I considered.

"We'll give it a go," I said.

He smiled, clapped me on the back.

"That's great, cobber," he said.

For some reason, that set my teeth on edge a bit. There's no reason I should object to someone using a 'Stralian phrase, and normally I don't, if it's used correctly.

But for some reason I couldn't yet determine, I didn't like anything about Kilbrew.

Not that it showed. If every client I have was required to be a bosom chum, there'd be no Rivers & Aiyar firm. I'd most likely be running a popgun gallery in some tourist trap somewhere around Bondi Beach.

I was slightly busier than a one-legged man at an ass-kicking contest at the time, since times were . . . and are . . . a little strange.

Increasingly, the number of safaris I've been taking out have been photo-only. I guess you'd think that bothers me, but lately I've been wondering what god-given right someone has to go out potting creatures not for his daily meal, but just so he can feel his testicles are bigger than his neighbor's.

My partner, the proper, if never to be acknowledged Rajah of Janpur, Chandra Aiyar, has been feeling much the same. Actually, more so. He's seriously been contemplating retirement, to take up the begging bowl and a life of prayer, as so many successful Indians do in their mid years.

I think he's a bit mad, and keep reminding him that anyone who tucks into a steak the way he does would be miserable on a diet of vegetables and rice.

But it's his life, isn't it?

The first thing I made sure was a proper slot in the Jurassic was available, remembering that law prohibits anyone traveling within a month of anyone else.

There was no problem there.

But remember that point, Paul. And pour me another one while you're remembering.

The other thing to keep in mind . . . and both of these pertain to my story . . . is that for some reason, Professor Prochaska's machine doesn't work within 100,000 years of today.

That's to keep paradoxes from paradoxing. Since this is a logical universe . . . stop laughing . . . you can't go back and murder your father.

You'd just explode in the attempt.

Ask the man who's had a client get stroppy and do just that, back when we were first getting started.

There have been some suppositions that this paradox-preventer isn't as bulletproof, and yes, I'm making a joke, even though it's deadly serious, as was thought.

There's never been a law about that, however.

There probably will be one very soon, though, and all because of Peter Kilbrew.

But it didn't happen on this trip.

We took the usual crew—Ming the cook, Beauregard Black the camp boss and two helpers. Including Kilbrew, we should have been able to make it in two trips—one for the people, one for the gear.

Instead, it was three. Kilbrew showed up with two men I'd never met, but I knew who they were instantly.

Both were tall, in their thirties, athletically built. They never seemed to smile and always wore dark glasses.

Good guess, Paul. And now I'll always have to wonder about your background. They weren't plainclothes coppers, but bodyguards. Both of them were Boers, from that fading enclave in South Africa that can't fade soon enough for my tastes. They were named Nicholas and Hendrik, no last names ever offered.

I asked Kilbrew, who I had to force myself to call by his first name, why he needed them. The allosaurs we were going after would kill any of us, not just the lead billionaire.

Unsmilingly, he said his insurance company insisted on it.

Batshit, of course. But I chose not to argue.

The two were armed with small machine pistols, which wouldn't do diddly against a dinosaur, and .375 semiauto Magnum rifles. I thought of saying something, caught myself.

And so we trundled into the chamber, and Bruce Cohen punted us back in time.

It was, is, always a shock to see the chamber door

shut on the University of St. Louis, and open again on rolling, wet plains, with the Kansas Sea in the background.

We hiked a klick or two away from the camp to a swamp, potted and staked a hypsilophodon for our bait, and went back to camp.

Beauregard had shot a small sauropod, and had butchered it out into steaks.

Kilbrew turned a bit green.

"Reggie, we're going to actually eat lizard?"

"We are," I said. "First you get one sundowner, no ice, then a nice, thick steak. Contrary to what they tell you, it doesn't taste like chicken, but dinosaur."

"I think I'll be happier with something we brought with us."

I shrugged. His business if he wanted to eat compo rations picked up from the military.

Dinner was, as always with Ming cooking, excellent. He'd done the steak with small baby greens and a real Roquefort.

I tried not to look at Kilbrew, eating some species of mystery meat loaf that came out of a pak.

"You really ought to try this," I said.

Kilbrew shook his head.

"My mother had no more than five dishes in her recipe book, all of them well done. And my father never seemed interested in food. So I grew up a bit of a retard in the gourmet department."

I refrained from saying "pity," helped myself to another slab of dinny.

When I'm in civilization, I watch my diet fairly closely. Great white . . . or any other color . . . hunters aren't supposed to have a prosperous paunch about them.

But not in the wild. If nothing else, the adrenaline keeps me from getting fat.

I noted Kilbrew's bodyguards didn't have any of the dietary prejudices of their boss.

Dessert was a wonderful cobbler, made from freeze-dried apples we'd brought with us.

Beauregard was pouring coffee, and, leaning across the fire, somehow managed to knock a metal plate off Hendrik's knee.

The last bite of cobbler spilled on the ground, and Hendrik glowered up at Beauregard.

"Bloody *kaffir*!" he snapped.

Black jerked back. He started to say something, but I was there first.

"That is language not used in any camp of mine, sir," I said. "I would appreciate your apology. At once."

Hendrik bristled, turned red, bulged a muscle.

I smiled, but there was no humor at all on my face. I shifted my weight forward, and got ready. Bodyguard my ass. I wondered how he'd handle a good solid fist to the voicebox.

"Hendrik!" Kilbrew said.

Hendrik's face stilled.

"I'm sorry," he said, in a voice that said very damned well he didn't mean it.

But Beauregard, being a professional and having heard worse, no doubt, nodded, and went for his tent.

I knew the damned Boers weren't content with having mucked up their share of Africa with absurd racism, but figured that, after almost a century of being driven back and back into their enclave, they were learning better.

How wrong I obviously was.

After a moment, both of the Africans got up, and went for their own tent.

I went to Beauregard's.

He was sitting on his cot, staring into the night.

"I'm sorry," I said.

"Why? You din't say shit."

"It was on my watch, as I understand you Americans say," I told him.

Black sat for a minute, then shook his head.

"You think they learn, Reggie. But they don't. Goddamned Kluxers! We ought to do to all these sheet-head bigots what the liberation armies did thirty years ago in Africa."

"*That's* bloody enlightened," I said sarcastically.

"Ain't no enlightenment about it, boss," he said. "You can't convince a no-neck racist of nothin', not ever. Might as well put a .375 to the back of their necks and have done."

"Well . . . that's one approach," I said. "But do me a favor and don't start shooting people 'til their bloody check clears."

Beauregard smiled slowly.

"For you, Reggie, I'll do that. I'll do just that."

I went out, and saw Kilbrew sitting alone by the fire. He'd gotten a bottle of cognac from the supply chest, and had poured himself a small shot.

There was an empty glass beside him.

One job a hunter has is being willing to drink with the sahib, especially if there's nothing for the morrow except waiting for an already dead dinosaur to get stinkier.

We sat in silence for a moment.

"People sure go out of their way to find trouble," he said.

"They do," I agreed. "There ought to be a law against us."

He didn't smile.

"Words are only words, and don't have any real harm."

"I can think of a few people . . . blacks, Jews, Irish, Italians, Asians . . . who wouldn't agree with that."

"*I* never let anything like that bother me."

I thought of saying that was easy, since he was bone white, but didn't reply.

"Wouldn't it be a blessing," he said, "if somebody took a time machine to Africa, and jumped back a few thousand years to the first primitive black man?

"One squad of infantry, and there wouldn't be any Africans to worry about. Wouldn't ever have been. And maybe Africa would still be flush with all those wonderful animals nobody can hunt any more. Can't, in some cases, even find them to take pictures of."

"A lot of animals would like that," I said, trying to keep the shock from my voice. "No humans ever to see them as dinner on the hoof."

"You really believe that all life came from Africa?" Kilbrew asked.

"The theory seems to have every scientist I've met believing it."

"Bullshit," Kilbrew said mildly. "I made my money not listening to anything any scientist said as being absolute. And this belief that everything started up, where, in Ethiopia is obvious nonsense."

"Why?" I asked.

"It's only common sense!"

I started to argue, remembered what Beauregard had said a few minutes ago, and remembered there's many, many ways to package racism.

If he wanted to believe in spontaneous evolution, or a pure-white God, I suppose that was his business.

"Best we put our heads down," I said. "Your allie might just decide to wander up a little early, and your monster gun probably isn't any easier when you touch off a cap when you're hungover."

Maybe I didn't watch my voice, because Kilbrew gave me a cold look. I smiled, and went for my tent.

The allosaur didn't materialize, so we spent the next day getting some more meat for the camp.

I was just as happy. The third day would hopefully be the charm, especially as the transition chamber would make its first check on us then.

Kilbrew was chill, formal to me. I suppose, even as mildly as I thought I'd spoken, I must've been the first person to disagree with him since he made his first billion. His pet thugs weren't any more friendly.

As much for a little punishment as anything else, I decided we'd build a blind near our nicely-reeking hypsilophodon that night, and hope for results the next morning. Some smaller sauropods had already been sniffing around the carcass, and I hoped for some luck.

It rained most of the night, and then dawn was chill, gray and foggy.

It's always a surprise to be reminded how softly a carnivore moves. One minute, there was nothing in the small clearing but a very dead dinosaur, then, almost as tall as the cycads around him, the dark gray bulk of our theropod was there.

It couldn't scent us . . . the rotting hypsilophodon would mask the stink of a regiment of Napoleonic infantry on the march.

I touched Kilbrew. He jerked . . . I think he was dozing . . . and saw the allosaur.

Kilbrew came up, just as Nicholas also saw the brute.

I moved to the side, and eased the safety off my .600 double.

But Kilbrew didn't panic.

The allosaur saw movement, turned, and its jaws gaped.

Kilbrew sent his first round down the beast's mouth.

It stumbled back, fell on its side, came back up, screaming rage, hate.

I was holding steady on where its tiny brain was, and Kilbrew's rifle went off again, putting a fist-size hole where I'd been aiming.

The allosaurus staggered, and Kilbrew's third round went in just below its eye.

It bellowed, and fell.

Kilbrew started forward.

"No!" I shouted, pulling at his arm, and then Hendrik had him.

"Reload," somebody shouted, probably me, and Kilbrew obeyed.

I stood, waiting, while the dinosaur thrashed about, its body taking a good long time to realize it was dead.

Finally it lay still.

"Now," I told Kilbrew. "Put one in the back of its head, to mak' siccar."

"No," he said. "I don't want to ruin the head any further."

I admired him as a cool one, even if a few minutes later, he had a very impressive case of the shakes.

The shots brought Black and the two handlers, with the butcher's kit, and in less than an hour we had the head and a good section of the snaky neck off.

We went back to the camp, and, right on schedule, Bruce was there with the chamber.

Even success didn't defrost Kilbrew.

It didn't matter much to me, other than I figured the bonus clients normally pay wouldn't come forth this time.

But it wasn't as if I'd expected many customer recommendations from Kilbrew anyway.

Surprisingly enough, not only did he pay the fee promptly, but there was a very fat bonus attached. I split my share with Beauregard, and told him it was for his vast brotherhood and gentility.

It was a good fifteen minutes before we stopped laughing.

We went back to business, and business was suddenly very good and very interesting.

Over the past few years, there had been transition chambers set up in other places than St. Louis: Australia; the Japanese one in Ulan Bator, Mongolia; and now the University of Nairobi was building one, a very big one. The one Rivers & Aiyar used was big enough only for people and a mule or two. No more.

Surprisingly, Professor Prochaska was mad enough to bite beer bottle necks.

Bruce Cohen explained why.

"He was one of the first consulted by Nairobi, and wasn't at all taken with the people in charge of the project."

"Why not?"

"The first thing is that he doesn't think they're that honest, which may or may not be the truth.

"But the second thing is really worrisome. The project is especially designed to benefit anthropologists and archeologists."

"Uh-oh," I said.

"Yeah," Cohen said. "There's been some interesting math theories done lately that suggest our nice and comfortable belief that nature won't allow a paradox may not be precisely true.

"So all of a sudden we're going to have these soft science . . . I'm not talking about archeologists here . . . wandering around Northern Africa."

"Looking," I said, "for a chance to get a really good look at primitive Man."

"Exactly," Cohen said. "Prochaska and I went to a conference a couple of months ago, and the savants, as I think they'd like to be known as, swear most piously they won't be bothering any early Man.

"But they might be hiding cameras in bushes.

"Someone running across a nice Nikon whirring away in the brush might think differently than he did before or after, might he not?"

I nodded, then remembered a rather disastrous trip I'd made a few years ago.

"At least that'll shut up the bible-shouters."

"You wanna make a big bet on that?" Cohen asked. "They've been able to deny science for a few hundred years now. What makes you think there'll be any change from the nonsense they spout that God created everything as is in 1883 or whenever it's supposed to be.

"I tell you, Reginald, I can see some really interesting problems coming up from all this."

I decided to do a little research.

The people with the trowels and dust brooms had slowly but surely inched man's beginnings back and back, as I discovered after a few minutes on my computer terminal.

Right now, the oldest example of close-to-Man, Australopithecus afarensis, is about four million and a bit old, in the Middle Pleistocene.

One colony only, if that's what it should be called, some thirty, hairy shorties a bit more than a meter tall, but who were human enough to use appropriately-jagged flints for tools.

It had been labeled Awash man, after the Ethiopian National Park it was found in.

Interesting, but I always thought Cohen worried too much.

Chandra and I were quite busy, for with a whole new continent opening up, many of my longtime clients came swarming back, eager to blast an entirely new species.

I discovered something that made me a bit unsettled. This new time machine in Nairobi had been supposedly built for scientists. Scientists, of course, who could afford the rather steep ticket. Transition chambers use a lot of power, especially one big enough to hold a helicopter.

But all of a sudden, through hunting circles, I

started hearing stories about hunters who'd managed to get themselves back to prehistoric Africa, hunters whose only claim to scientification was being able to calculate the cubic meters of their bank account.

I remembered what Cohen had said about Prochaska's worries, and started worrying myself.

Somebody might go back, and do something and suddenly I, and everybody I know, would be nonexistent. Or, on the other hand, we might all become peace-loving vegetarians, in tune with the Cosmos.

My bet went, very firmly, if cynically, on the former possibility.

But if there could be paradoxes, and if I could end up never having existed, it wouldn't be as if I'd have any time to get pissed, so I concentrated on getting some of my better-heeled clients on the list with Nairobi.

I did a little digging, and found the names of a couple of people who, if given an appropriately-sized check, would suddenly swear that you were a Doctor of Paleontology from the University of Fort Knox.

We'd been able to make two trips into Africa, when I got a call from Sir Peter Kilbrew, who wanted to hire me, instanter, to take him hunting again.

I'd seen his name on the news channels, and not just in the business section. He'd gotten himself involved in one of those schemes I understand you Americans come up with from time to time, offering blacks money to go back to Africa. As if they weren't at least, probably more so, as American as he was.

I laughed 'til I pissed myself when the organizer of this back-to-Africa nonsense turned out to be a scam artist, and disappeared into the woodwork with nobody-ever-said-for-sure how much of Kilbrew's money.

But as I've said, I try to stay out of my clients' politics.

Kilbrew sent two plane tickets, one for me, one for my wife, to come to Dallas and discuss things.

Since I'd told Brenda more than a sufficiency about Kilbrew, she passed on the trip.

The Kilbrew mansion sat on the south side of Dallas, on a half dozen acres of land that probably went for a couple of mil per acre, or more. The house was styled like a mansion out of Gone With the Breeze, or whatever that mawky book is, with columns, a bloody huge drive, outbuildings and such.

Kilbrew's two goons opened the door for me, and then Kilbrew appeared, wearing what he must have imagined old Hemingway wore in his Kenya days.

He introduced me to the Mrs. Kilbrew, who was a blond, walking monument to silicone. She simpered, pointed her cleavage at me, and said, "Call me Wandi."

I doubted that she was his first wife. Rich ones like Kilbrew generally take a few tries before they hit the proper combination of brainless and rutting ability.

Kilbrew showed me his trophy room, packed with mounted trophies. I noted with some satisfaction "my" allosaur head had pride of place. Oddly, the furnishings in the room were more suitable to a corporate board room than a living room.

"My negotiating room," he said. "I put 'em in here, underneath your boy's fangs, and you've no idea how amenable they get to my offers."

I made an understanding sort of noise, and he poured me a drink.

"Let me show you my latest," Kilbrew said, unlocking one of the gun cabinets, and taking something that looked like a black powder shotgun from its huge bore. But it evidently fired smokeless powder, for it had a curved magazine below the receiver.

"You figuring on doing some serious poaching around here?" I joked. "That ought to land you enough ducks, one blast, to feed the neighborhood."

"It wouldn't be bad for that, now would it?" Kilbrew said, again with his forced smile. "No. I may offer this to the UN Military. Eight gauge, and of course my now-patented buffer group. Twenty rounds, either shot or solid. Cyclic rate of fire about three hundred rounds per minute."

The shell he showed me was as long as the palm of my hand, and I've got a rather large paw. The shell's diameter was about 2 cm or so.

Kilbrew took it back, and held it with a rather unpleasant smile.

"A nice riot agent, don't you think?"

"I don't know," I said. "I try to stay away from riots."

Then we had dinner, which of course was as mid-American and dully inedible as you'd imagine, and after Mrs. Kilbrew had simpered her way to her "sewing room," and what that might have been, I've not a clue, Kilbrew got to business.

"I want you to take me out again," he said. "To Africa."

"I'm pleased you thought to call," I said. "Might I ask why you haven't consulted any of the local lads?"

"I did." Kilbrew harrumphed. "They were damned amateurs. The main hunter, of course being black, couldn't find any game where he'd said it'd be, and the camp staff were a bunch of numblebums, and most of the equipment was jerry-built. We even had to abandon one of our hovercraft, as a matter of fact."

"About what you'd expect, given who they were," Hendrik put in.

I ignored him.

"I'd gone in after one thing, and didn't get it," Kilbrew said. "Of course, when we got back, the billing was twice the estimate, which I'm in litigation about right now.

"I should have gone to you in the first place, but I didn't know until recently you've had experience in Africa."

"What were you after?" I asked.

"I want a giant hippopotamus."

I managed to hide my wince.

I don't like hippos.

I've shot a couple of contempo hippopotami with clients who managed to get permission to hunt on one of the great African preserves.

A hippo, as one client put it, is a mean piece of work.

The only good things I'll have to say about them is their steaks are among the tastiest meat in the world, and their hides make extraordinarily tough and, properly cured, pliable leather.

Beyond that, nothing.

With the exception of the black mamba and the crocodile, I doubt if any animal, including those few remaining lions and buffalo, kills more Africans every year.

And no one, yet, has hired me to hunt either the mamba or crocs.

Hippos, which in this time get to be about 4–6 meters long and 1.5 meters tall, weighing in at about 3–4 metric tons, are a long ways from the funny fatties of animated films.

In the water, if they yawn at you, that's not sleepiness, but a threat, most generally a precursor to biting your boat—and you, if they can get away with it—in half.

But that's not where they're most dangerous.

Hippos graze on land at night.

God help you if you get between them and the water. Because they can move almost as fast as an antelope. And if you're in their way, you'll be lucky if you're only trampled. The hippo's fangs are jagged, misshapen, and the length of your forearm.

They won't eat you, but once they get a good hold or three you might wish they had.

I rate the hippo's temper as being only just shorter than that of the Cape buffalo, and his intelligence is quite a bit higher.

As I said, I don't like them, from the day one sent me into the Pafuri River, to watch all my gear, including a beautiful Purdy double that had cost me a year's wages, to the bottom, as a phalanx of crocodile slithered into the water from the opposite bank.

A hippopotamus of the Pleistocene (*Hippopotamus gigans*, to use the new and rather obnoxious taxonomy) gets at least twice as big as one of today's brutes.

I'll underline that at least, since all these eras are being explored, and no one really knows how big any prehistoric creature actually grew.

Remember that Pleistocene riverine croc they found about six klicks north of here five or six years back? Twenty feet long, when nobody thought those monsters had ever gotten over 15 or so.

"That might be an interesting hunt," I managed.

"Sure as hell will be, especially because, with Nairobi's chamber, we'll be able to bring the whole damned thing back," Kilbrew said.

"Won't that jolt 'em, standing in my foyer?"

I nodded. "Whereabouts do you want to hunt?"

"There's a lake, a great big one, in Ethiopia, near where a little town named Abomsa is."

I didn't know the location. Nicholas got an atlas. I whistled.

"Damned close to Awash," I said. "I'm surprised they're willing to let any hunting go on there."

"The . . . blacks," Nicholas said, and I noted the pause, "will let anybody do anything over there, so long as you've got the dollars to pay for it."

I looked at Kilbrew, his two bodyguards. A smile went between them, as if they were sharing a secret.

I smelt something strange.

But stronger, I smelt money.

And so, for the filthy lucre, I took the contract.

Before we left St. Louis, Beauregard Black took me aside.

"You owe me for this one, Reggie."

"Come on, Beau," I protested. "You'd think I was throwing you in a den of murderers."

"Nary a den, boss," Black said. "Three of 'em's enough."

"Look, I'm giving you a chance to see the land we all came from."

"Only land I come from is right here in Saint Louis," he said. "Men who go lookin' for their past likely to find out some skeletons or worse.

"Besides, I hear Ethiopia these days is about as attractive as a good plague of locusts. You best be thinking of just how huge a Christmas bonus I'll be getting."

And so everyone assembled at Kilbrew's house, and packed for the expedition.

It was hot in the Texas sun, and we worked stripped to the waist.

I noticed with some amusement that Wandi Kilbrew was particularly fascinated with Beauregard Black's rather rugged build. Beauregard, happily married with four children, never noticed.

I don't think Kilbrew saw Wandi's interest. It wouldn't have improved matters any.

Everything packed, and the packing list checked twice, we left for Africa.

Beauregard was right about Ethiopia. It seemed that every five or six years somebody else laid claim to Addis Ababa, and came in with guns to back up their demands.

We did an overflight of Awash, even though I knew it'd look seriously different in the Paleolithic, although I did an automatic check on two extinct volcanoes that could be used to locate the site.

The pilot pointed out where the Awash Man dig was going on, then we went back and grabbed a jet down to Nairobi and the time chamber.

Even as big as the chamber was, we still needed four trips. The first was Black and the workers we'd hired for the campsite, then two huge Daimler hovercraft, since we would be traveling a ways to the lake. Last came the sahibs.

It was just after dawn when we loaded up outside the chamber, and took off north.

"I've heard that the Ethiopians have an armed guard back here in the Pleistocene, making sure the scientists don't cheat around the Awash colony," I said.

"Not my concern," Kilbrew said casually. "I'm after hippos, not scientists."

In the rear seat, Hendrik laughed. Not pleasantly.

Probably one of the countries with the biggest differences between now and then is Ethiopia. Now it's arid desert, with deep ravines rutting the landscape. Water, when you can find it, is brown, brackish.

It feels like an old, tired country, a country who died a long, long time ago, and is now nothing but a desiccated corpse.

Its people move slowly in the heat, conserving their energy and the low calories they're able to scrub up from the soil.

Pleistocene Ethiopia is brawling, alive. It's still hot, of course, near the equator, but muggy. There are swamps everywhere, opening into lakes.

I looked as we flew on, and counted three active volcanoes.

The hunting camp was to be on the northern shore of this lake . . . "No name," Kilbrew said. "If I were an egomaniac, I'd think about naming it after myself."

"Or Wandi, your wife," I suggested.

He looked at me, didn't smile, and stared back out the side of the open hovercraft.

I'd given Beauregard a copy of the map Kilbrew had made when he was here the first time, and picked up his beacon after about two hours' flight.

I followed it, and set down next to the tents that had already sprung up.

Beauregard and Ming were quite used to changing scenery, but the workers we'd picked up in Nairobi weren't. They were working, but kept looking over their shoulders, as if expecting some horrid monster to burst out of the ferny swamp around us.

I did a reccie down to the lake, saw no signs of hippos at all. I didn't hear their honk, but I didn't know if *Hippo gigans* called out the way modern beasts did.

I asked Kilbrew what evidence he had there were giant hippos floating around out there.

He said from a survey he'd gotten from an Ethiopian.

"But if it's wrong, we'll search on south until we find what we're after."

Strangely, he didn't seem particularly disturbed at the thought of losing a few days.

Quite surprisingly, he then announced that this first day he'd throw a barbecue. A proper Texas barbecue, and he and his bodyguards would do the cooking and serving.

I found it almost impossible to believe that these three would actually wait on blacks, but after Ming had set up the serving line, Kilbrew opened up a large container, and took out cow-type steaks, baked beans that'd been made in the twenty-first century, coleslaw and cherry pie. He fired up a charcoal grill, and the trio set to work, cheerful as diggers on the inside when the innkeeper calls time, winks and locks the door.

"The whole meal's just like the men, real men, who settled Texas, ate at their roundups," Kilbrew shouted. "Including the Rocky Mountain oysters."

For some reason, I wasn't that hungry, and ate lightly, only having a couple of the deep-fried calves' testicles Kilbrew called "oysters," and some tea.

I felt unaccountably sleepy, and yawning, begged off dessert.

"Maybe a bit of a nap?" Kilbrew suggested. "Give us some rest, and get up later, and figure out what happens tomorrow."

I nodded, and, almost stuporous, stumbled off to my tent.

I was almost instantly asleep.

I had terrible dreams that had me tossing, dreams of someone or something entering my tent. I kept trying to wake up, to reach the .600 I always kept at bedside when I was on safari, but couldn't.

The thing, whatever it was, was getting closer, then it had me, was shaking me.

I tried to shout for help, but then my eyes came open, and I was awake, and Beauregard Black was the one shaking me.

"Come on, boss. Wake up. Come on, Reggie," he was saying. "The bastards tried to poison us."

The shock brought me up into a sitting position.

"Come on, man. Wake up. That Kluxer took one of the hovercraft and took off north."

"Why . . . what . . ." and then I had it, remembering

that conversation on our first trip, when Kilbrew had talked about how one infantry squad could have wiped out Awash man, and prevented any blacks from being born.

I stumbled up, seeing two and three Beauregards, made it out into the campsite.

There were bodies sprawled here and there.

"Poison," Beauregard said. "I don't know why. Ming's the only one who's still alive."

"Why . . . what about you?"

"I swore I'd be damned if I'd take anything in the way of food from that bastard," Black said. "Then, when one of the workers fell over, and one of those Boer bastards started laughing, I figured his game.

"I pretended to be sleepy, went for my tent, and ducked into the brush, trying to figure out what to do.

"One of the helpers must've figured something was going wrong, because he went for Kilbrew. One of his goons shot the poor son of a bitch with one of those monster guns they brought along.

"I didn't look back 'til I found something to hide under. Then I saw them lift, and came back, hoping I could find somebody alive who might know what the hell is going on."

I stumbled down to the lake, and fell on my face, splashing about, hoping the tepid water would wake me up, not giving a damn about prehistoric bilharzia.

"Where are they going, Reggie? They've only been gone a few minutes. We've got to go after them or something."

I managed to find the words and explained.

"Those mothers are just plain wack!" he said. "Wipe out those puppies, and everybody goes."

"Maybe," I said. "Or maybe not. Maybe the paradox thing will work. Or maybe it won't. If it doesn't work . . . can you fly that Daimler?"

"There hasn't been anything I can't drive or fly," Black said. "Come on."

"No," I said. "First we'll need guns."

We took my .600, and Black a camp .375, plus boxes of shells.

I flopped into the passenger's seat, and Beauregard got the hovercraft started and airborne.

"Where are we going?"

I was suddenly grateful for that overflight over contemporary Awash Park, and my rather adept sense of direction.

"East-northeast," I said. "And keep it as low as you can. And I don't give a damn if you fry the turbine."

Beauregard shoved the power quadrant up to its stop, and the hovercraft nosed over and accelerated.

I was scanning the sky ahead, hoping Kilbrew would keep it at a sensible altitude, and we could spot him.

But my eyes were still blurring. I was still under the effect of that bit of whatever poison that'd been in that ever so bloody kindly barbecue.

"There," Beauregard said. He pointed, and then I could see a dot ahead of us.

Kilbrew's hovercraft had an additional passenger, and maybe ours was in a little better tune, for we were closing on them.

Someone must've seen us, because the hovercraft climbed, banked and came down on us.

"Reggie, I ain't no fighter pilot! Gimme some help here!"

I thought.

"Go straight for him, like we're going to ram the bastard."

"And then what?"

"Then he'll break first."

I didn't add "I hope."

I had my .600 loaded, and the safety off.

"I don't like this," Black muttered, but held firm.

We were within a few hundred meters of the other ship, closing fast. I heard a pair of shots, but we were out of effective range of either Kilbrew's .577 or those damnable shotguns he'd had built, all the while dreaming of mass murder, murder that might include the entire human race.

"Closer . . . closer . . ." I was muttering, wondering if maybe I'd been wrong and maybe whoever was flying the hovercraft had rock-solid nerves.

Only a moment before *my* nerve broke, about to shout to Beauregard to dive, the other hovercraft banked steeply to the right.

"Go right," I called, and Beauregard obeyed.

I had a perfect shot at the bottom of the other ship, and put a left and a right into its bottom.

Anything that will set a behemoth on its hind legs will, rather thoroughly, put paid to machinery.

The hovercraft bucked, spun, almost out of control.

I was shoving new rounds into the .600.

"There, you shitheel!" Black shouted, and I looked up, and saw one of the Boers fall out of the hovercraft.

It was a few hundred feet, and he screamed all the way down.

Kilbrew's ship was wobbling, going in.

"Stay on its ass!"

Beauregard nodded.

I heard another bang, saw the other Boer . . . Hendrik, I recognized, leaning out, at the driver's seat of the hovercraft. He fired at us twice, one-handed, with one of the alley sweepers Kilbrew had devised.

The windscreen of our ship starred, then blew out, and Black swore, and ducked as Kilbrew himself fired once, then again with his monster gun.

I chanced a shot back at him, missed.

We were dropping, and the ground was coming up fast.

Beauregard flared it just above some brush, and we came in for a stickery, if soft, landing.

"Now," I said. "Now we go after them."

I tossed Beauregard his rifle, reloaded the empty chamber of my .600 and we jumped out of the hovercraft. Black had the presence of mind to grab the ignition keys and shut the engine down.

Then it was silent, silent except for the high whine of the other ship, turbine spinning out of control, down somewhere to our right.

The land was mucky, ferny, with cycads that looked much like the ones around prehistoric Saint Louis.

Beauregard looked scared. He wasn't a hunter, didn't pretend to be.

Nor was I a mankiller. But I was about to learn how. I'd better.

I motioned silence, waved Beauregard to my left rear, and we started forward.

I moved slowly, as slowly as I'd ever stalked. Even Tyrannosaurus doesn't shoot back.

I saw Hendrik as he saw me.

He had one of those super shotguns.

I stepped sideways, into the slight cover of a drooping fern, and had my gun up.

I fired just an instant before he did.

My .600 round took him in the mouth, and took off most of his head.

His shot went wide. At least most of it did.

One of the pellets got me in the forearm, and I jerked, dropping my rifle.

Kilbrew came up from a crouch, behind Hendrik's body. He was carrying the .577.

I went for my .600, but it was far, too far away.

He had me cold.

Being Kilbrew, he savored the moment, aiming carefully.

There was a tight grin on his face.

"Fuck you!" I managed, damned if I'd give him the satisfaction of any fear.

I braced for the shock, even though I knew there wouldn't be any pain.

Just instant death.

He was less than ten meters away when he fired.

The bullet sprayed muck a meter away from me. Kilbrew gaped at the impossible miss, worked the bolt, and then Beauregard shot him in the guts.

The bullet, intended for one-shot kills of anything short of an elephant, almost cut Kilbrew in two.

Kilbrew went back, and down, completely motionless.

Illogically, since there was nothing left to kill, I

scrabbled for my rifle, broke it, fumbled another slug in, and snapped the action closed.

Then I looked up.

Coming out of the brush to the side was a small, hairy biped. It had a furred face, and wide, lemur-like eyes that were watching me curiously, not afraid, not worried.

I froze, seeing *Australopithecus afarensis*.

He, for I could see it was a male, eyed me calmly, then looked up at Beauregard, who stood, petrified, rifle in his hand.

Afarensis nodded then, as if making a judgment, and was gone.

Bloody hell.

I felt like I'd just met my own grandfather. I know with that tiny head he couldn't have been very intelligent, but to me he looked as if he had all the wisdom of all mankind.

Paul, I've been dry for ten minutes, and I really need another, very badly . . . thank you.

Better. Some better.

I walked over, picked up Kilbrew's rifle. I'd been right. There aren't any free lunches in physics. That few centimeters Kilbrew had so cleverly designed had also given the gun's recoil a chance to get a little momentum, enough to shock-shear one of the scope mounts. Kilbrew hadn't noticed it, but the scope was twisted about 20 degrees to the side.

Sometimes, the scientists are right. . . .

So we piled the bodies into our hovercraft, and went back to our camp.

It wasn't quite as bad as we thought.

Only four of the help died. The others, after

careful nursing by us, then shuttled back to where the transition chamber would come, and rushed to the best hospital in Nairobi, all lived.

I told an inspector of the Kenyan police what had happened.

"One of the richest men in the world . . . murdered. This is not good," he decided. "Did he say anything about having bribed the Ethiopian guards around Awash?"

"Nothing," I said. "But we weren't on chatting terms by then."

He turned everything over to the local UN representative, who turned everything in turn over to the US ambassador.

Surprisingly, no one leaked.

At least, not yet.

But suddenly there's mention of laws completely closing off Ethiopia from any time travel under ten million years ago. Or maybe closing it off completely.

I don't know.

I don't really care, since I'll never go back to the Pleistocene again.

One look at those eyes, and that was enough for me forever.

Of course, Wandi Kilbrew refused to pay the bill, and lawyers are now talking. When his estate eventually comes through, you can bloody bet Beauregard Black will get a bonus that will stagger his people for half a dozen generations.

And I'm thinking that maybe from now on I'll do nothing but sightseeing or photo safaris.

Father Figures

Susan Shwartz

"I have been a word in a book
I have been a book originally"
("*Cad Goddeu*," "The Battle of the
Trees," attributed to Taliesin)

EMRYS SAT ALONE UNDER A tree trying not to panic.
If he really were a prophet, he'd have no cause to
panic because he'd *know*. But all Emrys knew was
that Uther's men, who watched him from a hundred
vantage points near the great circular embankment,

133

whispered that he was damned well prophet and wizard and they'd kill him if he proved them wrong.

And then there were the black-robed priests who had called him a devil's son and longed to send him back to hell. They bore a remarkable resemblance to Vortigern's evil wizards who'd been ready to sacrifice him for being the boy without a father. So far, he'd managed to bite his tongue on that observation.

So maybe Emrys was a prophet, and maybe he'd just been damned lucky—unfortunate as the choice of words was.

What he was now, beyond all doubt, was a fool. What had possessed him to declare at Aurelius Ambrosius' funeral feast that he would deck the High King of Britain's grave with nothing less than the light itself?

The boy's drunk. He could see Uther's warriors mouthing that to one another and, pretty much in their cups themselves, grinning at the idea. Emrys had almost been insulted. You could expect that kind of stupidity from a descendant of Hengist or Horsa, drunk out of what few wits they had. Besides, Emrys hadn't even had *that* much to drink. He'd been blind with grief, not mead.

Uther had to understand that; with a gesture like the slash of a knife, he'd silenced his retainers. But he couldn't silence young Gildas, whose limp made him as useless a warrior as Emrys. And Gildas had his brother monks to protect him and honey over his mutterings that Emrys had been Aurelius' catamite.

For all that, some gossips probably believed him. Uther Pendragon wasn't one such, at least not toward the end. But he had never loved his brother's son.

"Let's just see what you can do, bastard," the new High King had muttered out of the side of his mouth. He'd barely spoken except to hail his brother's memory as one might salute an emperor. And even then, he could barely control his voice.

Bastard. Emrys had never known his father or, for that matter, who his father was. So he'd been ripe for the taking when Vortigern's wizards proclaimed that only a boy without a father could shore up the renegade king's fortress' foundation. They had expected to use his blood: his counterplan had been to use his wits and some scanty engineering knowledge pried from watching engineers who treasured learning said to have been handed down from the days when the Legions occupied Britain.

Instead, he'd blacked out. By the time he'd waked, Vortigern's wizards were shorter by their heads; masons were rebuilding the foundations with stone and mortar—but no blood; and Emrys had been named prophet—an honor he could have lived without and run considerably fewer risks—to a traitor.

Fearing that his next summons by Vortigern would be the death of him, Emrys eluded his guards and fled to join the High King, new-come from Little Britain. If he'd been a true prophet, would he—the boy without a father—have truly been so astonished to learn who his father had actually been? Emrys had felt like he was living in a dream. In the twinkling of an eye, he'd been promoted from potential sacrifice to king's son—even if he had been born on the wrong side of the blanket. Filial loyalty replaced hero worship, at least most of the time, and Emrys, called Merlinus by the High King's Romanized troops after the hawks he loved, had served Aurelius as faithfully as any true-born son might serve his father.

And then the High King died.

Being what they were, wary and even jealous of each other, Uther and Emrys couldn't even comfort each other for the loss of the man who'd been an absent father to his son, and raised his brother as if they, not Ambrosius and Emrys, had been parent and child. Uther had never forgiven Emrys the bastard for existing, let alone claiming a share of his elder brother's love. No doubt he'd be glad to see Emrys fail. Uther was a practical man, with no use for histrionics or failures, especially those standing too near his Purple. Unless Emrys could make good on his boast, he didn't have to be a prophet to know Uther would rid the world of him.

What if he succeeded? Wouldn't he be even more of a threat?

Quite probably. But the problem was: he had made a solemn vow that he'd be damned if he didn't keep. In more ways than one.

For now, though, Emrys was alive and boy enough to rejoice in the beauty of the day and a handful of moist, crumbling cakes (his servants liked him even if no one else did and were constantly trying to fatten him up so he wouldn't look like some changeling from under the hill). Munching, he glanced out over the curved embankment, trying to see massive stones, bigger than those in the circles in Little Britain, jutting up from Sarum Plain. He hadn't just been an idiot; he'd been an idiot in detail, vowing to cross the sea, uproot the Giants' Dance from Eire—over what were likely to be emphatic armed objections of the local fighters, no doubt—and float them back to Britain before dragging them over land and setting them up here above Ambrosius' grave. No doubt Uther's men expected the stones to swim or dance the whole damned way.

The late afternoon sun pierced through the cloud cover, half-blinding Emrys. Or maybe it wasn't the sun after all.

If he ran away, Uther would send men after him, to haul him back in disgrace. Perhaps, if he admitted what Uther most likely knew—that he might be his bastard nephew but no kind of a wizard at all and flung himself on the High King's mercy—Uther might merely pack him off to a monastery. Or kill him quickly, disgusted at his cowardice. Either might be better than this silent apprehension while he waited to be found out.

A raven, larger brother to the brand of the Legion's God that Emrys bore, flew across the plain. Emrys raised a hand in salute, knowing that men would mark the gesture and report it to the new High King. Young Gildas was probably lurking somewhere, scribbling, eternally scribbling. The fact that both he and Emrys were always writing or reading something should have been a bond between them. But Gildas never forgave himself for being less than perfect: he forgave Emrys even less.

And then he heard voices on the plain. A man's voice, a woman's, quarreling in no language he had ever heard. It bore some resemblance to Latin and some to the Saxon's tongue. He'd always been quick at music, quick at speech, quick to learn languages. Even his earliest teachers had called it a gift of

God (when they didn't attribute it to the devil). In either event, they tended toward plans to shut him in a monastery to work off the sin of his birth as a harmless scribe.

Emrys set himself to listen. There were no crystals here, as there'd been inset in the womb of the cave that had been his study and his refuge when he was a child, but he stared into the sunlight until sweat scalded down his sides and tears ran down his face. As his vision whited out, a blaze of comprehension engulfed him.

"Something went wrong. The last time I . . ." The man's voice was well-modulated and restrained, as if he had studied rhetoric in Athens itself.

"The last time you and Fletcher Pratt went off on one of your little jaunts, you didn't just miss dinner, I didn't see you for three months. Isaac was ready to write a detective novel about it, and Robert managed to sell that time-travel story to *Astounding*!" The lady's voice, higher pitched and angry, cut across her companion's.

Emrys crept closer, to spy as well as eavesdrop on the quarreling strangers. A good thing he was thin and lithe and could crouch in what was exceedingly inadequate cover. He saw a tall, lean man who carried himself like one of his father's war leaders. But for all his leanness and energy, the man was quite old—oh, sixty, if he were a day. Strong lines bracketed his mouth, and his temples, below a plume of silvering hair, were hollowed.

"I'm sorry, Catherine, to drag you into this. There's one consolation, however. We are most definitely in

England. Britain, I should say. Look at that henge. They haven't even begun to erect the stones. Neolithic, I should guess . . ."

"Lyon Sprague de Camp . . ." The lady stamped her foot. It wasn't much of a stamp, but then, it wasn't much of a foot: the lady was smaller than her lord by shoulders and a head. Her hair was gilded, but she could hardly be a Northerner, not with the saint's name she'd been called. "Oh, Spraguie, after all these years, do you think I'm going to let you go charging off into time again without me? At least, if things go wrong, we're together."

"We may be here for quite some time," the man said, pointing toward Aurelius' grave. "The transfer point's got to be there, or nearby. Along with what looks like a considerable war band."

Emrys squinted so he could examine the lady, in her strange white clothing and necklace of silver twisted in interlocking spirals, shells, and water-smoothed gems, more closely. Her hair was fair, her skin pale, and her lips red, almost the color of rowan in autumn. She carried herself like a queen.

Think, Emrys, the boy told himself. The lady's named after a saint, and the man bears several names. Or perhaps, the first name was a title. After all, Lion was one of the degrees of initiation into the cult of Mithras—and a higher degree at that than Raven, to which Emrys had attained.

Emrys came to what Bleys, his tutor, called a paradox. What was a senior initiate of Mithras doing with the Lady? The God of Legions had few dealings with women.

"The ground looks freshly turned in there. Probably a

tomb from the size of the excavation. The installation's bound to be in there. But we're going to have to be careful finding access."

"I can't imagine the people here don't have . . . stringent punishments for tomb robbers." The lady flared her nostrils in distaste.

"Do you regret coming with me?" asked the man. He wore a gray robe, a little short for him, but then, he would have towered over any but the largest Saxons. *And there were giants in the earth in those days . . .* no, Emrys cautioned himself. *You have no evidence to support that assumption. Mortal man, if unknown to me, and the Lady could be newly come from Rome. In that case, she'd probably be Christian, and it still makes no sense for her to consort with the Lion.*

Emrys could not doubt her humanity, however, or at least her perfect use of human form, when she quite audibly sniffed. "Nonsense! I would regret only if we were parted, as I told you. And I have every expectation that we will either figure out a way to return, become Philadelphia Yankees in King Arthur's Court, or whenever we are, or that we'll be rescued by our friends. Besides, the sight of you stealing those clothes . . ."

She laughed merrily, like a much younger woman. "I suppose we shall have to find allies soon. And shelter. If the weather holds, I would truly prefer to sleep outside. Wattle and daub holds bugs, and old stonework probably even worse. And you can smell that camp from here . . ." She widened her eyes, and turned her head sideways, as if looking through Emrys toward where Uther's men were camped.

"There is one advantage," said her companion. "As

you know, at this time in Britain's history, the climate could sustain viniferous grapes."

Lady Catherine laughed again and held up a hand. "Spare me the expository lump, dear. It all adds up to 'don't drink the water . . .' Still, the air is very sweet. No smog." She nodded at what Emrys finally decided had to be her husband. With a speed Emrys hadn't expected in a man his size or age, the tall man whirled, leapt forward, crashed through the bush, grabbed him, and dragged him out to drop him, ignominiously, at the lady's feet.

Lady Catherine instantly leaned forward. "Why, he's only a boy!" she cried. "Can we help you?" She grimaced, bit her lip, then repeated the question in curiously accented Latin.

"Interesting choice, my dear," said the Lion, or Sprague of the Camps, as his lady had called him. "Why Latin?"

"Look at his knife and tunic. They look Celtic enough to me, but I never studied Welsh. Iron, no less. And that fibula's studded with garnets. We've taken ourselves a high-ranking hostage."

"Better keep back, in that case, dear. Teenagers were fully qualified fighting men in Dark Age Britain."

Lady Catherine sniffed. "I don't think he'll hurt me. I know teenagers, after all."

Sprague snorted, but didn't release his hold on Emrys' arm in the slightest. "Answer the lady, *fili mei*," he ordered. "Catherine, did I get the vocative right?"

"You know you did," she said. She looked narrowly into Emrys' eyes, then spoke in the odd jargon that she and her husband had used since Emrys had first heard them.

"Sprague, I think he's understood every word we said since we . . . arrived."

Emrys attempted innocence and suspected he didn't achieve it. It never had worked for him when he'd been growing up, the last of a gaggle of princelings, legitimate and otherwise.

"In that case, give me one good reason why I shouldn't take this wretched little spy out and slit his throat with his own knife?" Sprague laughed as Emrys jerked against his restraining arm. "'Oh, what a tangled web we weave, when first we practice to deceive,'" he added to Emrys. "Catherine, I agree. The boy's a natural linguist and the fastest study I've ever seen. Damn, I wish Professor Terman could have observed *him*; he makes the Stanford study group look like a class full of slow learners."

"Stop scaring him, Spraguie," said Catherine his wife. "Look how dirty you got him." She leaned forward and, taking a clean white cloth, rubbed at the Raven brand on his forehead until he squirmed.

"Stay still now," she scolded . . . "But that's not dirt."

"No," her husband said. "It's a brand. A raven. 'Mithras, God of the morning . . .'"

His grip relaxed momentarily, and Emrys scrambled to his feet, saluting him as befitted a lower- to a higher-grade initiate.

The Lion raised an eyebrow.

"He must have heard me call you Lyon, dear, and jumped to the obvious conclusion," said Catherine. "The one time I actually use your first name . . ."

"No good deed goes unpunished. And he may have done us a favor. In any rate, as Lion to Raven,

I owe him protection. Can we help you?" Sprague asked again.

Emrys bowed his head. "No one can help me," he muttered despite inward, conflicting exhortations to stand straight and bow to his elders, or run as if the Wild Hunt were on his trail. Or tail, as the case probably was.

"That's as may be," the Lady Catherine said with some sharpness. "Why don't you tell us the whole story and let us be the judge of it."

"You won't believe me," Emrys said. "Nobody ever does." Except for the time, the first time in his life, he'd boasted as a man among men at his father's funeral feast. Nevertheless, he turned and led the way to the tree where he'd stretched out on his cloak and cursed the day he'd been born. He wasn't surprised to see that no one had touched his leather bottle of wine or the honeycakes, wrapped in a damp coarse cloth, that one of the cooks had pressed on him with a sigh of "poor lad, I mean, my lord."

After he and the older man had seated the lady carefully on the cleanest part of his cloak, he dropped to one knee, poured wine into the flask's attached cup and offered it to Lady Catherine. After she sipped and nodded politely, he wiped its rim and offered it to Lord Sprague.

"I suppose wine's a natural antiseptic," Catherine said as she watched her husband pour a libation before he drank.

"Not a bad week," Sprague said, wiping his lips, then his eyes. "Enough tannin in this to cure a vat of hides."

Catherine grimaced. "Well, cheers!" she said, taking

the cup back. She sipped, grimaced again, and drank once more. "You know, I could get used to this," she said and broke off a piece of honeycake so that Emrys, too, could eat.

"Let's have the whole story, young man. Why were you spying on us? For that matter, why are you sitting out here all by yourself and looking as if the hounds of hell are about to be set loose? Sprague, tell him we won't let anyone hurt him!"

"I find myself unable to tell him anything of the sort, unless he cooperates with us," the man said. "Starting with the truth, the whole truth, and nothing but the truth. We're waiting. Let's start with your name, seeing as you've already learned ours."

Emrys hunched his shoulders as he had when he was a boy trying to postpone the moment of his inevitable thrashing for one of the misdeeds that had always come as natural to him as breathing.

Are you a man or a bastard brat? He scolded himself, and straightened before it all came out in a rush. "I'm called Emrys. After my father Aurelius Ambrosius. I told you you wouldn't believe me."

"Son, you'd be amazed at what we might believe. Six impossible things before breakfast," the man said.

Catherine drew a fast, deep breath and glanced out over the plain. "That looks like Stonehenge. But where's the standing stones?"

"In Ireland," said Emrys. "And that's the whole problem. I promised I'd bring them back to Britain and set them up here. In honor of the High King. He's buried there." He pointed with his chin, his hands busy with wine and honeycake.

"The High King Ambrosius," said Catherine, raising

a hand to her lips. "Oh my. What're those lines from Keats? 'Like stout Cortez when with eagle eyes, He stared at the Pacific—and all his men Looked at each other with a wild surmise—Silent on a peak in Darien.'"

Neither Emrys' teacher Bleys nor any Druid he'd met had ever uttered such words, but Emrys recognized them as a song.

"It was Balboa, not Cortez," the man replied, "but I do understand the 'wild surmise' part, my dear. You think we're 'first looking into Chapman's Mallory'?" he asked.

"Perhaps not Mallory, but definitely Geoffrey of Monmouth, or even Nennius," Catherine replied. She looked out across the plain where no standing stones had ever risen nor, if the task were left to Emrys' feeble powers, ever would.

She paused, then grinned at her husband.

"Sprague, don't you know Merlin when you see him?"

Her husband laughed a mighty laugh, then wiped his eyes. Emrys hastened to offer him more wine. "'There really *are* more things in heaven and earth . . .'" the man murmured. "Catherine, let's look at the data at hand. In our world and our time, the stone circle we know as Stonehenge predates Dark Age Britain by . . . a considerable amount. Say two thousand years. And the menhirs and dolmens were transported not from Ireland but from the Prescelly Mountains in Pembrokeshire, while the altar stone probably came from Milford Haven. Possibly the idea was to throw down the cult of the death goddess in Wales . . ."

"Oh, Sprague . . . surely you're not going to quote *The White Goddess* at me?"

Emrys made the Sign.

Sprague snorted. "The words are marvelous, but the whole book's superstitious nonsense."

"Occam's Razor," swore his wife. "Least common denominator. We see a boy who calls himself Emrys. He's vowed to deck his father's grave with the light itself, assuming Mary Stewart will forgive me for stealing that line. If we were in our own world, Stonehenge would already be standing. But it's not, so, I think we've got to assume we haven't just traveled back in time, we've jumped universes."

Maybe Emrys had only thought he understood what the newcomers were talking about. Now, they were talking as if they'd been translated from some other world. Some happier world, no doubt, where boys like him were spared the consequences of their bragging.

The sunlight was slanting down on the henge. Sooner, rather than later, he'd have to go in and face sidelong looks, questions about "well, when do we set off for Ireland?" and whispers, hissing closer and closer until one night, men and knives would come for him, or he'd convulse and die with wolfsbane in his wine or some such.

Such a world probably didn't exist. Emrys shook his head to clear it, then returned to the problem at hand: his boast, his impending failure, and the doom that would surely follow.

"I swore it by the king's grave. You should swear things like that," he muttered.

"No, you shouldn't," said the man. "So it looks very

much as if you're honor bound to have to assemble the Giants' Dance here. Can't say I envy you, interesting problem in engineering though it is. But it may be that I can help you. In fact, I'll have to help you if Catherine and I are to have any chance of getting home because I don't believe our meeting is a coincidence at all."

Emrys started to throw himself to the ground in the prostration given to the emperors in the East. "I prayed, and you were—you *were* sent to help me!"

That the man called Sprague had said that "it"—and surely "it" must be some great power or talisman—rested near his father's grave made him shudder. Emrys told himself that Sprague and Catherine had sat at his table, warmed themselves at his hearth, and couldn't possibly mean to defile it or betray him. And he believed it, he told himself. He believed it.

"Oh dear God, Spraguie, if you don't set him straight, he's going to decide we're gods or demons, and I don't know which one would be worse. Look at the boy. He's shaking like a leaf."

The man's hand was on his shoulder, traveling to his chin, turning his face up. "Boy," he called. "Emrys! I give you my word, we're not gods or demons, but flesh and blood like you. Look!" He drew Emrys' knife and cut his hand. "It bleeds. Would a god bleed? Would a fraud show you blood or try to convince you that he had powers you lacked?"

"It didn't work for the man who would be king in Kafiristan," Catherine muttered, drawing a flashing grin from her husband. One day, Emrys promised himself, he'd have read enough that he'd know the heroes the lady talked about.

"But you *knew*. I didn't tell you, and you knew," Emrys protested.

"We're students of history. And we know a story . . . very like your own. Besides, in addition to history, I studied at Caltech—that's a school, lad, where they train engineers like you get in the Legions. I served in the Navy. And I've been to Easter Island where they have standing stones sculptured like giant heads. I've even seen the pyramids in Egypt. Let us help you."

The Giants' Dance was supposed to have come from Africa, and Emrys' guest was an engineer. For the first time, Emrys felt not just the stirrings of hope, but real hope that his guests might help him devise some practical plan.

Emrys looked away from the tall man to the seated woman whose eyes and jewels glowed in the light of late afternoon. A breeze sprang up, drying the cold sweats that had hit Emrys from time to time ever since he'd blurted out his idiot boast.

The lady was watching him. For all their brightness, her eyes were soft and very kind. "I think you've been through some rough times," she said. "It sounds to me as if you found your father after you'd been missing one for a long time. And you loved him very much. And now you're alone again."

"No, I'm not," Emrys said, furiously knuckling away what he told himself was *not* tears. "They're watching me. Uther's men and the monks. That Gildas. They're always watching me."

"Kind of young to have the ward heelers on your tail, aren't you, son?"

"What demons are those?"

"The very worst," said Sprague. "Petty demons."

"Now, Spraguie . . . stop playing word games. Let's help the boy move mountains, and then we can go home." She smiled at the tall man and at Emrys himself, and he thought it might not be the worst thing in the world—in all the worlds these strangers talked of—if they had to stay. If he could stay with them.

One thing about being even a bastard prince: Emrys could bring in guests, and they would be well treated. After they were warmed at his hearth, offered food, water, and linen, he realized his servants had decided they should be treated royally.

His guests looked magnificent. Lady Catherine's white linen, now topped by a great cloak, swept the ground, and she wore bracelets and earrings of amber the color of her hair. Sprague fastened a huge penannular brooch on a cloak in subtly woven plaids atop a green tunic. A sword that looked like the ones carried by Uther's guards hung at his belt.

Emrys pulled up heavy chairs for his guests at the trestle table that groaned with food: chickens, venison, a roast of boar, bread that tempted even Emrys' fledgling appetite, and grapes.

"I haven't been this dressed up since Bob and Pam Adams' wedding!" Sprague announced. "When they fired up the baths, did you see how they operated? It was just fascinating."

Catherine tapped her foot against the battered mosaic of the floor. In the soft shoe she now wore, it wasn't as impressive as her foot stamps earlier in the day, but she made her point.

"Now," said Sprague, "let's sit down and eat. Then, we'll make some plans."

"I have to confess," Emrys said. "I'm not really a prophet."

"That's as may be. One thing's certain: You're a scared boy, and you've got reason to be scared. Let's look at the situation. You may not be a magician, but you're shrewd. And any art that is sufficiently advanced is indistinguishable from magic."

Never mind the bards. Martial himself could not have composed a better aphorism, Emrys was sure. He waved away the servants, and cut his guests' meat with his own hands.

The lady leaned over the table. "From what I gather—that story in our own world, as we told you, plus the scrolls and codices I see you've collected, you're a good mathematician. What you've got here is partly an engineering problem. For that, Sprague can help you, none better. And the rest of it is logistics: getting your people where you need them and making sure they have what they need to do what they have to do."

"What we haven't got is time!" Emrys protested.

"*We* have all the time in the worlds," said Sprague. "But you're grieving, you're way out on a limb, and naturally, at your age, you're in a hurry. You won't believe me now, no one your age ever does, but you'd be wise to plan now so you won't have to play catch-up later. And listen to my wife: she studied economics at Columbia along with languages."

"Emrys, you may as well accept that moving these stones is going to take time. The more people, the less time. That's only logical. But, if you have too many people, you'll run into a whole other set of logistical problems: they'll get in each other's way, and if you've picked the wrong people, from warring clans or people who aren't honest, they'll probably start a war."

A chill ran down Emrys' spine. He had not lived among ill-wishers, either in his grandfather's house, Vortigern's household, or now without being able to sense—no magic about it, just sharp eyes and ears—when he was being spied on. "*They're watching,*" he mouthed at his guests.

Sprague raised an eyebrow, then dropped a hand to the pouch at his finely tooled belt. He rose and went to the fire, began to chant, and extended his hands. The fire erupted with a roar loud enough to drive the eavesdroppers away.

"*Not* the catalogue of ships again," his wife complained. "We may get a spy who's read Homer, and then what will you do? To say nothing of what happens when you run out of filings. No, don't tell me you've brought along iron or magnesium filings, too."

"The thing about clichés, my dear," said the man, "is that they work."

Emrys went to the door, where one guard, more valiant than the rest, lingered by the wall.

"Young Gildas almost pissed himself when that fire went off," the guard said, grinning. Did Emrys really have allies among the guards? That was useful to know. "It's worth being that close to . . . what you do to have seen the expression on his face."

"It is forbidden to interfere when I and my guests speak together. They are great teachers."

Emrys could practically hear the guard's jaw clench as he snapped to attention and closed the door.

"Nice going, son," said Catherine. "But I wouldn't get

any ambitions about being a boy actor, if I were you, though. They're a dime a dozen in Hollywood."

"What shrine is the Holly Wood?" asked Emrys. He should have known the lady was a priestess. Since the monks had swarmed all over Britain, he had known few Druids who dared to speak this openly.

"Never mind," she said, a little sharply. "Let's talk about logistics."

As Sprague watched with an expression of pleased— no, he wasn't surprised—he expected her to take charge, Emrys blinked. He supposed he should have been able to puzzle out "logistics" word from the Greek he'd learned.

"Robert—he's a . . . a wise man of our acquaintance, Emrys—says that dilettantes talk strategy, amateurs talk tactics, and real professionals talk logistics. Let's evaluate the situation."

"How could I have been so stupid as to say I'd adorn Aurelius' grave with the Giants' Dance?" Emrys lamented again. "The stones are enormous, and there's no one alive strong enough to move them."

"Man makes engines," said Sprague. "Pity you couldn't think of stones closer to home."

"It had to be these stones. It couldn't be stones from Little Britain; besides, they're allies. These stones belong to Gillomanus, a king in Ireland. They're big enough and important enough to be a proper monument for my . . . my father. Besides, if you pour water over them and bathe in it, they'll heal you. Or the water can be mixed with herbs and used to cure wounds. There isn't a single stone in the whole Giants' Dance that doesn't have some medicinal property." He paused to draw a breath.

"And besides," he said, "I promised. I've been doing some calculating . . ." He reached for wax tablets and stylus, rough parchment and pen, and pulled them forward, the wax half-smoothed from the last time he'd used it, the parchment already smudged and scraped. "Uther says he's damned if he's going to give me the fifteen thousand men he says it'll take to do the job right."

"The job being what? War with Gillomanus' Ireland or bringing home the memorial stones?"

"Probably both," Emrys said. "Gillomanus will never surrender the stones, I know that. We'll have to take them by force."

"You're a noncombatant," said Lady Catherine. "After they have their war, your work starts. Now, I don't need to be an engineer like Sprague here to know that brute strength won't work on those stones. You're going to need cranes and levers and ropes. Probably sledges or logs to get the stones to the ships once you take them down. But you men can talk," she said, rising and stretching, lithe as a cat. "I'm going to bed."

The Lion of Mithras who called himself Sprague paced in front of the dying fire, discoursing of siege engines and the Bible. At least, that's what the talk of the megalithic yards, fathoms, and cubits as opposed to what he called the "Stonehenge cubit" sounded like. "As my . . . my *magister* for these arts, Aubrey Burl, a learned man who went up and down the Isles seeking out these stones, taught . . ." Lord Sprague went on. "Oh never mind! It's in Pythagoras. I'm assuming you've studied geometry. The square of the hypotenuse . . ."

Emrys scrambled down from his chair, snatched a charred stick from the fire, and sketched the right triangle that had been one of his earliest lessons.

"Good boy!" the man approved. "Now," he said, "what do you know about counting and arithmetic in different bases . . ."

Emrys settled his chin on his hand, smearing ash over his face, he had no doubt, and listened as if his soul depended on it. As his life assuredly did.

Sprague continued to pace before the flames, occasionally dropping down beside Emrys to correct his triangles. The light waxed and waned, waxed and waned. Emrys' charred stick fell from his hand, and he stared into the fire. No white dragon. No red dragon. Not even a salamander. He'd been prophet to two kings, and he couldn't even summon up a damn lizard.

Back and forth.

"It's a formula," came the man's voice from a distance that sounded far greater than his height. "Perhaps the old curates' theory that you can attribute everything to solar myths actually means something. Hmmm. If I remember right, the meaning of the thirty posts of the inner circle is plain. Last time I let Catherine tease me about *The White Goddess*. Let's see if I can remember what Graves said."

Sprague's voice took on the cadence of a Druid, summoning wisdom from his trained memory. " 'The thirty arches of the outer circle and the thirty posts of the inner circle stood for the days of the ordinary Egyptian month; but the secret enclosed by these circles was that the solar year was divided into five seasons, each in turn divided into three twenty-four day periods, represented by the three stones of the dolmens' . . . hmmm, hmmm, and what's the point? 'For the circle was so sited that at dawn of the summer solstice the sun rose exactly at the end of the avenue in dead line with the altar and the Heel Stone; while of the surviving pair of the four undressed stones, one marks the sun's rising at the winter solstice, the other its setting at the summer solstice.'"

Emrys could see it now: the massive arches, darker for the brilliance of the dawn, with the great fire of the sun blazing through the entryway and glorifying his father's tomb with long beams of light.

It would be beautiful. It would be breathtakingly simple, a matter, as Lady Catherine had said before retiring, of fulcrums, levers, ropes, and enough men to do the heavy lifting—assuming they survived the war they'd have to fight with Gilloman. And the honor would be his, all his . . . just as the blame would be if he failed.

The hearth seemed to expand before Emrys' eyes, then spin as the room around them went darker than the sky right before dawn. The air glittered, and his temples pounded the way they'd done as he'd stood before Vortigern in a ruined fortress and the tale of the white dragon and the red ripped out of him.

They were back, those winged creatures, fanning his hearthfire; although they were much too big to occupy the firepit, they would rend the room from its foundation as they had done the traitor's fortress . . . .

Dimly, Emrys heard the Lion shout, "Catherine, get me a cloth! Boy's having some sort of seizure," before the roar of the comets that dazzled him as they exploded somewhere behind his eyes engulfed his consciousness.

He felt his mouth stretch open—"Get that cloth in there before he bites his tongue; what's that he's saying?"—and he fought to get out the infinitely important words: "This world is profitless, uncertain, a transient possession of everyone in turn, every day. Everyone that has been, everyone that will be, has died, will die, has departed, will depart. Each night I behold fire-breathing Phoebus with Venus, and watch by night the stars wheeling in the firmament; and they will teach me about the future of the nation . . ."

"This isn't epilepsy, Sprague," came the lady's voice. "He's hallucinating. It can't be ergot; the bread they served us was white bread, at any rate, or we'd be showing symptoms too."

"Emrys," came Sprague's voice, close to his face. "Boy . . . Merlin! Can you hear me?"

I can hear you, my lord, Emrys wanted to say. Other words tore out, hurting as they fled the prison of his skull. "I was taken out of my true self, I was as a spirit and knew the history of people long past and could foretell the future. I knew then the secrets of nature, bird flight, star wanderings and the way fish glide."

Hard hands were holding on to him, keeping him from flying through the fire and up into the night. *Let me go, let me go!* He thought he screamed that before the blackness, tinged with red and flame at the edges, engulfed him.

Emrys found himself lying upon stone, warmed by a fire onto which his guest heaped fresh wood so that it roared up like something in Emrys' visions. His visions . . .

The room reeked of his sweat and worse. At the last, he'd lost control again, like a baby or a man in his second childhood.

"It is quite all right," Lady Catherine spoke over the level of his aching skull to people visible only as long legs and shadowy robes. Some of them were black. "Nursing is the province of women."

As her husband bent to poke the fire, he turned and his shoulders shook.

The monks murmured, but Emrys' head hurt too badly to follow. Damned blackrobes: why couldn't they speak up like a man, or like the lady there?

"I have raised young children, I'm used to caring for the sick," Lady Catherine said. White ringed hands bathed his forehead, attesting the truth of her words. "Rest easy, brothers. Between the prince's servants and me, he will fare well enough."

More muttering, to which Emrys added words of his own. "Get those damned stormcrows out of here."

"You really shouldn't swear. But what's that you say, dear?" Lady Catherine asked. She raised his head so that it rested against her breast, effectively muffling his words. "Sprague, if you could hand me that cup . . ."

Her husband bent with a speed that must have made him a formidable warrior in his prime and handed her the cup with a bow. Neither allowed the blackrobes to come anywhere near it.

"Drink," the lady murmured, and he obeyed.

Willow, Emrys thought, and herbs heavier and darker. No wine. How had people that wise prepared a potion and left out the wine?

His head felt heavy, as it always did when the fits struck him.

Her arms, holding him, tightened. "I told you, we will care for him. We have no wish to draw you from your prayers. To which you have our leave to return." The lady's voice whipcracked, sending them away. Gildas turned in the doorway, glaring in a way Emrys knew well, then limped out.

The Lady had taken his enemies upon herself and her husband. Why? Emrys took the enigma down into a deep, black sleep like a well. If fortune favored him, he would find a solution at the bottom.

I'm getting better at this, Emrys told himself the next time he struggled out of a sleep about the size and depth of a pit. Someone—and he suspected he could put names to the people, because his servants were too afraid of him to tend him that intimately—had bathed him, wrapped him in a fresh robe, rolled him onto a pallet of silky furs, and covered him warmly. He had broken into a light sweat as you do when you get over a fever. His head no longer ached, and the vile taste in his mouth seemed remote, as if no concern of his.

He felt curiously light, his thoughts more clear than they had ever been.

Behind him, at the table, a chair scraped back, and long strides brought the man over, towering above him. "I copied over our triangles," said his guest. "When you fell, you smeared the drawings on the hearth. Are you well?"

"Better than I have a right to be," said Emrys. "Of

your kindness, sir, please lend me an arm. I want to stand."

"Catherine!"

"What's he doing, Spraguie? Standing up? Oh, no, you don't, child. You're going nowhere but your own bed today," she told him, taking him by the arm and leading him toward his room.

"But I must," he said. He was unsteady on his feet, and that was not good. He would have to be in shape to walk some distance and, if needs be, run and even fight. But he would need strength and for that, rest. He surrendered and allowed himself to be put to bed like a child. He would let himself enjoy the illusion of being a favored, well-tended child. Just for a little while.

The lady bent over him, smoothing back his hair in a gesture that made his throat tighten. His mother had given herself to holiness when he was very young; he could not remember a time when she had cared for, cosseted him the way a mother would care for a beloved child. He would have asked little better than to let her soothe him, perhaps feel her lips brush his forehead, then watch as she bustled about his room. Instead, as she bent closer, he whispered, "I've got to get you out of here tonight. Tell the Lion."

Emrys' guests carried their chairs into his room as if watching over him, concerned for his illness. He let himself fall into a doze, secure in their protection, knowing how much stronger he would feel when he awoke. From time to time he woke and measured the day's passage by the way the sunbeams drifted across his face.

When he woke for the fourth time, it was late afternoon. His guests had drawn their chairs closely together and were speaking, low-voiced, in the odd language they had used before they first saw him.

"He's concerned for us, Catherine. You were perhaps unduly harsh with those monks—"

"And this is the man who laughed when I said 'nursing is the province of women'? Better I than men who hate him and have access to an herb garden. Remember that monkshood took out King John."

"And none too soon," the man agreed. "But it couldn't be better. I wish we could stay and see the boy through this project of his, but I've given him everything he needs, except perhaps, confidence to do it. So I think it's only fair: let the lad keep his bargain and help us get home. Two strangers, wandering by the High King's grave? They've got two chances to enter it: slim and none. The guests of a bastard prince who's known to be a wizard? They'll be so afraid we'll turn them into toads that we'll have a free hand. Catherine, we could be back in Philadelphia before dawn!"

"I admit, I would like that. The people here are perfectly charming about heating water, but I *would* like a bath that's less labor-intensive. And I do not like the way those monks looked at young Emrys."

"When you're in a court, it's only necessary that there are court intrigues. Fascinating as it would be to meet King Uther, I think we'd better go home. And if Emrys is willing to help us, I think it's our best opportunity."

His first teacher had showed him how to keep his breaths regular, to appear to be sleeping, or preparing to meditate before the fire. But it was a struggle not to try to see his guests from beneath his eyelashes.

Light footsteps, a drift of fragrance, and Lady Catherine rose to check on him, then return to his chair. "I hate to leave him like this," she said. "He's a good boy. Sprague . . . ?" Her voice arched up in a question.

"In our world, this lad is absolutely essential to the future of the British Isles. If we took him back with us, we'd be meddling with history . . . I like him too . . ."

Emrys' eyes were welling. In a moment, the tears would spill out, and they'd know he'd been listening.

"But we can't take the risk. *It's not our world.*"

Both adults sighed heavily, and something in Emrys' heart chilled, probably forever. He let his awareness drift away. At least, when his guests went back to their rightful place in that Philadelphia—how civilized it must be, like Egypt, perhaps, or Athens, he'd be able to remember that they wanted to take him home with them, but he had a destiny to fulfill.

Damn his destiny. Whatever it was.

None of his servants thought it at all amiss that Emrys would wish to show his guests, who had been so kind to him, the High King's grave. But his servants all went in healthy awe of him, Emrys thought. The real test would be whether he could guide his friends through the labyrinth of guards and other unfriends and hold them off while they sought whatever shrine they claimed lay within the henge.

He had not had their company that long; but the

certainty that they wished to depart, coupled with what he knew the need for their departure was—for their own lives, if not for his—weighed on his heart even more than the day, remembered now as a sorrow long ago, his mother had left for the convent, abandoning him to his grandfather's fosterage.

In those days, he'd gone up into the hills and found Bleys, his master.

It was not inconceivable that, in the years to come, he would find others, equally as dear.

He unfastened his pouch and handed it to Emrys. "As a parting gift, my bag of tricks," he said. "You may find some of them useful after we leave."

He handed it to Emrys and clasped his arm, as if they'd been warriors together. Then, he held up his free hand. Light gleamed from off a gold ring.

"We're close," he whispered to his lady. "Look for any stonework that looks more . . . more modern than the rest." He stopped and turned to face Emrys again.

"I want to thank you," he began, as Catherine drew closer, setting her hands upon Emrys' shoulders.

"You know," said Lady Catherine, tightening her hands, "it isn't inconceivable we could meet again. In the tales of our world, you disappear, shut up in an oak tree, underground . . . Yes, none of it sounds particularly pleasant, but consider the possibility that you come to us instead. It wouldn't hurt . . ."

"No?" asked her husband. "My dear, you're breaking the prime directive. And besides, if Emrys came to us in Philadelphia, you'd only drag him to the dentist."

No real mirth underlay their laughter, but Emrys made himself laugh too.

And then, too quickly, fell silent.

"We're being followed," he said. He froze where he stood, listening with all his being. One step, then a pause, then a drag, as if the man who followed them limped.

"Gildas," he said, more in exasperation than fear.

Would the young monk never leave Emrys alone? Was it just that they were rivals for a scholar's praise? Or that Emrys wore the Raven's brand? Probably, he would never know.

One thing he did know: let Gildas find him aiding his friends to enter Aurelius' tomb—or let Gildas concoct a plausible tale of grave-robbing—and swift death, far preferable to execution, could be the best that he—or all of them—could hope for.

He took the torch Lady Catherine carried and snuffed it on the ground. Let Gildas find them in the dark: he carried light; he could be tracked.

He gestured his friends on ahead. What if he did not see them depart? If all went well, they would be gone and he—this was his world. He had coped with its spites, petty and great, before.

The Lion set out across the turf, his wife at his side. Quickly, she turned, rushed back to Emrys, and kissed him, fast and hard, then followed her husband. The tomb was ringed with fire. Emrys could remember when it was built and where—atop ancient stonework. Perhaps hidden in that wall was the door they sought to their home. He would have to have faith they succeeded.

He would never know now, he thought.

He turned to wait for Gildas, watching the light bobbing toward him as the monk limped as fast as he could. He should never have come out alone, Emrys thought. If he were what Gildas thought, what qualm should he have about killing him?

Not very logical, his Gildas, but a good hater. Emrys dropped a hand to the pouch the Lion had given him, withdrew what he sought, and waited.

Gildas' torch drew closer, close enough for the monk to see that Emrys stood alone, as always.

"Where are your demons?" demanded the young monk. He stood unevenly, the firelight gleaming off the cross hung round his neck. "I heard them speaking of forbidden magics."

Forbidden to whom? Gildas never quite understood that not everyone was a Christian. Or cared.

"My *guests* are gone." *Where you will never find them.*

"To rob the High King's tomb?"

"Have you been swilling sacramental wine again?" Emrys asked. No need to waste what he was coming to think of as his gift, or curse, or even logic when insults would do.

"Blasphemer!" With the high, hot temper of the Celt, Gildas rushed him, torch out to strike and maim.

It was the moment Emrys had been waiting for.

He threw the handful of metal filings he had drawn from the Lion's pouch onto the torch, then hurled himself back as it exploded into violent light.

Gildas shrieked and fell, but not before the torch set his robe ablaze.

Emrys kicked out the fire—perhaps more vigorously than need be. Thoroughness, his teachers had always said, was a virtue.

When the fire was out, and Gildas safely unconscious, Emrys hoisted him over his shoulder and carried him to the nearest guards, dropping hints the monk had wrestled with a demon and been saved through Emrys' wisdom.

After all, if Gildas was going to hate him, he might as well have some grounds for his grudge.

He could just imagine how his guests would smile if only they knew.

If only.

He waited until the guards had left before he sighed and returned to his quiet rooms.

None of the servants had touched the triangles inscribed the night before: how should they dare? Emrys set the pouch down, and carefully arranged the parchments.

He clapped his hands for his body-servant. The man entered so fast that Emrys knew he was under constant scrutiny. He knew that, from now on, he would always be watched, and awe—maybe turning to respect should he deserve it—struck him as better than hatred and suspicion.

"Set out clean clothes for me. Then go and ask whether the High King will receive me."

He washed, then smoothed his hair and dressed as neatly as if Lady Catherine were going to approve him. He was attaching his new pouch to his finest belt when the word came: Uther would indeed grant him audience.

Picking up the parchments that showed him how to satisfy his boast—perhaps for all times, he swung his cloak about himself and went to see the king.

He had a vow to fulfill.

Tom O'Bedlam and the Mystery of Love

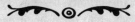

Darrell Schweitzer

Love is madness and madness is love,
and never the twain shall part.
> — *Anonymous the Elder*

WINTER. LONDON. FIFTEEN HUNDRED AND
Something-Something. In his bed at Whitehall, King
Henry VIII dreamed of love, of lovely maidens who
became his numerous queens, some of them now
minus their heads . . . which sometimes happened in

the entanglements of love, a way of cutting through the
Gordian knot of the heartstrings, so to speak. . . . He
dreamed of dancing, of songs, of roistering, of maidens
and meat pies.

Courtiers, with their heads in their hands, serenaded
him with lines he'd stolen from another but of which
he was nevertheless inordinately proud, *"Alas, my love,
you do me wrong . . ."*

He sniffled. He started to sneeze.

Tom O'Bedlam dreamed. Nick the Lunatic dreamed
with him, his bosom and boon companion, whom Tom
had redeemed long since from the labors of Reason,
from the ardors, the cruelty, the slavery of Sanity. This
same Nicholas, who had once been gaoler in Bedlam
before Tom spoke to him with the true Voice of the
place and set him free, which is to say mad; AHEM!
This very Nicholas walked with Tom O'Bedlam in the
dream they both dreamed together, in the cold and
the dark of the night.

They passed a troop of the Watch, pikes and armor
gleaming in the pale moonlight; but sober watchers
do not affect to see madmen, particularly madmen
abroad in dreams; therefore, dreaming, Tom and Nick
went on their way without any interference.

Dreaming still, they reached the countryside, drifting down empty lanes, past trees naked of all but
their last leaf. And that last leaf rattled mournfully,
one leaf per tree, as it was the custom among trees
in winter to retain but one.

Tom and Nick jangled their bells, mournfully, by
moonlit midnight, as was their custom to reply; but
they felt, the both of them, a certain emptiness, a

melancholy, and remarked on it without words, for two madmen dreaming the same dream surely do not have to trouble themselves to *speak*.

Alas, for great loss.

Something burning where the heart is broken, where joy is stolen away, like the last spark sputtering when the fireplace is swept clean.

Aye, and swept clean of all hope, but beautiful in its tragedy, its sorrows like intricately-carven black onyx.

Is there any other kind?

You got me.

They passed through a forest of branchless trees, the naked trunks like enormous, tangled blades of silver grass. A wind rustled through the forest, sighing far away.

The forest gave way to open country, but like none Tom had ever seen. The ground was white in the moonlight, but not covered with snow; more leathery than earthen. It had a distinct bounce to it.

Nick did a handstand, bells jangling. He clapped the sides of his soleless shoes and wiggled his dirty toes, then flung himself high into the air as if from a trampoline . . . high, high . . . until great black, winged things began to circle him hungrily, eclipsing the Moon as they passed.

He called out to Tom, who leapt up to catch Nick as he tumbled and caught him by the ankles and hauled him down, out of the clutches of the fiery-eyed, softly buzzing flyers with their gleaming-metal talons; down, down—

They bounced for several miles, soaring over another stand of forest, coming to rest before what seemed a vast mountain with two oval caves in it, side by side. Here yawned the very abyss, the darkness which swallows up even madmen.

Fortunately, more of the silvery strands grew thickly about. Tom and Nick clung to them, at the very edge of the abyss, to avoid falling in.

And standing there, gazing into the depths, Tom O'Bedlam had a vision, as if he were dreaming his own dream *within* the dream and had now awakened from it.

He understood, as only a madman could.

It was this: he and Nick had become as *lice*. They had travelled for what seemed like hours across an enormous *face*, through the forest of the *beard*, escaping the flying peril of the *gnats* (or perhaps flies) until they found themselves deposited at the very lip of *No! No! That wasn't it. Abysses may have lips but nostrils don't!*

He and Nick clung desperately to a giant's nose hairs as their presence had unfortunate consequences.

"AH—AH—AH—!"

Now the wind roared more profoundly than all the world's hurricanes—profound, yes, though it didn't actually say anything; for the hurricane is the philosopher among storms, Tom always said, or one day would, or so said in his dreams (some confusion on this point), and its profundity is so profound that even the hurricane cannot fathom it—

"AH—AH—AH—!!"

—the one certainty being the thunder of its blast, as the eye of the storm passed, or in this case perhaps you might say it was the nose of the storm; and the winds reversed themselves and Tom and Nick lost their grip and went tumbling into an abyss vaster than any that yawns between the grave and the world, between the world and the stars—

"CHOOO!!!"

Burning the midnight oil that would never expire, because this midnight would never pass, Peter the Poet paced petulantly in his drafty garret. He sat down at his desk again.

His fancies raged. But words would not come.

His quill scratched across the page:

> *Alas, my love, you do me wrong,*
> *to cast me off discourteously . . .*

Rubbish, he knew. Anybody could do better than that, even, he fancied, a pair of lice crawling up someone's nose.

King Henry sneezed and awoke briefly. He thought of love. His royal wrath roused. He considered shouting for the headsman and finding someone's head to lop off, just for the exercise, but, no, 'twas late, 'twas cold, and he could do it in the morning. For now he turned and sank back into the deep recesses of the royal bed, and dreamed of meat pies, and so does not figure largely in our narrative.

> *"And I have loved you so long,*
> *delighting in your company . . ."*

Tom O'Bedlam sneezed and awoke. Nick lay beside him, still asleep, sniffling, but not for long, as the not-so-kindly innkeeper, who hadn't so much allowed them to stay through the miserable cold of the night as failed to eject them because he was himself entirely

too drunk (and customers lay snoring across the tables
and benches of the common room; here and there
somebody sneezed; a belch; flies or fleas or gnats hovered); verily, i'faith, this same innkeeper, arisen early,
unsteady on his feet with an ugly expression on his face,
approached them in his thundering, clumping boots
with a bucket of slops in hand that he *might* manage
to heave out into the street and then again maybe not,
as he would have to step over the recumbent Tom
and Nick to make his way to the door—

"Nick," Tom said, nudging him.

Nick sneezed and swatted a louse off his cheek.

"Nick, we have to go."

The innkeeper loomed clumpingly.

Nick swatted again.

Just in, as he thought to phrase it, the nick of time,
Tom hauled his companion up and out the door and
into the street. The innkeeper slipped or tripped, or
out of sheer spite threw the slops after them. Foul
liquid landed with a splat in the snow.

Still Peter the Poet gazed out his window into the
darkness, which he fancied to be the darkness of his
own melancholy.

The words would not come.

He scratched more rubbish on the page.

> *I have been ready at your hand,*
> *to grant whatever you would crave . . .*

He watched the Moon set. He watched it rise. The
night would never end.

"Is it morning, Tom?"

"It should be, yes."

"But, look—"

Tom looked. The full Moon was setting in the west, but to the east another Moon was rising where the Sun should be. Birds in the eaves of the houses around them twittered and began to sing, then hesitated, uncertain of what to do next.

"That's not right, Tom," said Nick.

"No, 'tisn't."

They had to scramble aside as a troop of guards with pikes and armor, with banners flying, with moonlight gleaming off their silver helmets, came tramping down the street, screeching "Make way! Make way for our great lady!"

They bore their lady in a sedan chair. She gazed out through the curtain, resplendent in her finery, jewels gleaming, regarding the two madmen through a glass of some sort, which only magnified her hideous face, which was that of a naked skull.

Her guardsmen screeched because their heads were not those of men, but of ravens and crows.

"That's not right either," said Nick.

"No, 'tisn't."

They stared after the company as it passed.

And so the day passed too, though it was a misuse of the term to call it a day, as there was no daylight in it, as the Moon passed again across the sky amid stars which seemed subtly out of place. And the Moon made to set, and yet *another* rose in the east; and the cold of the night continued; and though Tom and Nick half-heartedly capered at times, and did their tricks in the cold and the snow—Nick lit a candle at both ends and swallowed it, and spat it up again, still burning—no one gave them any pennies for their pains. There were only ghosts abroad, and ghouls, skeletons, the King of Faerie with his rout, the occasional furtive wizard, the former Lord Chancellor of England in all his state (but minus head) and frequent lunatics—there being such a surfeit of Moons that for the moonstruck it was a very special occasion indeed.

Yet the respectable folk of England were still in their beds, still asleep, in the night that would not end.

Peter the Poet paced, not asleep at all.

King Henry dreamed of meat pies.

Tom and Nick came upon a man who sat calmly on a low wall. As they approached he rolled his eyes and shook his head, made a gobbling noise, and fell over backwards into a snowy rubbish heap.

Tom looked down over the wall.

"Never mind the formalities. Can't ye tell we're as mad as thou art—?"

"Forsooth," said Nick. "Or possibly fivesooth."

But the other merely groped among the rubbish, crooned, and said, "Do not wake me from this wondrous dream, for I lie in the arms of a beautiful maiden!"

Nick regarded him, then turned away.

"Is it sooth he says?"

"No, 'tisn't."

"You keep saying that."

"That's because a madman must be obsessed, Nicholas. Therefore he hath tics and twinges and odd tatters of phrase, which he repeateth anon and anon, as, well, one whose wits are diseas'd—"

"Oh, aye."

"You ought to do it more yourself. Keep your madness in good trim, for Madness, though the most natural and unpracticed thing in the world, requires practice, which is a paradox, as 'twas told to me by a pair o' doxies once in a particularly friendly fashion—"

But before Tom could continue his discourse, lunatic as it might be, Nick tried to remind him that none of this would matter a jot if they both froze to death in the dark.

"That nears dangerously close to common sense," said Tom. "Stop it."

But even as he spoke there came One with hooded robe and scythe and hourglass.

"Do I not know you two?"

Tom shook his head and jingled his bells.

"We've met before, perhaps?"

Tom and Nick shook their heads in unison.

"Let me look it up." Bony fingers flipped through a notebook made of tiny tombstones, which clapped thunder as the pages turned.

But Tom reached over and flipped the pages back, with a thunder, a crackle, and a crack, losing the place.

"This gets so confusing sometimes."

"Aye," said Tom. "It does at that."

Tom and Nick ran. Nick continued his discourse on how the world was ending, the sunrise would never come, there would be no more pennies, warm cups of ale, or inn floors to sleep on. He started to sob. His tears froze and fell down like sparkling diamonds. He stopped to scoop some of them up, wondering if he might be able to use a few to buy ale and mutton.

Tom turned to him and shook him.

"Nick. You're almost making *sense*, a fearful thing from a madman."

"Saint Fibberdeygibbet preserve us! What shall we do?"

"I think we should sleep on it."

"Are we not already dreaming? That makes no sense at all!"

"Exactly."

So they lay down in the street, in the snow and mud, and again slept, and again dreamed, though they were never sure they had ever awakened. A coach ran over them almost at once, but it was a phantom coach, drawn by flaming, headless horses, conveying a bishop of London speedily to Hell (or possibly a bishop of Hell speedily to London), and so it hardly disturbed their rest.

Meanwhile the poet rose from his desk and paced the room, mournfully, yet again. His fancies gathered all around him, thick as gnats, or fleas, or flies . . . he would decide which later on . . . and he imagined himself no more than vermin, crawling on the face of mankind . . . and all ladies gazed upon him as if they were foul specters, or he was . . . and he yearned for someone who could understand the burning yearning he had in his breast . . . *that* phrase, he knew, would have to go into the rubbish heap, as soon as he found the words, as soon as inspiration returned . . .

Tom O'Bedlam slept, and dreamed that he rode in a phantom coach drawn by flaming, headless horses (there were a lot of them on the streets this night;

business was booming for spectral conveyances of all sorts) and that a queen in all her finery sat across from him.

The coach sped; it jostled and swayed as it rattled over the rough streets.

The queen's head, which had been in her lap, bounced to the floor at Tom's feet.

"Oh dear," she said. "You must excuse me."

Gently, Tom placed the queen's head back in her lap. There was no room to bow, but he swept his hat from his head in a gallant gesture, bells jingling.

"Are you a Fool?" she asked.

"Are they the ones who say 'i'faith' and 'hey, nonny-nonny,' and call everybody 'nuncle'?"

"Yes. My husband had one like that."

"Tiresome lot. No, I, Your Highness, am a madman."

Her Highness found that to be something of a relief. It was a relief, too, to have a sympathetic ear to talk to, as she recounted how the King had wronged her, jilted her, and lopped her head off for good measure, which didn't even let her enjoy the afterlife, because of the constant, tedious obligation to rise from her grave and haunt him.

"We ghosts wail and sing a lot," she said. "Not that it does much good. No matter how off-key we are, *I think he likes it.*"

Tom commiserated. He did remark, incidentally, on how the sun did not rise and the world seemed to have come to an end, but only incidentally, remaining focussed on what really mattered, which is to say the lady's sorrows, lost love, broken hearts, and the miscarriage of romance.

"Ah me," the ex-queen sighed. The coach bumped. This time her head bounced into Tom's lap.

"Ah, you . . . by the way, while you're here . . . are these *your* fancies that fill and haunt the night, that forbid the sun to rise . . . ?"

She groped forward and took her head back.

"You have been a friend to me, sir. I would grant you any favor I have within my power . . . but, alas, my powers have been much curtailed by, by . . . you know." She hefted her head and gestured with it. "All I can offer you is the advice, that, being a madman, you alone understand the mystery that is love, and that if you find the one who is most wounded in love, and somehow heal that wound, then the world will go on as before . . . though I can't see why even a madman would want that."

"You'd have to be mad to understand, Majesty. Being dead isn't enough."

"Ah, yes, of course—"

Just then the coach hit a particularly large bump, the door flew open, and Tom tumbled out into a snowbank.

He sat up, sputtering, awake (relatively speaking), though some distance from where he had lain down with Nick.

On his way there he passed a line of monks who chanted solemnly and hit themselves on the forehead with wooden tablets. He passed pure maidens, gallant highwaymen, dashing pirates, honest politicians, and other such persons as inhabit dreams.

He came again upon the One with the scythe, hood, and hourglass, who hissed at him, *"Ssayyy . . . don't we havvv an appp-pointmenttt?"*

He spun the hourglass with his finger and hurried on.

Above him, there were now *eight* moons in the sky. A ninth seemed to have become stuck somehow on the spire of St. Paul's, like an apple on the tip of a knife. The Man in this particular Moon complained vehemently. His dog barked. He dropped his lantern into the street, where it exploded into glittering shards, each of which, Tom knew, was filled with enchantment and could lead someone on a magical, romantic quest, or provide some great and impossible revelation, or boon—but he didn't have time for that.

The air was thick with melancholy. Gloom hung over the city like a damp fog, dimming the outlines of the rooftops to a dull blur. In the houses as he passed, he heard sleepers cry out and sob in their dreams, dreams which might never, ever end at the rate things were going.

He found Nick lying in the street. Several pigs nuzzled around him. But sufficient Melancholy had puddled there (a foul, dark fluid, like slops) that they were the most sorrowful pigs Tom had ever seem. They merely gazed at him reproachfully as he shooed them away.

He shook his friend. "Nick! Nick!"

"Oh alas," said Nick, awakening. "I was dreaming of meat pies. I almost had a bite when—"

"Come on!"

"Come whither?"

"Hither. Thither."

"Blither."

"Oh, yes. Do so Nicholas. Absolutely. Your madness is like a rare sapling, gently nurtured, which now grows into a vast forest that shall not be cut down in a single night."

"But what if that night never ends, Tom?"

Tom told him what the headless queen had suggested.

"Now *you're* almost making sense, Tom. Beware! Beware!" Nick jangled his bells in warning.

Tom urged him to consider the source. Such advice might have been sound, but *how* it had been obtained put it safely within the allowable bounds of madness.

Now all they had to do was find the one so wounded in love that all the rest had followed.

It wasn't hard.

They went where the fancies were thickest, where the melancholy filled the streets like black syrup, rising above the windows, splashing over walls, while Tom and Nick swam in it amid bobbing skulls thick as foam on a stormy ocean.

They glimpsed the Hooded One with the scythe again, who was standing in an upper window, surveying all that passed below, looking rather pleased with himself.

But when that One saw Tom and Nick paddling by in a washtub, he shouted something and ran downstairs.

But Tom looked ahead, not behind. He saw that he and Nick had come to a forest of gallows, from which skeletons hung, all singing as the wind passed through their bones.

I have both waged life and land
Your love and goodwill for to have . . .

They beheld knights on quests, always failing, maidens pining away at tombs which bore the effigies of those same knights. A dragon, quite pleased with itself indeed, gobbled down the maidens one by one.

There were ten moons in the sky, eleven. They bumped into one another. The various Men in the Moons quarrelled furiously.

The skeletons sang:

> "*I brought thee kerchers to thy head*
> *That were wrought fine and gallantly . . .*"

Nick tugged on Tom's sleeve. "What's a kercher?"

"Rubbish!" someone shouted from a loft, high overhead.

"I think we have arrived," said Tom.

Introductions were in order.

"Peter the Poet, I'm Completely Mad. Completely Mad, this is Nick the Lunatic."

"Actually his name is Tom O'Bedlam," said Nick.

"Ah me!" said the Poet, half in a swoon, hand to his forehead.

"Poets do that a lot," said Tom to Nick. "It's part of the trade."

"Sort of like being mad."

"Yes! Exactly!" said Peter the Poet. "Even more so because I am *in love!*" He paced back and forth, gesticulating, waving pen and paper in the air. Tom and Nick stretched and bent, trying to read what was written, but the page never stood still long enough. Meanwhile Peter explained how he had been smitten, indeed, with the madness of love, which burned him, from which his life bled as if from a wound, as fortune's wheel turned but would not favor him, as his fancies raged forth into the night on the holy quest of love (several hundred metaphors followed; we need not list them all), how he had given his heart away—

Indeed, this was so. He undid his doublet, unlaced his shirt and showed them the hole in his breast where his heart used to be.

"Good place to store cheese," Nick remarked.

And in a great storm of words then, in thunder and fury, in drizzling melancholy the Poet told the whole soppy, sorry story, which had no end, and could only be interrupted to further explain that a Poet's fancies come from the heart, and if he has already given his heart away, and does not possess it, those fancies must arise in some place other than the residence where the poet resides; *ergo* a problem of uncontrollable proportions, which the Poet can hardly be expected to do anything about; ahem, since he, therefore, struggling with the Muse, with inspiration, can hardly be expected to recapture and rein in his fancies because what he writes *has no heart in it* and the result is likely to come out more like:

> Thy gown was of the grassy green,
> Thy sleeves of satin hanging by,
> Which made thee be our harvest queen.
> And yet thou wouldst not love me.

"Doesn't even rhyme," said Nick.

"It could be worse," said Peter the Poet bitterly. "It could be *Hey nonny-nonny.*"

"I shudder to think," said Nick.

"Does she have a name?" Tom asked.

"Who?" said Peter.

"Your lady love. Now I too have some experience in the madness of love, for I was wounded in love myself, when I loved a giantess who was unfortunately moonstruck when she stood up too tall one night and the Moon hit her on the head and knocked her over the edge of the world—'twas a sad thing, but not entirely tragic, for still she tumbles in the abyss, among the stars, and she rather enjoys herself—I hear from her on occasion, as she dreams of me, or sings love songs in her dreams, though she has fallen so far now that sometimes they take years to reach me—but as I was saying, ahem, it is my experience that in these cases the beloved usually has a *name* . . ."

"It's Rosalind," said the Poet.

"Ah."

"At least that's her poetical name. I spied her from afar. I fell instantly, madly in love—something you can appreciate, I am sure—and I declared her my Rosalind. I set her on a pedestal, as my inspiration, my Muse. I gave her my heart, as you've seen, but still she loves me not, and my poetry cannot speak of the sorrows I suffer—"

"But you haven't actually ever *spoken* to her, have you, much less inquired of her name?"

"What else can she be but my Rosalind?"

"Her name might be Ethel," said Nick.

"You haven't actually—?"

"I poured my love into a poem, and thus I gave her my heart. It melted into the paper like butter into toast. I followed her to where she lived, and slid the poem under the door—"

"Where for all you know the scullery maid found it, and used it to wipe her nose when she sneezed."

"All gooey with melted butter?" asked Nick.

"*Alas, for unrequited love!*" said the Poet. "Now

sorrows and fancies pour from my heart, which is somewhere else, so what can I hope to do about it?"

"I think I know," said Tom.

And One who bore a scythe and hourglass, and
had to hold both rather uncomfortably under his
bony arms as he paged through his notebook, stood
on the doorstep of the house where the Poet lived
in the loft. There were by now twenty-seven moons
in the sky, but the night was still somehow dark, the
light itself steely, gleaming of death, the air chill,
Doom and Gloom and Melancholy flowing by in the
street like a vast river from an overturned witch's
cauldron. (In fact every witch in the kingdom rushed
out with a jar or a jug to get a sample.)

At last he found the page in his notebook. *Yes*, he
did know these two, who were due and overdue and
had evaded the ravages and reapings of himself and
all his kind. These two had escaped all the tyranny
of Time, for entirely too long.

Now would be a reckoning.

He passed through the door of the house and began
to ascend the stairs to the loft, his scythe scraping
awkwardly as he held notebook in one hand, hourglass in the other, and in situations like this wished
for a third.

Just then Tom, Nick, and Peter the Poet came
padding or clattering down the stairs (depending on
condition of footwear) and nearly collided with the
One who ascended.

The Poet let out a frightened cry. Nick just tugged
on Tom's sleeve as if to say, *Do something*, and Tom,
calmly, with the assuredness of madness, snatched

the gravestone notebook out of the apparition's hand,
flipped through it back and forth, laughed at a few
things he saw in there, sighed at a few others, and
said, "Oh, alas, I have lost your place."

While the Hooded One was still sputtering "Stop
that!" and trying to find his place again, Tom said,
"May I borrow this?" and took the hourglass. He
popped off the top, wet his finger with his tongue,
and reached in to draw out a few of the Sands of
Time on his fingertip.

He touched his finger to his tongue, then turned
to Nick and Peter and touched their tongues also.

It was a beautiful spring day, the sky so bright it
was almost booming, *"Hey! Look how bright I am!"*
Birds sang, not one of them with a *hey nonny-nonny*
either. The air was filled with the scents of flowers
wafting as such scents traditionally do (as a poet
would describe it); and on such a day, Tom, Nick, and
Peter the Poet came to a country fair. There, amid
the bustling country folk, among the motley of jesters
and clowns, the fantastic costumes of the players (who
noisily out-Heroded Herod), the puppets, the banners,
and funny hats with exotic feathers, *there,* shining
before them all like a beacon, her beauty parting the
mass of confusion as the staff of Moses parted the
Red Sea, stood none other than Rosalind.

"That's her," said Peter the Poet.

Thus she had appeared to his eyes when first he
saw her.

"I am without words," said the Poet, enraptured
once again.

So it was Tom who went up to the lady, bowed

low and gallantly, did several somersaults, stood on his hands with his toes waving in the air, while he said, "Your pardon, gentle maid, but if you will take the word of a poor madman, there is a poet yonder who is mad for love with you—"

But the lady merely shrugged and said, "Why, of course. I *am* of radiant beauty, am I not? Poets appreciate that sort of thing."

She laughed. Tom fell over onto his feet. He found himself with Nick and Peter, back in London. The sky darkened and was once again filled with dripping melancholy and intermittent droplets of *ennui*, which rattled off windowpanes like sleet.

"That didn't accomplish very much," said Nick.

"I feel a *hey nonny-nonny* coming on," said the Poet.

Again, Tom held up his finger and touched their tongues.

The Hooded One flipped through his notebook furiously. These things had to be done according to protocol. He would have to be patient. But not *too* patient.

Now it was past high summer, with just a touch of autumn in the air, nighttime but a proper nighttime, with only one moon (a crescent) in the sky, and the Hunter rising to gaze over the horizon onto the fields and towns of England.

Tom, Nick, and the Poet came to a cottage. They knocked on the door and a plump, middle-aged woman met them.

Tom introduced himself, did a few handstands,

pulled an egg out of his ear (which hatched in his hand; he gave the woman the resultant chicken) and explained why they had come.

"Ah, madmen," she said. "Of course. Enter."

"I'm not mad," said Peter. "I'm a poet."

"The same."

They entered in, and before Peter could launch into another of his flowing, poetical, and very long speeches, the lady broke in and said, "My name really is Rosalind, which is but happenstance. You, young man, are too wild-eyed for me, too like these other madmen. You speak of love. I remember love in all its rages. I think of it sometimes, on quiet evenings by the fire. But my life is not like that now. I count the days. I count sheep. I go to market on market day. The seasons follow one another the way they should. I am content. I might have cared for love once, but not now. Why bother?"

She served them warm ale and bread. They sat by the fire for a while, but said little.

Peter the Poet began to weep. Then he stood up, and swept his arm back as if he were about to declaim.

"Quick!" said Nick in alarm. "It might be one of those *hey nonny-nonnies*—!"

Tom bowed politely to the lady and touched Peter's tongue with the last grains of the Sands of Time, then Nick's, then his own.

The Hooded One had it *figured out*. All he had to do, ultimately, was *wait*. Time, after all, was on his side. They were relatives. They saw each other occasionally at parties and family reunions.

Yes, wait. He reset his hourglass and thumbed his scythe blade with a bare, pale bone.

In London again, in the snow, Tom, Nick, and the Poet walked along the dark streets. There was no moon at all in the sky this night, only stars, but there were lights in windows, wreaths on doors, and groups of people singing carols. It must have been close to Christmas. From the taverns came the sounds of more singing, and of much roistering.

Nick held up his foot. His bottomless shoes flopped around his ankles. He wiggled purplish toes.

"Couldn't we go in and roister for a while? I'm getting cold."

"Not yet," said Tom. "Not quite yet."

They came to another house, in the city, and climbed along long, dark flights of stairs, the bells on their caps jingling softly, the Poet's boots scraping.

Gently, Tom pushed open a creaking door, revealing a room where an old woman lay in a bed under thin, ragged blankets, by the light of a single sputtering candle.

She sighed as they entered, *"Alas, my love, you do me wrong . . ."*

"I beg your pardon," said Peter the Poet.

"Had I known when I was young what I know now," she said, "I would have found a time and place for love. It is the one thing which is both constant and most fleeting. We clutch it like gold, but it trickles away like water. A poet told me that once. I never met him, but he wrote many things, in notes and poems he slipped under my door. I guess he was too shy. I never found out who he was. I could have loved him."

"Oh, alas!" said Peter, sinking to his knees at her bedside.

"Yes, alas," said the old woman. She fumbled in a drawer by her bedside. She unfolded a piece of paper, and, though it was too dark to read in that room, she recited what was written thereon, for she had memorized it long, long before.

> *Well, I pray to God on high,*
> *That thou my constancy mayst see,*
> *And that yet once before I die,*
> *Thou wilt vouchsafe to love me.*"

Her hand went limp. She let the paper fall onto the bedclothes.

"Not very good," she said, "but written with real feeling. That's what matters."

There on the paper was something that shone like a brilliant jewel, like a star fallen to earth and captured in the hand, a thing as delicate as a snowflake, but all of fire. It was his soul, his heart, the very source of his inspiration, which he had given away in hopeless love so long ago.

First he reached under his clothing, removing a bit of cheese from where his heart used to be, putting the cheese into a pocket. Then gently, reverently, he took up the glowing thing and replaced it within himself, where it belonged.

Now his fancies were under control.

He looked at the lady sadly, but hardly weeping, and began thinking of the words to a sonnet he would write about this night, something elegant in form, like a deftly carven jewel.

"*Now I've got you!!*" hissed the Hooded One, stepping out of the shadows, bones rattling, swinging his scythe wide. *"I've figured it out! All I had to do was wait! Ha!"*

"And you shall have to wait a little longer," said Tom O'Bedlam, "as anyone who is completely insane can understand readily enough."

He tapped the hourglass and sent it spinning, end over end. But as the lid had not been secured properly after Tom had opened it during their previous encounter, the Sands of Time spilled out all over the room, and there was much confusion.

"That's not fair!"

Tumbling, then, back through the days of their lives and the days they had never lived, Tom, Nick, Peter the Poet, and Rosalind found themselves once more in a London street, under the bright sky of summer (which is somewhat less obstreperous than many spring skies you could meet). It was an ordinary day. People went about their business. There was talk that the King was going to chop off another queen's head, or maybe had invented a new kind of meat pie. No one seemed entirely sure. Rumor, painted in tongues, wagged idly.

The poet got out pen and paper, sat on a wall. Beyond the wall lay a lunatic who had shaped a lady out of rubbish; but she had come to life and the two made passionate love, each of them perfect in the other's eyes.

The poet started to write a sonnet.

Tom, with the insight that comes only to the mad, stayed his hand, and said, "Have you considered becoming an accountant? Lots of lovely numbers in neat rows. Steady wages. No heartbreak or raging metaphors."

(The lunatic behind the wall and his lady love began to sing, something with *Hey nonny-nonny* in it every other line. It was time for Tom and the others to move on.)

The ending was this: Peter married Rosalind, after a proposal that added up their accounts neatly and showed how one side balanced the other. They lived quietly and happily together for a long time. If theirs was not a fiery, all-consuming passion, it was just as well, for such love is only for madmen, as Tom O'Bedlam knew so well. It deprives one of reason by its very nature, but even so, you have to have a knack for it, as you do for really inspired madness.

He explained as much to the Man in the Moon (there was only one) at night when he climbed to the top of the spire of old St. Paul's and helped free the Moon, which had gotten stuck up there, like an apple on the end of a knife.

One for the Record

Esther M. Friesner

I BELIEVE THAT I AM safe in saying that no one was more gratified than myself when the Club arose so promptly, phoenixlike, from the figurative ashes of our last unpleasant incident. One might argue that the worst was averted, and depending upon one's priorities and point of view, one might be right. The harm that Dr. Sonoma's incursion did to our reputation was minimal, yet the havoc his visit wreaked upon us purely in terms of demographics was incalculable.

So many murders, so little income. Though Dr. Sonoma was long gone from our midst, his residual influence had provoked several of our membership to the injudicious slaughter of several more. Although the celebrity dead often may be espied as alive and well by all the best tabloids and the plebeian dead may vote in Chicago, the better class of corpses seldom keep up their membership dues at the Club.

Dawkins was bemoaning this very fact to me as the two of us scanned the small, utterly discreet slips of paper which were being handed out to all members that bright April day. Stafford "Pinch" Dawkins was one of our relatively newer members, having joined our ranks after the Sonoma incident. He was, by all accounts, a gentleman of excellent bloodlines and impeccable breeding, but one whose family fortunes had suffered a plummet in the lattermost tenth of the nineteenth century due to injudicious investments. *La famille* Dawkins had spent nigh unto a hundred years crawling back out of the mire of middle income, finally reclaiming their rightful place in society in the person of young Stafford, who was a veritable wizard among the pork bellies, a Delphic oracle *par excellence* to whom the futures (*nota bene* my intentional usage of the plural) were an open book. Had he turned *haruspex* (that variety of augur who peeks at our tomorrows by studying the flight of swallows or the prancing of barnyard fowl) he would read the omens solely in the conduct of the goose that laid the golden egg.

Alas, while the spectre of Poverty may be exorcised within a single generation by the laying-on of Neiman-Marcus credit cards, the ghost of Bourgeois Lifestyle Past tends to linger like the aroma of a senile Gorgonzola. The rich who have been rendered simply "comfortable" do not forget. No matter that the disaster befell their many-times-great-grandsire, they live with the fear that what happened once before may well happen again. They have lost their precious sense of invulnerable entitlement and that, in turn, makes them ... *careful*. Not cautious, certainly not prudent or even particularly wise, just ... *careful*. There is a difference.

We called him "Pinch" for a reason: It was what he did. Not to women—that would be merely coarse—but to pennies, which was unspeakable. Of course we told him the nickname came from how certain we were that we could count on his help "in a pinch." It was an explanation as credible as a courtesan's smile, but Pinch was so eager to be accepted back into the societal bosom that he gulped it down whole.

The printed notice which we had just received, however, stuck firmly in his craw.

"A *raise*?" Pinch's eyebrows elevated themselves to such a height that they looked ready to crawl under the brim of his golf cap for sanctuary. The two of us had been on our way to a jolly round of the sport when we were waylaid by the news. "But our dues are astronomical now. How have they conjured up these obscene numbers? There haven't been any new property tax assessments, there are no legal matters outstanding, and no improvements to the plant are currently scheduled." Pinch knew whereof he spoke. He did Spartan service on almost every Club committee; not so much from altruism as from the hag-ridden drive to keep a close and personal eye upon any developments potentially perilous to his capital.

I sighed. I was none too enamoured of the hike in dues either, but there are some matters of which one does not complain. Clearly this was one aspect of good manners which had been woefully absent from Pinch's upbringing. I therefore viewed it as my duty to supply this want. I fancied myself the young man's mentor and sought to cultivate him. Apart from his Dickensian frugality, he was a pleasant companion and the only Club member, male or female, against whom I had a sporting chance in a round of golf.

"I can explain," I offered. "Before you joined, we suffered a precipitous drop in membership due to . . . certain unfortunate circumstances."

"Ah." Pinch laid a finger aside of his nose. "Say no more," he said rather unnecessarily. I had no intention of saying a single syllable more about our beloved Club's past vicissitudes, although I was gratified to note that Pinch knew enough to let slumbering scandals lie.

"In view of this," I continued, "the Board has obviously noted a comparable drop in income. To maintain our budget, they are redistributing the burden of the deceased members' obligations across the living membership."

"Why don't we simply mount a campaign to attract new members?" Pinch suggested.

I made a face. Perhaps I was mistaken; maybe he was stupid after all. "A *campaign*?" I echoed. "My dear Pinch, you can not be serious. The Club is like the fabled Hesperides: If you can not find your way to our door without seven yards of red carpet and a roadmap, you do not belong here. Our membership is exclusive in all the finer senses of the word. We do not actively shun any person or persons due to their ethnic background or religious affiliation. The very fact that they have heard tell of the Club implies that they stand upon an intimate footing with current members. A *campaign*." I clucked my tongue and shook my head over such chimerical fancies. "Why not take out a full-page advertisement in the tabloid press and attach a giveaway offer? One free debutante with each membership purchased."

I had hoped that my sarcastic diatribe would have the salutary effect of making Pinch fully aware of just how far beyond the bounds his suggestion had flown. I expected at the very least a lengthy apology, coupled with a satisfactory measure of abasement. If nothing more, I hoped that he would drop the subject and turn the conversation into more meaningful channels, such as the introduction of small side bets to our regular golf game, just to keep things interesting.

Instead, with a tenacity of life a cockroach might envy, the topic suffered a gross resurgence from his lips. "I can understand your not wanting to bring in the wrong sort of people," he said. "But surely the exorbitant price currently set on Club membership ought to be more than enough to discourage them."

Lacking a mirror at that moment I could not hope to see the scowl that darkened my brow, but to judge from the way in which Pinch gasped, flinched, and startled away at the sight of it, it must have been a oner.

"*Money?*" I thundered. "Is that all you think is at stake here? Not money, but the *love* of money is the Biblical root of all evil. A love which, my dear Pinch, seems to have laid hold of your heart with both hands and a divorce lawyer. There are worse things than going out-of-pocket in a good cause. I suggest you reflect, reconsider, and repent any schemes you might have entertained for lightening your own pecuniary obligations towards the Club by bringing in new members." With that, I turned on my heel and strode off, bristling smartly.

It was a marvelous snit, if I do say so myself, although its effect was rather ruined by the fact that I only stalked off as far as the first tee. Righteous indignation is all very well, but a gentleman honors his golf dates.

Pinch did not play well that day, even for him. I flattered myself into believing that his mediocre performance on the links somehow betokened contrition of soul. Clearly he had taken my words of chastisement to heart; there would be no more talk of grubbing up new members for the Club as if they were so many blue-blooded radishes.

I was wrong, of course; in all his sorry, short lifetime, Pinch never did truly heed any words save *Buy Low, Sell High.* He showed up with his "find" approximately one week later, much as a cat will display a mangled rat upon the doorsill.

This is not to say that Renée Speranza in any way resembled a dead rat. Far from it. She was as toothsome a morsel of femininity as might have been discreetly salivated over in a less enlightened, more enjoyable epoch. It was not her physical beauty alone which had the power to charm. Besides the attractions of a well-formed leg, a dainty waist, and a gloriously proportioned bosom, there clung to her also a certain air of mystery, of spirituality, almost of melancholia, that subtle breath of the tomb that makes all Romantic poets and certain Vassar girls so damnably intriguing.

And she was rich, as Pinch made haste to inform anyone who would listen. "Bundles of the stuff," was the way he put it to me.

I sighed. "Pinch, my dear fellow, do you think it *wise*?"

"Do I think *what* wise?" he asked. The two of us were alone at a table in the Club bar, the hour still being early, the premises still being relatively underpopulated. Miss Speranza had excused herself to seek out the Ladies' Lounge.

"Well, you know: To speak so freely of—of—of your escort's economic condition."

"Good Lord, what's wrong with that?" Pinch exclaimed. "If she were in debt, then I could see the need for discretion, but—"

I sighed again, deeply. Knowing Pinch was turning into a crash course in aerobics for me, improving my lung capacity by the moment. Certain subjects are not the meat of public conversation nor inquiry. One's sexual exploits may be expounded *carte blanche*, the more boring aspects of one's career are common fodder for all the best dinner parties, even one's political affiliations may be commented upon before the general ruck (provided, of course, that one has not committed the ghastly *faux pas* of belonging to one of those hideous, crackpot, fringe parties, such as the Socialists, the Libertarians, or the Democrats), but one's *money*—? I sighed and then I shuddered.

I suppose it all came back to the fact that Pinch's forebears had been too long in exile from the proper circles. The poor lad simply did not know any better.

One does not swat a puppy for irrigating the Aubusson, one trains it gently away from such behavior. Thus I attempted to do with Pinch. As delicately and as expediently as possible, I attempted to show him his error.

It did not work. "Now look, old man," he told me, "I honestly don't see the harm in anything I've said. When Renée rejoins us, I'm sure she'll agree with me. The lady wants to join the Club; won't she be investigated by the Board? Won't *they* want to know about her fiscal status?"

"Just as that charming nurse from the insurance company wanted to know whether I indulged in recreational pharmaceuticals and the love that dare not speak its name," I replied coldly. "This information I provided willingly, but I do *not* think I would want her speaking of it *ad libitum* whenever the conversation flags."

"Her money's *clean*, if that's what's troubling you," Pinch persisted. "None of it earned in *trade*." It was his turn to shudder. Apparently some of the old Dawkins breeding had survived the lean years. "Inherited, every last shilling and shekel. Apparently her first husband was successful in his chosen field of endeavor."

"Which was—?"

"Oh, she didn't get around to telling me *that*." Pinch swirled the dregs of his Scotch around the bottom of the glass and tried to look coy. He made a sorry hash of it.

"Let me guess," I said. "You want to marry her."

"Am I so transparent?" He was hurt.

"I've known martinis more opaque than you. And I don't mean those noxious modern variants." (A chocolate martini? Why not marshmallow-flavored *foie gras* as well? O rank madness!)

"Ah, well." He shrugged. "Can you blame me? I love her. I fell in love with her when first we met. She's beautiful, she's genteel, and she's got oodles of—"

"Please." I raised a staying hand before he could expound upon the lady's nummulary virtues once more. "In that case, I fail to see why you are trying to promote her membership in the Club. Why not wait until after you are wed and purchase a joint membership?"

Pinch showed a disquieting smile. "Because the Club, in its wisdom, does not *offer* joint memberships. It offers *single* memberships and *family* memberships, and the family membership includes privileges for two children, whether you have them or not."

"Is that so?" I mused. Really, the matter had never crossed my mind, being as I am a contented bachelor.

Pinch nodded with vigor. "And because the family membership covers two children, it costs much more than if you were to purchase two individual memberships."

"I see." I nodded. "Then your course of action is clear."

Pinch's face fell. "I wish it were."

"It's not?"

"Hardly. You see, I wish to marry Renée with all due haste."

"Good Lord, man, you do not mean to imply that the lady is—?" I leaped to the inevitable conclusion that perhaps the happy couple soon would be getting their money's worth out of a family membership after all.

Pinch turned a stunning Harvard crimson. "I should say *not*," he snapped. "If I wish to wed Renée swiftly it's solely on account of the dictates of love, not the unreliability of latex."

"Marry her, then." I honestly failed to see the problem.

"Oh yes, that *would* be nice." His words had the bitter tang of a grapefruit rind. "Except for the fact that the Club forbids married couples from purchasing anything but family memberships."

"Do we?" It came as news to me. Like most of my fellow members, I had never read the Club's charter and bylaws in their entirety. I paused to savor the cleverness of this profitable wrinkle in our Rules before replying, "Still, nothing to prevent you and Renée from cohabiting without benefit of prenuptial agreement."

"Are you out of you mind, man?" Pinch's fine nostrils flared with abhorrence at my lightly spoken suggestion of extramatrimonial cohabitation. "How would it look?"

"That presumes that anyone would care enough *to* look," I replied mildly. "We do know how to tend to our own knitting here at the Club."

Pinch snorted his skepticism. "Then someone's dropped a stitch or two. My friend, either you are the victim of a charming though potentially toxic naiveté, or else you are speaking just to hear your jaws clatter. I am neither blind nor deaf: I know how matters stand at the Club and I tell you that the wind one feels so constantly at one's back hereabouts comes from the clandestine waggling of every tongue on the premises. No, sir, I assure you that my union with

Miss Speranza will be as open and aboveboard as it will be legal, moral, and—"

—*financially rewarding?* I thought. But of course I said nothing of the sort aloud. Instead I clasped Pinch's hand, shook it firmly, and reassured him that I had intended no offense to him or the lady. A few further social pleasantries, an assortment of good wishes for the favorable pursuance of his courtship, a swift-yet-delicate change of conversational topic to the neutral ground of fly fishing, and the sweet breath of Elysium blew o'er our colloquy once more.

We had been debating the merits of dry versus wet flies for approximately twenty minutes when I thought to remark, "I say, Pinch, it's been rather a long time since Miss Speranza left us. Do you think all's well?"

"All is quite well," said Miss Speranza.

I am not the highly strung type. I do not start at shadows nor am I known to be especially goosey in even the most trying circumstances (of which, I admit, the Club seems to have more than its proper share). My *sangfroid* is almost as legendary as my tailor. Thus my reaction to Miss Speranza's abrupt utterance was all the more significant.

In brief, I jumped out of my skin, off my chair, and halfway to Greenwich.

My startlement was so great that it caused me to thrust a very comfortable leather chair out from under myself. The chair was set on impeccably oiled brass casters, which conveyed it almost the length of the Club bar until it bumped into a wall. My own trajectory was more of the simple what-goes-up-must-come-down variety. It brought me to land on the carpet, an accomplishment that did neither my dignity nor my coccyx any favors.

I waited to hear Pinch's laughter ring out at my expense. It did not. The unexpected irruption of Miss Speranza's voice had caused him to react in much the same way as myself.

"Oh my," said the fair cause of our discomfiture as she gazed down at us. "I'm so sorry. I didn't mean to frighten you like that."

We got to our feet and reassured her in unison that no apology was necessary. "Our fault entirely for not having remarked upon your charming presence, my dear," I said.

Pinch hastened to retrieve his chair, which had traveled almost as far away from its launch point as my own. He swiftly turned a gaffe into gallantry by offering it to his lady before pulling over another seat for himself. I passed a few minutes' chat with them, for manners' sake, then made my excuses. If the light of love gleamed in Pinch's eye, it positively radiated from Miss Speranza's. As I strolled off, I admit to feeling a passing pang of envy.

"Ah, what a precious thing it is to find one's soul mate," I murmured, wending my lonesome way into the Club rose garden.

I was making the closer acquaintance of a blushing Mamie Eisenhower (the rose, *bien sûr*) when I became aware of a rustling among the thorns that could not be ascribed to gophers nor Green Card-*manqué* groundsmen, both of which are renowned for knowing how to keep a low profile in chancy times.

"Who goes there?" I demanded, my hand dropping automatically to my Club-issued dog whistle.

(The Board had distributed these devices as a service to members who frequented the more isolated areas of the grounds. In the event of assault, one brief hypersonic tootle would fetch the immediate attention of several roaming packs of Bichons Frisés. Your Bichon is small, curly-topped, and akin to the poodle. The assailant rash enough to linger once he saw that he was not to be torn limb from limb by Dobermans, pit bulls or any of their ilk soon learned the error of scorning attack-lapdogs. Affection can be fatal. At least one would-be footpad met an unspeakable demise, first battered senseless by violently wagging tails, then drowned in a veritable flood of canine drool.)

The rustling in the bushes stopped. "'Sokay, man," came a hoarse voice. "'Sokay, no sweat, be cool."

"If I wished my perspiration to respond to the commands of strangers, I would purchase an exercise video. Show yourself!" I cried.

The bushes rustled more and yielded up their prey. The young man thus disgorged from their thorny snare looked much the worse for wear and tear. His pale face was scored with scarlet scratches, his long, shaggy black hair bedecked with serrate leaves and a sprinkling of pink and crimson petals. There was a certain air of lost Arcadia about him, an image reinforced by the fact that he was clad not in the dungarees and rudely worded T-shirt that are the standard plumage of such *rara avis* as he, but in a *chiton*. (It is, alas, a sorry commentary on our times that the masses would not recognize the Greek *chiton* unless a rerun of Paul Newman in *The Silver Chalice* bit them on the fundament.)

He also wore sandals and carried an electric guitar.

"Who are you?" I demanded. Courtesy forbade me from likewise asking *what* he might be and *why* he was being it among our roses. "What are you doing here? This is private property!"

"Easy, man, easy," he said, swaying somewhat on his feet and blinking up into the sky as if he had never seen anything so wondrous as the sun. "Gotta get my bearings, gotta think things through. Oh wow, talk about your head trips." With that cogent observation, he laid one hand to his brow, rolled his eyes back in his head, and fainted.

I used my cellular telephone to summon aid. Specifically, I called young Langley, whom I knew to be somewhere about the premises at that time of day. As soon as I saw that guitar, I knew he was the man for the job.

Like Dawkins, Benet Owen Langley was a recent addition to the Club's membership rolls, though he joined our companionable establishment under circumstances every bit as distinct from Dawkins's as they were extraordinary in their own right. He might have claimed the honorific of Youngest Member had such a designation existed, for he was no more than twenty-one years of age. Through intense application he had graduated Harvard in three years rather than the customary four and thence proceeded to sweep through the Law School with as much dispatch as that venerable institution might allow. He ignored the jibes of such straw-headed idlers as pronounce *overachiever* with contempt and made Partner in a prestigeous New York City firm of corporate attorneys in record time.

This in itself was no great miracle. The phenomenal

nature of young Langley's accomplishments became apparent only when one was privy to the fact that he was the offspring of one Thrash Gordon, late luminary of that genre of *soi disant* music known as Heavy Metal rock and roll. Before Mr. Gordon departed this life in the wake of a tragic tuning fork accident, he managed to break seventeen guitars, fifty-seven hotel suites, eight drummers, and Dorothea Langley's heart. Dorothea had retained her maiden name throughout the course of that ill-considered marriage and, upon her husband's death, returned to the estranged bosom of her family to raise her boy properly.

It worked. Albeit Benet Owen (so named by his father in a moment of cold-cough-and-flu-medicament-induced religiosity, commemorating both St. Benet Biscop, one of the lesser-known patron saints of musicians, and St. Owen of Rouen, invoked against deafness) had passed the first eight formative years of his life as a junior-rank roadie, once free of his father's world he embraced his mother's roots with a convert's holy passion.

Yet swear as he might that he had turned his back irrevocably on the realm of popular music and all it entailed, he could not deny he had retained much knowledge of that shadowy otherworld.

Now, as he knelt beside the apparition in the rose garden, his first remark proved that he had not removed himself so far from the late Thrash's sphere as he might have preferred, viz:

"Whoa. That is one *bitchin'* ax!"

"I beg your pardon?" I remarked.

Young Langley promptly re-collected himself and

withdrew his hand from the guitar with all alacrity (though also with some obvious reluctance). "I mean to say, this is *quite* the costly musical instrument: *Too* costly to be in the hands of someone like *that*. It's probably stolen. We must alert the authorities."

Alerting the authorities was not in accord with Club policy. Despite repeated *contretemps* that had at the last ditch demanded the intervention of local law enforcement personnel, the Board still preferred *not* to bring in outsiders to settle matters until sufficient quantities of members-only blood had been shed to make such action unavoidable.

"How can you be sure?" I asked.

"Well, just *look* at him!" young Langley replied with a fine *que voulez-vous?* gesture of his impeccably manicured hands. "He's in possession of one of the priciest guitars on the market, yet he's unkempt, uncombed, and in rags!"

"He is not in rags," I corrected him. "He is wearing a *chiton*, which is—"

Young Langley had no respect for a Classical education. "Have you searched him for identification?" he inquired, interrupting me.

"Where?" I countered. "The *chiton* was never confected that had pockets, as you *would* know if you'd bothered to hear me out." I confess, I was a bit acidulous, but his cavalier disregard for my hard-won erudition irked me out of all knowledge.

Young Langley made an impatient sound, then checked our uninvited guest for vital signs. He was just prying open the victim's eyelids when these flew wide of their own accord. Our visitor sat bolt upright and let out a shriek of abject terror that scattered the petals from a good half-dozen of the nearest rose bushes.

"Oh wow, man, I'm sorry," he said after he recovered his self-possession. "It's just, like, I thought I was still back down *there*, you know?"

"Back down where?" I inquired.

"The Underworld."

Young Langley and I exchanged a look of trepidation. Although I fancied myself a kind-hearted soul and was willing to believe the same of Langley until proved otherwise, we did not feel that it would be wise to offer the Club as a refuge for anyone unfortunate enough to have run afoul of Organized Crime. The police were too regular a fixture on Club grounds as it was, and were as tired of seeing us as we were of seeing them.

Langley, bless him, took all this into consideration and acted like a gentleman: His checkbook was out and open with an alacrity that would have set Alumni Fund solicitors to helpless drooling.

"What's the problem, old man?" he asked. "A loan come due? Piper to be paid and all that? Perhaps if you were to give me some general notion of how best we might aid you and see you on your way . . ." (Of course he was never crass enough to mention the M-word, nor how much of the M-word our uninvited guest might need to assuage his pursuers.)

"Huh?" The man brushed hair out of his eyes and gaped at Langley. "Oh, you think I need *money*?" The M-word! There it was, naked and blushing in the marketplace! Beyond all other external factors, this was proof positive that we were not in the presence of one of Our Kind. (True, I had used the M-word myself repeatedly, and not so long ago, but there is a great difference between mentioning it when you are speaking in the abstract and naming the Ineffable Name when you are dealing with concrete sums. The former is finance, the latter, vulgarity.)

"Ah . . . don't you?" young Langley asked.

"Naaah. I got millions. Hey, look, I'm real sorry about all this, me showing up wherever the hell I am now, dressed like this, scaring the crap out of you, but I tell you what: You get me to a phone and I'll make it all better, fast. 'Kay?"

I pursed my lips and glanced at Langley, one eyebrow raised ever so slightly. I could tell that we neither one of us believed the apparition before us to be in possession of a million anything, saving perhaps fleas, but ours was not to reason why. Ours was but to get the fellow off of Club property in good order, with a minimum of fuss and no public notice taken.

With this in mind, young Langley reached into his trouser pocket, pulled out his cellular telephone, and handed it to our guest with a gracious: "At your service, sir."

The bedraggled man stared at the instrument with a most disconcerting lack of comprehension. He took it from Langley's hand, turned it over a time or two, and by main chance happened to flip it open. A ludicrous grin stretched itself from ear to ear as he held it to his lips and loudly declaimed into the receiver: "Kirk to Enterprise!" Then he returned the telephone to its owner and added, "Cool toy, man. So, where's the phone?"

A terrible realization set its Louis Vuitton suitcases down on the doormat of my consciousness and lightly rang the bell for admission. I assumed a false air of insouciance and did my best to make it sound like a casual question when I inquired, "I beg your pardon, friend, but would you happen to know today's date? Year included, if you don't mind."

His answer told all.

"Not *again*," said Beddoes, the head of our Membership committee. He leaned his elbows on the bar, covered his face with his hands, and moaned softly over his brandy.

"Afraid so, old man," I said, though *terrified so* might have been more accurate.

"What *is* it about this place?" Beddoes exclaimed, demanding an answer of the stuffed porcupine above the bar, which one of our local Nimrods had contributed to the Club décor. (Granted he had found the poor dead creature at a Provincetown yard sale rather than between the crosshairs, but a hunt is a hunt.) "Why do we keep attracting this sort of thing?"

He was of course referring to the fact that the Club had, for some time now, become a magnet for beings whose like had not been seen heretofore outside of Greek mythology. In some cases they had assumed a semblance less apposite to Doria than to Darien. The most recent incident, of which I have already made passing mention, involved a Dr. Dion Sonoma whose true identity proved what every maenad worth her frenzy already knows: *In vino* there is often too damned much *veritas* for comfort. No matter their appearance, those refugees from Attic shores, the havoc they inevitably wrought was all of a piece.

I blamed Simpson. We all did. His case had been

the first, him and his notion that bringing a Greek sphinx onto Club property did not violate the No Pets rule. Had we but known, and been less enraptured by the novelty of it all, we might have spared ourselves much. Riddles are no fun when the wrong answer ends in disembowling.

However, past errors and their ensuing regrets would do nothing to ameliorate current difficulties. No use crying over spilled entrails. All of us then present in the bar were experienced survivors and knew we must deal with the situation at hand before it managed to get out of same.

"What are you guys talking about?" our uninvited guest wanted to know. He was seated a little farther along the bar, in company with Langley. I had given our Youngest Member the task of standing watch and ward over the man as soon as I realized who he was and what it meant.

"You," I replied cheerfully.

"Yeah? What? The whole to-hell-and-back thing or just my music, man?"

"A bit from Column A and a smidge from Column B, as they say." I spoke with an airiness I did not quite feel. One of the first things our new friend had done upon discovering *when* he was, was to recount how he had come to be absent from the surface world for so long.

He had done it before. After all, his name *was* Orpheus.

I ought to clarify: Orpheus was not just his name, but his identity. He never had bothered to disguise or conceal it in any way. As he remarked, it made for all sorts of in-one's-face irony whenever he opened for

Styx. Yes, he had enjoyed a renewed career in music, or what passes for music among some people, and had made a tidy sum at doing what he did best. No fool he, at least in matters of business. In time, he fell in love and married a beautiful girl who somehow managed to die in a freak concert accident. A freak fell on her while stage diving from the top of one of the speakers.

Some people simply refuse to learn from past mistakes: Believing more in recycling than rewedding, once more Orpheus took the road to Avernus and confronted grim Hades upon his iron throne. He used his gift of enchanted song to beguile the lord of the dead to release his lost love's spirit so that she might return to life.

There was no arguing with the power of Orpheus's music, though the idea of being forced to truckle repeatedly to a paltry demigod put a king-sized knot in Hades' loincloth. His divine displeasure was for naught. Orpheus had the upper hand, and it could span three octaves. And so, with epicly exasperated undertones of *Here we go again*, great Hades gave him back his new bride under the same condition as for his previously lost spouse, Eurydike: That Orpheus must ascend from the Underworld never once looking back to confirm that his beloved was in fact following him into the light of day.

As many a schoolboy knows (of the sort who have received a *proper* education) Orpheus did not trust Hades. Just as the exit from Avernus was within sight, he looked back. This violated the hellish compact. Eurydike's shade vanished, weeping, into the Underworld once more, and Orpheus was forbidden from returning for her. It is a little-known fact that the phrase, *No do-overs* originated with the lord of the dead.

I am sorry to report that Orpheus had not used his renewed career as an earthly musician to cultivate a better sense of trust. This time, too, he looked back before he had removed his new bride fully from Hades' realm. Some people might not learn from past mistakes, but some gods do. When Orpheus turned his head this time, instead of his bride's fleeing ghost he beheld Hades himself.

With astonishing speed the lord of the dead slapped a gag on the celestial singer so that not one hemi-demisemiquaver might escape his lips, then declaimed *How* dare *you think that I am not a demiurge of honor? Your bride was eager enough to escape Avernus, but you had to look back.* Again. *I forgave your petty skepticism once; now I am insulted. Since you seem so fond of gazing into the depths of my kingdom,* stay *here!*

And so he did, until the lucky day when at last he was able to work the gag off, belt out a few bars of *Sloop John B.* (the "I wanna go home" verse in particular), and take his leave.

The rest is Club rose garden history.

"Yeah," said Orpheus, nodding sagely. "I guess the whole thing is pretty cool. Think maybe I could finally get some coverage on VH1? It'd make a kickass episode of *Behind The Music.*" He grinned and ordered another tequila shooter. It was his sixth, though the liquor seemed to have no appreciable effect on him. I suppose a lengthy and enforced residence in Avernus will do much to increase one's tolerance for mere earthly intoxicants.

Beddoes leaned close and whispered urgently in my ear, "Are you *sure* he's who you claim he is? Mightn't there be some mistake?"

I shook my head. "He is that demigod musician beyond compare, sweet-voiced Orpheus whose songs had the power to charm the very stones of the earth. I can not help it if now he has chosen to sing rock *music* rather than music *to rocks*."

"But Orpheus isn't just mythic, he's dead," Beddoes protested. "See here, I've had a Classical education as well as you and I know the story: He was torn to shreds by the women of Scythia over some silly trifle or another. Touchy things, women."

"Not quite so dead as all that," I said, a shade pedantically. "His severed head lived on and continued to sing despite the ladies."

"Granted, but look at him *now*, would you? He's got a head *and* a working body! How did he manage *that*?"

"He got better?" young Langley suggested.

We both gave him a withering look ere I proceeded to say: "However our musician friend managed to recoup his corporeal deficit, the fact remains that he is here now. It is with the here and now that we must deal."

Beddoes would not be assuaged. "How can you be *sure* he's Orpheus?" he insisted.

I sighed. "You are evidently an empyricist. So be it." I turned to Orpheus and said, "I beg your pardon, old man, but would you mind favoring us with a little song?"

He smiled. "No problem. Whaddaya wanna hear?"

I told him, though not before I stuffed my ears with a shredded cocktail napkin and covertly signaled both the bartender and young Langley to do the same. Then Orpheus sang.

Some time later, a dripping wet Beddoes was a believer. As he wiped soapsuds from his eyes with a bar towel, he grumbled, "Did you *have* to make him sing *that* song?"

"My dear Beddoes, it was the most illustrative item I could come up with off the cuff. I thought you liked *South Pacific*?"

"That's beside the point. I neither have nor do I desire a man to wash out of my hair."

"Granted. But I think you must admit that finding yourself lathering up in the Gentlemen's locker room while fully clothed should be confirmation enough as to our visitor's, ah, professional chops?"

It was so. There was no gainsaying the matter. Remained to be answered only the pertinent question:

"Now that we know he's Orpheus, what do we *do* about it?"

I smiled. Although the presence of the bard was evidence that the Club's uncanny knack for attracting trouble of the mythic stripe was undiminished, for once we were ahead of the game. We had identified the amanita among the shiitake before anyone could exclaim, *My, doesn't that mushroom look tasty*, pop it in his mouth, and perish. Being thus aware of potential peril, we now had the option of preventing the same. It was a heady feeling, and one that I meant to exploit.

"My dear Beddoes, we have in our midst and in our debt a man whose song can lure the birds from the trees, the fish from the waters, the Liberals from their benighted insistence upon helping the less fortunate. What do you *think* we do about it?"

"Oh man, these tunes are *lame*." Orpheus looked up from the sheaf of sheet music I had just put into his hands and regarded me with the eyes of a basset hound betrayed.

"It can not be helped," I replied. "No doubt you would prefer melodies more suitable to, ah, head-booming and, er, mash pits, is it? But this is a wedding."

Young Langley suppressed a snigger. He did a wretched job of it, but at least he tried. "I think you mean *mosh* pits and head-*banging*," he said, leaning in to adjust Orpheus's bow tie.

"Besides," Beddoes put in, "you really have no choice. You're destitute. You're going to have to earn a living again sooner or later."

"I just can't understand what happened, man." Orpheus scratched his head and frowned. When he had contacted the institutions safeguarding his financial resources they had all reported the same disquieting news: The accounts were empty, the contents of the safe deposit boxes pilfered, the investment portfolios ravished. Nor was this situation to be accounted for by Orpheus's tenure in Avernus. True, he had been declared legally dead, but the gutting of his bank accounts, *et cetera*, had taken place rather soon after his disappearance from the waking world.

To quote Orpheus's own assessment of the situation: "Bummer. Being poor sucks."

Suck howsoever it might, Orpheus's misfortune

was our opportunity, since it left him amenable to our plans. We would have him sing at the wedding that promised to be *the* event of the social season, encompassing as it did a guest list that included all of our wealthiest members. It was a simple scheme: To use the bard's compelling voice to induce the guests to pony up enough of their capital to put the Club back on a secure financial footing. Such a plot not only would relieve our beloved Club of all fiscal anxiety, but also would have the added benefit of putting paid to the complaints of such cost-conscious creatures as Stafford "Pinch" Dawkins.

Perhaps the thought of good old Pinch's tiresome whinging was what possessed me to propose his wedding to Miss Renée Speranza as the perfect place to put our plan into action. If you empty your checkbook publicly, in company with the most influential members of the Club, you are not apt to carp about it afterwards. That would look bad.

Pinch's parsimonious proclivities notwithstanding, for him, appearances were still trumps. Of this we had proof: Had not he bitten the figurative bullet and proposed to Miss Speranza despite his dissatisfaction with Club policy concerning family memberships? Very well, then.

Thus it was that we found ourselves in the Club's ballroom, waiting for the newlywed couple to arrive. The guests were likewise there assembled, having been already processed by the reception line. The bar was doing a land office business despite Pinch's insistence that it be cash only. The canapés were gone. Our host had paid only for enough to feed three-quarters of the guests a maximum of two apiece.

In that corner of the room sacred to music, Orpheus and his backup band were keeping up an innocuous tweedling suitable to any elevator or *Your call is important to us; please continue to hold* directive. Apart from Orpheus, the other musicians were the *ne plus ultra* of mediocrity, harmony hacks whose iridescent green polyester suits were scarce penance enough to atone for what they could do to a harmless Streisand tune. We did not know where Pinch had found them nor did we care to know. They were cheap, which was all that mattered to him. Beddoes, Langley and I persuaded him to include Orpheus among their number by promising to pay for the band's services as our wedding gift. He leaped at the chance like a starved trout rising to a dry fly.

A stir from the doorway heralded the approach of the bride and groom. Beddoes gave me the high sign, I relayed it to Langley who in turn told Orpheus to lead the band in one round of "Here Comes the Bride" before segueing into the first of his cash-flow carols. We had taken the liberty of tampering with several existing tunes, setting our give-to-the-Club-until-it-hurts words to already extant music. (Respect for copyright is a quaint concept, reserved for lesser breeds without the lawyers. Information wants to be free when I am the one who does not feel like paying for it.)

The last brassy chords of Wagner's treacly *oeuvre* were just sinking beneath the waves of applause for the newlyweds when disaster struck.

"YOU!"

Orpheus leaped from the platform and rushed upon Dawkins and his bride. Seizing the lady roughly by the shoulders, he shook her like a dust mop and thundered, "What are *you* doing here?"

Before the former Miss Speranza could reply, her new husband intervened. Stiff-arming Orpheus aside, Pinch demanded, "Are you crazy? Get away from my wife!"

"*Your* wife?" Orpheus laughed. "Sure, why not? If that's what you're into."

"If *what* is what I'm into?"

"Doing it with dead things."

"Now, see here—!" Pinch had gone almost as white as his bride's gown, which was only a shade or two darker than the lady's complexion. Orpheus took advantage of Pinch's sputtering outrage to get in a word edgewise with Renée.

"Hey, babe, long time no see. I kinda wondered what became of you after I screwed up and looked back. So you didn't turn and run back down the road to Hell? What happened? Trip over a good intention?" He chucked her under the chin so hard that her bridal headpiece went flying.

Pinch made a grab for Orpheus's arm, and his groomsmen moved into formation behind him to render assistance as needed. We could have told them to save their breath: Though they were one and all veterans of the finest rugby team to ever scrum for the honor of Harvard, they could do nothing against Orpheus. He merely eyed them for a moment before launching into "It's Raining Men." Immediately there was a peal of thunder followed by the sound of bodies dropping from a great height. From what we glimpsed through the windows of the reception room, these were highly attractive male bodies. The brawny groomsmen raced outside, uttering shrieks of glee and calling dibs on the blonds.

A furious Pinch stood his ground and cocked back a fist intended for Orpheus, but the bard took care of him temporarily, bidding him "Stop! In the Name of Love." While Pinch was thus rendered immobile, Orpheus returned his attention to the bride.

"All those years I thought you were down in Avernus with me. Man. At least that explains why you never came by to visit. No, you were up here, sucking my bank accounts dry like a good little lamia. Well, guess what, babe? I'm back and I'll see you in court!"

Miss Speranza—now Mrs. Dawkins—gave her former husband the cold and clammy eye. "Don't be a fool," she bade him. "You can't sue the dead."

Her cavalier admission to being one of the Respiratorily Disenfranchised caused Pinch to go stark white as to the face, but helpless to do more. At least public acknowledgment of her decedence explained her eerie gift for sneaking up on a man so silently.

Orpheus's eyes narrowed. "Then maybe I won't leave it to a mortal court of law," he said. There was a most disturbing note in his voice and, seeing as it was *his* voice, the aforesaid disturbing note was pitched perfectly. I felt the small hairs on the back of my neck stand up like West Point plebes on parade.

Pinch's bride was made of sterner stuff. "You don't scare me. I used to have an apartment in Jersey City."

"Sure you did, before you took *my* money and ran. I entered the gates of Avernus for you and this is the thanks I get?"

The newly pledged Mrs. Dawkins rolled her eyes.

"Oh, puh-*leeze*! I'd *still* be down there if I'd relied on you. He *told* you not to look back: Twice! I can't stand a man who won't learn from his mistakes."

"I'm learning from one of them right now," Orpheus said grimly. His fingers curled and uncurled. I could not tell whether he were plucking the strings of an invisible lyre or rehearsing her imminent strangulation.

"Shouldn't we do something to stop this before it gets any worse?" Beddoes was at my elbow, his face the color of eggshell. "This has all the earmarks of a pending bloodbath. The Club can't take many more."

"What do you propose we do?" I replied, assuming a stoic air I did not truly feel. "Lest you forget, that is Orpheus. So long as he has the power of his voice, no one may stand against him."

"She seems to be doing a fair enough job of it." Beddoes nodded at the former Miss Speranza. "Why isn't he singing *her* into submission?"

"Perhaps because she is—or should I say she *was*—his wife," I replied. "Even a bachelor understands how wives often have the power to blot out the sound of their husbands' voices when it suits them."

As we conferred, the tension between Orpheus and his second wife mounted apace. "Just tell me one thing before you get what's coming to you," he demanded. "How *did* you manage to get out of Avernus?"

Her laugh had all the charm of a creaking lich-gate. "How do you think, sweetheart? I walked. Don't stare at me that way; you look like a trepanned catfish. *You* fixed it so I could get out. That whole don't-look-back shtick was to test you, not me. You think

Hades wanted me hanging around after he'd processed all the paperwork? Half the reason he was so mad at you for looking back at me was because of what happened the first time! She's a sweet kid, Orpheus, but she never was very independent, was she?"

"What are you talking about?" Orpehus asked. The whites of his eyes showed all around the irises, after the manner of a badly spooked horse. "*Who* are you talking about?"

"That would be me."

She irrupted among us with the same abruptness and stealth as Renée Speranza had formerly used to such devastating effect in the Club bar lo, those many weeks ago. She was a fetching creature of Classic beauty, which made perfect sense given her identity.

"Eu—Eurydike?" The divine singer really did resemble a mentally deficient fish when startled.

The lady crossed the room and brought her husband the gift of renewed eloquence via a swift slap to the face. "Love me *forever*, hm?" she said, pointing at the smirking bride. "You got over your broken heart pretty damn quick, you swine! Since when does *forever* end after a lousy two, three millennia?"

Renée stepped up to put an arm around Eurydike's shoulder. "I found this poor girl all by herself in one of the saddest, darkest corners of Avernus. None of the other shades would come near her because of what *you'd* done to her. They can smell the taint of life; it puts them off their wailing. I introduced myself and we got to talking. When I found out who she was, I asked her how come she was still hanging around a dump like Avernus when she'd been cleared for emigration. Poor baby never even thought to *try* getting out without you being there to lead her every step of the way. I told her, *Eury*, I said, *what's the worst that can happen to you if you try to get out on your own? What's Hades gonna do?* Kill *you?* It was the first time I saw her smile. Of course she stopped smiling as soon as I told her who I was. Not that she was mad at *me*, of course."

"Certainly not!" Eurydike gave Renée a sisterly hug while glowering daggers at Orpheus. "Renée gave me the strength to stand up and help myself, for a change. She was the only one who cared. Not like *you!*"

"Aw, babe, now come on, *I* cared!" Orpheus had the look of a man who was starting to miss the peace and quiet of the Underworld. "Was it *my* fault you didn't know you could've just walked out of there even after I blew it? *I* didn't even know that was possible."

"If you really cared about me you could've made an *effort*; done something like, oh, I don't know, maybe *ask* someone for advice about making a second try to get me out of Hades' kingdom? Someone like the *Delphic Oracle*, maybe? Seeing as how your father was *Apollo*? You know, Apollo the sun-god? Ring any bells? Apollo who *established* the shrine at Delphi and had the Oracle in his *back pocket*?"

"Chitons don't have pockets," Orpheus said. It was neither the time nor the place for such observations.

Musicians.

This time Eurydike belted him with a closed fist. He sailed across the room and knocked over a swan ice sculpture that had cost Dawkins a pretty penny. He moaned softly, a sound overwhelmed by the cheers of all the women present.

"Baby, I couldn't do that." Orpheus struggled to

his feet, slipping on bits of shattered swan, and staggered back toward his wives. "I was too upset to think straight, and then I ran into the Scythian women and they tore me to pieces and for a long time all I had to my name was my head. I mean, that was *totally* bogus. And then—"

Eurydike thrust out her hand, palm foremost. "Spare me. Which is more than I'm going to do for you." Her fingers curled into claws. There was an ugly glint in her eye. Maenads tear their living victims to shreds while under the influence of the grape, and Scythians were known to operate under the influence of hemp, but Eurydike's murderous rage was more terrifying, being the product of ice-cold sobriety.

Female empowerment is not a pretty thing. Not for the men involved, at any rate.

Lest any think that Orpheus stood ready to accept the dire punishment that Eurydike was about to deal him, I must correct that misapprehension. Apollo's son was already preparing his defense. I heard him begin to hum under his breath, preparatory to bursting into omnipotent song, though for the life of me I could not identify the composition.

"Heaven help us, I can name that tune!" Beddoes voice constricted with terror. "'It's The End of the World As We Know It.' If he's going to die, he's going to take us with him!"

"Coward," Eurydike snarled. "Apocalypse is the last refuge of the scoundrel. You forget that I'm not afraid to die. Been there, done that." She took another step forward. A fine dew of nervous perspiration spangled Orpheus' brow, a look of desperation lit his eyes, and he opened his mouth to sing.

"*Stop!* Stop in the name of the Law!" Langley's shout broke Orpheus' concentration and interrupted Eurydike's relentless approach. The bold young man threw himself between the two of them with a fine disregard for his own safety. A slip of paper, blazing white as Zeus' own thunderbolt, flashed under Eurydike's nose.

"Madam, my card," he said. "Why settle for wreaking mere physical mayhem on this churlish Party of the Second Part when I can see to it that his sufferings last for decades?"

"Huh?" said Eurydike.

Langley gave her his most jury-swaying smile. "My dear nymph, I assure you: Disembowelment is a walk in the park next to a good old-fashioned lawsuit." He linked arms with her and led her away, to the plaudits of the crowd.

The case never did make it to court. That was a mercy, considering how poor Dawkins was on the verge of death by humiliation at the thought of his bride being a material witness in so scandalous a legal proceeding. In fact, he was actually smiling and very much at his ease when next we two met one another at the Club some three months later.

"Good heavens, Pinch," I exclaimed upon seeing him. "You are looking remarkably content."

"And why shouldn't I be?" he countered. "Married life agrees with us."

"I am heartily glad to hear that you and Renée have managed to overcome the recent unpleasantness at your wedding and forge on undaunted," I said.

"Yes, she's a fine little woman, Renée. Oh, sometimes

she gets a fit of the sulks, but whenever that happens we can always count on Eurydike to jolly her out of it."

"What?" I said.

He continued as though I had not spoken. "Of course Eurydike's problem's her temper—no surprise given what she went through, abandonment issues, *et cetera, et cetera.* Every so often she'll give Orpheus one of those looks that says 'If you leave your wet towels on the bathroom floor one more time, I'm going to rip your arm off and beat you over the head with it,' but then I pop the two of them into the Beemer and drive them to their Anger Management session and it all works out."

"Eurydike?" I repeated. "Orpheus? But— But— You can not possibly mean to say that they are living under the same roof with you and Renée!"

"Why not?" Pinch replied. "We're married."

And so they were. So young Langley informed me, at any rate. Although under normal circumstances death is the finale for most marriages, the return to life by three of the parties involved legally negated any such termination. (There was a precedent for it somewhere in Southern California. There would be.) I attempted to argue the point with him, but he showed me his briefs and left me speechless. That was that: They were married. All of them. To each other.

"Really, Pinch, how can you accept all this so calmly?" I pressed. "Surely Orpheus claims conjugal rights with the ladies?"

"Certainly. They're his wives, too."

"This does not bother you?"

"I admit, it does, particularly when the girls make

certain . . . comparisons. But hey, whenever Orpheus goes on the road, I get them both all to myself, so I can't complain. Honestly, old man, sharing the affections of your wives isn't such a big thing if you view it in the light of the greater good this marriage has accomplished."

"Ah," I said, nodding wisely. "So true. For once in our history, the Club has met the challenge of a mythic incursion and emerged unscathed."

"Even more important than that," Dawkins said, "I've finally found the way to get my money's worth out of that damned unfair family membership!"

I sighed. *Fiat pecunia, ruat caelum*, as Dawkins would have it. *Let there be the M-word, though the heavens fall.* Clearly the man had dropped beyond the Pale, if he had so abandoned all pretense of social propriety in favor of mere monetary advantage. Despite his fortune, he had plunged willingly into his own pecuniary Avernus, never to emerge. He was, alas, no longer one of us.

I did what any right-thinking gentleman would have done under the circumstances: I made a golf date for next Thursday at twenty dollars the hole.

The Haunted Bicuspid

Harry Turtledove

HERE'S TWO DOLLARS AND FIFTY cents—in gold, by God, George M. A quarter eagle's plenty to buy drinks for every body in the place. Tell me when you need more. I'll do it again.

What's that you say, my friend? You see more gold now than you did just a few years ago? Well, I should hope you do, by thunder. It's all coming from California, way out West. I don't suppose any one would have thought the world held so much gold until they stumbled across it on that Sutter fellow's land.

But I don't feel like talking about gold right this here minute—except that that's *my* gold on the bar.

If I'm buying, part of what I'm buying is the chance to talk about any blamed thing I please. Anybody feel like quarreling about that?

No? Good.

All right, then. Here goes. Friends, my name is William Legrand. Most of you know me, and most of you call me Bill. I'm a plainspoken man, I am. Nothing fancy about me. Yes, I'm partial to canvasback duck and soft-shell crabs when I can get 'em, but what Baltimorean isn't? That's not fancy—they're right good eating, and who'll tell me they aren't?

I was born in the year of our Lord 1800. Last year of the eighteenth century, that was, and don't you believe any silly fool who tries to tell you it was the first year of the nineteenth. As of the twenty-seventh *ultimo*, that makes me a right round fifty-one years of age. I am not ashamed to say I have done pretty well for myself in that half century and a little bit. If there's a single soul who sells more furniture or finer furniture in Baltimore, I'd like to know who he is. Helen and I have been married for twenty-eight years now, and we still get on better than tolerably well. I have three sons and a daughter, and Helen was lucky enough never to lose a baby, for which I thank God. One of my sons went to Harvard, another to Yale. I wasn't able to do that kind of thing myself, but a man's children should have more chances than he did. That's the American way, don't you think? And I have two little granddaughters now, and I wouldn't trade 'em for anything. Not for the moon, do you hear me?

If it weren't for my teeth, everything would be perfect.

I see some of you wince. I see some of you flinch. I see I am not the only man in this splendid establishment to find himself a martyr to the toothache. I am not surprised to make that discovery. People laugh about the toothache—people who haven't got it laugh at it, I should say. And Old Scratch is welcome to every single one of those laughing hyenas.

I was still a young man the first time I faced the gum lancet, the punch, the pincers, the lever, and the pelican. They sound like tools for an old-time torturer, don't they? By God, gentlemen, they *are* tools for an old-time torturer. Any of you who ever had dealings with a dentist more than a few years ago will know what I am talking about. Oh, yes, I see some heads going up and down. I knew I would.

Here's another quarter eagle, George M. You keep that river flowing for these gentlemen, if you would be so kind.

People would say, You try this, Bill, or, You do that, Bill, and it will not hurt so bad. I would drink myself blind before I went to have a tooth yanked. Or I would take so much opium, I could not even recollect my own name. Or I would do both those things at once, so that my friends would have to steer me to the latest butcher because I could not navigate on my own.

And when the damned quack got to work, whoever he was that time, it would hurt worse than anything you can think of. If he grabs a tooth with the pincers, and instead of pulling it he breaks it, and he has to jerk out all the fragments one at a time, what else is it going to do? I ask you, my friends, what else can it *possibly* do?

I tell you frankly, I was more relieved than sorry when I lost the last tooth down below—ten years ago it was now. My bottom false teeth fit tolerably well, and I don't mind 'em a bit. But I wanted to hang on to the ones I have up top. I still do want that, as a matter of fact. If you have a full plate up there, they hold in your uppers with springs, and that is another infernal invention. There are plenty of ways I would like to be like George Washington, but that is not one of them.

But God does what He wants, not what you want. Not what I want, either. About six months ago, it was, when one of my top left bicuspids went off like it had a fire lit inside it.

What's a bicuspid? On each side, top and bottom, you have got two teeth betwixt your eyeteeth and your grinders. Ask a dentist, and he will tell you they're bicuspids. I have done a powerful lot of palavering with dentists over the years. I know how they talk. I am a man who likes to learn things. I want to find out just precisely what they are going to inflict on me before they go and inflict it.

And a whole fat lot of good *that* has done me, too.

I kept hoping the toothache would go away. Might as well hope the bill collector or your mother-in-law will go away. You stand a better chance. Before long, I knew it was time to get me to a dentist—that or go plumb out of my mind, one. I had not had to lose a chopper for five or six years before that. The last quack I had gone to was out of business. Maybe the folks he tormented strung him up. I can hope so, anyhow.

So I found me another fellow, a Dutchman named Vankirk. He grinned when he saw my poor sorry mouth. *His* teeth, damn him, were as white as if he soaked 'em in cat piss every night. For all I know, maybe he did.

He poked at my poor sorry chopper with one of those iron hooks his miserable tribe uses. You know the type I mean—like out of the Spanish Inquisition, only smaller. He had to pry me off the ceiling afterwards, too. You bet he did. Then he gave me another shiny smile. "Oh, yes, Mr. Legrand," he says, "I can have that out in jig time, and a replacement in the socket, and you will not feel a thing."

I laughed in his face. "Go peddle your papers," I says. "I am not a blushing bride at this business. I have been with your kind of man before. I have heard promises like that before. I have stupefied myself with every remedy known to nature. And it has hurt like blazes every single time."

"Every remedy known to nature, perhaps," says Vankirk. "But what about remedies known to man? Have you ever visited a dentist who uses chloroform?"

Now, I had heard of his stuff. It was written up in the *Baltimore Sun* not so long before. But, "Just another humbug," says I.

Vankirk shook his head. "Mr. Legrand, chloroform is no humbug," he says, solemn as a preacher at a millionaire's funeral. "They can take off a man's leg with it—never mind his tooth, his *leg*—and he will not feel a thing until he wakes up. I have been using it for six months, and it is a sockdolager."

In my day, I have been lied to by a good many

dentists. I am familiar with the breed. If this Vankirk was lying, he was better at it than any other tooth-drawer I have had the displeasure to know. I felt something I had not felt since my very first acquaintance with the pincers. Friends, I felt hope.

"You can pop a replacement tooth in when you yank mine, you say?" I ask him. "I have had that done before, more than once, and never known it to hold above a year."

"Plainly, you have been visiting men who do not know their business," says Vankirk. "From examining your mouth, I believe I have the very tooth that will make a perfect fit in your jaw."

He opened a drawer and rummaged in a box of teeth and finally found the one he wanted. It looked like a tooth to me. That is all I can tell you. It did not have blood and pus all over it, I will say that, the way mine do when one butcher or another hauls them out of my jaw. I ask him, "Where did it come from?"

"Out of the mouth of a brave young soldier killed at the battle of Buena Vista," Vankirk says. "This tooth, Mr. Legrand, is good for twenty or thirty more years than you are. You may count on that."

I never count on anything a dentist tells me. I say, "In my day, I have had teeth put in my head from men slain in the War of 1812, the Black Hawk War, and the war the Texans fought against Mexico before the US of A decided to teach Santa Anna a lesson. Not a one of them lasted. Why should I think this here one will be any different?"

"It is not the tooth alone, Mr. Legrand. It is the man who puts it in," he says, and strikes a pose.

He did not lack for confidence, Vankirk. And the one I had in there had to come out. I knew that. I would not have been there if I didn't. But, says I, "Tell me one thing—is this here tooth an American's or a Mexican's?"

"An American's," he answers right away. He was all set to get shirty about it, too. "Do you think I would stick a damned greaser's tooth in your jaw? No, sir."

"That was what I wanted to know," I say, and I sat down in his chair. "Go ahead, then. Let us get it over with."

George M., I see there are folks with empty glasses. Why don't you keep them filled? We can settle the score when I am done. You know me. I am good for it. If I am not, no man in Baltimore is. Thank you kindly, sir. You are a gentleman, as I have cause to know.

Where was I? Oh, yes—in that blamed dentist's chair. Says I, "Won't you strap down my arms so I can't punch you while you are pulling?"

"No need. I was not lying when I said it would not hurt," Vankirk says. He opened that drawer again, the one the tooth came out of. This time, he had hold of a bottle and a rag. He soaked the rag in the stuff in the bottle—it looked like water, but it wasn't—and then he hauled off and stuck that wet rag over my nose and mouth.

The chloroform—that was what it had to be, chloroform—smelled sweet and nasty at the same time. It did not smell like anything I had ever known before. When I opened my mouth to yell, it tasted sweet, too. It tasted *unnaturally* sweet, to tell you the truth. It tasted *so* sweet, it burned.

What I meant for that yell came out like a gurgle.

It was like all of a sudden I was drunker than I had ever been before. Well, no. It was not *just* like that, you understand. But it was closer to that than to anything else you will know if you have not been under chloroform yourself. And then I was not drunk any more. I was *gone*.

When I woke up, at first I did not realize I was waking up. I did not know I had been asleep, you see. My senses were still reeling. I started to ask Vankirk when he was going to start. That was when I realized my mouth tasted all bloody.

I also realized I could not talk, not for hell. I wondered if the chloroform had scrambled my brains for fair. But it was not the chloroform. Vankirk had stuffed a wad of cloth in there to soak up some of the blood. I spat it out, and did not land it on my breeches, for which I was grateful.

Says I, "This *is* no humbug. It did not hurt."

"No, sir," Vankirk says. He held up his pincers. In it, he still had the black ruin that was my tooth. Its bottom end was all smeared with blood, like I knew it would be. He took it out of the pincers and flung it in the rubbish. "No use putting this old wreck in another man's head."

"I reckon not," says I.

"The one I put there in its place fit as though it was made there," Vankirk says. "I have been doing this for a while now, Mr. Legrand, and I have never had a transplanted tooth go in so well."

"Good," says I. I felt around with my tongue. Sure enough, the new tooth was in there. It was fixed to the one in back of it by fine wire. Not to the one in front. That there one is long gone.

Vankirk says, "You will feel some pain now, as the chloroform wears off. You see, I do not lie to you. Have you got some laudanum with you?"

"That I do," I says, and I took a few drops. I know about the pain after a tooth comes out. I ought to. It is not so bad. Laudanum—which is opium in brandy, for any one who does not know—laudanum, I say, can shift that pain all right.

"As your jaw heals, that tooth will become a part of you," Vankirk says. "Because it fit in there so exceedingly well, I think it will last a long time."

Like I said, friends, I have had teeth transplanted before. Not a one of them stayed in place long. I had said as much to the tooth-drawer. I started to say so again. But then I shut my mouth, and not on account of I was still bleeding some. He knew what he was talking about with the chloroform. Maybe he knew what he was talking about here, too.

"Can you walk?" he asks me. "Are you all right to go?"

I got to my feet. The room swayed some, but it was not too bad. I have felt drunker than I did just then. "I am fine, thank you," says I. "And I *do* thank you—believe me, I do." I think this was the first time I ever thanked a tooth-drawer after escaping his clutches. I confess, though, I may be mistaken. Now and then, I have been suffering sufficient so as to thank one of those brigands no matter what he did to me.

"Walk around my room here a bit. I want to make certain you are steady on your pins," Vankirk says. So I did that. It was not too bad. On my third or fourth circuit, I caught the dentist's eye. He nodded, for I had satisfied him. Says he, "Come back in a fortnight.

I will take the wire off that new tooth I put in there. It should do fine on its own. With any luck at all, it will last you the rest of your life."

"I will do just as you say. Let us make the appointment now," I answer him. So we did. He wrote it in a book he had, and he wrote it for me on a scrap of paper. I put that in my waistcoat pocket. "And after that," says I, and I planted my beaver hat on my head, "you will see me nevermore."

Looking back, I do believe that to be the very commencement of my troubles, the beginning of a descent into the maelström from which I was fortunate in the extreme to escape unscathed, or nearly so. But at this time I knew nothing of what lay ahead, nothing of the ordeal to which I was to be subjected.

My head still whirled a bit from the chloroform and from the laudanum. I could walk, however, and knew where I was going. And I was leaving the dentist's, and it did not hurt. *It did not hurt.* Since the Passion and Resurrection of our Lord, I do not think God has wrought a greater miracle.

When I returned to my house, Helen flew into my arms. "Oh, Bill! Poor Bill!" she cried. "How are you, you sorry, abused creature?"

"I am—well enough," I answered, and regaled her with the tale of my experience. As she hearkened to the story, her eyes, the outward expression of her soul, grew ever wider in astonishment. Kissing her tenderly yet carefully, I continued, "And so you see, my dear, I am in a state to be envied rather than pitied."

"No one who loses a tooth is to be envied," she

said, which is true enough, "but I am gladder than I can express that it was not the torment you have known too many times."

"So am I, by all that is holy," I replied. "He told me the chloroform was no humbug, and he told me the truth. Who would have expected such a thing from a dentist?"

My three sons, my daughter, and her husband, knowing I was to be subjected to this latest bout of toothly torment, came to call upon me in turn to learn how I was, and were pleasantly amazed to discover me so well. I am, as I have previously observed, fortunate in my family.

They all exclaimed to no small degree on observing me to be free of the agonies I had hitherto endured during and subsequent to the forced removal of that which Nature purposed to endure for ever. And Benjamin, my eldest, on learning in full what had transpired, said, "So you have another man's tooth in your jaw in place of your own?"

"I do indeed," I replied.

"And from what unlucky soul came the mortal fragment?" he inquired.

"Why, from a fallen hero of the late war against Mexico," I informed him. "So, at any rate, said Mr. Vankirk. He seeming otherwise veracious, I have no cause to doubt his word— But why do you laugh? What have I said or done to inspire such mirth?"

"You will know, dear and loving Father," said Benjamin, "that my particular friend is Dr. Ernest Valdemar, with whom I studied at Harvard College. Owing to your dental miseries, we have found occasions too numerous to mention on which to discuss such matters. He has, generally speaking, a low opinion of transplanted teeth."

"As has Mr. Vankirk, generally speaking," I replied. "*Exceptio probat regulam*, however, and he believed I would do well with this new tooth inserted into my jaw. Since he spoke the truth—indeed, if anything, less than the truth—regarding the analgesic and anaesthetic properties of chloroform, I see no reason not to hope, at least, he likewise had cause to be sanguine about my long-continuing use of a tooth now valueless to the soldier who once bore it."

He held up a hand to forestall my further speech, and then declared, "Dr. Valdemar has also a low opinion of those who gather these bits of ivory for the tooth-drawers' trade—harvesters, he styles them. He says, and he should be in a position to know, that the bulk of the teeth employed in dentures and in transplantation come not from battlefields but from graveyards and even from the potter's field, stolen at night in the dark of the moon by those whose deeds must not see the light of day. Whose tooth, then, Father, dwells now in that socket once your own?"

I will not—I cannot—deny the *frisson* of horror and dread shooting through me at this question. If the donor of the dental appendage was not the stalwart soldier to whom Vankirk had animadverted, who was he? Who, indeed? Some fiend in human shape? Some nameless, useless, worthless scribbler, his brief, strutting time on earth all squandered, his soul gone to fearful judgement, and his fleshly envelope flung now into a pauper's grave?

My laugh holding more heartiness than I truly felt, I essayed to make light of my beloved Benjamin's apprehensions. "In a fortnight's time, I shall see Vankirk again; it is then he will remove the wire affixing the new tooth to its neighbor, that neighbor being one of the handful of sound instruments of mastication remaining in my upper mandible," I said. "That will be time enough to discuss the matter with him, and, I pledge to you, I shall not omit doing so."

Setting a kindly hand upon my shoulder, my eldest said, "Let it be as you wish, then, Father. My concern is only for you; I would not have you—contaminated by some unclean bit of matter rightfully residing on the far side of the tomb."

My own chief concern after receipt of the new tooth was not contamination but suppuration, the almost inevitable bout of pus and fever attendant upon such rude intrusions upon the oral cavity as the tooth-drawer is compelled to make. Having suffered several such bouts—having, indeed, lost a cousin at an untimely age as a result of one—I knew the signs, and awaited them with the apprehension to be expected from a man of such knowledge. Yet all remained well, and, in fact, I healed with a rapidity hardly less astonishing to me than the anodyne of chloroform itself. By the third day after the extraction, I was up and about and very largely my usual self once more.

Fourteen days having passed, I repaired to the illustrious Vankirk's so that he might examine the results of his ministrations upon me. "Good morning, Mr. Legrand," he said. "How fare you today?"

"Exceeding well; monstrous well, you might even say," I replied. "Undo your wire, sir, and I shall be on my way."

"If the socket be healed sufficiently, I shall do just as you say. In the meantime"—here gesturing towards the chair whence I had been fortunate enough to make my escape half a month before—"take a seat, if you would be so kind."

"I am entirely at your service," I said, reflecting as I sat upon how great a prodigy it was that one such as I, with my fear both morbid and well-earned of those practicing the dentist's art, should allow such a pronouncement to pass his lips as any thing save the most *macabre* jest.

A tiny, sharp-nosed pliers of shiny iron in his hand, Vankirk bent towards me—and I, I willingly opened my mouth. "Well, well," quoth he, commencing his work, "here is a thing most extraordinary."

"What is it?" I enquired—indistinctly, I fear me, on account of the interference with my ejaculation arising from his hand and instrument.

First removing the wire, as he had told me he would, he answered, "Why, how very well you have recovered from your ordeal, Mr. Legrand, and how perfectly the tooth I have transplanted into your jawbone has taken hold there. If I—if any man—could do such work with every patient, I would serve kings, and live as kings do; for kings are no less immune to the toothache than any other mortals."

"You did better with me than I had dreamt possible, Mr. Vankirk, and should I again stand in need of the services of a tooth-drawer—which, given the way of all flesh, and of my sorry flesh in especial, strikes me as being altogether too probable—you may rest assured I shall hasten hither to your establishment as quickly as ever I may; for, rendered insensible by the miracle of chloroform, I shall at last be able—or rather, happily unable—to cry out, imitating the famous and goodly Paul long ago in his first letter to the Corinthians, 'O pincers, where is thy sting? O torment, where is thy victory?' and knowing myself to have triumphed over the agonies that have tortured mankind for ever and ever."

Still holding the pliers, Vankirk cocked his head to one side, examining me with a keenness most disconcerting. After a moment, he shook his head, a quizzical expression playing across his countenance. "Extraordinary indeed," he murmured.

"Why say you that, sir, when I—?"

I had scarcely begun the question ere the tooth-drawer raised a hand, quelling my utterance before it could be well born. "Extraordinary in that you are, to all appearances, a changed man," he said.

"Why, so I am—I am a man free from pain, for which I shall remain ever in your debt, figuratively if not financially," I said.

"Our financial arrangements are satisfactory in the highest degree," Vankirk said. "By every account reaching my ear, you are and have always been a man of the nicest scrupulosity in respect to money, and in this you seem to have altered not by the smallest jot or tittle; not even by the proverbial iota, smaller than either. But your present style—how shall I say it?—differs somewhat from that which I observed in you a fortnight previously. And, as the illustrious Buffon (not to be confused with any of our present illustrious buffoons) so justly remarked, '*Le style c'est l'homme même.*' I trust you would agree?"

"How could any man disagree with such a sage

observation?" I returned. "As an apologia, however, I must remind you that my faculties at the time of our last encounter were more than a little deranged by the pain of which you so skillfully relieved me."

"It could be," he replied, studying me with even greater keenness than before. "Yes, it could be. Yet the transformation seems too striking for that to be the sole fount wherefrom it arises."

"I know none other, unless"—and I laughed; yes, laughed! fool that I was—"you would include in your calculations the tooth of which you made me a gift in exchange for my own dear, departed bicuspid. Tell me, if you would—what is the tooth's true origin? Some source closer than a sanguinary field from the late war with Mexico? Am I correct in guessing you obtained it from some local—harvester, I believe the term is?"

"Well—since from some source or another—"

"My eldest son, whose particular friend is a doctor."

"I see. Since you have learned the term from your son, then, I shall not deny the brute fact of the matter. Yes, you have a Baltimore tooth, not one from the Mexican War. But I insist, Mr. Legrand, that it is a tooth as sound as I declared it to be when first I showed it to you, the truth of which is demonstrated by the rapidity and thoroughness with which it has incorporated itself into the matrix of your dentition. That last you cannot possibly deny."

"Nor would I attempt to do so," I replied, rising from the chair in which I had, on this occasion, neither suffered the tortures inflicted upon those condemned to the nether regions by the just judgement of the

Almighty nor experienced the miracle of complete insensibility granted through the agency of the dentist's chloroform, but merely undergone some tiny and transitory discomfort whilst Vankirk removed the wire tethering the transplanted tooth to its natural neighbor. "Truly, I have a better opinion of you after your frank and manly admission of the facts of the matter than I would have had as the result of some vain and pompous effort at dissembling."

Vankirk scraped a match against the sole of his shoe to light a cigarillo; the sulfurous stink springing from the combustion of the match head warred briefly with the tobacco's sweeter smoke before failing, just as the Opponent of all that is good, he who dwells in brimstone, shall surely fail at the end of days. Pausing after his first inhalation, he said, "Your style has indeed undergone an alteration; and what this portends, and whether it be for good or ill, I know not—and, I believe, only the sequential unfolding of the leaves of the Book of Time shall hold the answer."

"I am but a man; a featherless biped, as the divine Plato put it; though not, I should hope, Voltaire the cynic's plucked chicken; and, as a man, I can only agree that the future is unknowable until it shall have become first present and then past; while, as a man named William Legrand—commonly called Bill—I can only assert that no change perceptible to me other than the relief of my distress through your art has eventuated in the time that is now the recent past, this time being as impalpable as the future but, unlike it, perceptible through memory, whatever sort of spiritual or physical phenomenon memory may one day prove to be."

"God bless my soul," the tooth-drawer declared, and then, upon due reflection, "yes, and yours as well."

"Yes," I said, "and mine as well."

On leaving his place of business, I truly believed all would be well, or as well as it might be for one with my notorious dental difficulties. The only cloud appearing upon the horizon of my imagination was the fear—no, not really the fear; say rather, the concern—that the tooth transplanted to my maxilla, whencever it first came, would weaken and abandon its adopted home. This showed no sign of eventuating. Indeed, as day followed day that tooth became attached ever more firmly to my jaw. Would that my own had been so tenacious of adhesion to the jawbone from which they sprang.

For some considerable while, then, all seemed well. No—again I misstate the plain truth, which is that for some considerable while all *was* well. Not every thing was perfect; we speak of a man's life, after all, not an angel's. But all went as I would have hoped, or near enough. The most that occurred of an unusual—certainly not uncanny, not yet—nature was that one or two or perhaps even several individuals imitated Vankirk the tooth-drawer in remarking upon what they perceived as an alteration to my accustomed forms of speech.

"What ever can you mean?" I enquired of one of these, a newspaper man by the name of Thomas Bob. "I note no variation from my utterances of days gone by."

"Whether it be perceptible to yourself or not, your prolixity, I must tell you, has increased to a remarkable degree," Thomas Bob replied. "Were that not so, would I remark upon it?" He laughed immoderately; such were the jests of which he was enamored.

"My prolixity, say you? Why, am I not the same simple, straightforward fellow I always was, a man to call a spade a spade, and not, with Tacitus, an implement for digging trenches—you will, I pray, forgive my failing to append the original Latin, which unfortunately I cannot at the moment—"

"Enough!" He committed the sin of interruption, sometimes merely a peccadillo of the most venial sort, but at others approaching the mortal. So I felt it to be now. This notwithstanding, my acquaintance continued, "Do you not see, Legrand, how for you have gone down the road towards proving my assertion?"

"No," I said—only this and nothing more.

Again, Thomas Bob gave forth with the heartiest expression of his mirth, which increased my liking for him, for a man who will laugh when the joke is on himself is more highly to be esteemed than one who either cannot imagine the possibility of such a thing or who at once is inspired to hatred on becoming the butt of another's wit. We parted on the friendliest terms. I asked him to convey my regards to his son, who has lately attained to prominence as an editor of magazines.

Several days after my meeting with this distinguished gentleman, I had a dream of such extraordinary clarity—indeed, of such verisimilitude—as to surpass any I had ever known before. Some of these, whether they spring from the lying gate of ivory or the true gate of horn to which Homer animadverts, are fonts of delight. Not so the one darkening my slumbers on the night I now describe.

I was black, to begin with. Now, I will not speak to the issue of whether the negro should by rights be slave or free; that is a discussion for another time and another place, and one that, the Compromise of 1850 notwithstanding, seems to be as likely to be decided by shot and shell as by the quills and quillets of fussy barristers. Suffice to say, the Legrands have not, nor have we ever had, the faintest tincture of colored blood flowing in our veins.

Yet I was black, black as soot, black as coal, black as ebony, black as India ink, black as midnight in a sky without stars or moon, black as Satan's soul. And, when I first came to myself in this dream, I found I was high amongst the branches of a great tulip tree. Glancing down for even the briefest instant engendered terror which nearly sufficed to loose my grip upon the trunk and send me hurtling to my doom, as Lucifer hurtled from the heavens long, long ago.

Quickly gathering myself, I managed to hang on, and to climb. The branch upon which I was at length compelled to crawl shuddered under my weight, not least on account of its rotten state. Whoever would send any man, even a worthless negro, on such a mission deserves, in my view, nothing less than horse-whipping. Yet I had no choice; I *must* go forward, or face a fate even worse than the likelihood of plunging, screaming death.

Crawling on, I came upon a human skull spiked to the said branch (a skull with, as I noted enviously, teeth of an extraordinary whiteness and soundness; whatever had pained this mortal morsel, the dreaded toothache had kept apart from his door). I dropped through one of the skull's gaping eye sockets a scarabaeus beetle of remarkable heft; it glinted of gold as it fell.

And then, as is the way of dreams, I found myself on the ground once more, digging at a spot chosen by extending a line from the center of the trunk through the spot where the beetle fell. Imagine my delight upon discovering a wooden chest banded with iron, of the sort in which pirates were wont to bury treasure. Imagine my despair upon discovering it to be full of—teeth.

Yes, teeth. Never had I seen such a marvelous profusion of dentality all gathered together at one and the same place. Incisors, eyeteeth, bicuspids, molars; so many, they might have been a flock of passenger pigeons turned to rooted enamel. Under the bright sun of my imagined sky, they shone almost as if they were the gold and jewels for which I had surely hoped.

I reached down and ran my hand through them. The not unpleasing music they made striking one against another suggested something to me, something not merely musical but reminding me of— Of what I never learned, for I awoke then, and the answer, if answer there was, vanished and was lost for ever, as is the way of dreams. Yet the dream itself remained perfect in my memory, suffering none of the usual distortion and diminution attendant upon these nocturnal visions in the clear light of morning.

A few nights later, I dreamt once more; once more I found myself in a world seeming perfectly real, yet assuredly the product of a dreadful and disordered imagination. My enemies—vile ecclesiastics of some inquisitorial sect better left unnamed—had captured me and condemned me to a death of cruelty unparalleled, a death wherein the horror of anticipation only added to the innate terror of extinction lodged in the breast of brute beast and man alike.

I lay on my back, strapped to a low wooden platform by the securest of leather lashings, at the bottom of a deep and but dimly lighted chamber. And above me—as yet some distance above me, but slowly and inexorably lowering towards my helpless and recumbent frame—swung an immense pendulum, hissing through the air at its every passage. The heavy metal ball weighting it would have sufficed—would far more than have sufficed—to crush the life from me when its arc should at last have met my yielding flesh, but that, apparently, was not the doom ordained for me.

For, you see, affixed to the bottom of the weighty ball was an enormous *tooth*, sharpened by patient and cunning art until its cutting edge glittered with a keenness to which the patient swordsmiths who shaped blades from finest Damascus steel might only have aspired. And when that tooth—I do not say fang, for it came from no lion or serpent or grotesque antediluvian beast, but was in form a *man's* tooth, somehow monstrously magnified—began to bite into me, I should without fail have been sliced thinner than a sausage at a lunch counter.

Closer and closer, over what seemed hours, descended the pendulum and that supernally terrifying instrument of destruction at which I could but gaze in dread, almost mesmerized fascination. Already I could feel the sinister wind of its passage with each swing. Soon, soon— Soon, how much more I would feel!

From far above, a soft but clear voice called, "Will you not return that which you have stolen?"

"Stolen?" I said, and my own voice held a new terror, for I pride myself, and with justice, on being an honest man. "I have stolen nothing—nothing, do you hear me?"

"I hear lies; naught save lies." The inquisitor, I thought, spoke more in sorrow than in anger. "Even now, that which you purloined remains with you to embellish your person and salve your vanity."

"Lies! You are the one who lies!" I cried, my desperation rising as the pendulum, the terrible pendulum, perceptibly descended.

"Having granted you the opportunity to repent of your crimes, I now give you the punishment you have earned both for your sin and for your failure of repentance," the inquisitor declared. "I wash my hands of you, Legrand, and may God have mercy upon your immortal soul."

Again the pendulum lowered, and lowered, and, Lord help me, lowered once more. Its next stroke sliced through some of the lashings binding me to that sacrificial platform. The one following that would surely slice through me. My eyes arced with the inexorable motion of the ball and its appended cutting tooth. I watched it reach the high point of its trajectory, and then, moaning with fear at what was to come, I watched it commence its surely fatal descent. I screamed—

And I awoke with Helen beside me, warm in my own bed and altogether unbisected.

After these two most vivid dreams, I trust you will understand why from that time forward I feared and shunned slumber no less than a hydrophobic hound fights shy of water. The hound in due course expires of his distemper. Not being diseased in any normal sense, I did not perish, and the natural weakness of my mortal flesh did cause me occasionally to yield to the allurements of Morpheus despite my fear of what might come to pass if I did.

One night, asleep despite all wishes and efforts to remain awake, I fancied myself—indeed, in my mind, I *was*—guilty of some heinous crime. I had done it, and I had concealed it, concealed it so perfectly no human agency could have hoped to discover my guilt. Yes, officers of the police had come, but purely *pro forma*. That the crime had been committed at all was even, in their minds, a question; that I was in any way connected to it had never once occurred to them.

We sat down to confer together in the very chamber where the nefarious deed was done. I was, at first, charming and witty. But something then began to vex me, something at first so slight as to be all but imperceptible—certainly so to the minions of the law with whom I was engaged. And yet it grew and grew and grew within the confines of my mind to proportions Brobdingnagian. It was *a low, dull pain—much such a pain as a tooth makes when commencing to ache*. I gasped for breath—and yet the officers, lucky souls, felt it not.

I grew nervous, agitated, *distrait*, for the pounding in my mouth grew worse and worse. Soon I felt I must cry out or perish. It hurt more and more and more!—and at last, unable to suffer such anguish for another instant, I cried, "I admit the deed! Tear out the tooth!"—and I pointed to the one in question. "Here, here!—it is the paroxysm of this hideous bicuspid!"

Then, as before, I awoke in a house all quiet and serene; all quiet and serene but for me, I should say, for I lay with my heart audibly thudding as if in rhythm to the tintinnabulation of a great iron bell, my nightclothes drenched with the fetid perspiration brought on by terror. I slept no more until dawn, and not a wink for two days afterwards, either.

I had begun to steel myself towards a course of action I should have called mad in any other, yet one seemingly needful in my particular circumstance. Yet still I hesitated, for divers reasons that appeared to me good, beginning with my unwillingness to undergo yet more pain and suffering and ending with my disinclination to credit the conclusion towards which these nocturnal phantasms were driving me—or, it could be, I should say, beginning with the latter and ending with the former. So many dreams pass through the mendacious gate of ivory, it is easiest to believe they all do.

Whilst equivocating—indeed, tergiversating, for I knew in my heart of hearts the right course, yet found not the courage to pursue it—I again found I could no longer hold eyelid apart from eyelid despite the heroic use of every stimulant known to man. I yawned; I tottered; I fell into bed, more in hope than in expectation of true rest; I slept.

And, once more, I dreamt. I had thought my previous nightmare the worst that could ever befall any poor mortal, of no matter how sinful a character. This proves only the limits of my previous power of imagination, not of the horror to which I might subject myself in slumber—or rather, as I had begun to suspect, the horror to which some increasingly unwelcome interloper and cuckoo's egg might subject me.

I seemed to awake, not from sleep, but from some illness so grave and severe, so nearly fatal, as to have all but suspended permanently my every vital faculty. And, upon awakening, I found myself not in the bed in which I had surely had consciousness slip away from me, but lying on rude, hard planks in darkness absolute.

It was not night. Oh, it may have been night, but it was not night that made the darkness. This I discovered on extending my hands upwards and encountering, less than a foot above my face, more boards, these as rude and hard as the others. Reaching out to either side, I found, God help me, more still. *I had been laid in the tomb alive!*

But one question beat upon my mind as I beat uselessly, futilely, upon the inner confines of the coffin housing what soon would become in truth my mortal remains unless I found some means of egress—would I go utterly mad ere perishing of asphyxiation, or would I take my last stifling breath still in full possession of the faculty of reason and aware to the end of my imminent extinction? The devil and the deep sea are as nothing beside it.

My screams rang deafeningly loud in the wooden enclosure so altogether likely to enclose me forever. Perhaps God was kind, and I did not have earth surrounding me on all sides, six feet above and how many thousands of miles below? Perhaps some merciful soul, hearing the cries of one in his last extremity, would hurry to his rescue as the Good Samaritan did in our Lord's parable so long ago. I did not believe it, but what had I to lose?

Only after some little time had elapsed did I note what I was screaming, and in so doing startled myself even in the midst of the unsurpassable horror of interment untimely. No such commonplace expostulation as *Help me!* or *In God's name, let me out!* passed my lips. No; what I shouted in that moment of terror inexpressible was, "I will give it back! So help me, I will give it back!"

A monstrous shaking commenced, as from the earthquake that ravaged New Madrid in the days of my green youth. Was I saved? Had I lain in the mortuary after all, and was some kindly soul tipping over the casket to facilitate my liberation? Was that light—sweet, blissful light—beating on my eyelids, or was it no more than madness commencing to derange my sense?

With a supreme effort of will, I opened my eyes. There above me, more sublimely beautiful than any angel's, appeared my sweet Helen's face, illumined by a candle bright and lovelier, altogether more welcoming, than the sun. "Are you well, Bill?" she inquired anxiously. "You gave some great, convulsive thrashes in your sleep."

"I will give it back!" I said, as I had when I lay entombed, even if only within the bounds of my own mind. Helen laughed, reckoning me—as any reasonable person might—still half swaddled in my slumbers. Yet never in all my days was I more sincere, more intent, more determined.

As soon as I thought there was any probability, no matter how remote, of bearding the illustrious Vankirk in his den, I hurried thither as fast as shank's mare would carry me. Finding him there—a commendation to his diligence, a trait of character frequently allied to skill—I was so rude as to seize him by the lapels, at the same time crying, "Take it out! Take from my jaw this ghastly, ghostly fragment, untimely ripped from the maxilla of a man who, even from beyond the grave, has made it all too plain he desires—no, requires—a reunion of his *disiuncta membra.*"

"My dear Legrand!" quoth Vankirk. "You desire me to remove the bicuspid I successfully—indeed, all but miraculously—transplanted to your jaw? What madness do you speak, sir?"

"If miracle this be, never let me see another," I replied. "A miracle is said to be a happening for the good, but no good has come to me of this. On the contrary; never have I known such nightmares, which word you may construe either metaphorically or literally, as best suits you." I spent the next little while explaining all that had eventuated since that tooth's taking residence in my head, and finished, "This being so, I implore you to get it hence; get it hence forthwith. I have returned to you because of your knowledge of chloroform and skill with the anaesthetic drug, yet were you to tell me you needs must extract this accursed bicuspid with no such alleviating anodyne, I should not hesitate in begging you to proceed."

"You are in earnest," Vankirk observed, and my answering nod, I dare say, closely approximated to that of a madman in its vehemence. He was for some time silent, examining me closely. "To eschew the use of chloroform in an extraction would show a beastly and barbarous cruelty to which no man aspiring to the merciful calling of dentistry should sink," he declared. "Come; seat yourself in my chair. I shall do as you wish, and charge not a penny for it; never let it be said I leave those seeking my services unsatisfied in any way."

I seized his hand. "God bless you," I said fervently, and of my own free will placed myself in the seat in whose counterparts I had undergone so many exquisite excrucations. As he took the bottle of liquid Lethe from its repository, I held up one finger. "A moment, if you please."

"Yes? What do you require now?"

"Have you any notion, any true notion, of the provenance of this tooth? The more precisely you can return it, once drawn, to its former and even now rightful owner, the better, I think, for everyone."

"I know from whom I bought it," Vankirk answered, "and have a good notion of the haunts she frequents. I can, I believe, make nearly certain to deliver it to the proper cemetery—or, I should say, paupers' graveyard. Will that suffice you?"

Although staggered at the notion that the person who took the tooth which had so tormented me from the reeking jaw of some dull-eyed, swollen corpse could possibly belong to the fair sex, I nodded once more. "You must do that very thing," I said. "You must swear by whatever you hold most dear and holy that you *will* do it; else I cannot answer for the consequences, either to you or to myself."

"By my mother's grave, Mr. Legrand—a fitting oath here, in my opinion—I shall do what you require of me," Vankirk said. The solemnity with which he spoke not failing to impress me, I lowered my head in agreement, as Jove is said to have done in days of yore. He commenced to removed the stopper from the jar of chloroform, but then, arresting the motion, sent my way a glance instinct with curiosity. "I trust I do infer correctly that you would have me extract the offending bicuspid—the suppositiously offending bicuspid—without attempting to implant in your maxilla another intended to replace it?"

"Not for all the gold in California, not for all the cotton in Alabama, not for all the swindlers in New York City would I ever again have some other man's dental apparatus rooted in my own jaw. This being so, yes, sir, your inference is accurate."

"Very well. You must be aware, your bite will suffer."

"Worse things than my bite will suffer should you disregard my wishes here. Go on, man; go on."

Bowing courteously, he said, "I obey," and did at last expose to the open air the contents of that small yet potent bottle. Once more he steeped a scrap of cloth in the oily liquid contained therein; to my nostrils came the heavy, sweetish odor of this incomparable product of human sagacity and ingenuity, this even before he pressed the cloth to my face and brought with it—oblivion.

When I woke up, my mouth was full of blood. Vankirk held up a basin for me to spit in. I did. Soon as I could talk straight, I asks him, "Is the blamed thing out of there?"

"It sure is," Vankirk says. He held up his pelican to prove it. I couldn't swear that was the same tooth.

But it was all over blood and there was a hole in my mouth in the right place, so I expect it was. He goes on, "I will tell you something downright peculiar, Mr. Legrand. Is your head clear enough to follow me?"

"I will follow you wherever you may go," says I. "You may count on it. Tell me this downright peculiar thing."

"I have had to take out a good many transplanted teeth," Vankirk says. "They most often fail. You know this yourself." I nodded, on account of I know it much too well. He goes on, "They are not in the habit of taking root. By the nature of things, they cannot be. They are dead. That means they come out easy as you please. But not this one here."

"Is that a fact? Somehow, Mr. Vankirk, I am not much surprised."

"By what you have told me, I can see how you would not be. This tooth here hung on with both hands and both feet, you might say. It made itself a part of you, and did not want to leave. I have never seen that before in a transplanted tooth. I never expect to see it again. I feared I would harm your jawbone getting it out. It was clinging that tight—it truly was. But it is gone now," he says.

"A good thing, too," says I. "I will not miss it a bit, and you can bet on that. Now—are you sure you got it all?"

He held up the pelican again. There was the tooth. It looked pretty much like a whole tooth, I will tell you that. Vankirk, now, he took another look at it. He frowned a little. Says he, "I suppose it is just barely possible some tiny little piece of root may have got left behind. I do not think so, but it is just barely possible. If it troubles you after this wound heals up, you come back, and I will go in there after it."

"I will do that very thing. You may rely on it," says I.

But that was a while ago now, and my teeth have not given me any trouble since. Well, that is not true. I have had some of the usual sort. I have the measure of that, though. With this new chloroform, I hardly even fear going to the tooth-drawer. I have not had any trouble of the other kind. I have not had any dreams of the sort I had with that tooth in my head. Those dreams would stagger an opium eater, and that is nothing but the truth.

They are gone now. Thank heavens for that. Vankirk is a smart fellow, but this time he outsmarted himself. He did yank every bit of that miserable tooth, and he fooled himself when he thought he might not have. I am glad he fooled himself, too, which is one more thing you may take to the bank.

In fact, George M., I am so glad that dreadful tooth is truly gone and will trouble me no more, I am going to ask you to set things up again for everybody, so my friends here can help me celebrate.

Amontillado, all around!

Return to Xanadu

~~~◉~~~

Lawrence Watt-Evans

THE LIFE OF A DANCING girl in the Great Khan's service in the pleasure dome of Xanadu was not turning out quite as Dunyazad had expected.

Her mother and her older sister had always told her that it was really a simple enough existence—you trained in the womanly arts, and when the opportunity arose you draped yourself over your chosen lord and practiced those arts as best you could, pampering and enticing him. You made yourself an obedient plaything for a time—a few days, a few months, perhaps a year or two—and then, when he tired of you, you were consigned to his harem with his other women, to raise his children and train the younger girls. It wasn't a particularly exciting life, but there were certainly comforts and compensations.

No one had ever said anything about being snatched entirely out of Xanadu by strange magic, transported into a chilly wooden house where a hostile woman flung you a strange and difficult dress to wear, and where you were neglected, left alone by the hearth while your chosen lord, Walter Bayard, spent all his time talking with the other men.

Dunyazad had no idea why that woman, Kylliki, had seemed to be angry at her, but the attitude was unmistakable. The woman had *hissed* at her, like a serpent! And she acted in such bold and forward ways, not at all properly submissive, even while she kept herself wrapped up in heavy clothes that hid her charms from the men.

She seemed angry at *everyone*, really, but most especially at Dunyazad, yet Dunyazad was quite certain she had never done anything to upset the woman. Perhaps Kylliki had wanted Walter Bayard for herself? But she was married to the strange magician . . .

It was all too complicated for Dunyazad, who had never expected to need to think about such things. She lay wrapped in a bearskin by the hearth, staring in the direction that her Walter Bayard had gone, in the company of that horrible woman and the man her lord called Harold. She hadn't said a word when Kylliki and Harold had led Walter Bayard away—it was not her place to interfere in anyone else's business—but she did wonder what was going on. The oddest noises had drifted back to her.

And now the big bearded magician was chanting

some long and complicated spell, and she couldn't hear anyone else at all.

That wasn't right. What had happened to her Walter Bayard? Why was he not speaking? Was he still with the others? Worried, she pushed away the bearskin and got to her feet. She padded quickly to the door of the room where the magician was speaking and glanced in.

Walter Bayard was not there. The big magician was there, working himself up into a frenzy, and Harold was there, and Kylliki, but not the man whose possession she had become.

She stepped through the door and asked, "Have you seen my lord?"

At that moment the magician completed his spell, and Dunyazad was swept up in a sudden whirlwind; color and light and sound swirled about her, and she felt herself falling.

And then she tumbled onto a familiar floor of tesselated black and white marble, landing in an awkward sprawl that neatly missed a nearby pile of cushions that would, had they been but a few inches to one side, have broken her fall nicely.

She blinked, then sat up and looked slowly around.

She was back home in Xanadu, amid the familiar pillars and arches of the main hall in the Khan's pleasure dome, pale in the light of a waning moon. The orchestra was in its accustomed place, but no one was playing; they, and half a dozen of her fellow handmaidens, were instead all staring silently at Dunyazad.

"What has happened?" she asked.

The others exchanged glances; then her cousin Aliyah spoke.

"O Beloved, surely thou knowest better than we what has transpired and brought thee to us once again."

"Indeed, I do not," said Dunyazad. "Tell me, I pray, what thou hast seen since last we spoke."

Aliyah glanced at the other women, and two or three of them nodded at her.

"O dearest cousin, know, then, that yestereve, when we sought thee and thy lord, thou wert nowhere to be found, and we wondered greatly thereat. It was as though thou had vanished 'tween one instant and the next. And from he of the breathing mouth, our lord Pete Brodsky, went up a lamentation that he had once more been foully deceived by Walter Bayard and by Harold Shea, whom he pronounced to be scoundrels, thieves and kidnappers and perhaps murderers. We bade him calm himself, and offered him freely of honeydew and milk, but he would have none of it. He railed at us and called us bawds and worse, in league with his tormentors, and thus he raged through all the night.

"And then, scarce a moment ago, as he once more fled my touch, and as my sisters and these musicians sought to calm him, Pete Brodsky vanished as if carried off by djinni, and thou, O Beloved, appeared in his place."

"I thank thee, O cousin," Dunyazad said. "Thy words are as clear as the ice far beneath our feet." It seemed plain enough what had occurred; that great bearded magician had first snatched Walter Bayard and herself to his other realm, and then sent her back in exhange for Pete Brodsky.

But why? And what was she to do now, with her chosen lord gone?

Aliyah cleared her throat.

"O Beloved," she said, "why art thou dressed so strangely?"

Dunyazad blinked, and looked down at herself and the odd dress she wore. "This garment they gave me to wear, in the place in which I found myself," she said. She tried to snatch it off, but the heavy fabric snagged and bunched, and she succeeded only in catching it into a bundle beneath her arms.

"And what place was this? Where hast thou been?"

"Indeed, I know not," Dunyazad said as she tugged at the dress. "My lord and I were whisked thither in an instant by magic, and I was given this to wear but told nothing of my fate nor the nature of the land in which I found myself. I did as I was bid, but in the night my lord was awakened and led away, and when I sought him out a great black-bearded magician spoke a spell that sent me hither."

The other women exchanged glances.

"This sounds not unlike the doings of djinni or ifrits," said a woman named Zubaidah.

"O daughter of the moon, you speak words of unmistakable truth," Aliyah replied. "I fear my cousin has been deceived by enchanters. Surely these men, Walter Bayard and Pete Brodsky, and the others who appeared with them at the first, were not men at all, but demons! Remember thee, how a great voice spoke from nowhere, and said a mistake had been made? This must certainly have been an ifrit that had sent the strangers to us in error, for they were demons condemned to some dire netherworld!"

"My lord a demon?" Dunyazad asked, eyes wide. She had freed one arm from the entangling dress, but now she stopped her struggles with the garment still around her neck and her left arm still in its sleeve. "Think you so? But nay, he was kind-spoken and gentle, and sought to please me even as I served him!"

"Ah, the better to deceive you!" Zubaidah said. "And indeed, this marks him as a demon or ifrit, for what mortal man troubles himself with the desires of his slave?"

"I fear Zubaidah speaks truly, my cousin," Aliyah said. "You have been debauched by demons, and there is naught for it now but you must be slain, ere you further defile the Khan's refuge."

Dunyazad tensed. "Slain? *Slain?* Nay, sisters, I am unchanged, and as pure of a demon's taint as any of you!"

"O daughter of heaven, we cannot take that risk," said Aminah, who had not previously spoken. She raised her hands and clapped them sharply, three times, over her head.

Dunyazad did not wait for the scimitar-bearing eunuchs thus summoned; instead she sprang to her feet and ran, her bare feet slapping on the cold marble. The strange dress still hung from her shoulder, flapping behind her with every step.

She had seen the eunuchs at work before. Anything that disturbed the order and tranquility of Xanadu brought out the scimitars, and the *best* the creator of the disturbance could hope for would be to be flung into the frigid dungeons to await the Khan's whim. A mere slave, like herself, was more likely to be beheaded on the spot.

Dunyazad preferred to keep her head attached. She knew this was an indication of a certain perversity in her nature, a reluctance to be properly submissive to the will of those above her in the natural order, but nonetheless, she ran.

A moment later she emerged from the pavilion into the gardens, where the air was sweet with the scent of the trees; she stumbled across the grassy slope toward the chasm where rose the sacred river. Running hard, she burst through the cedars that guarded the stream's source; half running and half sliding, she staggered down the rocky banks, down toward the mighty fountain where the waters of the Alph sprayed up from the earth.

She hoped that the eunuchs would not follow her there; the place was both sacred and feared, and there was a very real danger that anyone caught in the water's blast would be drowned, or swept away, carried down through the forest and into the caverns beneath Xanadu.

As she neared the river's edge she stopped, throwing herself down on the bank; she had no desire to be washed away, into the icy caves five miles below. She lay panting for a moment, too stunned by her situation to think or speak or move.

Then she raised her eyes to the heavens, to the thin sliver of dying moon above. She saw no prospect of help there.

She knew she could not hide here forever. What would she eat? Where could she sleep? The air was cold, and she did not think she could bear it for long.

But if she came out of the chasm the eunuchs

would find her, and chop off her head with their great curved swords. In fact, in time they would undoubtedly find her and drag her out and behead her even if she did *not* emerge; the river and fountain were not *that* greatly feared. She could scarcely expect them to not find her; all of Xanadu was but ten miles around.

She could not hope to escape from great Kubla's pleasure garden entirely; it was girdled with walls and towers. She was trapped.

And this, simply because Zubaidah thought that her lord Walter Bayard was a demon, rather than a man!

Dunyazad did not believe that; she was quite sure that he was a mortal. That black-bearded magician might be an ifrit, but surely not Walter!

She remembered how the magician had called to Pete Brodsky and pulled him from Xanadu into that other world, and wished she could summon her lord back to her side, so that he could prove to the eunuchs and the other women that he was only a man, and not a demon.

A thought struck her. Perhaps she *could* summon him, just as the black-bearded enchanter had. After all, the Alph was sacred and therefore magical, and perhaps that magic would allow her lord to hear her.

There could be no harm in trying.

"Walter!" she cried. "Oh, my lord Walter Bayard, return to me! Come to me, I beg you!" She could scarcely hear her own wail over the roaring torrent of the river—but still, she received an answer.

"Who calls?" a man's voice asked.

It was not the voice of Walter Bayard, nor that echoing voice from nowhere, but Dunyazad was not so foolish as to waste any opportunity. "It is I, Dunyazad," she cried.

"Dunyazad? I know no Dunyazad," the voice replied. "Who are you?"

"I am but a dancing girl in the service of the Great Khan, Kubla."

"A dancing girl?"

"Indeed, your most humble slave. Pray, to whom am I privileged to speak?"

"Why, none other than the Khan you serve."

Dunyazad's eyes widened, and she dropped her head, pressing her forehead against the grassy slope. "Your pardon, noble Khan! I did not mean to disturb you!"

"Nonetheless, you have done so—and I am in truth disturbed that I hear your voice, but cannot see you. Where are you, my slave Dunyazad?"

"I . . . I am in the chasm where the sacred river rises from the earth, O Great Khan."

"Indeed! That is almost a mile from where I sit; surely, this is magic at work. And why are you in this place? For surely, you know it has been forbidden you."

"Of a certainty, O dread master! Yet I bethought me I had nothing to lose, for my own sisters in your harem have risen against me, and condemned me to death—and have made the gravest of errors thereby, I assure you, O Light of the World!"

"Have they? Tell me your tale, O Dunyazad, that I may see how you came to be where you should not, and perhaps why the magic of this place allows me to hear your voice—though in truth, yours is not the first voice I have heard thus. But a few days ago I thought I heard my grandfather's voice, prophesying war . . ." His voice trailed off, and Dunyazad hesitated, but then the Khan spoke again.

"Tell me your tale, woman!"

Dunyazad did her best to gather her wits, and then began.

"Some days ago, O lord, there appeared among us four men, clad in strange garb. In accordance with our customs and your instructions, the household made them welcome with song and dance, and fed them upon honeydew . . ."

She went on to describe how a great voice had spoken, whereupon Harold Shea and Vaclav Polacek had vanished, never to return, and how she and the other women had tried to comfort the remaining two, Walter Bayard and Pete Brodsky, upon the loss of their companions. She explained that she had found her breast broadened in the company of Walter Bayard, and that she had served him as best she could during his stay—and how when he, in turn, had been snatched away by magic, she had been taken with him, but only briefly, before being sent back in exchange for Pete Brodsky.

And she admitted how this had been seen as demonic by her compatriots, and how she had fled to the chasm, where the magic of the place had carried her voice to the Khan.

"Surely, O Khan," she concluded, "this is a sign from the heavens. Why would my voice be heard by the lord of all Xanadu, emperor of China and Asia, if not because you alone have the power to make right what is wrong, and rescind the sentence of death my sisters have passed upon me?" Sudden inspiration struck, and she added, "Perhaps this is in some way connected with your grandfather's prophecy. Perhaps my death will bring about this war, and sparing me will avert the catastrophe! I have dealt with strange lords and powerful magicians, and they may have caught me up in their schemes. Why risk angering them by slaying me?"

"Why, indeed?" the Khan mused. "In truth, your story concerns me, and I am inclined to let you live—but how are matters best put right? Perhaps there will be war if you die—or perhaps if you live! And if I allow you to live, can I send you back to the harem without stirring discontent among the women there? Perhaps a squabble among my concubines is the promised conflict, and no more than that."

Dunyazad started to speak, but before she could get a word out the Khan continued, "I do not pretend to omniscience; that is not within the sphere of mortal men. I think we must consult another. I have sent my court magician, my aide de camp, a mighty sorcerer, to find you. Let us ask him what he would suggest."

A new voice spoke, and Dunyazad looked up at the sound to see a trim, white-haired man in a fine robe standing over her. He wore a small triangular beard and an elegant mustache.

"Ah, my pelagic young spark, cast up on a strange shore in this dark valley," he said. "We must choose your destiny wisely, lest darkness fall upon Xanadu, eh?"

"As you say, my lord," Dunyazad replied, though she did not understand all the words he had used. This man was oddly reassuring; his expression seemed kind and full of humor.

"You say your name is . . . Dunyazad?"

"Yes, O master."

"Whatever is someone named Dunyazad doing in Kubla Khan's Xanadu?"

Dunyazad blinked in surprise. "I am told I was born here. Where else should I be, O lord? Surely not in that strange wooden house . . ."

"No, of course not. You're clearly more suited for a marble palace—but Xanadu? I would say you would be more at home in perhaps Samarkand-in-Asia, don't you think?"

"I . . . I do not know, O learned master."

"Well, *I* know, and I'd like to see things put right. I think we can find a better home for you."

"As my lord desires."

"Are you happy in your role as a dancing girl? You certainly have the figure for it, but you speak well—might you do better in another line of work?"

"I live but to please my master." She prostrated herself again.

"Yet you had the spunk to run out here to the chasm, didn't you?"

"As you say, O moon of wisdom."

"I can see that someone's been flinging people hither and yon through other worlds—the black-bearded magician, these four men, these are clearly not any of the Khan's subjects! Perhaps *you* belong in another realm entirely. Sending you to one would remove you from Xanadu, so that you could create no more disturbance, but would not require your death—which I'm sure would please you!"

Dunyazad did not dare reply to this.

"Hmmm . . ." the magician said, clasping his hands. "A beautiful young woman named Dunyazad who can tell a story when the need arises, and who dares to speak even to a king in order to preserve her life—where can we find a place for you?" He closed his eyes thoughtfully, then opened them and smiled. "My dear," he said, "I think I know *exactly* where you belong."

"At the side of my lord, Walter Bayard?" Dunyazad asked. "Or with my sister in the Khan's harem?"

"I think not. Oh, a lord you shall have, and a sister, but not Walter Bayard, nor a place in the Khan's harem. Now, sit up, child, and let me do this properly."

Dunyazad obeyed, as the magician began to chant. He walked around her on the grassy slope, gesturing, until he had woven a circle around her thrice—a magical circle that glowed golden in the gloom.

"I'll keep an eye on you at first," the magician said, as he completed the final circuit. "Just call out if you think I have it wrong, and I'll fetch you back to Xanadu."

And then there was the now-familiar feeling of dislocation, and she found herself falling.

This time she landed squarely on waiting cushions, and looked around.

At first she did not recognize her surroundings. She was clearly in a palace; the walls were gleaming marble, pierced by dozens of pointed arches adorned with fine filigree, and the furnishings were extravagantly fine and beautiful.

She frowned, puzzled. She was sure she had never been in this place before, yet it somehow seemed familiar.

And then a beautiful dark-haired woman entered through one of the arches, and said, "Sister? Are you well?"

Dunyazad turned and recognized her older sister, Shahrazad. "I am not certain," she said.

"Our husbands await us in the courtyard; shall I tell them you are ill?"

"Husbands?" Dunyazad knew that she had never married in Xanadu—but her life there was already beginning to seem distant and dreamlike, while the world around her grew ever more familiar.

"Of course—my beloved lord King Shahryar, and his brother, your own King Shahzaman. We were to ride to the hills for a holiday; had you forgotten? Has a fever blurred your thoughts?"

A king, her husband? That seemed like a childhood fantasy, but it also somehow seemed *right*. "Perhaps it has," Dunyazad said as she rose from the cushions. "I dreamed of a stately pleasure dome, with caves of ice . . ." Then she shook her head. "But that's nonsense."

Her memories of Xanadu were fading, memories of her life in this palace returning. She dimly recalled the magician's final words, offering to snatch her back to Xanadu—but why would she ever want to return *there*?

This was where she belonged. She knew that beyond any possibility of doubt.

Somewhere else, a magician smiled. "Well, *that's* put right, finally! Whatever was she doing in Xanadu, I wonder?" He shrugged, and turned his attention to other matters.

In the palace, Dunyazad flung aside the dress

Kylliki had given her and accepted the robes a servant held out. "Come, sister," she said, taking Shahrazad's hand. "Let us join our husbands for our ride." She laughed. "And perhaps on the way you can tell me a story!"

The Apotheosis of
Martin Padway

~~~◉~~~

S.M. Stirling

"THIS IS THE *RIGHT* VECTOR," the computer insisted.

"If you say so," Maximus Liu-Peng replied. *Insolent machine*, he added to himself. *Still, there's something fishy here. Some sort of temporal loop?*

Luckily, the passengers were too occupied oohing and ahing at the screens to notice the interplay. The big holographic displays around the interior of the compartment showed a blinking succession of possible cities, all of them late-sixth-century Florence; cities

277

large, small, burning, thriving, an abandoned one with a clutch of Hunnish yurts . . .

They wavered, then steadied down to a recognizable shape; recognizable from maps, from preserved relics four hundred years old, and from the general appearance of an Early Industrial city.

Classical-era buildings sprawled across a set of hills with a river winding through it, all columns and marble around the squares and squalid tenements elsewhere; old temples had been converted into churches; city walls torn down and replaced by boulevards and parks; and a spanking-new railway station on the outskirts had spawned a clutch of factories with tall brick chimneys and spreading row housing for the workers.

"How quaint!" gushed somebody's influential cousin, officially an observer for the Senatorial Committee on Anachro-Temporal Affairs.

Maximus controlled his features. Several of the scholarly types didn't try to hide their scorn; either safely tenured, naïve, or both. A coal-black anthropologist cleared her throat with a *hrrrump*.

"You're certain this is our *own* past?" she said.

The operator's poker experience came in handy again. "That's a"—*bloody stupid question*—"moot point, *Doctore Illustrissimo*," he said. "It's definitely a past with Martinus of Padua in it. There are no other lines within several hundred chronospace-years that show a scientific-industrial revolution this early. Quantum factors make it difficult"—*fucking meaningless*—"to say if it's *precisely* the line that led to us."

"But will *He* be here?" an archbishop said.

That required even more caution. "Well, Your Holiness, that's what we'll have to find out. This *is*—"

he pointed to the July 14th, 585 A.D. readout "—the traditional date of the Ascension."

"I am not worthy to witness a miracle," the cleric breathed. "Yet that is why we have come—"

"We're here to find final proof of the Great Man theory," a historian answered, and they glared at each other. "Not to indulge in superstition. It's only natural that primitives, confronted with one of history's truly decisive individuals, should spin a cocoon of myth as they did with Alexander or Manuel—"

"Nonsense," the anthropologist said. "Martinus was merely there at the right time. Socioeconomic conditions were obviously—"

"I just drive this thing," Maximus muttered as the argument went into arm-waving stalemate, and checked the exterior deflector screens. It wouldn't do to have any of the natives see them floating up here. . . .

Lieutenant Tharasamund Hrothegisson, *hirdman* in the Guards of Urias III, King of the Goths and Italians and Emperor of the West, looked carefully at each man's presented rifle as he walked down the line.

Then he called his troop to attention, drew the long *spatha* at his side, turned to face his men and stood at parade rest, with the point of the blade resting lightly on the pavement between his feet. The street was flat stones set in concrete—nothing but the best for the capital of the Romano-Gothic Empire!—but not too broad, perhaps thirty feet from wall to wall counting the brick sidewalks.

"All right, men," he said, raising his voice. "This shouldn't be much of a job. Wait for the word of command, and if you have to shoot to kill, shoot low."

There were nods and grins, quickly stifled. Tharasamund had spoken in Gothic; that was still the official language of the army—though nowadays only about a fifth of the men were born to Gothic mothers, even in a unit of the Royal Guards, and that was counting Visigoths. There were plenty of Italians, other Romans from Hispania and Gaul and North Africa, Burgunds, Lombards, Franks, Bavarians, Frisians—even a few Saxons and Angles and Jutes, a solitary Dane, and a couple of reddish-brown Lyonessians from beyond the western sea.

None of them were unhappy at the thought of taking a slap at a city mob, though, being mostly farmers' sons or lesser gentry themselves. Good lads, but inclined to be a bit rough if they weren't watched.

"Deploy in line," he said, looking back over his shoulder at the guns for a moment.

There were two of them: old-fashioned bronze twelve-pounders, already unhitched from their teams and pointing forward. *And may God spare me the need to use them,* he thought. They were obsolete for field use, but as giant short-range shotguns with four-inch bores they were still as horribly efficient as they'd been in the Second Greek War, when they were a monstrous innovation and surprise.

The soldiers trotted quickly to make a two-deep line across the street, identical in their forest-green uniforms and cloth-covered steel helmets. The city was quiet—far too quiet for Florence on a Saturday afternoon, even with the League playoffs sucking everyone who could afford it out to the stadium in the suburbs. The wind had died, leaving the drowsy warmth of an Italian summer afternoon lying heavy;

also heavy with the city smells of smoke and horse dung and garbage. The buzzing flies were the loudest sound he could hear, save for a distant grumbling, rumbling thunder. Shopkeepers had pulled down their shutters and householders barred window and door hours ago.

"Load!"

The men reached down to the bandoliers at their right hips, pulled out cartridges and dropped them into the open breeches. They closed with a multiple *snick-snick-snick.*

"Fix bayonets!"

The long sword-knives went home below the barrels with another grating metallic rattle and snap.

"Present!"

The troops advanced their rifles with a deep-throated *ho!* That left a line of bristling steel points stretching across the street. With any luck . . .

Tharasamund took off his helmet and inclined his head slightly to one side. *Yes, here they come,* he thought.

He replaced the headpiece and waited, *spatha* making small precise movements as his wrist moved, limbering his sword arm. The first thing he saw was a man in the brown uniform of the City police. He was running as fast as he could—limping, in fact—and blood ran down his face from a scalp bare of the leather helmet he should have worn. When he saw the line of bayonets, he stopped and started thanking God, Mary, and the saints.

"Make some sense, Sathanas fly away with you," Tharasamund snapped.

He was a tall rangy blue-eyed man a few years

shy of thirty himself, with a close-trimmed yellow beard and mustaches and shoulder-length hair a shade lighter, but his Latin was without an accent—better than the rather rustic Tuscan dialect the policeman spoke, in fact. Still, his uniform and Gothic features calmed the Italian a little. They represented authority, even in these enlightened times of the career open to talents.

"My lord," he gasped. "Patrolman Marcus Mummius reporting."

"What's going on?"

"My lord, the Carthage Lions triumphed!"

Tharasamund winced. "What was the score?" he asked.

"Seventeen-sixteen, with a field goal in sudden-death overtime."

Oh, Sathanas take it, he thought, restraining an impulse to clap his hand to his forehead and curse aloud.

The Florentine mob *hated* losing, even when times were good—which they weren't. When times were bad, they were as touchy as a lion with a gut ache. For some reason they thought being the capital city entitled their team to eternal victory, and this was just the sort of thing to drive them into a frenzy. Particularly with defeat at the hands of an upstart team like the Carthage Lions, only in the League a few years—North Africa hadn't been part of the Western Empire until the war of 560, twenty-five years ago.

"We tried to keep everything in order, but when the Carthaginian fans stormed the field and tore down the goalposts, the crowd went wild. They would have killed all the Lions *and* their supporters if we hadn't put all our men to guarding the entrances to the locker rooms. Then they began fighting with all the men from other cities, shouting that foreigners were taking all the best jobs, and—"

"Sergeant, give this man a drink and patch him up," Tharasamund said, ignoring the Italian's thanks as he was led away.

There were thousands of out-of-towners around for the playoffs, plenty of material for a riot with the bad times of the last year—the papers were calling it a *recession*, odd word.

The first spray of hooligans came around the corner two hundred yards south, screaming slogans, banging on shop shutters with rocks and clubs. *They* were wearing leather helmets, the sort actual footballers used, but painted in team colors and with gaudy plumes added, and the numbers of their favorite players across their chests.

Their noisy enthusiasm waned abruptly as they saw the soldiers; then a deep baying snarl went up, and they began to edge and mill forward towards the line of points.

Tharasamund winced. That was a *very* bad sign.

"I've been too successful for too long," Martinus of Padua said as he lit a cigarette and leaned back for a moment in his swivel chair, looking at the neat stacks of paper that crowded his marble-slab desktop.

"On the other hand, consider the alternative," he told himself.

His voice was hoarse with age and tobacco smoke; the precise Latin he spoke was a scholar's, but it bore

the very faint trace of an accent that was—literally—
like none other in the whole world. He'd been born
Martin Padway, in the United States of America
during the first decade of the twentieth century, but
even he hardly ever thought of himself by that name
any more; it had been fifty-two years since he found
himself transported from Benito Mussolini's Rome to
the one ruled by Thiudahad, King of the Goths and
Italians, 533 A.D.

He gave a breathy chuckle; the city fathers of Padua
had even erected a monument to his supposed birth
in their fair town, and it attracted a substantial stream
of tourists. Quite a lucrative little business, all built
on a linguistic accident—any native Latin speaker
would hear *Padway* as *Paduei*, "of Padua." The chuckle
became a rumbling cough, and he swore quietly as
he wiped his lips with a handkerchief. The years had
carved deep runnels in his face, leaving the beak of a
nose even more prominent, but he still had most of
his teeth, and the liver-spotted hands were steady as
he picked up a file from the *urgent* stack.

He took another drag on the cigarette, coughed
again, flipped it open and read:

Item:

The East Roman armies looked like they'd finally
broken the last Persian resistance in Sogdiana, what
Padway mentally referred to as Afghanistan.

*Damn. I was hoping they'd be pinned down there
fighting guerillas forever. The way the Byzantines keep
persecuting Zoroastrians and Buddhists, they deserve
it. Plus the Sogdians are even meaner than Saxons.
Oh, well. Might be good for trade if they settle down
peacefully.*

The East Roman Emperor Justinian was even older than Martin Padway, and he'd never stopped hating the Italo-Gothic kingdom—what had become the reborn and expanded Empire of the West. The more it grew, the more bitter his enmity. Despite the fact that he personally would have been long dead without the doctors Padway had supplied, and never would have beaten the Persians or pushed the Byzantine frontier far north of the Danube without the gunpowder weapons and telegraphs and steamboats his artisans had copied from the models Padway had "invented."

That made absolutely no difference to Justinian's intensely clever but even more paranoid mind; he probably thought he'd have done it all anyway if Padway hadn't shown up. Or even more.

Maybe his grandnephew will be more reasonable. The old buzzard can't last forever . . . *can he? Note to State Department: get the spies working double-time to see if the Byzantines start shifting troops west to the Dalmatian frontier. He'd love to take another slap at us.*

Item:

Riots between pagan and Christian settlers had broken out again in Nova Eboracum, over in Lyonesse; what in another history had been called New York.

Maybe I was a bit too clever there.

Diverting the Saxon migrations from Britannia to the Americas had taken care of their land hunger and gotten a lot of inveterate pirates out of the Channel. It had even introduced them to the rudiments of civilization, since the new colonies were more firmly under the Empire of the West's control than the North Sea homelands.

What it hadn't done was lessen their love of a fight; "Saxon" meant something like "shiv-man," and the tribal ethnonym was no accident. These days they were just using different rationalizations, stubborn Wodenites bashing enthusiasts for the White Christ and vice versa and the Britanno-Roman and Gallo-Roman and Iberian settlers rioting against them all.

The current financial crisis didn't help either. People here just weren't used to the idea of market fluctuations—bad harvests and famine yes, the trade cycle, no. FDR hadn't been able to cure the one at home, and Padway hadn't found any way to do it here either, except spread a little comfort money around and wait.

Note to Royal Council: send a couple of regiments to Lyonesse. Not ones with a lot of Saxons or Frisians in the ranks. Push the troublemakers up west of Albany into the frontier townships and give them all land grants.

Then the transplanted Saxons could take out their pugnacity on the Indians. The British Empire had used that trick with the Scots-Irish, in Ireland and America both.

Item:

The Elba Steel Company was complaining about competition from the new mills in the Rhineland. *Nothing much I can do about that.*

Italy just didn't have much basis for heavy industry, and now that the Rhone-Rhine canal and railway were working . . . But the Elba Company *did* have a lot of important Italian and Gothic aristocrats on the board of directors. *They* had pull in the House of Lords. Plus he'd advised many of them to put their serf-emancipation compensation money into Elba stock, back when. Italian industry had spent a generation or two booming, because it was the only game around. Now the provinces were starting to catch up and all the established balances were shifting.

Wait a minute. We'll throw them some government contracts, and they can use the profits to tempt some of the new Gallic and Britannic steel firms to agree to cross-shareholdings. That would ease the transition—and keep those important votes sweet.

Item:

Down in Australia—

A knock came at the door, and his secretary Lucilla stuck her head through. "Quaestor," she said, having always refused to call him "excellent boss" like everyone else. "Your granddaughter is here."

"And it's my *birthday*, grandfather!" Jorith said, bursting through and hurrying forward. He rose—slightly painfully—and returned her enthusiastic hug.

His daughter's youngest daughter was just turned eighteen. She took after her father's side of the family in looks; he was the third son of King Urias I. She was nearly up to Padway's five-foot-six, which made her towering for a woman of this age and area, with straight features, long dark-blond hair falling past her shoulders and bright green eyes.

Actually, she reminds me of her father's mother, Padway thought. *Just as gorgeous a man-trap, and just as smart. Doesn't have Mathaswentha's weakness for lopping off people's heads, though.*

At one point, he'd come within an inch of marrying Mathaswentha himself. Urias' uncle Wittigis had tried to marry her by force, during the first Byzantine invasion, a few months after Padway was dropped back into Gothic-era Rome; as a princess of the Amaling clan, she made whoever married her automatically eligible for the elective Gothic monarchy. That was one reason he'd pushed the Goths into accepting a pure eldest-son inheritance system; it cut down on succession disputes.

Padway had rescued Mathaswentha from a forced marriage at the very altar, and for a while he'd been smitten with her, and vice versa.

Brrrr, he thought; the memory of his narrow escape never failed to send a chill down his spine. Luckily he'd wised up in time, and had had Urias on hand—a Goth smart enough and tough enough to keep that she-leopard on a leash, and a good friend of Padway's.

Gentle, scholarly Drusilla had been much more the American's style.

"Pity your parents couldn't get back from Gadez," he said, feeling slightly guilty.

The truth was he'd never much liked his daughter Maria. That was unjust. It wasn't *her* fault that Drusilla had died in childbirth. He'd tried to be a good father anyway, but between that and the press of business, she'd mostly been raised by relatives and servants. Jorith was the delight of his old age.

And doesn't she know it, he thought indulgently.

They walked out together through the Quaestor's Offices, her arm through his left elbow. He was slightly—resentfully—conscious of the fact that she was walking slowly and ready to catch him if he stumbled, despite the cane he used with his right hand. He was in his mid-eighties now. Moving hurt. He'd spent nearly six decades back here, and he wasn't that spry, brash young archaeologist any more.

Not even the same person, really. A few weeks ago he'd tried to make himself *think* in English, and found it horrifyingly difficult.

I should be grateful, he thought, as they walked down corridors past offices and clerical pools, amid a ripple of bows and murmurs. *I'm not senile or bedridden.* Or dead, for that matter. And he'd done a lot more good here than he could have in his native century; nobody who'd seen a real famine closeup, or what was left of a town after a sack by Hun raiders, could doubt that.

He ignored the quartet of guards who followed, hard-eyed young men with their hands on the hilts of their swords and revolvers at their waists. *They* were part of the furniture. Justinian and assorted other enemies would *still* be glad to see him go. He chuckled a little as they came out into the broad marble-and-mosaic foyer of the building.

"What's so funny, Grandfather?" Jorith said.

"That there are still men prepared to go to such efforts to kill me," Padway said.

"That's *funny*?" she said, in a scandalized tone.

"In a way. If they'd killed me right after I arrived here, they might have accomplished something—from their point of view; stopped me from changing things. It was touch and go there, those first couple of years. It's far too late, now . . ."

"But not too late for the theatre," Jorith said. "It's a revival of one of your plays, too—*A Midsummer Night's Dream* . . . what are you laughing at *this* time, Grandfather?"

❀   ❀   ❀

"There's nothing here," the archbishop fretted.

"Well, the Cathedral wasn't built until the 700s," the historian pointed out with poisonously sweet reasonableness.

The field wasn't empty, strictly speaking. There was a big two-story brick building, so new that the tiles were still going on the roof. The rest of it was trampled mud, wheelbarrows, piles of mortar and brick and timber and boards, and a clumsy-looking steam traction engine.

"But why should . . . marvelous are the works of the Lord," the archbishop said. "If His Son could be born in a stable, a saint can rise to heaven from a building yard."

"We're redirecting traffic, my lord," the policeman said, walking up to the door of the carriage.

"What for?" Padway said. *Mustn't get testy in my old age,* he thought. *And it was a pretty good performance.* Thank God for a good memory; he'd managed to put down something close to Shakespeare's text.

"There are rumors of riots," the policeman said, sweating slightly. Nobody liked having the Big Boss suddenly turn up on their beat when something was going wrong. "Riots among the football spectators, my lord."

"Oh. Well, thank you, officer," Padway said. As the carriage lurched into motion, he went on: "I keep outsmarting myself."

Jorith giggled. "Grandfather, why is it that all the other politicians and courtiers are dull as dust, but you can always make me laugh?"

It does sound funnier in Latin, he thought. Plus he'd gotten a considerable reputation as a wit over the past fifty years by reusing the clichés of the next fifteen hundred years. He chuckled himself.

And Drusilla swooned over things like parting is such sweet sorrow, *too.* That brought a stab of pain, and he leaned out the window of the carriage.

"What I mean," he went on, "is that I introduced football to quiet people down. Didn't think anyone could get as upset about that as they did over chariot races."

"I've never seen the point, myself," Jorith said. "Polo is much more exciting."

Padway grinned to himself. The Gothic aristocracy had taken to *that* like Russians to drink. In fact, they'd virtually reinvented the game themselves, with a little encouragement and some descriptions from him.

They remind me of horsy country-gentleman-type Englishmen, he thought, not for the first time. *Particularly now that they've taken to baths and literacy.*

They were out of the theatre crush now, the carriages moving a little faster as they moved downhill. The clatter of shod hooves on pavement was loud, but at least most of them had rubber wheels these days, which cut down on the shattering racket iron-clad ones made on city streets. He stopped himself from making a mental note to look into how automobile research was coming.

Leave it to the young men, he thought.

There were enough of them coming out of the universities now, trained in the scientific world-view. In the long run, it would be better *not* to intervene any more, even with "suggestions." There were enough

superstitions about "Mysterious Martinus"; he wanted
the younger generation to learn how to think rationally,
and for themselves.

He smiled, thinking of the thrill he'd had the first
time a young professor had dared to argue with him
about chemistry—and the whippersnapper had turned
out to be right, and Padway's vague high-school recol-
lections wrong, too. And after that . . .

Jorith was smiling at him indulgently. He blinked,
realizing he'd dozed off, lost in half dreams of decades
past.

"Sorry," he said, straightening on the coach's well-
padded seat, wincing a little at the stiffness in his
neck.

"You deserve to be able to nap when you feel like
it, Grandfather," Jorith said. "It's a sin, the way you
work yourself to a nub, after all you've done for the
kingdom. Why, I remember only last month, how
everyone cheered in the Senate when you made that
speech—the one where you said we had nothing to
fear but fear itself—"

A short crashing *baaammm* rang out ahead. Padway's
head came up with a start, the last threads of dream
slipping away. He knew that sound of old—was respon-
sible for it being heard a millennium or so early.

Rifles, firing in volley . . .

"*Fire!*" Tharasamund said reluctantly.

The sound of fifteen rifles going off within half a
second of each other battered at his ears. The front
rank reloaded, spent cartridges tinkling on the pavement, and the sergeant bellowed:

"Second rank, volley fire present—*fire!*"

Dirty-white powder smoke drifted back towards him, smelling of rotten eggs and death. Ten yards away the crowd milled and screamed, half a dozen lying limply dead, twice as many more whimpering or fleeing clutching wounds or lying and screaming out their hurt to the world. The rest hesitated, bunching up—which meant a lot of them were angry enough to face high-velocity lead slugs.

"*Cease fire!*" he said to his men, with enough of a rasp in it to make them obey. To the mob, he went on in Latin.

"Disperse! Return to your homes!" he called, working to keep his voice deep and authoritative, and all the desperation he felt out of it. "In the Emperor Urias' name!"

"Down with the Goths!" someone screeched. "Down with the heretics! *Dig up their bones!*"

"Oh-oh," Tharasamund said.

That was call to riot, an import from Constantine's city . . . The religious prejudice was home-grown, though. Most Goths were still Arian Christians— heretics, to Orthodox Catholics—and the Western Empire enforced a strict policy of toleration, even for pagans and Jews and Nestorians, and for Zoroastrian refugees from Justinian's persecutions.

I hate to do this. They're fools, but that doesn't mean they deserve to be sausage meat. Drunk, half of them, and a lot of them out of work.

"Clear firing lanes!" he rasped aloud.

The soldiers did, shuffling aside but keeping their rifles to the shoulder to leave a line of bright points and intimidating muzzles facing the crowd. The artillery-men stepped aside from their weapons—they'd recoil ten feet each when fired, on smooth pavement—with the gun captains holding the long lanyards ready. Those four-inch bores were even more intimidating than rifles, if you knew what they could do.

"Ready, sir," the artillery noncom said. "Double-shotted with grape."

Tharasamund nodded. "Disperse!" he repeated, his voice cutting over the low brabbling murmur of the crowd. "This is your last warning!"

He heard a whisper of *why give them any fucking warnings?* but ignored it; there were some times an officer was wise to be half-deaf.

The noise of the crowd died down, a slow sullen quiet spreading like olive oil on a linen tablecloth. A few in the front rank tossed down their rocks and chunks of brick, turning and trying to force their way back through the crowd; the slow forward movement turned into eddies and milling about. He took a long breath of relief, and felt the little hairs along his spine stop trying to bristle upright.

"I should have stayed home in Campania and raised horses," he muttered to himself. "But no, I had to be dutiful . . ."

He half-turned his head as he sheathed his sword; that let him catch the motion on the rooftop out of the corner of his eye. Time froze; he could see the man—short, swarthy, nondescript, in a shabby tunic. The expression of concentration on the man's face as he tossed the black-iron sphere with its long fuse trailing sputterings and blue smoke . . .

"*Down!*" Tharasamund screamed, and suited action to words—there was no time to do anything else.

Someone tripped and fell over him; that saved his

life, although he never remembered exactly what happened when the bomb fell into the open ammunition limber of the twelve-pounder.

"What was *that*?" Jorith exclaimed, shock on her face.

Neither of them really needed telling. *That* was an explosion, and a fairly big one. The driver of the carriage leaned on the brake and reined in, but the road was fairly steep here—flanked on both sides by shops and homes above them. Padway leaned out again, putting on his spectacles and blinking, thankful that at least the lense grinders were turning out good flint glass at last. Then another blast came, and another, smaller and muffled by distance.

"God damn that bastard Justinian to *hell*," he growled—surprising himself by swearing, and doing it in English. Normally he was a mild-mannered man, but . . .

"Grandfather?" Jorith said nervously; she wasn't used to him lapsing into the mysterious foreign tongue either.

"Sorry, kitten," he said, then coughed. "I was cursing the Emperor of the East."

Her blue eyes went wide. "You think—"

"Well, we can produce our own riots, but not bombs, I think," Padway said. "Dammit, he can try and kill *me*—he's been doing that for fifty years—but this is beyond enough."

Shod hooves clattered on the pavement outside. One of the bodyguards leaned over to speak through the coach's window.

"Excellent boss," he said. "There are rioters behind

us. We think it would be best to try and go forward and link up with the soldiers we heard ahead, and then take the Equinoctal Way out to the suburbs. There will be more troops moving into the city."

"As you think best, Hermann," Padway said; he'd commanded armies in his time, but that was forty years ago and more, and he'd never pretended to be a fighting man. He tried to leave that to the professionals.

Tharasamund shook his head. That was a bad mistake; pain thrust needles through his head, and there was a loud metallic ringing noise that made him struggle to clap hands to his ears. The soft heavy resistance to the movement made him realize that he was lying under several mangled bodies, and what the sticky substance clotting his eyelashes and running into his mouth was. He retched a little, gained control with gritted teeth and a massive effort of will, and pushed the body off. Half-blinded, he groped frantically for a water bottle and splashed the contents across his face while he rubbed at his eyelids. The blood wasn't quite dried, and the flies weren't all that bad yet; that meant he hadn't been out long. A public fountain had broken in the blast, and water was puddling up against the dam of dead horses and men and wrecked equipment across the road.

As he'd expected, what he saw when he *could* see properly was very bad. Nobody looked alive—most of the bodies weren't even intact, and if one of the field guns hadn't taken some of the blast when both limbers went off, he wouldn't be either. Nobody but the dead were here—a tangle of the mob around where the last of his soldiers had fallen. All the intact weapons were gone, of course, except for his sword and revolver; he'd probably looked too thoroughly like a mangled corpse to be worth searching for men in a hurry. The fronts of the shops on either side were smashed in by the explosion and by looters completing the work; a civilian lay half in and half out of one window, very thoroughly dead.

"Probably the shopkeeper," Tharasamund muttered grimly, his own voice sounding muffled and strange. The pain and the ringing in his ears were a little better, but probably he'd never have quite the keenness of hearing again.

That was another score to settle, along with the cold rage at the killing of his men. He staggered over to the fountain and washed as best he could; that brought him nearer to consciousness. The first thing to do—

He hardly heard the coach clatter up, but the sight brought him out into the roadway, waving his sword. That brought half a dozen pistols in the hands of the mounted guards on him, and a shotgun from the man beside the driver. The men were in civil dress, country gentleman's Gothic style, but they were a mixed lot. Soldiers or ex-soldiers, he'd swear; from the look of the coach, some great lord's personal retainers. None of them looked very upset at the carnage that was painting the coach's wheels and the hooves of their horses red . . . best be a little careful.

"Tharasamund, Captain in the *Kunglike-hird*, the Royal Guard," he snapped, sheathing the blade. "I need transport, and I call on you to assist me in the Emperor's name."

"Straight-leg, we don't stop for anyone," the chief guard said—he had a long tow-colored mane, a thick bull-neck, and an equally thick growling accent in his Latin: Saxon, at a guess. "The only thing I want to hear from you is how to get our lord to someplace safe."

Tharasamund looked around. He could hear distant shouting and screams and the crackle of gunfire. That meant they were *loud*. And he could see columns of smoke, too. It might be an hour—or four or five—before enough troops marched in from the barracks outside town, between the built-up area and the royal palace, to restore order. Someone had screwed up royally; he'd be surprised if there wasn't a new urban prefect soon.

Not that that will be much consolation to the dead, he added to himself.

He was opening his mouth to argue again—he had to get back to regimental HQ, to report this monumental ratfuck, and get some orders—when a young woman leaned out of the half-open carriage door.

Not just any young woman. Her gown and jewels were rich in an exquisitely restrained court fashion, but that face would have stopped him cold if she were naked—*especially* if she were naked. His gesture turned into a sweeping bow.

Wait a minute. They said their lord, *not their* lady.

The girl's eyes widened at the sight ahead, and she gulped. Then she fought down nausea—he felt a rush of approval even in the press of emergency—and looked at him. There was a faint feeling like an electric-telegraph spark as their eyes met, gray gazing into blue, and then she was looking over her shoulder.

"Grandfather," she said, in pure upper-class Latin. "There's been a disaster here."

"There's been an attack on Imperial troops here," Tharasamund said firmly, pitching his voice to carry into the interior of the vehicle. "I must insist, my lord—"

It seemed to be a day for shocks. The man who leaned out in turn, bracing himself with a grimace, certainly looked like a grandfather. Possibly God's grandfather, from the wrinkles; he'd never seen anyone older and still alive. The pouched eyes behind the lenses and big beak nose were disconcertingly shrewd. It was a face Tharasamund had seen before, when his unit was on court duty; anyone who saw magazines and engravings and photographs would have recognized it as well, these past two generations and more.

Martinus of Padua. Quaestor to three Emperors of the West; king-maker, sorcerer or saint, devil or angel—some pagans thought him a god—and next to Urias II, the most powerful man in the world. Possibly more powerful. Emperors came and went, but the man from Padua had been making things happen since Tharasamund's grandfather was a stripling riding to his first war, when the Greeks invaded Italy in Thiudahad's day.

Tharasamund saluted and made a deep bow. "My apologies, my lord. I am at your disposal." He managed a smile, a gentleman's refusal to be disconcerted by events. "And at yours, my lady."

"Jorith Hermansdaughter, noble Captain," she said,

a little faintly but with courtly politeness. A princess, then, and the old man's granddaughter.

This *definitely* took precedence over his own troubles. . . .

Ouch, Padway thought, pushing his glasses back up his nose and giving thanks, for once, for the increasing short-sightedness of old age. He'd seen worse, but not very often.

"Captain, pleased to see you," he said. "What happened here?"

"My lord," the young man said crisply. He looked suitably heroic in a battered way, but it was a pleasure to hear the firm intelligence in his voice. "A detachment of my company was ordered by General Winnithar of the Capital City garrison command to suppress rioters in aid to the civil power. We were doing so when a bomb thrower dropped a grenade into the ammunition limber. I suspect the man was a foreign agent—the whole thing was too smooth for accident."

As he spoke, another explosion echoed over the city. Padway nodded, looking like an ancient and highly intelligent owl.

"Doubtless you're right, Captain. Do you think the Equinoctal Way will be clear?"

Tharasamund made a visible effort. "It's as good a chance as any, my lord," he said. "It's broad—rioters generally stick to the old town. And it's the best way to get to the garrison barracks quickly."

Broad and open to light, air and artillery, Padway thought—a joke about the way Napoleon III had rebuilt Paris, and part of his own thoughts over the years planning the expansion of Florence.

"Let's go that way," he said. "Hengist, head us out."

"I never wanted to have adventures," Padway grumbled. "Even when I was a young man. *Certainly* not now."

Jorith looked at him and gave a smile; not a very convincing one, but he acknowledged the effort.

"This is an adventure?" she said. "I've always *wanted* adventures—but this just feels like I was walking along the street and stepped into a sewer full of big rats."

"That's what adventures are like," Padway said, wincing slightly as the coach lurched slowly over something that went *crunch* under the wheel and trying not to think of what—formerly who—it was, "while you're having them. They sound much better in retrospect."

The young guardsman—Tharasamund Hrothegisson, Padway forced himself to remember—chuckled harshly.

"Oh, yes," he said, in extremely good Latin with only the faintest tinge of a Gothic accent, then added: "Your pardon, my lord."

Jorith looked at him oddly, while Padway nodded. He might not have been a fighting man himself, but he'd met a fair sample over the years, and this was one who'd seen the elephant. For a moment youth and age shared a knowledge uncommunicable to anyone unacquainted with that particular animal. Then a memory tickled at Padway's mind; he'd always had a rook's habit of stashing away bits and pieces, valuable for an archaeologist and invaluable for a politician.

"Hrothegisson . . . not a relation of Thiudegiskel?"

The young man stiffened. Officially, there had been an amnesty—but nobody had forgotten that Thiudegiskel son of Thiudahad had tried to get elected King of the Goths and Italians instead of Urias I, Padway's candidate; or that he'd gone over to the Byzantines during the invasion that followed and nearly wrecked the nascent Empire of the West.

"My mother was the daughter of his mother's sister," he said stiffly. "My lord."

That didn't make him an Amaling, but . . .

"Ancient history, young fellow. Like me," he added with a wry grin. "What are you doing, by the way?"

The young Goth had gotten up and was examining the fastenings of the rubberized-canvas hood that covered the carriage.

"I thought I'd peel this back a bit at the front, my lord—"

"You can call me boss or Quaestor or even sir, if you must," Padway said. He *still* wasn't entirely comfortable being my-lorded.

"—sir. I'd be of some use, if I could see out."

"Not all the way?"

"Oh, that would never do," Tharasamund said. "You're far too noticeable . . . sir."

Tharasamund finished looking at the fastenings, made a few economical slashes with his dagger, and peeled the soft material back from its struts, just enough to give him a good view. Warm air flowed in.

"Uh-oh," he said.

I know what uh-oh *means,* Padway thought. *It means the perfume's in the soup . . . or the shit's hit the fan.*

"Give me a hand," he snapped.

Something in his voice made the two youngsters obey without argument. Grumbling at his own stiffness and with a hand under each arm, he knelt up on the front seat and looked past the driver and guard.

"Uh-oh," he said.

"It's in the soup, right enough, excellent boss," Tharasamund said.

One advantage of Florence's hilly build and grid-network streets was that you could see a long way from a slight rise. The view ahead showed more fires, more wreckage . . . and a very large, very loud mob about half a mile away, milling and shouting and throwing things. Beyond that was a double line of horsemen, fifty or sixty strong. As they watched, there was a bright flash of metal, as the troopers all clapped hand to hilt and drew their *spathae* in a single coordinated movement to the word of command. A deep shout followed, and the horses began to move forward, faster and faster . . .

"Oh, that was a bad idea. That was a *very* bad idea," Tharasamund muttered.

Sensible young man, Padway thought.

A big man on a big horse waving a sword and coming towards you was an awesome spectacle; scores of them looked unstoppable. Armies had broken and run from the sheer fear from the sight, including one memorable occasion when Padway had been in command, trying to make a mob of Italian peasant recruits hold a pike line against charging Byzantine heavy cavalry.

The problem was . . .

The horsemen struck. Sure enough, the front of

the mob surged away in panic, trying to turn and run. The problem was that there were thousands of people behind them, and they *couldn't* run. There wasn't room. The swords swung down, lethal arcs that ended in slashed-open heads and shoulders, but the horses were slowing as they moved into the thick mass of rioters. Horses were all conscripts, with an absolute and instinctive fear of running into things, falling, and risking their vulnerable legs.

A line of brave men with spears could stop any cavalry ever foaled. A mass of people too big to run away could do the same, in a messy fashion, by sheer inertia.

Padway shifted slightly, keeping his body between Jorith and the results, and noticed that Tharasamund did the same. People stopped running as the horses slowed; they turned, started to throw things, yelled, waved their arms. The cavalry horses were bolder than most of their breed, but they backed, snorting and rolling their eyes; a few turned in tight circles, caught between their riders' hands on the reins and an inborn need to run away from danger. The rain of bits of stone and iron and wood grew thicker; a soldier was pulled out of the saddle . . .

And at the rear of the mob, a purposeful-looking group was turning towards the carriage halted at the top of the hill.

"Guards cavalry," Tharasamund said tightly. *They never did know anything but how to die well. Though I grant they do know how to do that.*

He looked at Padway, back at the white, frightened, determined face of the girl, then at the mob.

"Obviously, there are agitators at work," he said, "not just hungry rioters sparked off by a football game."

Padway nodded. The Saxon chief of his guardsmen bent down from the saddle and pointed to a narrow alleyway.

"That way, I think," he growled. "Liuderis, Marco, get that cart and set it up."

The coachman turned the horses' heads into the narrow, odorous gloom of the alley. The guardsmen grabbed a discarded vendor's pushcart, dumped out its load of vegetables in a torrent of green, and pulled it into the alleyway after the carriage before upending it. Most of them crouched behind it, drawing their pistols.

"We'll hold them here," Hengist said grimly. "Excellent boss, you and this gentleman—" he nodded to Tharasamund "—and the young mistress get going."

Gray eyes met blue, and Tharasamund nodded sharply. Padway seemed about to protest, and the Saxon grinned.

"Sorry, excellent boss, that's not an order you can give me. My oath's to keep you safe—obedience takes second place."

He slapped the rump of the rear horse in the carriage team, leaping back to let the carriage lurch by in the narrow way. Tharasamund lifted a hand in salute, then used it to steady Padway; the Quaestor sat down heavily, sighing. Jorith helped him down, and braced him as they lurched across cobbles and then out into rutted dirt.

Think, Tharasamund, the soldier told himself. They weren't out into the country yet, and wouldn't be for half an hour, but the buildings were very new, some

still under construction. No people were about; with
a holiday and then a riot there wouldn't be, and this
area had few residences, being mostly workshops.

He looked back; nothing to see, but then came
a snarling brabble of voices, and a crackle of pistol
fire. *By Christ and His mother, that's a brave man,*
he thought. *And true to his oath. Saxons may not be
civilized but they're stubborn enough.*

Jorith looked behind them as well. "Is that—" she
said, and swallowed.

Tharasamund nodded. "Yes, lady. They can hold
them quite a while, in that narrow way. Not many
rioters will have firearms, and there can't be many
agents of the Greek emperor. Just enough."

She shivered. "It sounds . . . different, in the epics.
Last stands."

Padway mumbled something in a language Tharasamund didn't recognize, though a couple of the
words had a haunting pseudo-familiarity, sounding
like oaths. For a moment he thought the old man
was dazed, and then he spoke sharply—loud enough
for the coachman to hear.

"If any of you get out of this, and I don't, take
a message to the King and Council: this means Justinian thinks he's ready for a showdown. I should
have—never mind."

There was a mutter of assent. *The Quaestor is a
brave man too, in his way,* Tharasamund acknowledged.
He's thinking of the Kingdom's welfare. And, from the
way his eyes darted her way, his granddaughter's.

An idea blossomed. "Sir, I have an idea. Some of
those men who turned our way were mounted, and
they've identified this coach. What we need to do

is to get you to a place of safety for a few hours, until the city's brought back to order. Do you see that half-built whatever-it-is on the hill up ahead? We can . . ."

"This doesn't look much like what I'd anticipated," the archbishop said, peering at the wide screen.

Maximus snorted. He wasn't an expert, but he *had* scanned the briefing. This was the beginning of the Wars of Reunification; what did the cleric expect, a festival with wreaths and flowers and incense?

The pilot's long nose twitched. There would be incense down there, all right, of a type he'd seen on previous expeditions. Things burning; people too, possibly. That sort of thing happened, if you went this far back. For a long time to come, too.

"There!" he said aloud, and everyone crowded up behind him; he ran a hand through a light-field to make sure nobody tripped a control by mistake. "There, that's *him!*"

The screen leapt, magnification increasing as the computer obeyed his intent—that was a virtue of the more modern types; they did what you wanted them to do, not just what you told them.

A carriage drawn by four matched black horses galloped out of an alley and turned westward, swaying as the coachman stood on his seat and lashed them with a whip. The overhead cover had been partly cut away; Maximus froze a portion of the screen to show the face of an old man. The computer helpfully listed the probability of this being the man they were after. It was as near unity as no matter. This was also the earliest era when photographs of famous men were available, and enough had survived into modern times to be digitized.

Somebody made a half-disgusted sound. "He's so . . . so *ugly*," one said. The archbishop made a reproving sound. Maximus nodded, agreeing for once. It wasn't the man's fault that regeneration therapy wouldn't be invented for another two hundred years, or perfected for three. One thing time travel taught you was how fortunate you were to be born in the tenth century A.D.

"And he's stopping!" the historian cried. "I wonder why?"

Maximus hid another snort, and swung the viewpoint. "At a guess, most learned one, because those cutthroats are after him, and he's planning on hiding before they get here."

"Are you sure this is a good idea, Captain?" Padway said.

The young Goth shrugged. "No, sir," he said, helping the older man down from the carriage. "But they ought to follow the coach. It's much more visible."

Padway wheezed a chuckle as they hurried into the unfinished building, around the heaps of sand and bricks and timber; it was always nice to meet a man who didn't promise more than he could deliver. The carriage spurred off, making a great show of haste but not moving as fast as it might. He made two mental notes: one to see that the coachman got something, if he made it out of this, and another to put in a good word for Captain Tharasamund. He'd had a *lot* of experience judging men, and there were never enough good ones around.

The first floor of the building was an echoing vastness smelling of raw brick and new cement, with a concrete slab floor, thin brick walls, and cast-iron pillars holding it all up. A lot of timber was piled about, and a rough staircase led to the second story. Tharasamund and Princess Jorith half-lifted Padway up the stairs and propped him against a pile of sacks of lime mortar; then the Gothic soldier ran to a window, standing beside it and peering out through boards nailed over the unfinished casement.

"Oh, Sathanas take it," he said.

"They didn't follow the coach?" Padway asked.

"Most of them did. Two mounted men are turning in here, and a crowd of what look like ruffians after them. My apologies, sir," he finished, with bitter self-reproach.

"You took a chance. I agreed. If you bet, you lose sometimes."

Tharasamund saw Padway's eyes flick to Jorith's face and then away. His own lips compressed. *Damned if I'll let a mob get their hands on a royal princess,* he thought. *But by all the saints, what can I do about it?*

Fighting was the only thing that came to mind. Tharasamund had a healthy opinion of his own abilities in that line, but fighting off what looked like fifty or sixty men wasn't in the realm of the possible, even with a narrow approach and slum scum on the other side.

"Do what you can, then," he said to himself, looking around.

He had six shots in his revolver, and three reloads in his belt pouches . . .

He heard voices below and set himself. One of the men he'd seen riding came into view, urging his followers on, a short muscular-looking fellow in respectable but drab riding clothes, with a neatly trimmed black beard. The Goth let the long barrel of his revolver drop over his left forearm, squeezed . . .

Crack. The man toppled backward, screaming, and then screaming that his leg was broken—screaming in Greek. An educated man's dialect, but a native speaker's, as well. There were such folk in the Western Empire—parts of southern Italy and much of Sicily spoke Greek as their first language—but he would have bet his father's lands against a spavined mule that the man had been born not far from Constantinople.

Tharasamund dodged back as someone emptied a pistol at him; probably the other Greek. Whoever he was, the shooter started exhorting his men to attack; "Gothic heretics" and "two hundred gold crowns for their heads—each" seemed to be about equal inducements. It took a while, and he thought he knew the reason when he heard hasty sawing and hammering sounds.

"They're building a mantlet," he said grimly. At the confusion in the young woman's eyes, he went on: "A wooden shield, the sort they used to use in sieges. Wouldn't do them much good against a rifle, but a few layers of thick planks will turn a pistol ball."

Jorith raised her head. "I know I can rely on you, Captain," she said quietly. Tharasamund winced; he knew what she relied on him to do, and he didn't like it.

Well, that's irrelevant, he thought. *You'll do it anyway, and make it quick.*

Then her eyes went wide. "What's that you're leaning against, Grandfather?" she asked.

"Mortar," Padway said, raising a curious white brow.

"Lime," the girl said. "In the old days, during sieges, didn't—"

"They threw quicklime on men climbing siege ladders," Tharasamund half-whooped, with a strangled shout to keep the rioters and foreign agents below in the dark.

Padway moved himself aside, grinning slightly. Tharasamund moved towards the pile of sacks; Jorith halted him with an upraised hand.

"Wait," she said, and whipped off a gauzy silk scarf. "Those gauntlets will protect your hands, but your face—"

He bowed his head, and she fastened the thin cloth across his face like a mask; with the fabric close to his eyes, he could see out of it well enough. Then he worked, dragging the rough burlap sacks over towards the stairwell, carefully avoiding exposing his body to sight from below.

"Let's see," he muttered. "I'll stack them up here"— he made a pyramid of four, carefully weakening the lacing that held each sack closed at the top—"at the back of the stairwell, so they'll be above and behind anyone coming up the stairs. My lady Jorith? I'm afraid I'll need you to push."

He tried to keep his voice light, but there was a grave knowledge in the way she nodded.

"You up there!" a voice called. "Send us the old man, lay down your weapons, and we'll let you go!"

"And we can believe as much of that as we want

to," Tharasamund called back. "No, thank you. Here's our deal: if you run now, before the troops come, I won't shoot you in the back."

"You'll be dead before then, you whipworthy barbarian!" the voice snarled. "You and your drab and the sorcerer too! *Take them!*"

The stairs were steep; Tharasamund had to go down on his belly to reach the upper one without exposing more than his eyes and gun hand. The mantlet—it was a door, with layers of planks nailed across it—came staggering upward. The hale Greek stood behind, firing over his mens' heads to keep the Goth's down; he was half-concealed behind an iron pillar, and had his weapon braced against it.

Tharasamund swallowed against a dry throat and ignored him, ducking up to shoot at the feet of the men carrying the wooden bracer instead. Most of the shots missed. The targets were small and moving, and he had to snap-shoot in an instant, with no careful aiming. At last one hit, and the mantlet wavered and stalled as a man fell backward squalling and clutching at a splintered ankle.

"*Now, Jorith!*" he shouted.

The girl had lain down behind the sacks, with her slippered feet braced against them. She shoved, and they wavered and toppled forward. Momentum took over, and the sacks tumbled down. Acrid white dust billowed in choking clouds, and Tharasamund reflexively threw an arm across his face, coughing. One of the toughs behind the mantlet looked up and shouted, gesturing frantically—and his comrades followed the pointing arm, which was the worst possible thing they could have done.

Screams sounded sweetly, and strangled curses. The mantlet was thrown aside to crash on the hard cement floor beneath, and men ran—up out of the cloud of alkaline dust, or down and away from it. The Goth grinned behind his protecting face mask as he bounded erect and drew his *spatha*. A man staggered up the stairs, coughing and wheezing, his eyes already turning to bacon-rind red.

He swung a club. Tharasamund skipped neatly over it and lunged, his point skewering down over the thug's collarbone; muscle clamped on it, and he put a booted foot on the other's chest and pushed him back onto his fellows. More cursing and crashing; then two came forward, with their handkerchiefs held over their mouths. Both had swords, and one even had some idea of what to do with it. For a long minute it was clash and clatter and the flat unmusical rasp of steel on steel, and then the Goth sheered off half a face with a backhand cut.

"Ho, *la*, St. *Wulfias!*" he shouted exultantly, then found himself coughing again; some of the dust had gotten through the silk, and his eyes were tearing up as well.

Jorith came up beside him and offered a flask. He drank; it was citron water, and he used some to wash his eyes as well. The acid in it stung, but it would be better than leaving lime dust under his eyelids.

"Saw them off, sir," he wheezed to Padway, and Jorith clapped her hands and rose on tiptoe to kiss him. At another time, he would have paid more attention to that, but . . .

"For now," Padway said. "But if Justinian didn't

send idiots, and his *agents in rebus* usually are fairly shrewd, they'll—"

The noise below had mostly been bellowing, cries of pain and shrieks of *I'm blind!* and departing footfalls as many of the strong-arm squad decided there were better things to do in a riot-stricken city than have quicklime poured over their heads.

Now a crackling sound arose as well. All three looked at each other, hopelessly hoping that someone would deny that the sound was fire. When smoke began to drift up from between the floorboards, no doubt at all was left.

"Captain," Padway said.

"Sir?"

"I'm going to give you an order," he said. "You're not going to like it, but you're going to do it anyway."

"Sir—"

"Grandfather—"

"Take Jorith and get out of here," Padway rasped. "No, shut up. I'm an old man—a very old man—and I haven't six months to live anyway."

Jorith went white, and Padway waved a hand and then let it fall limp. "Didn't want to spoil your birthday, kitten, but that's what the doctors say. My lungs. Maybe I shouldn't have sent that expedition to find tobacco . . . I've lived longer than I ever had a right to expect anyway. Now get out—they won't have enough men to chase you, not when they see I'm not with you. I put my granddaughter in your hands. That is your trust."

A racking cough, and a wheeze: *"Go!"*

Tharasamund hesitated, but only for an instant. Then he brought his sword up in a salute more heartfelt than most he'd made, sheathed it, and put a hand on Jorith's shoulder as she knelt to embrace her grandsire.

"Now, my lady," he said.

She came, half-stunned, looking back over her shoulder. Tharasamund snatched up a coil of rope, made an end fast, looked out to the rear. Padway had been right; there were only two men out there, and they backed away when they saw the tall soldier coming down the rope, even hindered with a woman across his shoulder. He landed with flexed knees, sweeping the princess to her feet and drawing steel in the same motion.

"Follow me . . . and *run*," he said.

"No!" He turned, surprised that she disobeyed. Then he stopped, forgetting her, forgetting everything.

Light speared his eyes, and he flung up a hand and squinted. Light, not the red of flames, but a blinding light whiter than the very thought of whiteness in the mind of God. In the heart of it, a brazen chariot shone mirror-bright, turning gently with a ponderous motion that gave an impression of overwhelming weight—it must be visible to all Florence, as well.

The roof of the building exploded upward in a shower of red roofing tile and shattered beam, and through it he could see a form rising.

It was Martinus Paduei. It could be nobody else. Borne upward on a pillar of light . . .

Dimly, he was aware of the remaining rioters' screaming flight, followed by their Greek paymaster. He was a little more aware of Jorith beside him, tears of joy streaming down her face as she sank to her knees and made the sign of the cross again and again. He sank down beside her, holding up his sword so that it also signed the holy symbol against the sky. The light was pain, but he forced his eyes open anyway, unwilling to lose a moment of the sight.

There was a single piercing throb of sound, like the harp of an angel taller than the sky and the light was gone, leaving only the fading afterimages strobing across his vision.

"He was a saint!" Jorith sobbed. "Oh, Grandfather—"

"Yes," the young man said. "I don't think there's much doubt about that now. He *was* a saint."

He looked down into the girl's face and smiled. "And he told me to take care of you, my lady Jorith. We'd better go."

Martin Padway opened his eyes, blinking. For a long moment he simply lay on what felt like a very comfortable couch, looking at the faces that surrounded him. Then two thoughts sent his eyes wide:

I don't hurt. That first. All the bone-deep aches and catches were *gone*, all the pains that had grown so constant over the years that he didn't consciously notice them. *Yes, but* how *I notice them now they're gone!* he thought.

The second thought was: *They're all so* young! There were a round dozen men and women, every color from ebony-black to pink-white via a majority of brown that included several East Asian types. But none of them looked over twenty; they had the subtle signs—the flawless fine-textured skin, the bouncing *freshness* of movement—that were lost in early adulthood. It was far more noticeable than the various weirdnesses of their clothing.

Behind them were what looked like movie screens showing aerial shots, or various combinations of graphs and numbers, all moving and in different colors.

"Time travelers, right?" he said. *After all, I know time travel is possible. I've had going on fifty years to get used to the concept.*

One man—young man—gave a satisfied smile. "Instant comprehension! Just as you'd expect from a superior individual. I told you that the Great Man theory—"

He seemed to be talking upper-class sixth-century Latin, until you noticed that his lip movements weren't quite synchronized with the words and there was a murmur of something else beneath it.

Fascinating, Padway thought. *And that's an academic riding a hobbyhorse, or I was never an archaeologist.* Evidently some things were eternal.

Some of the others started arguing. Padway raised a hand:

"Please! Thank you very much for saving my life, but if you wouldn't mind a little information . . ."

"Yes, excellent sir," another man said—he was in a plain coverall, albeit of eerily mobile material. "From four hundred years in your future. We are—well, mostly—a study team investigating a crucial point in history . . . your lifetime, in fact, excellent sir."

"Four centuries in which future?" Padway said. "Gothic Rome, or my original twentieth? Twentieth century A.D.," he went on, to their growing bewilderment.

There was a long moment of silence. Padway broke it. "You mean, you didn't *know*?" he said.

The argument started up again, fast enough that

Padway caught snatches of the language it was actually in, rather than the who-knew-how translation. His mind identified it as a Romance-derived language; something like twentieth-century Italian, but more archaic, and with a lot of Germanic loan words and other vocabulary he couldn't identify.

A slow, enormous grin split the ancient American's face. "Fifty years," he murmured.

Fifty years of politics and administration and warfare and engineering. None of them his chosen profession, just the things he had to do to survive and keep the darkness from falling. If this bunch were from only four centuries ahead in the future *Padway* had made, he'd done that, with a vengence; they were from the date that in Padway's original history had seen the height of the Vikings.

He'd kept the darkness at bay, and now . . . now he could go back to being a research specialist. The grin grew wider.

Better than that, he'd actually get to *know how things turned out*! Making history was all very well, but he'd always wanted to read it more.

The Deadly Mission of P. Snodgrass

Frederik Pohl

THIS IS THE STORY OF Phineas Snodgrass, inventor.
He built a time machine.

He built a time machine and in it he went back
some two thousand years, to about the time of the birth
of Christ. He made himself known to the Emperor
Augustus, his lady Livia and other rich and powerful Romans of the day and, quickly making friends,
secured their cooperation in bringing about a rapid
transformation of Year One living habits. (He stole

the idea from a science-fiction novel by L. Sprague de Camp, called *Lest Darkness Fall*.)

His time machine wasn't very big, but his heart was, so Snodgrass selected his cargo with the plan of providing the maximum immediate help for the world's people. The principal features of ancient Rome were dirt and disease, pain and death. Snodgrass decided to make the Roman world healthy and to keep its people alive through twentieth-century medicine. Everything else could take care of itself, once the human race was free of its terrible plagues and early deaths.

Snodgrass introduced penicillin and aureomycin and painless dentistry. He ground lenses for spectacles and explained the surgical techniques for removing cataracts. He taught anesthesia and the germ theory of disease, and showed how to purify drinking water. He built Kleenex factories and taught the Romans to cover their mouths when they coughed. He demanded, and got, covers for the open Roman sewers, and he pioneered the practice of the balanced diet.

Snodgrass brought health to the ancient world, and kept his own health, too. He lived to more than a hundred years. He died, in fact, in the year A.D. 100, a very contented man.

When Snodgrass arrived in Augustus' great palace on the Palatine Hill, there were some 250,000,000 human beings alive in the world. He persuaded the principate to share his blessings with all the world, benefiting not only the hundred million subjects of the Empire, but the other hundred millions in Asia and the tens of millions in Africa, the Western Hemisphere, and all the Pacific islands.

Everybody got healthy.

Infant mortality dropped at once, from ninety deaths in a hundred to fewer than two. Life expectancies doubled immediately. Everyone was well, and demonstrated their health by having more children, who grew in health to maturity and had more.

It is a feeble population that cannot double itself every generation if it tries.

These Romans, Goths and Mongols were tough. Every thirty years the population of the world increased by a factor of two. In the year A.D. 30, the world population was a half-billion. In A.D. 60, it was a full billion. By the time Snodgrass passed away, a happy man, it was as large as it is today.

It is too bad that Snodgrass did not have room in his time machine for the blueprints of cargo ships, the texts on metallurgy to build the tools that would make the reapers that would harvest the fields—for the triple-expansion steam turbines that would generate the electricity that would power the machines that would run the cities—for all the technology that two thousand subsequent years had brought about.

But he didn't.

Consequently by the time of his death conditions were no longer quite perfect. A great many people were badly housed.

On the whole, Snodgrass was pleased, for all these things could surely take care of themselves. With a healthy world population, the increase in numbers would be a mere spur to research. Boundless nature, once its ways were studied, would surely provide for any number of human beings.

Indeed it did. Steam engines on the Newcomen

design were lifting water to irrigate fields to grow food long before his death. The Nile was dammed at Aswan in the year 55.

Battery-powered street cars replaced oxcarts in Rome and Alexandria before A.D. 75, and the galley slaves were freed by huge, clumsy diesel outboards that drove the food ships across the Mediterranean a few years later.

In the year A.D. 200 the world had now something over twenty billion souls, and technology was running neck-and-neck with expansion. Nuclear-driven ploughs had cleared the Teutoberg Wald, where Varus' bones were still mouldering, and fertilizer made from ion-exchange mining of the sea produced fantastic crops of hybrid grains. In A.D. 300 the world population stood at a quarter of a trillion. Hydrogen fusion produced fabulous quantities of energy from the sea; atomic transmutation converted any matter into food. This was necessary, because there was no longer any room for farms. The Earth was getting crowded. By the middle of the sixth century the 60,000,000 square miles of land surface on the Earth was so well covered that no human being standing anywhere on dry land could stretch out his arms in any direction without touching another human being standing beside him.

But everyone was healthy, and science marched on. The seas were drained, which immediately tripled the available land area. (In fifty years the sea bottoms were also full.) Energy which had come from the fusion of marine hydrogen now came by tapping the full energy output of the Sun, through gigantic "mirrors" composed of pure force. The other planets froze, of course, but this no longer mattered, since in the decades that followed they were disintegrated for the sake of the energy at their cores. So was the Sun. Maintaining life on Earth on such artificial standards was prodigal of energy consumption; in time every star in the Galaxy was transmitting its total power output to the Earth, and plans were afoot to tap Andromeda, which would care for all necessary expansion for—thirty years.

At this point a calculation was made.

Taking the weight of the average man at about a hundred and thirty pounds—in round numbers, 6×10^4 grammes—and allowing for a continued doubling of population every thirty years (although there was no such thing as a "year" any more, since the Sun had been disintegrated; now a lonely Earth floated aimlessly towards Vega), it was discovered that by the early part of the twenty-first century the total mass of human flesh, bone and blood would be 6×10^{27} grams.

This presented a problem. The total mass of the Earth itself was only 5.98×10^{27} grams. Already humanity lived in burrows penetrating crust and basalt and quarrying into the congealed nickel-iron core; by the twenty-first century all the core itself would have been transmuted into living men and women, and their galleries would have to be tunneled through masses of their own bodies, a writhing, squeezed ball of living corpses drifting through space.

Moreover simple arithmetic showed that this was not the end. In finite time the mass of human beings would equal the total mass of the Galaxy; and in some further time it would equal and exceed the total mass of *all* galaxies everywhere.

This state of affairs could no longer be tolerated, and so a project was launched.

With some difficulty resources were diverted to permit the construction of a small but important device. It was a time machine. With one volunteer aboard (selected from the nine hundred trillion who applied) it went back to the year 1. Its cargo was only a hunting rifle with one cartridge, and with that cartridge the volunteer assassinated Snodgrass as he trudged up the Palatine.

To the great (if only potential) joy of some quintillions of never-to-be-born persons, Darkness blessedly fell.

The Garden Gnome Freedom Front

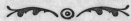

Laura Frankos

ANYONE NOTICING THE THREE YOUNG women dining in the café in the Norman village of Saint-Clément would have assumed they were students from the nearby university at Rouen. They *were* students, but they were also commandos in a secret organization devoted to freeing an oppressed people.

"Are all our esteemed members present?" asked Alizon Riand.

Raquel Guibert snorted. "Given that there are only

three of us, that should be obvious. Becca, put away the sketchbook and pay attention."

Becca Milleron lifted her curly head from her work. "Are we ready? I'm nearly finished." She scrutinized her drawing—a dragon with a perplexed expression somewhat like the artist's—and bent to add some cross-hatching.

Alizon tapped on a glass with her fork, causing Becca to stop. "Ahem. I hereby call this month's meeting of the Garden Gnome Freedom Front to order. Raquel, do you want to give your report first?"

"Sure. Our rivals in Torgon have struck again, no doubt jealous of our successes this summer. They seized a dozen gnomes, along with their wheelbarrows, windmills, hedgehogs, and deer. A week later, the gnomes reappeared in the town square."

Alizon's long slender hands gripped the edge of the table. "I'm braced. What did they look like this time?"

"It's truly depraved. They had been repainted so it looked like they were wearing pinstriped business suits. One poor gnome even had a briefcase. The wheelbarrows were flipped over and painted beige to look like computers. Thank heavens they didn't turn the hedgehogs into computer mice—something Cinderella's godmother never dreamed of."

"Wheelbarrow computers?" asked Becca, trying to envision the scene. "But what about the wheels? Wouldn't they stick up and spoil the effect?"

"The ceramic wheelbarrow did look dreadful. But two of them were plastic wheelbarrows, so they simply removed the axles. They even stuck squares of clear plastic on them to mimic monitors."

Alizon shook her head. "Plastic wheelbarrows! How tacky. One could almost applaud our rivals' actions. After all, they claim they are defending France from kitsch."

"Taking the gnomes from their gardens and inserting them in the corporate world is *not* improving their situation," said Raquel. "Pinstripes and briefcases! Ours is a much more noble purpose."

"To free the gnomes from the tyranny of human owners and return them to their native woodland home!" cried Becca.

"Huzzah!" all three cheered, then broke into laughter. The waiter hardly gave them a glance; they were regulars at the nearly deserted café.

In the nineties, many organizations devoted to garden gnomes sprang up in France, rather like mushrooms. A few were meant for aficionados of the ceramic figures, of which there were at least 100 million worldwide. Others, like the rivals in the nearby town of Torgon, snatched gnomes and set them in absurd displays as a protest against tacky art. Still other groups, of a more violent terroristic nature, smashed gnomes to bits. The Garden Gnome Freedom Front had its own specific objectives. Its handbook included sections on the Origins of Gnomes and Their Destiny, the Uselessness of Accessories (including wheelbarrows and deer), Distinguishing Characteristics of Gnomes, and, most important, their treatise, Why Support Gnomish Independence?

The G.G.F.F. had begun as a joke a year before, in 1995, when the three friends contributed to a science fiction fanzine. Alizon, who was majoring in history, and Raquel, whose specialty was folklore, concocted silly ideas for the text. Becca, the artist, illustrated each section. It won them notoriety in the French science fiction community, and Becca got an award for fan art at a convention when she displayed the handbook's cover painting.

None of them could remember who first suggested making their fictional organization a reality. It was in spring, when they were celebrating the end of examinations with a bit too much wine. Their flat looked over the oldest section of Saint-Clément, filled with small cottages, quaint gardens . . . and gnomes. One minute they were drinking a fine Bordeaux, the next they were scrambling over stone walls, absconding with bearded ceramic figures. Alizon declared that the best place for the rescued gnomes was a woodland glade. An avid bird watcher, she knew the right spot, some two miles outside the town. Even with her expert guidance, getting there in the dark was hard. Tromping through bracken eradicated the effects of the wine, but the exhilaration returned when they placed the newly independent gnomes in a fairy ring of mushrooms.

They struck two more blows for gnomish liberty over the summer, and on this balmy September day had gathered to plan another mission.

"Next on our agenda: local gnomish doings," Alizon announced after their giggling subsided. "I've spotted two new houses with gnomes in the gardens, on rue Michelet and rue Maréchal-Foch. The benefits of being a bird watcher: nobody knows I'm doing surveillance for our cause with my binoculars."

Raquel and Becca exchanged looks. "You can't fool us," Raquel said at last. "You were out watching birds and accidentally spotted some gnomes."

"Well, what if I did? I saw two green woodpeckers, a kingfisher, six chaffinches, and four gnomes. Not bad for a half hour's stroll."

"Yes, but were there any dogs in those gardens?" asked Becca. "That Hound of the Baskervilles nearly ate me last month. If it came any closer, I was going to pitch the gnome at it, and say the hell with our cause."

"No dogs, and the families are on vacation," assured Alizon.

"Good. Now here's my news," said Becca. "I've got the early edition of the *Saint-Clément Chronicle*. My cousin's a reporter and gave it to me because he remembered my gnome painting. He thought I'd be amused. Lord, it was hard keeping a straight face. Poor Claude has no idea I'm behind this 'evil plot.'" She produced the newspaper, which featured an article and an editorial about the Front's raids. "Our successes are starting to work against us."

"You're right," said Alizon. "It says some people are taking their gnomes inside at night. No wonder they've been harder to spot lately."

"And it says a hiker found the first ring of gnomes we liberated, and that two have been reclaimed by their owners. All that work for nothing," said Raquel.

Becca said, "Well, they've had a taste of freedom. We'll just have to rescue them again. But I'm warning you: if the gnome from that house with the wolfhound ever returns to his garden, he's staying there."

They fell to preparing the next attack.

The nighttime raids of the Garden Gnome Freedom Front were difficult undertakings. Scrambling through unfamiliar gardens in search of gnomes resulted in ripped clothes and skinned knees. The night of September 26th offered them a full moon, which would make it easier to see where they were going, especially when they entered the woods in the wee small hours, but it also made them more visible. Alizon wanted to wait for a darker night, but the others disagreed. "When there's more moonlight, we can see if the yards are safe," Becca said.

"And where we're walking," Raquel said. "Not all of us are skilled woodland wanderers, Fearless Leader."

Alizon just grinned and handed out the assignments. Raquel and Becca were to free two gnomes apiece, and Alizon, three. Raquel had insisted on seven as the target number. "It's a significant number throughout folklore," she observed.

"Not only that, but seven freed gnomes look splendid in a fairy ring," said Alizon. "More would look crowded; less, not enough."

After emancipating the gnomes, they planned to meet on the western edge of the town. For once, everything went smoothly. No dogs, no sharp-edged gates, no unexpected mud puddles, no sudden shouts from outraged gnome owners. The streets of Saint-Clément were empty and silent. Alizon was the last to arrive, lugging a totebag. "I found one of the ugliest little bastards ever made at the house of that retired American businessman." Her flashlight shone on a gnome holding an oversized lavender watering can. He wore black and yellow checked breeches, an olive green shirt, and his hat wasn't the traditional red, but pinkish.

"He's got a good face," Becca said. "Just a crummy wardrobe."

"Pack up Ugly Togs and let's go," said Raquel. "The sooner we're away from the town, the better."

After nearly an hour's walking, Becca complained, "How much farther, Alizon? I'm exhausted."

"Another three kilometers. I'm sorry it's so far, but it's the absolute best place yet. Any gnome would be honored to celebrate his liberty in it. Hey, listen! That's a tawny owl calling."

Raquel stumbled over a tree root and swore. "For God's sake, it's just a bird, Alizon!"

"If your folklore professors heard you talking like that, they'd drum you out of the program," said Alizon. "Don't owls foretell dire omens and such?"

"That particular owl foretells that I won't go to bed for hours," Becca said dryly.

Eventually, they crossed a weathered footbridge and climbed a low rise. Alizon led the way through a dense grove of birches, ghostly white in the moonlight. A haphazard array of huge stone columns suddenly rose before them. Only one remained upright; the rest had toppled, with shrubs surrounding them like blankets wrapped around sleeping toddlers. Water softly gurgled from a nearby spring.

"A bunch of big rocks in the middle of the forest?" Becca asked. "This is your great surprise?"

Raquel caught on. "This must have been one of the druids' sacred groves! Oh, that's cool, Alizon. It's worth the blisters."

"Druids? Like Panoramix in the Asterix comics?" asked Becca. "Are these menhirs?"

"They're properly called *stelae*," Alizon said. "They

date to the Iron Age, but scholars think later generations of druids used them for religious purposes. This
ring is mentioned in a few books, but nobody's ever
excavated here."

"I imagine if you've seen one menhir, you've seen
them all," said Becca.

"Obelix would disagree with you," Alizon teased.

By the glow of their flashlights, the trio began
removing gnomes from their bags. Ugly Togs came
first, followed by his companion, a pudgy, bushy-
bearded gnome with a book tucked under one arm.
Alizon's third rescuee was a complete contrast to the
first one: a freshly painted gnome with red hat, brown
apron, and a shovel. "A classic, and in outstanding
condition. Even his pupils shine. I had the feeling
he was watching me when I nabbed him."

Raquel's pair included a poorly made gnome in
a belted blue jacket and a female gnome wearing
a white apron and carrying a bowl of fruit. Becca
produced a squatting fellow with a chip missing from
one shoulder and a hatchet resting on the other, and
a rosy-cheeked gnome, clad mostly in yellow, holding
a lantern. Alizon exclaimed when the last one came to
light. "I liberated him on our first raid! He must have
been one of the pair mentioned in the article."

"Are you sure?" asked Becca. "We were all potted
that night."

"I remember his lantern. There were two deer and
red ceramic mushrooms in the garden, right? The
mushrooms had spots."

"You never forget a detail." Becca lifted the gnome
up high. "Hey, little guy! You're free again. Wonder
what you think of that?"

"I'm certain they're very happy," said Raquel, walking to the center of the ring with the female gnome tucked under her arm. "Ladies first." She set the gnome down in the patch of bare soil Alizon had cleared on an earlier trek.

They arranged the gnomes in a circle, Becca straightening them until they were evenly spaced. "They look charming," said Alizon. "It's nice to think of them standing where the ancient druids once practiced their magic."

"It's the moonlight," said Becca.

Raquel was staring at the sky. She took off her glasses and wiped them on her shirt. "Is it my bad eyes, or does the moon look funny around the edge?"

"Oh, I forgot!" said Alizon. "There's an eclipse tonight. The weather's so clear, we should be able to see it perfectly. Damn, I wish I brought my binoculars."

"Can't we just go home?" asked Becca.

Raquel climbed a menhir and yanked off her shoe. "There's no point going home until after the eclipse. That lovely moonlight is disappearing, and I, for one, have no desire to crash through the forest in utter darkness."

A crestfallen Becca joined Raquel on the fallen menhir. "Oh, well. How long do these things last?"

"A big chunk's gone already," said Alizon. "Totality could last about an hour."

Becca groaned.

"Could be worse," Raquel said, rubbing her foot. "We've got a dry place to sit, and I brought a snack." From her backpack, she produced a slightly squashed baguette, a thermos, some Camembert, bananas, and chocolate bars. "I am always prepared, even in the middle of a forest."

"Huzzah!" cheered Becca, falling on the food.

The beauty of the phenomenon, the natural surroundings, the circle of their liberated gnomes, and especially the thermos of hot *café recoiffé*—coffee liberally spiked with Calvados—greatly improved everyone's moods. "You know, this is actually helpful," Becca said. "If I ever paint an eclipse, I'll know how the light looks and how the moon gradually disappears."

"Ah, this is research for you," Raquel said. "The only folklore I know about eclipses says that they are associated with magic and witchcraft. A hooting owl, an eclipse . . . We're doomed."

"Nonsense," Alizon said. "The spirits of the Celtic Druids are watching over us. They were obsessed with celestial movements, so they'd love a juicy lunar eclipse like this. Look, it's nearly gone."

"Amazing," Becca whispered as the moon vanished from sight. "I really am thankful we're here."

"We are most grateful, too," said a gruff voice behind them.

The three women whirled around, but saw no one. Then Alizon's sharp eyes caught some movement near the edge of the stone circle, close to the ground. *A hedgehog,* she thought. *Perhaps a badger.* Then she realized she couldn't see the gnomes any longer. Something grunted at the base of their menhir.

Raquel directed her flashlight at the noise. Seven gnomes blinked at them. The one in the center, the gnome with the checkered breeches, bowed, his hand over his waist. His partner, the rotund fellow with the book, doffed his hat, and the girl gnome curtsied. The others pleasantly nodded.

"How much Calvados did you put in that coffee?" Becca asked in a tiny voice.

Raquel didn't answer, but swept the flashlight over to the empty clearing, then back at the small figures directly below them. They squinted. The blue-garbed gnome threw up his walking stick to ward off the beam and cowered. The other six were smiling, but he looked as blue as his buttoned jacket.

"Please do not shine that in our faces," said the spiffy gnome with the shovel. His French was flawless, but for a faint German accent. "We see very well at night."

"Hans! Let me pass! After all, only I, Anton of der Lamp, haf been rescued by them twice," the one in the yellow shirt said in a thicker accent. "If you haf matches, my lantern ist more gentle to the eyes."

The blue one moaned something that wasn't German *or* French. Handsome Hans said, "Hush, Vaclav," and patted him on the back.

The young women looked at one another. "This is no dream," said Alizon, trying to sound convincing. "I just pinched myself."

"But how?" Raquel's voice trailed off.

The fat gnome pointed skyward. "Dear ladies, like most denizens of Faerie—and many such are abroad tonight—we are subject to the powers of the moon. Indeed, every month, on the night the moon reaches its ripest, we come to life, albeit briefly, in your gardens. Sadly, we revert to these absurd poses at moonset." He adopted his original form: thick book lodged under his arm, one hand resting on his brown belt. "But this is a place of ancient magics, and it too is governed by the moon. Had you taken us elsewhere—"

"Such as der glade vere you placed me last spring," interjected Anton of the Lamp.

"—our period of animation would have been as brief as its usual monthly course. This sequence, however, has resulted in a permanent effect," concluded the pudgy gnome. He gave Anton a sour look for interrupting his lecture.

"Professor Gottfried talks too much, as usual," growled the old gnome with the dinged shoulder. "Though how you can hear anything through that thatch of fuzz amazes me. What he's trying to say is, we're alive, and for keeps. Many thanks to you ladies from Old Otto." He too removed his hat, revealing a bald scalp with a fringe of white hair.

"You're truly alive?" Becca asked, drawing her feet up. Old Otto seemed charming, but his hatchet looked nastily sharp.

The girl gnome giggled. "As alive as you, dearie. I am Gretchen, at your service. Care for some fruit? I hope I never see another apple or bunch of grapes in all my days." She hoisted her bowl to the young women. Somehow the solid heft of the bowl and the juiciness of the apple convinced Alizon of the reality of the scene more than the talking, laughing gnomes did. From the slow, thoughtful way Becca and Raquel nibbled on grapes, Alizon could tell they felt the same. She slid off the menhir to stand beside the gnomes. A few moments later, her friends joined her. The gnomes rushed up to shake their hands. Their small fingers were warm and soft, not cold, hard ceramic.

Gretchen poked Ugly Togs in the belly. "No more watering can, eh, Karl?"

"Wretched thing!" Karl savagely kicked the lavender can. His boot connected with a metallic *thunk* and it sailed into the brush. Something chittered angrily in response, causing Vaclav, the blue gnome, to start whimpering again.

"Do not anger the *fées*!" Professor Gottfried exclaimed.

"My apologies, small ones," Karl called. "Stupid little gits," he added in a low voice. The bushes parted, and five tiny humanoid figures emerged, carrying baskets of linens. One grimaced at Karl. They walked to the edge of the spring and began washing the clothes.

"I know where the gnomes came from," Becca said, "but *what are those*?"

"The *fées*," Raquel said. "A kind of fairy. Legend has it they do their laundry in springs and . . . hang it on druidic stones to dry." Which was exactly what the *fées* were doing. How many other folk legends were based on reality? She racked her brain for anything else she could remember about *fées*. "Don't go dancing with them or leave a newborn child where they can get it."

"You can see them?" The Professor asked, his voice sharp with surprise.

"As well as I can see you," Alizon said. "It's strange, but I can see you more clearly than I could a few minutes ago, though the eclipse is still total."

Gottfried scratched his beard. "Odd. You *should* be able to see us, as you brought about, however unwittingly, the magic that gave us life. But the *fées* . . ."

"Fairy fruit!" Raquel gasped. She stared at Gretchen's

bowl in horror. "What have we done to ourselves? Must we live in Faerie for eternity? Are we cursed?"

The female gnome drew herself up to her full height of two feet. "Certainly not! My fruit is of the highest quality, and very healthful. It's no doubt improved your eyesight. You can probably see all manner of things, if you only look in the right way."

"Cool!" Alizon muttered, glancing around. *There* was that tawny owl, in that oak, and *there*, a barn owl, its white feathers blending in with the birches. How could she have missed them before? Becca, too, was looking around as if seeing things in a new light, though the woods were still quite dark.

Raquel removed her glasses, put them back on, then removed them again. She didn't need them, and she could see much better than she should have been able to in the darkness. "Is it permanent?" Her earlier outburst embarrassed her, but a lifetime of reading about the dire consequences of eating fairy fruit no doubt conditioned her.

The gnomes—excepting mournful Vaclav, who was wringing his hat—didn't know. Handsome Hans said, "Forgive our ignorance, but none of us have ever shared a meal with humans before."

"Speaking of meals," said Anton, *"Ich habe Hunger, und hier ist nichts* to eat, excepting roots *und* bugs."

"I'm famished, too," said Karl. "I'm as empty as Vatsy's head."

"Jà chci jìt domu!" Vaclav moaned.

"What's he saying? Why doesn't he speak French?" asked Becca.

Old Otto grunted. "He was born in Prague, that's

why. The rest of us are from Germany. Just look at him! Shoddy Czech workmanship."

Gretchen put her arm around Vaclav. "Be nice, Otto. He can't help being cracked. He says he wants to go home." She murmured in Czech, and Vaclav nodded and sniffled. "I speak his tongue; my husband was a Czech gnome, and Vatsy lived next door. Jiri, who unfortunately got dropped on the paving last year, wasn't as thick-headed as Vaclav. He learned French the way most of us do, spending years listening to the humans. Most of us are good at languages. Gottfried and Karl even learned English and Spanish in Miami. Anton's our most recent immigrant, which explains his dreadful accent." Anton, ever irrepressible, waggled his fingers in his ears and stuck out his tongue.

Alizon pondered the matter. "Do you consider yourselves German?"

"Only by birth," said Professor Gottfried. "We are naturalized French gnomes."

Old Otto shouted, "I'm no German! You see this?" He pointed to his chipped shoulder. "A damned Nazi did this."

"Otto, they don't want to hear about your old war wound," said Handsome Hans. "I believe Mademoiselle Raquel still has food in her sack. Perhaps she will share with some hungry gnomes?"

Raquel hurriedly opened her backpack, and the gnomes, even Vaclav, devoured the remains of her snack. Anton lit his lantern with a match. While the gnomes ate, Raquel edged close to her friends. "What are we going to do with them?" she whispered.

"Beats me," Becca hissed back. "Have them invade

the office of the *Chronicle* and demand a retraction of their editorial? Sic them on my ex-boyfriend?"

"Let's ask them what they want," Alizon said, direct as always. "O gnomes, now that you are alive and free, what do you want to do?"

"*Jà chci jìt domu!*"

"Well, we know what Vaclav wants," said Raquel. She got down on her knees and handed him a tissue. "If you want to go back home, we'll take you." He trumpeted noisily and looked at her gratefully.

"He's too dim to appreciate freedom," Gretchen said. "Besides, his human, Madame d'Aulnoy, fusses over him. He gets mugs of ale, dishes of cream, and tasty tidbits, though he can only enjoy them once a month. She even sings to him."

"She's as great a cabbagehead as Vatsy," Karl snickered.

Handsome Hans brushed crumbs from his immaculate pants. "There are owners and owners. My Georges is a fine chap. He paints me every winter and washes me every day. His garden is the finest in the village, and he talks to me while he tends it."

Karl planted his pudgy form in front of Hans. Karl's tacky appearance was improved after jettisoning his lavender watering can, but any gnome would have looked dingy next to the pristine Hans. "You want to go back?"

"*Jà chci jìt domu!*"

Hans blushed until his cheeks were nearly as rosy as Anton's. "No disrespect meant, ladies. I value your effort; and I'll enjoy being alive. But Georges is old. Every solstice, when he returns me to his beautiful garden, he says, 'So, Hans, we live to see yet another spring.' Then he sits there, on an oak bench, right by me, and drinks a glass of cognac. He spends the whole winter looking forward to that. I couldn't disappoint him. Perhaps, after he dies, I'll take advantage of my altered state and travel the great sites of gnomish history or make the pilgrimage to the Black Forest."

"You vant to stay?" howled Anton. He rolled on the ground beside Karl, kicking his feet in the air. "*Sind Sie verrückt?* To spend your days stuck in a garten, mit die Vogel shitting on you und snails leaving tracks of slime on your boots? All for some human?"

"What if I do?"

Anton jerked a thumb at Vaclav. "You're as bad as him!"

"Worse," Karl sneered. "He's like a slob of a brownie, endlessly slaving for humans."

"Who you callin' a brownie?" Hans raised his shovel as if to strike. Karl snatched Vaclav's stick in defense. Anton put up his fists, daring Hans to come on.

Alizon hastily intervened before they came to blows. "Wait! We didn't work this magic to have it end in violence. You're all free and independent gnomes now. If Hans and Vaclav want to go back to their garden, that's their right."

"*Jà chci jìt domu!*"

"And the rest of you?" asked Becca. "Do you also want to return?"

"*Himmel*, no!" shouted Anton. "I've escaped it twice. I vant to get as far from that cold, muddy hellhole as possible."

Professor Gottfried had been picking over crumbs while the others quarreled. Now he looked up. "Perhaps you would care to come to America with me and Karl.

That's our fondest dream: to return to Florida to help others sorely in need. Such a lovely, sunny spot."

Anton asked, "Sunny?"

"The average annual temperature in Miami is twenty-four point four degrees," the Professor mumbled through his whiskers. "Americans say seventy-six degrees Fahrenheit."

"I'm your gnome! Let's go!" Anton capered around his lantern, making weird shadows and startling the industrious *fées* from their laundry.

Becca broke into a fit of coughing as tanned gnomes in Ray-bans and Bermuda shorts came to mind.

Raquel said, a trifle nervously, "We're poor students. Air fare to America is beyond our means, unless you have fairy gold somewhere." She was only half-joking. If gnomes and *fées* were real, and fairy fruit somehow magically altered one's perception, what about legends of lost treasures?

But she was disappointed. "How could we gather treasure, dearie?" said Gretchen. "Until now, we've been limited to roaming Saint-Clément one night a month. Hardly enough exercise to keep one's figure, even dining on the best fruit."

The Professor flicked through his book and began discoursing about his dwarvish cousins in the Alps, but Karl squelched his lecture. "We'll find a way, ladies. Gottfried and I have big plans."

"Perhaps we could make plans for more food?" asked Gretchen. "I hate to admit it after all the ladies' kindness, but I'm still hungry."

The other gnomes eagerly seconded this, and the G.G.F.F. couldn't refuse. Who knew what could happen if the gnomes took offense? They trekked home, carrying the stubby-legged gnomes again, since their pace was half that of the humans.

Once back in the flat, the gnomes devoured a gigantic omelette and all the baked goods in the pantry, even stale crackers. They had appetites worthy of beings three times their size. They also insisted Raquel make some more *café recoiffé*, as there had only been a swallow left in the thermos. Nor did they want her to be stingy with the Calvados. Even Vaclav loosened up after a few cups and smiled crookedly.

Old Otto smacked his lips. "Ah! That banishes the chill from my aged bones."

"So come to sunny Florida mit us," Anton said. "Varm as toast!"

Alizon leaned forward. "Yes, what will you do, Otto? You've been here the longest. Will you stay, or find a new home?"

The elderly gnome's bushy eyebrows shot up. "For you to understand my desires, I must tell you a little story."

Some of his companions reacted with dismay. "*Little?*" Karl asked in disbelief, while Anton buried himself under the sofa cushions.

"If I had a franc for every time I've heard this . . ." Hans said.

Gretchen patted Hans' knee. "Be kind. I'm sure our benefactresses will enjoy hearing Otto." The humans nodded, and Otto, after another long swig, began.

"I was born in 1905, and have lived with many different families over the years. I saw my first home overrun during the Great War, and my owner and his son cut down before my eyes. I vowed if it ever were in my power, I wouldn't let such a thing happen again."

Gottfried clucked at this, but subsided after Otto glared at him.

"When the next war erupted, I lived some distance west of here. On the night of July 5, 1944, the moon was full, and every gnome alive knew there was trouble afoot. We could see the American patrols sneaking through our gardens and streets, just as you did tonight. We could see the Nazis, too. There was a sniper in my human's potting shed. I knew he was waiting for the Americans to come around the garden wall, so just before they did, I leaped off the wall, drawing his fire. He winged me, but gave away his position. The Americans killed him."

Professor Gottfried exploded. "This was a terrible breach of Faerie etiquette! There are *rules* governing our conduct with humans, and meddling such as Otto's is strictly forbidden!"

"Do you think the Nazis played by the rules?" Otto retorted. "Besides, who says they were human? I've met demons I liked better. I could have done worse; I wanted to cut that bastard's throat with my hatchet. Could have done it. They would have blamed it on the Resistance." Gottfried looked appalled at that notion, his mouth a tiny red *O* in his chubby face.

"What happened then?" asked Alizon, wondering if any other Faerie folk assisted in the Normandy invasion. *Talk about rewriting the history books . . .*

"The patrol commander, a huge blond named Sgt. Sven Faelling, returned to our house after the Americans had taken the village. He said, in atrocious French, 'Madame, your gnome saved our lives.' He believed I had accidentally tumbled off the wall, startling the sniper into firing too soon. Madame tried giving me to the sergeant, but Faelling refused, saying he had more fighting ahead. But he scratched his name on my boot, so he could claim me again someday, if he lived. See?" He held up his foot and the women could see the name carved into the sole. "Now that I am able, I will go to America and find him."

"It's been fifty-two years, Otto," said Raquel. "He's probably dead."

Otto shook his grizzled head. "I'd know it. You see, I forestalled Death's taking him once before. If I can, I should be there when Death returns. It's only fitting."

"I bet we'll find Sgt. Faelling on the Internet, if you know his regiment," said Becca.

"I do. What is this Internet?" asked Otto.

Alizon chuckled. "A treasury of information, much of it useless, but some valuable."

"Like Gottfried's book," Karl said with a sly look at his companion. The Professor harrumphed.

Raquel surveyed the seven gnomes sprawled about the room. "So that's two gnomes staying, and four going to America. What about you, Gretchen?"

The female gnome demurely studied her white apron and spoke without looking up. "My fondest wish is not to be parted from the best, the handsomest gnome in all Saint-Clément."

Hans visibly preened, only to deflate as Gretchen turned to Karl, who was rubbing at a chocolate stain on his breeches. "Karl, dear, may I aid your quest?"

Karl turned as pink as his untraditional hat. "I thought you'd never look at another gnome after Jiri's tragic accident!"

"A girl gets lonely," Gretchen said, sounding rather

like a gnomish Mae West. They romantically stared into each other's eyes as Anton made smacking noises and Vaclav muttered something Czech that definitely wasn't *Jà chci jìt domu*.

Raquel whispered to Becca, "There's one girl gnome for every thirty boy gnomes in town. She could have her pick of them. She wants Ugly Togs?"

"No accounting for taste. *You* used to date Emil Dubois."

"For two weeks!"

"It's late," Alizon hastily said. "Let's get some sleep."

The gnomes grimaced. "When you're frozen in place for days on end, you do plenty of dozing," said Otto. "We'll stay up."

"And Vaclav and I will go home," said Hans, "so our humans won't worry."

Karl started to say something rude, but Gretchen murmured, "Mind your manners, love." Alizon suspected boisterous Karl would soon be hearing a lot of that.

Hans and Vaclav made their farewells. The handsome gnome promised the humans he'd visit often, and Vaclav sniveled over everyone. After they'd left, the women staggered into bed. None of them believed they would sleep, but they did.

"Trink, trink, Brüderlein, trink!" Raquel rolled over and looked at the clock, which read ten past eight. Too damn early any day, much less one after a wild night like the last, dreaming about live gnomes singing German drinking songs . . . And how could she see the clock so clearly without her glasses? Something about Faerie-sight . . .

Her mental fog lifted as she heard Becca silencing the singers. "Quiet!" she hissed. "Do you want our landlady to hear this gnomish revelry?"

"Or Denis. God, what will Denis think?" Alizon asked, thinking of the hunky student who lived across the hall. "The whole building must have heard that yodeling."

Raquel stumbled into the front room. It was full of gnomes and empty bottles—the quintet had discovered the liquor cabinet. "Everyone will think we're having orgies," Raquel said. "Drunken orgies. With a bunch of *really* short older men."

"Sorry to disturb you," Anton hiccuped. "Ve vanted to celebrate."

"You must keep quiet," Becca said. "We could get in trouble if anyone finds you. It wouldn't be easy explaining five living, breathing, *singing* gnomes."

Otto adopted his squatting pose with his hatchet on his shoulder. "We're quite good at hiding, but if caught, we freeze, the way we do on the nights of the full moon. No one without Faerie-sight could know we were truly alive."

"But if your owners found you, they'd arrest us for theft," said Alizon.

The gnomes grudgingly accepted the need for silence while the women attended their classes and went shopping. The gnomes wanted more baked goods and beer, the darker the better.

The women had trouble paying attention to their lectures that day, each of them fretting about what the gnomes might do in their absence. Returning to the flat that afternoon, they were relieved not to see police cars or television news vans on their street. Nor had they heard anything in the market about stolen gnomes or Little People wandering through the town in the night. They'd peeked in Madame d'Aulnoy's garden, where Vaclav winked at them, and spotted an old man weeding in Hans' garden, not far from the splendid gnome.

They hardly recognized the flat when they opened the door. It probably hadn't been that clean right after it was built. Gretchen, Karl, Gottfried, Anton, and Otto stood at attention as they entered, their sleeves rolled up and their hands reddened, as if they'd been scrubbing all day. The floor sparkled. Laundry had been picked up, washed, and put away. The myriad stacks of papers and books had been straightened. Even the ancient faucet fixtures gleamed—and no longer dripped.

"Wow!" Becca breathed. "It's gorgeous! You could give it the white glove test."

"We wanted to atone for our earlier inebriation," Professor Gottfried said, "and decided this was the best way. Though not all of us agreed at first."

"Brownie work," Karl muttered. "I'm nobody's slave, you know."

Otto shook a finger at him. "Nothing in the rules says a gnome can't show gratitude by doing a spot of cleaning or bringing a bit of good luck to a human. And speaking of luck, did you ladies find Sgt. Faelling for me?"

"He's in a veteran's hospital in California," said Alizon. "We thought we could mail you straight to him, saying we learned the story about the 'Gnome-andy Invasion.'"

"Brilliant notion," Otto said. "Easier than me making

my way there alone. Somehow, I have the feeling I'd better hurry if I want to see him in time."

The women agreed to send Otto by air express after his supper. The gnomes could go months without food, but now that they could eat more than once a month, it was the thing they most enjoyed. After consuming a magnificent dinner prepared by Becca and emptying many bottles of beer, everyone said *adieu* to Old Otto, who nestled himself cozily in a large box, with Raquel's cover letter to Sgt. Faelling tucked by his side. Alizon carried him to the post office, sent him on his way to California, and returned home.

"And then there were four," Raquel said, smiling at the remaining gnomes. "How do you intend to get to Florida?"

"We'll hitch a mail truck to the Paris airport and find a plane for Miami," said Karl. His air of supreme confidence left no room for doubt. "Trust us. Faerie folk are skilled at keeping hidden. How many *fées* had you ever seen before last night? Well, the woods are full of the little buggers, to say nothing of woodland gnomes, elves, White Ladies, and *lutins*."

"What are they?" asked Becca.

"Goblins. Be very polite if you meet one. Address him as *Bon Garçon*," said Raquel.

"They're all in my book, *The Standard History of Gnomes and Their Relatives*," mumbled the Professor. "I shall leave it with you ladies, as a token of my thanks. After all, I doubt I'll have time to write in Florida, freeing an oppressed race!"

Alizon said, "You mentioned this last night. What oppressed race?"

"In the suburbs of Miami, living amid the humans

even as we gnomes do, are poor unfortunates known as the phony copterids."

Alizon wondered what made those copterids different from the real ones. Perhaps the relationship was something like that of the ceramic garden gnomes and their woodland cousins. The name bothered her. It sounded vaguely familiar, but Raquel was the expert on folk legends. She glanced at her friend, but Raquel clearly didn't know what Gottfried was talking about.

The Professor continued: "Their plight is a two-fold tragedy: even on nights of the full moon, they cannot move from their places of imprisonment. They are, I fear, stupider than Vatsy. And their feral cousins lurk in the nearby marshes, calling pitifully to their enchanted fellows. Ah, it rends the heart to hear them!"

Karl said, "So we shall find a place of ancient magics, perhaps one used by the Seminoles, and on the next eclipse, we'll rescue them along with the gnomes in our old neighborhood."

"How noble!" Gretchen gushed. "I can't wait to start!"

Fearing that Miami would be overrun by gnomes and whatever the other Faerie folk were, Becca asked, "They won't hurt people, will they?"

"Not at all," said Karl. "They just want to escape the humans, same as us."

"So let us go now!" said Anton. "Night has fallen, und no one vill spy us. *Vielen Dank*, lovely ladies. As long as Anton's lamp burns, he shall not forget how you saved him twice." The rosy-cheeked gnome bounced over and kissed all three women, as did

Gretchen. Gottfried and Karl shook hands, then all four scrambled out the window. A moment later, they were over the garden wall and gone.

Alizon broke the long silence that followed their exit. "As president, I propose the immediate disbandment of the Garden Gnome Freedom Front. Nor should we go a step from this flat during the next lunar eclipse."

"Second the motion!" Raquel and Becca chorused.

There were undoubtedly benefits from the gnomish rescue. Raquel no longer needed glasses, and the others found their sight improved in unusual ways. They did indeed encounter Faerie folk in the nearby woods, though Raquel lamented she couldn't very well convince her professors they were real. The trio decided to make the best of it: if the world wouldn't believe in the reality of what they knew about Faerie, they'd disguise the truth as fiction. They began work on a fantasy novel, using Gottfried's book as a major reference.

A month after the eclipse, they received a letter from Sgt. Faelling's son in California, thanking them for Otto. "My father was so pleased to see the gnome that saved his patrol," he wrote. "The little fellow sat by Dad's bedside for three weeks, watching over him until he peacefully slipped away. Now the gnome is in Mom's garden, under a palm tree and a hibiscus bush. He looks silly there, but Mom loves him very much."

"So Otto's warming his old bones, too," said Becca. "Wonder how the others are doing in Florida?"

"Keep watching for news of phony copterids after the next American eclipse," laughed Raquel.

Alizon, sitting at the table, dropped her fork with a clatter and ran to her room.

She returned with a book, her hands shaking. "I knew that sounded familiar! The Professor's beard muffled all his words."

"You know what they're doing?" asked Raquel.

Alizon flushed. "*Phoenicopterus ruber*. The greater flamingo. Heaven help the Americans. They've gone to liberate the lawn flamingos of Miami."

The Newcomers

Poul Anderson

EVENING SLOWLY BECAME WARM BLUE dusk. Trees on the south side of the Morokini, pine, river birch, alder, rose in delicate darkling tracery. They had been left standing along the bank, a jut from the woodlands to the west. It ended short of the house, giving an open view across the river itself. Beyond, New Tholis was already a mass of night, roofs, chimneys, watchtower silhouetted, windows aglow with candlelight. The water still sheened beneath the sky, tossing flashes of light where its cascades chuckled and gurgled across rocks, on its way east to the sea.

Lights appeared among the trees, soft, flickery,

iridescent, like mother-of-pearl come alive and aflight. Some of their scores flew out from under the leaves. Two cavorted near enough to the house for a man to see what it was that shone. Less than six inches long, they were almost like humans in miniature, borne on wings almost like a moth's but luminous and larger than themselves. Silver-pale hair flowed down over nude ivory-pale bodies, male and female. They darted and tumbled about one another and laughed for joy.

Suddenly the male streaked close to the veranda. "Hail, Arvel Tarabine! Welcome, stranger!" Though his cry was no louder than a fledgling's peep, high-pitched to the edge of audibility, it sang.

"Which are you?" asked Arvel curtly.

The ellil flitted to and fro. "Fiulo," he trilled. "That's Fiulo the Quick, not Fiulo the Zephyr or Honeysuckle-Fiulo. And yonder, behold Yuna, my love for tonight. Isn't she beautiful? Isn't she delightful? Don't you envy me? May you be half as glad."

He sped back to her. She held out her arms to him. He clasped both her hands. They kissed, let go, and danced off through the air toward the woods.

Arvel shook his grizzled head. "No longer can I tell them apart," he growled. "More and more every year."

"An enchanting sight," said Olavir Cyrac. "Never erenow have I spied so many." He had lately come across Ocean, a younger son of a noble house in Croy, eager to experience the New Lands. From Port Roncitar he had fared up the Morokini, taking hospitality where he found it, repaying with news from the mother cities.

A few centuries-old lines murmured from his lips:

"Love is no lady, but a wench with wings,
Fickle and fleet, the child of wind
  and sky,
Cool as a fall where tumbling water rings,
Brazen as sunlight and, like moonglow,
  shy—"

Cappen Varra had also been a romantic wanderer.

"I fear I can't help you there," said Arvel with a wry grin. "Lasses are in short supply throughout the colonies."

"You offer me aplenty else, sir," replied the visitor.

He had arrived today, leaving his bearers camped outside the town while he crossed the bridge to seek Arvel Tarabine. He had heard what a hoard of tales the old man kept from an adventurous career. Arvel received him well, asking pardon for the absence of his lady wife. She was off at the Vionne plantation to join in the naming rite for their newest-born grandchild. However, their cook set a good board. After dining, the men had gone to the veranda for a brandy and a smoke.

An indentured servant put the refreshment tray on a small table between two chairs. Another hung a lantern from the roof. Its light drowned the frail radiance of the ellils. Wicker creaked as host and guest sat down.

"Fair is all of Dordonia that I have seen," Olavir went on, "yet naught thus far compares with this. Well have you settlers wrought."

Arvel sipped from his goblet. "On the whole, we're

content. It was wilderness when I found it, which cost much toil and some grief in the taming."

Olavir stared. "*You* found it, sir?"

"With a few comrades, whom Sir Falcovan chose to survey these parts. I picked our Irroan guide. I'd been scouting for several years, you see; that was my gainful employ then. I was also spokesman when, having perused our report, the Company sent a party to buy the land from the natives." Arvel sighed. "Utterly unlike now, it was."

"Tanglewood and savage beasts, I imagine."

"Also after we'd cleared and planted. I miss—"

A hoarse, thunderous basso profundo rumbled and coughed from the stream. Olavir well-nigh dropped the pipe he was charging. "What's that?"

Arvel scowled. "A buha. I'd hoped none would come this early in the summer. The hideous noise frightens our fowl and livestock. Moreover, they spoil the fishing. Aforetime we went after 'em in boats, with cold steel, but since losing men to one that attacked, we've gotten us a wizard who drives 'em away. A pretty copper such a spell costs, too." He shrugged. "Well, otherwise he serves as schoolmaster."

"It's a Halfworld creature, then? A water dweller?"

"Aye, but formerly its haunts were in swampy feverlands where few folk have wish to go. The form of a toad, more or less; the size of a bear. Its tongue flies yards from its gape, to snap up any fish or birds that unwittingly pass too near. But it'll devour whatever else it catches. The first buhas here, oh, they feasted on the nuukai, they did. Crouched unseen below a fall—snap, snap, snap!"

"What brought them hither?"

"Earlier, they'd shunned this valley. We learned from the Irroans that they fear the werrows. When a werrow comes down to drink, any buhas thresh off, blind with terror. The Irroans say they can't endure such beauty. Not that this ever happened before, for werrows care no more than do men for those mires and muddy streams. There, I think, the buha's Halfworld prey is bog-wisps." Arvel drained his goblet, refilled it, topped his guest's, and reached into the jar to load his pipe. "At least the brute will soon fall quiet. It's belching the foul vapors from its last feeding."

"Never have I heard of these monsters."

"Nay, for like skunks, they're not of the Old Lands. Much that we found beyond Ocean was strange to us." Arvel grinned. "But we found no elephants or unicorns."

The booming did stop shortly after he dipped a pine splinter into a firepot on the table and ignited his smokeweed. Again the two heard the cascades and, barely, the lilting of the ellis.

"You saw—werrows—in those days agone?" the traveler ventured.

Arvel nodded. His tone turned wistful. "Say rather, in the gloamings and dawns, and on moonlit nights. A few, oftenest alone, for they were lordly beings, however lightly they moved upon the earth. Lightly, aye; they left never a track behind, unless in the dew or hoarfrost." Now Olavir thought he too was quoting, for he had not seemed given to flowery language. "Yet he was mighty of stature, was my lord werrow, like unto an elk. His coat was blue-white, silken, with a damascene ripple as he walked or as he soared in a leap, while his horse tail streamed and shimmered behind. His eyes were like full moons. His rack was like twin trees, ebon, many-branched. Along the tines gleamed their leaves, star points. Never would a one of us, nor the fiercest Irroan, lift hand against him. When we began to clear and cultivate, we left untouched the meadows of asphodel where the wer-rows pastured."

His gaze drifted to the river. "Nor did we willingly trouble the nuukai. Water sprites, they were, small, slender, changeable of hue and shape. They frolicked in the falls. When they sprang aloft, the drops and mists off them made fleeting rainbows by day, crystal flickerings after dark. They sang, easily heard, calls and melodies, choruses that wove together with birdsong but went on after the birds departed for winter, the year around."

He shook his head. "Mayhap a gaffer makes up certain memories, yet I do think they sweetened our dreams."

Olavir charged his own pipe. The two smoked and sipped in silence until Olavir asked, "When and how did this change, sir?"

"Not all at once." Arvel shook himself, as though shedding the mood, and said matter-of-factly: "Belike it struck me so hard because I'd often been elsewhere for weeks or months on end. I was more hunter, trap-per, and trader with the Irroans than I was a farmer. Thrice a soldier of sorts. Thus on returning I'd mark things that had stolen half unnoticed upon those who stayed the whole while."

"What were they?"

"In the beginning, for the better. It's rich soil.

Our crops flourished. Best were native plants, maize, squash, beans, and of course smokeweed, but seeds from the Old Lands also grew. Those suited to the clime, that is. We bred sleek cattle, fat hogs, and the finest of horses. Our orchards and honeybees did wondrous well. I could go on. Let me but say that sithence some things have supplanted others, and not complain. Despite any adversities, we've made good lives in Dordonia."

"You *won* them, really, not so, sir?" Olavir said in honest admiration. "During childhood I heard overseas tidings of terrible struggles in the earlier years."

"Aye, we were plagued with everything from wolves and rattlesnakes to venomous ivy. Nor was the Half-world always friendly. If we had no ogres or lupasks, we must cope with the likes of gnashers and ghost casts. Then there was the Red Leech—but that's a repulsive story."

"And the Irroans."

"A few clashes. One war, when the Kamaho confederacy invaded. That campaign took most of a year." Arvel broke off with a laugh. "Folk have wearied of my military reminiscences."

"To me they're new."

"If you care to stay for some days, I'll fill your ears." Again Arvel sat for a bit in thought. "The war was my longest absence. Thus I was the most jolted by what happened here meanwhile. It had waxed like an avalanche." He grimaced. "Nor was I pleased to discover, at last, what had begun it."

"Why not, if I dare ask?"

Arvel puffed hard on his pipe and said a little harshly: "Best you have the account from me. For it concerns a kinsman of my wife, and his own lady. Altogether ill hap. Nevertheless—it came about through them."

Aboard the merchant carrack *Illanda* Captain Ferain Grancy yielded to no man, storm, or monster. He had navigated her around the Middle Sea, along the eastern coasts of the Old Lands from Norren to Makango, and twice across Ocean itself. He had ridden out hurricanes, beaten off pirates and savages, quelled a mutiny, and once, by such adroit maneuvering that his guns all made their target, slain a menacing kraken. In port he was a shrewd bargainer for his cargoes, thus earning handsome commissions.

Otherwise, though, ashore he was apt to feel lost and lubberly, seldom more than now.

Sunlight slanted through leaded glass to make Aedra Niande's braids golden and limn her slenderness against brown wainscoting. The sleeves of a slightly threadbare gown slipped back when she raised her hands as if in defense. "What are you thinking?" she cried.

"Or are you?" muttered her father.

He had kept his chair when his daughter sprang up. Ferain had not yet seated himself. Eyes blue like hers, but in a sagging graybeard countenance. Shifted from one young person to the next and settled into a glower at the visitor. They saw rugged features, black hair shorter than was fashionable, a powerful frame well clad in kidskin doublet, silk blouse, tooled leather belt, and linen breeks tucked into substantial half-boots.

"Just what I said," Ferain answered. "You know I'm a forthright man."

Aedra clasped her hands together. "Nay," she whispered. "I beg of the gods—you've not gone mad? Surely you jest?"

"Dead serious I am." Ferain hesitated. "But, uh, mayhap I could've put it more softly. I lack your gift of fine words."

"As well that you do," snapped Recor Niande. "Always you rush forward like a wild boar. Now do you see how right about him I've been, daughter?"

"I—I—" Aedra caught her breath. "Nay, father. He's kind, is Ferain, and courteous to me, and—and it must take care and forethought to steer among reefs and trade with foreigners."

"Trade!" snorted Recor.

Ferain glanced around the big, sparsely furnished room. He glimpsed dust here and there. But despite the situation, Recor had stood against his courtship from the first. What, a child of Landholder Foxgrove to wed a common seaman, an agent of merchants? The fact that the Dynasts' War and its aftermath had ruined him as they did many others in Caronne, until little remained but his town house and a shrunken staff of underpaid slovens, while Captain Grancy had grown modestly prosperous, counted for naught. It was lucky that modern law gave women free choice of marriage.

Aedra rallied. "An honorable man, a strong arm to uphold us," she said. "Did not Rovald of old rise from lowlier origins to save the kingdom and win the crown?"

There she went again, Ferain sighed to himself: calling on legends, poems, stuff out of books, and what she believed was mystical insight; dreaming of antiquity and unearthly beauties.

Nay, that did her injustice. She had enough strength and wit to manage the household—better than her father could—and, however reluctantly, resist him for the sake of her love. Else Ferain's yearning would have been no more than a transient lust.

He cleared his throat. "Um, I claim naught so grandiose. I simply feel we two can gain a richer, happier life in the New Lands." To Recor: "Erelong we'd have wealth to spare, sending monies hither to build House Foxgrove anew." His pledge to give as much aid as he was able had helped win Aedra's affection.

The squire was unmoved. "From wilderness and wild men?"

Ferain suppressed an oath and mustered patience. "Sir, you know it's no longer thus on the seaboard. Colonies flourish." He launched the speech he had been preparing. "My ship'll ply between them, bearing furs of Ouranique, smokeweed and pure-bred livestock of Dordonia, cotton and cane sugar of Baray, or whatever, from town to town or to Port Roncitar for transshipment overseas. Such vessels are fewer than are wanted yonder. I'll gain high profit. *Illanda*'s owners agree."

Recor reddened. "My daughter crammed into a, a cubicle in a reeling, stinking hull, the one woman amidst a gang of ruffians, to perish miserably when it sinks—" He choked.

"Sir, my sailors may be rough, but they're trustworthy. Over the years I've winnowed out any who were not. True, the passage may prove stiff. But I wager not my life—" Ferain smiled an Aedra—"for never would I risk yours, beloved. I've made the crossing more than once, remember. We'll fare unscathed, save for possible seasickness. Soon afterward you'll dwell in a goodly home, a lady of more standing than ever you could hope for here."

"You presume!" said Recor.

Oh, gods of mischief, Ferain groaned inwardly, his tongue had blundered anew. "No offense, sir. I speak not of noble birth but of, uh, what may be attained."

"You already have your demmed coastwise trade. Why'll you forsake it?"

"Sir, on the east side of the Ocean the merchant mariners crowd each other and bid down their wares. Also, the Tauran League's stranglehold on the markets of Croy, its tarrifs and duties—"

"The tradesman speaks. Albeit no tradesman who knew his place would be this foolish." Recor addressed Aedra. "Think, girl. Supposing all went as well as his cracked pot bubbles of, still, you'd be afar, in a jumble of folk from everywhere and every station in life, an uncouth country without temples, scholaria, traditions, magical lore, any of the graces you treasure."

"Not so!" protested Ferain. "They have their learning and, and they print books, and the towns are cleaner and merrier than Seilles these days, I can tell you. Freedom's in the very air. I'll show you my cousin Lona Tarabine's letters."

Aedra had regained balance. "You've indeed given thought to this," she breathed.

He nodded vigorously. "For years. Most thoroughly since I met you."

She shivered. "And yet—away from what's old and dear—my greenwood—"

"Oh, erelong we can afford to build a house a ways inland, if you like. No dearth of forest!"

"But my little friends, the shining flower dancers—" Her voice trailed off. Tears trembled on her lashes.

Bitterness surged. "Are they so much to you?"

She winced. "I know not. This is too sudden. I'm bewildered. I must take counsel."

"Aye, do," said Recor. "We'll talk at length, you and I. You may go, Captain Grancy."

"Nay," stammered Aedra, "I mean I—must take counsel—with my heart. And with the spirit of the greenwood."

Oh, nay, thought Ferain. He'd known she sometimes went off woolgathering. But in earnest?

Aedra straightened. Resolution crystallized. Aye, thought Ferain, thus she was. Let her read her ancient books, sing her ancient songs, dream her daydreams, consort with silly Halfworlders and play with harmless minor magics. Who's perfect? She remained lovely, warm-blooded, clear-headed about mortal matters and as strong at the core as any husband could wish for.

"At once," she said, "lest I weep and grow afraid."

"The hour's too late," Recor demurred. "Darkness would overtake you."

She nodded, more calm by the minute. "As it should. The spirit I'd invoke would never come forth by day. The moon's close to full." Reverently: "Have the gods given us that?"

"Wh-where'd you go?" stumbled Ferain's own immediate fear.

"To the Well of Ardair in Samyr Wood. I've been there a few times, merely to muse. But it's known to be charmed. Likelier will I get a sign beside its moonlit clarity than under the roof of a temple." Aedra came back to earth. "The journey's as safe by night as by day. Father can affirm how the Duke's rangers keep rogues at their distance. A preserve of his, after all."

Recor understood when he must give ground before her. "Very well, if you insist," he grumbled. "I'll summon Paer to escort you."

Temper flared. She stamped her foot. "Never! Nor any other lout. I'm bound for Faerie and holiness."

Ferain's pulse quickened. "I'll go," he said.

It took her aback. "What? But I meant—"

His will stiffened. "I agree with your father. You'll not travel alone after dark."

"I've done it before."

"I didn't know she'd stay out after sunset," Recor said, almost plaintively. "My scoldings, my bans availed naught."

"But here I am," Ferain told Aedra. "Will you or nill you, alongside you or behind you, I'm coming too."

"Not even though I go to learn whether you and I—"

He interrupted her. "Not even then. I must needs live with myself." He braced his soul. "I could, however, give up this aim of a fresh beginning—if there's the one way we can find to one another."

Gentleness and a certain wisdom came over her. "Nay," she said quietly, "that would always lie between us and fester. Let me go tonight in peace. I think—I dare hope the Good One will manifest herself and tell me to give you your desire."

"Just the same, you'll fare with a guard, best me but anyhow a fellow who can fight, or stay home." It was as bold a gamble as any he had made, staking his whole happiness. "Otherwise I must bid you farewell. Mayhap some luckier man will prove worthy of you."

A part of him felt confident. And he had read her aright. "Well, this *is* a matter concerning us both—" He heard the reluctance, but the words were enough.

"Improper!" harrumphed Recor. "Scandalous! I'll not have it!"

Thus he tempered the steel. "Do you impugn Captain Grancy's honor?" she demanded coldly. "Or mine?"

He hunched in his chair, all at once aged. "Nay, of course not."

Victorious, she laughed, trod over to him, and ran a finger down his cheek. "There's my old dear. Stop fretting. Everything shall end well. Wait and see. Now, we have two horses left us. Have Paer saddle them. And, oh, aye, put some provisions in the bags."

They clattered over the cobblestones of Wheelbarrow Lane, beneath the overhangs of half-timbered houses, onto smoothly paved Tholis Way. This end of the avenue lay near enough to the Longline that Ferain had had time to hurry back to his ship and fetch a cutlass. He glimpsed her masts above a roof. A feeling akin to homesickness tugged at him.

Trolls and tribulation, he didn't *belong* on a horse! It knew as much, too. It skittered, balked, tossed its

ugly head, answered to the reins like a barge in rip-
tides to the helm. Traffic of pedestrians and wagons
made things worse. He hoped desperately that the nag
wouldn't shy and trample somebody, or throw him from
his seat. Aedra effortlessly controlled her own mount.
Her glances at him turned less than adoring.

Somehow they won across King's Newmarket, over
the Imperial Canal bridge, past the armory, and out
the Eastport. Seilles had long since spread beyond the
old walls, but not very far in this direction, for the
land rose steeply on the left, cliffs and crags, rocks
and ravines, gorse and scrub; and only two miles ahead
began Samyr Wood. Level sunlight soaked its green
with amber. Shadows stretched. The air lay quiet,
cooling though still mild, still bearing odors of spur-
rey and wild thyme. A few early swallows glided by.
Except for a faint buzz from their insect quarry and
the clop of hoofs on stone, silence deepened.

Aedra edged nigh, reached across, and stroked a
soothing hand along the neck of Ferain's horse. "Calm,
poor Udo, calm," she murmured. "He means you no
harm. This is but a small jaunt. Soon you'll graze on
savory herbs." She looked at her companion. "Don't
haunt on the reins like that. You hurt his mouth.
He's sensitive."

"Huh!" grunted the sailor.

"It would likewise help if you made better use of
your stirrups. You sit him like a sack of meal. And
that unnecessary sword of yours slats his barrel."

"His what?" If only the barrel held rum.

"Oh, no matter. He should feel easier in the forest,
when I'm leading. But do take care. We venture in
among beings shy and frail."

"I've heard that some are not," Ferain retorted, largely out of irritation. "The wolves may be gone, but don't goblins, drows, lupasks, and suchlike prowl the wildwoods yet?"

Aedra shivered. Her forefinger drew a fivepoint. "No ill-omened croaks, if it please you." She touched heels to her steed. It trotted faster, in front of his.

Aye, this outing had gone unlucky, Ferain thought. Sour, at least. She didn't really want his company. Even the sight of her legs, in tight hose under the hiked-up skirts, ceased to give cheer.

At the edge of the forest the highway bent east-southeast toward plowlands, meadows, and farmsteads. A path led off it, broad, for hunters and merrymakers. The last rays of sun were losing themselves amidst oak, elm, beech, and other sorts he had no names for. Soil muffled hoofbeats. Fragrance lingered.

After a while Aedra turned off onto a trail that wound away into the depths. Bracken rustled as the riders brushed by. Overarching, boughs and leaves made almost a ceiling. Yard by yard, the pair rode into a twilight that swiftly thickened. Ferain wondered how she proposed to find the bloody well, but caught the question between his teeth.

A nacreous glow hove in view, and another and another. They bobbed forward. It was their wings that shone. He dropped hand to hilt. "What the Pit!" he barked.

"Silence," she commanded over her shoulder. "Frighten them not. They're ellils."

He didn't ease much. Aye, though he'd never seen any before, he'd heard about them and that they were benign, playful but never actually tricksy. However, from childhood on he'd been taught wariness of the Halfworld. Certain happenings later had borne it out for him. What other things might stalk through this murk?

"I expected the little darlings would spy us, know me, and hasten to light our way," said Aedra with a tenderness that ought to have been aimed at him. She drew rein and lifted her free hand. "Why, you're Trillia, aren't you? How gladsome to find you."

The tiny female fluttered down to perch on her wrist. A dozen or so wheeled and dipped around, males as well. They seemed to fly in couples, often closing in for a brief caress. One male hovered near Aedra's friend.

Ferain could just catch what she sang: "Wondrous that you're back, sweet lady. What brings you? Who's yon hulk? If he's with you, may he have the welcome of the forest."

"Ferain Grancy is he, from off the sea," Aedra answered. "Fear not if in his ignorance he botches the wildwood peace a bit. He thinks I need him here for a guardian."

"Ooh, your lover?" Trillia giggled and gestured at the nearby male. "Behold mine for this while—Rani. You've not met him earlier, for he and a few more have newly come to this part of Samyr in their wanderings."

"But I've been told about you, my lady Aedra," Rani called as he whirled about her head. "How you bring garden flowers and tales from your world. We'll guide you twain to a bed of soft moss beside a purling brook, that you may rejoice with us." He flitted by Trillia and ran both hands over her.

Ferain, who had keen eyes, saw what was chiefly on what passed for his mind.

Probably the young woman blushed, though all he could discern through the gloom, by skittering Faerie lights, was that her lashes dipped. "Nay, I'm on a grave matter," she said quickly. "I regret having no roses or violets for your delectation, nor time for chatter and song. I'm urgently bound for the Well of Ardair to seek a sign."

Trillia fluttered up. Ferain read alarm on the dainty wee face. The ellils flapped around, agitated beyond their usual flightiness. They whistled and shrilled in some language not human.

Rani gathered courage, perhaps to impress his inamorata. Wheeling before Aedra, he piped, "You'd cast a spell—and there? Nay, I beg you! It could summon horrors forth from the night."

"What?" Aedra replied. "Surely not. It's, it's merely oracular." She drew breath. "No book I've studied holds that such doings are evil, or have such power. And hitherto I have but toyed with arcana. I've less skill than any village witchwife, and what can she do of more import than healing a minor sickness or forewarning against travel on some bespoken day? Does she thereby raise the Unseelie?"

"This is no village, this is the wildwood," wailed Trillia. "A spirit indwells at Ardair."

"Aye, that's been known from time beyond reckoning. But has it caused fiends to lair nearby? Why, yourselves are more magical than anything I can attempt."

"In wandering, we encountered—hunters," Rani replied with a shudder that seemed to go through them all. "That alone was cause to flee those territories."

"*Their* territories," Aedra said firmly. "My father possesses huntsmen's lore. I've gained some from him. Beasts of prey keep within bounds. You've never had trouble hereabouts, have you?"

"N-nay," confessed three or four together.

"Doesn't that show there's naught dangerous? We're not far from human habitation. I daresay it's scared them off long since. Were you but able to stay in place through your lifetimes, you'd suffer nothing."

Ferain snatched the opportunity to assert himself. "Besides, what Halfworld creature can withstand this cold steel I carry?" he declaimed.

The ellils fluted and scattered, like fallen leaves in a gust. "Come back!" Aedra called. "Come back, do. I said he's clumsy." She cast him what he guessed was a hard look. "And *you* keep back, hear you? Hold your brags bottled. If you spoil this undertaking, I'll incline to think father's right."

"I pray pardon," he forced.

She gazed aloft. "Would you not like to watch my spellcasting?" she suggested. Ferain judged glumly that she had a smile for them, if not him. "Even if it fails, you cannot have seen the likes before."

That lured their quicksilver tempers. Doubtless she'd known it would. They swept low to dance about earth and brush, in and out among the trees. Their laughter pealed, chimes at the rim of human hearing. Aedra clucked to her horse and rode onward. Ellils made a skipping glory around her head and lanterns leading her. Ferain followed as best he could.

Bracken screened a trail that branched off, still more pinched and twisty. The ellils led them down it. Often a horse stumbled on a root or a withe seen too late whipped a rider. Thus did Ferain lose his ostrich-plumed hat. He dared not ask for a halt. That fed his smoldering resentment. Humans must have trodden this way now and then, but not for many years, save Aedra. Her dreaminess appealed to these fantastical folk; they took her to everything marvelous that they knew of.

As his steed plodded on, Ferain saw lights come by twos and fours through the murk, from right and left but mostly from ahead. They waxed in sight, they gathered in shifting clusters, until perhaps half a hundred ellils had joined the party. Their merriment rang thin and sweet. He supposed their Halfworld senses had told them across miles that something interesting was afoot. With nothing better to do, he watched them. Over and over, he saw couples withdraw for a while. They returned with self-satisfied expressions.

Must they tantalize him?

After an interminable span, the trail abruptly gave on a glade about a hundred feet across. Forest loomed like a black wall around it. The moon stood almost full. Doubly bright after the nighted woods, it veiled most stars but frosted the leaves and silvered the grass. The well lay at the middle. It appeared to be actually a spring, walled by a low coping. Who had brought those lichenous boulders, how long ago, and why? Time had forgotten. From the saddle Ferain caught a glimpse of glimmer on the water within. Herbs crushed underhoof were pungent. The ellils swarmed into the open.

"Halt," Aedra said. "We are here."

"So I deemed," Ferain grumbled. By moonlight

and ellil light he saw her frown. "Oh, I'll hold my tongue."

She jumped to the ground. He climbed down, aware of a sore backside. "Shall I moor—shall I tie the horses?" he asked.

"Nay. Hang reins over muzzles, let them graze free." The note of exasperation was unfair, he thought. He wouldn't expect her to know a sheet from a halyard.

"You can then rest," she told him. "This may take hours. I've never essayed such a spell erenow, and what I've found in books is not very clear. But I trust a kindly spirit will respond." Her voice softened. "And I trust it will advise me to go abroad with you, Ferain."

"Won't you take food first?" he blurted. He was belly-growling hungry. And it had been her idea to bring supplies.

"Not until afterward. Fasting sharpens vision." Impatience broke through. "Eat if you must. Keep aside, though, in the shadows."

He felt stung anew. Yet as she left him, he saw in the moonlight the raptness coming upon her. What a many-sided soul she was. While life with her might occasionally be difficult, it could never become wearisome.

If the stupid spirit would rise and give the right answers. Why couldn't she simply think things over like a sensible person?

He took bread, cheese, and wineskin from a saddlebag and went to the dark side to sit down, rather gingerly. The ellils flurried above, everywhere along the perimeter. As Aedra paced to the well, they fell silent; but on those nearest him, Ferain read a child-like curiosity.

Aedra dropped to her knees, bowed her head above folded hands, and murmured. Moonlight whitened her athwart the blackness beyond.

She rose, lifted her arms to the sky, and spoke words unknown to him.

Thrice she solemnly danced around the well—a sort of bransle, he thought—while her chant soared lovely to hear.

She knelt again, leaned over the coping, and scooped up a double handful. She held it toward the moon before she drank.

Ferain tore off a chunk of bread and munched.

"O nameless Presence," Aedra crooned beneath heaven, "with my song and spell I conjure you, with my heart I make offering. Come of your mercy, come from your waters bearing your wisdom, grant me your insight as woman to woman, lover to lover. By the Great Mother do I summon you, by the Fates, and by the One Above All. Arise, arise, arise."

A mist flowed from the well. The ellils could not stay back anymore. They twittered, they fluted, they tumbled inward until their glowing hid the moon.

Out from under the trees, out from the unseen east, flew a darkness. The length of a man it was, with scything wings. Fangs gleamed bone-white. The eyes were fire pits. Swift as a wind, it was in among the ellils.

"Lupask, lupask!" they shrieked, scattering. The snaky neck swung, jaws snapped, talons clutched. It caught one, blood spurted in drops like stars, the little being struggled, flapped, and went down the gullet.

The hunter tilted, overtook another, and devoured her in passing. Air whistled.

Aedra reeled to her feet. Ferain dashed toward her. The mist retreated into the well. Prudently, flashed through him.

"Help them!" Aedra screamed.

As always when in peril, his mind ran so fast that time seemed sluggish. He saw that no ellil could outfly the lupask, that it would reap a score or worse before the rest had gotten away, and he knew it cared nothing about him or her unless they annoyed it, but then it would attack, and he must not endanger her, nor must he fail her— "Get it down!" he bawled. "Down where we can fight!" He hurried off to brandish his cutlass at a distance.

The horses neighed, panicked, bolted into the forest. It would be a long walk home, he thought. If he lived. May they fall over the reins and break their fool necks. But then he'd better compensate Recor—

"To him!" Aedra shouted. "To my lover! He'll save you!"

If an ellil alone lacked common sense, together they had the unity of bees. Or maybe her sympathy with them went deeper than he knew. They heard. Somehow, they understood. Even those who were escaping circled to rejoin the swarm. It aimed itself at Ferain and englobed him in light. The lupask came after.

He swung the cutlass. It bit into a wing. Iron seared through Halfworld scales, flesh, bone. Smoke puffed. The lupask yammered, a noise that pierced. Crippled, it fell to earth.

There it writhed into a new shape. A huge lizard

crawled against Ferain. Its gape was as wide and sharp as ever. It hissed geyser-loudly.

His weapon hewed.

Sprawled dead, the lupask slowly fumed away. Morning sun would dissolve its skeleton and strew the vapor into the wind. By then the smell should be gone. Meanwhile the moon spread an argent peace.

"Dearest, dearest, dearest!" Aedra toppled into Ferain's arms.

The impact nearly dumped him onto his aching rear. The battle had left him weak and chilled. His breath shuddered raw. His sweat stank worse than the carcass.

He kept stance, though, and then it was as if warmth and strength poured from her into him. "There, there," he mumbled, ruffling her hair. "Everything's well." Idiotically: "D'you want to start your gramarie afresh?"

Tears glistened on the face she raised to his. "No need," she gasped. "I'll be with you wh-wherever you go." A kind of laughter coughed. "Try to stop me!"

The kiss went on for a while. The ellils flocked back. They danced and chimed approvingly under the moon.

Lucidity lurched into the humans. Aedra laid her head on Ferain's breast. "I, I fear the lupask caught scent of my magic from afar and sped hither," she mourned.

"I'd say likelier he winded this many ellils gathered in one place," he replied. "They should have known better. Well, they're no intellects, are they?" He glanced at the joy surrounding them. "Grieve not for those lost. They're not doing so."

Brief lives at best, he'd heard tell; plentiful offspring
to make up for that; natures sprightly but shallow.

Also nevertheless, Rani and Trillia showed anxiety as
they drew nigh and hovered. "You saved us," sang the
female. "Broad is the range you've freed from fear."

"And yet the lupasks will return," worried the male.
"Again we'll fly in dread of them."

"You will be here to ward us, won't you?" warbled
Trillia.

"I'm sorry, nay," Aedra answered. "My man and
I shall shortly fare off to the New Lands overseas.
Refrain from large assemblies, and I can pray you be
safe in this neighborhood, at least."

"It's so narrow," complained Trillia.

Rani's wings quivered. "We're beings of the air.
Roaming means as much as life."

"Sad am I for you, then," Aedra sighed. "I can
only wish you well—" She tautened. She stepped
back from Ferain. It was as if the moonlight blazed
in her eyes.

"The New Lands," she breathed. "Refuge, bound-
lessness."

The ellils captured her thought at once. She had
talked in this forest about the discoveries yonder.
A nightingale chorus burst from them. They soared,
swooped, zigzagged, radiance alive. "Oh, aye, oh,
aye," they sang. "Take us with you. We'll love you
forever."

"I, I know not," Ferain stammered, astonished.
"What'd you do there?"

Trillia laughed, darting before his eyes. "What we've
always done. Dear Aedra will vouch for us. We live on
blossoms and nectar, a nibble of fruit in season, nuts

and seeds through the winter. We are love, we are loveliness. Take us with you!" Flying, she opened her arms to him. Her bosom was unutterably shapely.

"Oh, do," Aedra whispered. "I'd miss them so."

How could he refuse? "We can't carry them all—"

"Of course not. Nor should we deprive the motherland of them. A few score. To delight us, our children, our grandchildren in our new homes."

It would be a nuisance, he thought. Not that they'd require more than a bushel or two of whatever nourished them. But he'd have to dampen superstitious fears in his crew when they flickered like corposants on spars and rigging. No doubt he, or at any rate Aedra, would have to nurse them through storm and salt, and afterward help them get established.

Yet his darling desired it.

Arvel Tarabine blew smoke at the Faerie dancers. "Thus it was," he ended. "The intent was good. The outcome, though—you see."

"I'm not sure," said Olavir. "Everything here's strange to me. Would you explain?"

"That's easily done. Too easily. What nobody understood was that in the Old Lands, the lupasks keep the ellils down.

"Here nothing preys on them. They breed. And breed. And breed.

"We learned too late how fond they are of asphodel blooms. Killed that pasturage entirely. The werrows died off or departed, and the streams were clear for the buhas. Those destroyed the nuukai. You've heard what else they do.

"The ellils also go after apple blossoms. Our orchards don't bear. And clover blossoms. We produce no more honey. Feed for our livestock is leaner than aforetime.

"In Baray they're crowding the quetwa—native Halfworld creatures, which themselves terrify mosquitoes—out of existence. Northward in Ouranique, the fur trade suffers because the ellils find too many nuts and seeds; squirrels decline, which means fox do. Meanwhile they spread west unchecked. I've gotten rumors of maddened wendigos and of Irroan medicine men finding spirit flowers gone scarce.

"Oh, few of us lay blame on Ferain and Aedra," he added. "Who could have foreknown? They're doing well enough these days."

Olavir stared into the gathering night at the luminous merriment. "Can naught be done?" he asked.

Arvel shrugged. "Who'd want to try trapping and conveying lupasks? Nor can we say what might come of *that*."

He too gazed thence while he drained his goblet. "We must needs live with what is," he said. "And enjoy them, I suppose. But I miss the nuukai and the werrows."

Sprague: An Afterword

Robert Silverberg

HE WAS MY SENIOR BY only about a quarter of a century, but he always seemed to me like a figure out of another age, an unaccountable twentieth-century survivor of that great band of eighteenth- and nineteenth-century British scholar-explorers who went forth into Asia and Africa to uncover the secrets of antiquity and the mysteries of the world's remaining unexplored regions. Whenever he entered a room—and you could not fail to notice him, for he was a big man, a formidable figure indeed, strikingly handsome, with flashing eyes, imposing eyebrows, a distinguished close-clipped beard, a stentorian voice, square-shouldered military posture—I could easily imagine myself in the presence of someone who had moved on intimate terms with Richard Burton, who had gone to Mecca in disguise, or Austen Henry Layard, who dug up the ruins of Nineveh, or Henry Rawlinson, who deciphered the indecipherable cuneiform inscriptions of Mesopotamia, or the intrepid Dr. Livingstone, who cast so much light on Africa's dark interior, or Bruce of the Blue Nile, the formidable explorer of Ethiopia.

They were men who had traveled fearlessly into the darkest corners of the world, often under circumstances of the most extreme discomfort. Who were fluent in Arabic or Persian or Swahili or Amharic or Urdu or Turkish or perhaps all of them, along with French and Latin and Greek, of course. Who could quote at will (in the original, naturally) from Aristophanes or Homer or Petronius Arbiter or Michael Psellos or Firdausi or the Koran, as need arose in the conversation. Who had dined on crocodile meat and ostrich eggs and kookaburra tongues. To me, Sprague was one of that number. I often imagined him to have known them, to have marched with them through wilderness and desert and tropical forest, to have swapped gaudy tales of exploration with them by their campfires. It was hard to understand what he was doing in the midst of a gathering of science fiction writers in some hotel room of the America of the 1950s, when by rights he ought to be off in Baluchistan or the Negev or the outer reaches of the Gobi, seeking answers to questions that to others seemed unanswerable.

In fact Sprague was born too late—in 1907—to discover Victoria Falls or the wellsprings of the Nile, or to penetrate the unknown caves of Tun-huang, or to

unearth the ruins of the Mausoleum of Halicarnassus.
All those jobs had been done already. So, however
similar he may have been in temperament and scholarly attainments to the great Victorian explorers and
archaeologists, he had to be content with following in
their footsteps, retracing their paths, restudying what
they had studied. However much he looked like one
of those men who would come back to London every
ten years or so to report on their latest achievements
to the members of the Royal Geographical Society,
he had to be content to live a writer's life, not an
adventurer's, and his greatest feats of exploration were
carried out on worlds of his own imagining.

He was, I think, a fundamentally shy man. (So
were many of the great Victorian scholar-explorers, I
suspect, which is why they preferred to spend their
lives under the African or Indian sun rather than joust
in the drawing rooms of London society.) Not timid,
mind you: no timid man would travel to the places
Sprague liked to visit, or deal as capably as he did
with the often difficult Third World types he traveled
among. ("I boarded one of the 40-foot launches that
served as ferries, and scrunched down in the fantail
with a swarm of locals, from kids to graybeards. They
asked about my wives and children, and I showed
them my wallet photographs. A young schoolteacher
came aft to help me when I ran out of Arabic. At last
someone asked if I were a Muslim or a Copt—that
is, an Egyptian Christian. This was a tricky question.
There are many Copts around Luxor, and there is
mutual hostility between the religious comunities. I
racked my brains for a tactful reply. Just as we landed,
Allah sent me an inspiration. I said: '*Fi fiktri kull*

id-din kuwayyis.' ['In my opinion, all religions are good.'] Broad smiles all around again.") No, when I say Sprague was shy, I mean that there was a zone of fundamental reticence and reserve about him, a *noli me tangere* of the soul, that led him toward a highly formal manner of behavior, a dislike of small talk, an abhorrence of any sort of personal revelation. In that, too, he was somewhat Victorian. (Though on one memorable occasion in 1985, about which I will not tell you in detail, he startled me by abruptly initiating a discussion with me of the sort men more usually have in locker rooms—but this was conducted at a party, in a very crowded room, and, of course, at the very top of his lungs.)

Despite that unlikely moment, I always regarded Sprague more as a colleague than as a close friend. I had difficulties surmounting Sprague's highly formal manner and the gulf of nearly a generation in our ages, and over four decades of correspondence and encounters at conventions we maintained an amiable collegial relationship that only occasionally verged on becoming what I would regard as a friendship. Perhaps he was like that with almost everyone except a very few men of his own age. Yet I do recall his kindly show of interest to me, a 22-year-old newcomer, when we were both attending a small midwestern science-fiction convention long ago, and the genuinely warm weekend my wife Karen and I spent with Sprague and his lovely wife Catherine at a convention held more than thirty years later. (Theirs was a marriage that would last six decades, from 1939 until her death in April 2000, only seven months before his. Both lived on into their nineties.)

I had encountered his work a full decade before I first met him—in the late 1940s, it was, in such anthologies as *Adventures in Time and Space* (which included the short story "The Blue Giraffe") and *A Treasury of Science Fiction* ("Living Fossil"). Quickly he became a favorite of mine, and when I began hungrily to seek out back issues of such magazines as *Astounding Science Fiction* and *Unknown Worlds*, to both of which he had been a prolific contributor, it was always an occasion for rejoicing when a de Camp story turned up in one of them. I have continued to read and reread him to this day with unalloyed pleasure.

From 1938 on he had been a mainstay of the extraordinary stable of writers that the brilliant editor of those magazines, John W. Campbell, had gathered around him—people like Robert A. Heinlein, Isaac Asimov, A.E. van Vogt, Theodore Sturgeon, Fritz Leiber. De Camp was a central figure in that group, winning a large and enthusiastic following with a multitude of stories marked by high erudition and a wry comic sense, stories so characteristically de Campian that one could identify his hand after reading only a paragraph or two. Since from my early teen years onward I had regarded his work with special pleasure, it was, of course, one of the great delights of my precocious years as a science-fiction professional to find myself not only meeting L. Sprague de Camp but to be treated by him, as he did from the beginning of my career, as a fellow practitioner of the craft.

He wrote more than a hundred books, both science fiction and fantasy, along with a great many scholarly works and books of scientific popularization. Among his significant nonfiction books were such as *The Ancient Engineers*, *Ancient Ruins and Archaeology*, and *Lost Continents: The Atlantis Theme in History, Science, and Literature*—and he made splendid use of that scholarship in his fiction, which, as I have noted, was marked by a taste for whimsical erudition. I think my first choice among his books is *Lest Darkness Fall*, which John Campbell first published in *Unknown*, the short-lived fantasy companion to his more famous magazine, *Astounding*. It's the story, lighthearted and gripping at the same time, of a twentieth-century archaeologist transported by a bolt of lightning to the sixth century, where he strives to stave off the Dark Ages by introducing modern technology. Another notable de Camp story is *The Wheels of If*, (*Astounding*, 1940), a rollicking alternate-universe story that transports another modern man into a mysteriously transmogrified twentieth century in which, he eventually discovers, the New World is controlled by the descendants of the Viking explorers of a thousand years earlier.

Then, too, there are the famous Harold Shea fantasies that de Camp wrote in collaboration with Fletcher Pratt: *The Incomplete Enchanter* and its various sequels. Here again de Camp sends a man of our own time off into worlds of fantasy, this time worlds of epic poetry (the Norse sagas, Spenser's "Faerie Queen," etc.) And his fine historical novels—*The Dragon of the Ishtar Gate, An Elephant for Aristotle*, and three others—and his biographies of H.P. Lovecraft and Robert E. Howard, and his editions of Howard's "Conan" books, which introduced Conan to the postwar generation of readers, and ever so much more—

He lived a long and astonishingly full life, went everywhere and saw everything, and set it all down on paper over half a century for several generations of delighted readers. He was an extraordinary writer, a pillar of our field, and a remarkable man as well. You can find out more about him at the web site maintained in his honor—www.lspraguedecamp.com—or you could hunt up his enormous Hugo-winning autobiographical volume, *Time and Chance*, published by Donald M. Grant in 1996, which sets forth his colorful life and far-flung travels in four hundred huge pages.

The Science Fiction Writers of America, in 1978, named him as the fourth winner of its highest honor, the Grand Master award, following Robert A. Heinlein, Jack Williamson, and Clifford D. Simak. It was well deserved, for de Camp was one of the shapers of modern science fiction. (And helped to define it, in a magnificent book called *Science Fiction Handbook*, published in 1953, which I think is the best textbook on writing science fiction ever produced. Certainly I learned plenty from it.) His particular contribution to the field was his understanding that history and geography and linguistics are sciences, even as chemistry and physics and astronomy are. Though he was educated (at Cal Tech) as an engineer, his broad and deep knowledge of world literature and world history served him well in science fiction's primary extrapolative tasks: he was a superb storyteller, on a good day as compelling as Scheherezade, and a fascinating man as well. I'm glad to have had the privilege of knowing him and I share with you all the privilege and the pleasure of reading his work.

American freedom and justice versus the tyrannies of the seventeenth century

1632 *by Eric Flint*
Paperback • 31972-8   **$7.99** ___

"This gripping and expertly detailed account of an episode of time travel that changes history is a treat for lovers of action-SF or alternate history . . . it distinguishes Flint as an SF author of particular note, one who can entertain and edify in equal, and major, measure."
                                        —*Publishers Weekly*, starred review

1633 *by David Weber & Eric Flint*
Paperback • 7434-7155-5   **$7.99** ___

The greatest naval war in European history is about to erupt. Like it or not, Gustavus Adolphus will have to rely on Mike Stearns and the technical wizardry of his obstreperous Americans to save the King of Sweden from ruin, but caught in the conflagration are two American diplomatic missions abroad. . . .

1634: The Galileo Affair *by Eric Flint & Andrew Dennis*
Hardcover • 7434-8815-6   **$26.00** ___

The Thirty Years War continues to ravage 17th-century Europe, but a new force is gathering power and influence: the Confederated Principalities of Europe, an alliance between Gustavus Adolphus, King of Sweden, and the West Virginians from the 20th century . . .

And don't miss the Ring of Fire series anthologies:

The Ring of Fire *edited by Eric Flint*
Hardcover • 7434-7175-X   **$23.00** ___

Grantville Gazette *edited by Eric Flint*
Paperback • 7434-8860-1   **$6.99** ___

— —

If not available through your local bookstore send this coupon and a check or money order for the cover price(s) + $1.50 s/h to Baen Books, Dept. BA, P.O. Box 1403, Riverdale, NY 10471. Delivery can take up to eight weeks.

NAME: _____

ADDRESS: _____

_____

I have enclosed a check or money order in the amount of $ _____